Our Strange Endeavors

Riley Andrews

ISBN 979-8-218-44355-9 (paperback)
Cover design by David Gardias
Edited by Jennifer Herrington
Interior art by Mariia Ovsianikova

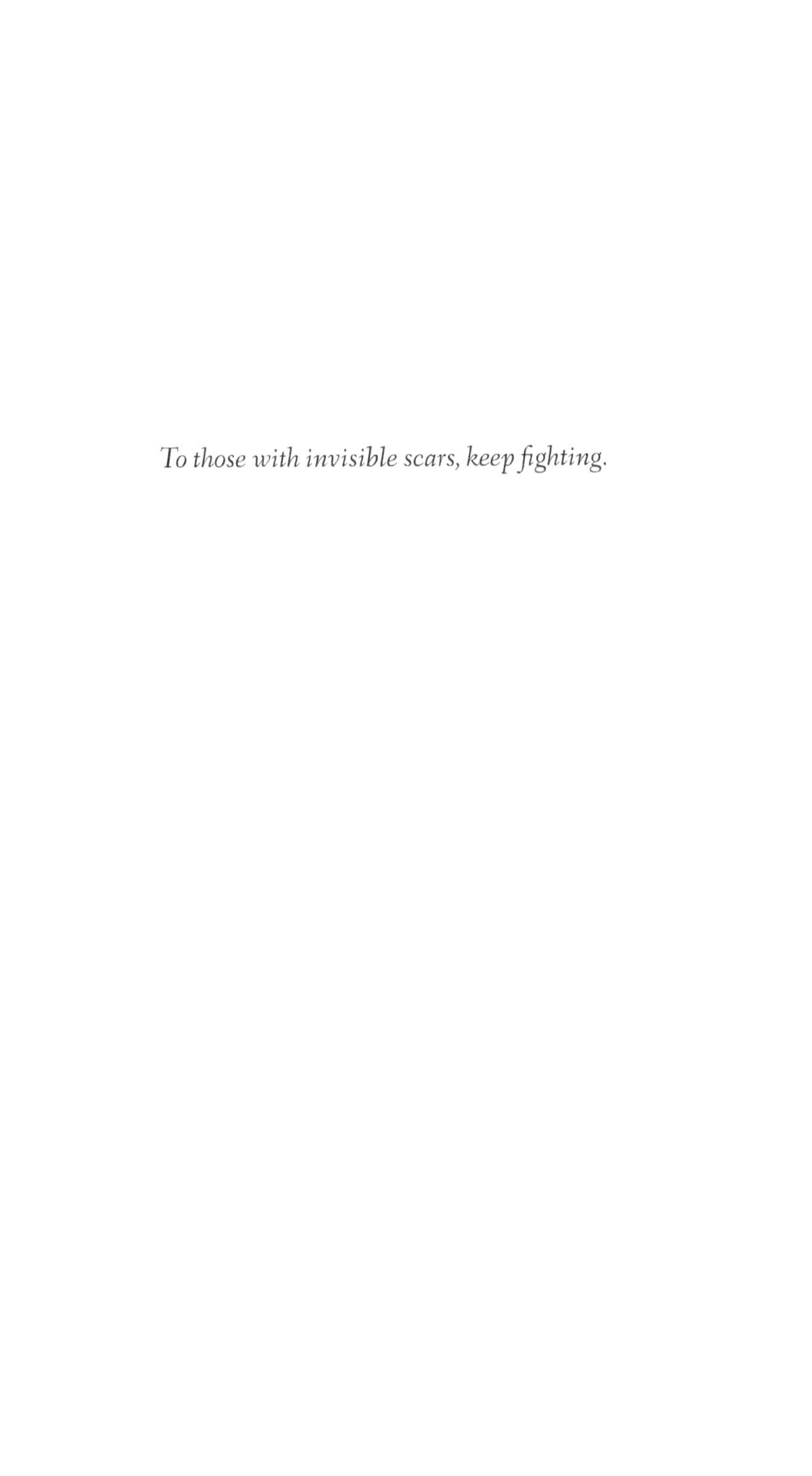

To those with invisible scars, keep fighting.

Author's Note

This book contains fictional depictions of violence, murder, emotional abuse, blackmail, mentions of physical abuse, explicit sexual acts, bondage, mentions of parental death, mentions of religious trauma, a character being drugged, mentions of sexual assault, and manipulation. Please be advised that the following content may not be suitable for all audiences.

The Lotte

The District

Krissy

The entertainment district was a bloodsucking parasite. An organism that fed off optimism and the star-studded dreams of others. For those brave enough to try their luck, very few made it out on the other side and lived to tell the tale. With cutthroat rivalries, limited roles to fill, and fierce owners hell-bent on carving out their slice of the ten-block radius, it was enough to wear down the most seasoned of talent. The parasite was keen on finding the most wide-eyed dancers, musicians, or singers, and draining them of their love for the arts until they had nothing left to give in return. Careers started and ended in the entertainment district, and for those of us who dared to keep trying, we learned rather quickly that only the strong-willed and the cunning could learn the truth of this industry.

If you lasted long enough, the relationship turned symbiotic—giving as much as it took.

For some, it was as vain as lusting after the thrill of performing center stage, while for others it was about money, power, or even sex. Whatever reason brought them here in the first place, it was always a front for what they truly desired. Like all those that had come before me, I was no different. I had my reasons for suffering through years of blatant favoritism toward others less deserving, shoddy background roles, and a sleazy boss who had no business working in the arts.

Aiden Hoffman, the owner of the theater I worked at, made his wealth in the early nineties and poured the majority of his capital into strip clubs and dive bars—the more unsavory side of all that the district had to offer. When that wasn't enough to sate his needs, he took his profit and purchased a cabaret on a whim with little experience running such a massive operation. He forcefully put himself at the bottom of a very short list of individuals who'd staked their claim in district property—making a few enemies along the way. Competition was fierce between the few nameless conglomerates that ruled over the concert venues, nightclubs, theaters, and musical productions that kept the beating heart of the city alive and well.

Similar to the other buildings on this block, The Lotte was a living, breathing piece of history adored by many, and respected by few, that never deserved to be kept in such careless hands. I was inclined to say Hoffman was the worst thing to happen to the theater, had he not appointed Samantha Wilson to be his leading lady solely for the reason that she was also warming his bed.

Partisanship wasn't unheard of in this industry, but at least in other companies, when they favored one employee over the other, their talent was worth a damn.

The red-haired dancer had no business headlining with her mediocre dance routines and lip syncing that did little to fool the audience. She lacked any sense of authenticity that would have rightfully earned her the honor of fame she so desperately craved. And had the circumstances been different, I could have easily seen a reality in which Samantha and I had something more than a petty rivalry. Unfortunately for her, she had very few allies within the company and wholeheartedly believed it was above her to even try to mend the relationships she'd destroyed along the way.

The arrogant rarely see the problem when it's staring right back at them.

Despite the innate flaws of the industry and the people who made my life hell, something about the promise of a better tomorrow made me endure it all without question. A tomorrow that allowed the pieces to fall into place—for a life I'd only dreamt of. The theater offered me a home in a city as vast as it was cruel when no one else would take me in. The theater provided me with a family when I never imagined I'd get another shot to make things right. The theater provided a taste of what opportunities awaited me before an adoring crowd. I'd been luckier than most when it came to pursuing a dance career, but as much as the theater gave, it wasn't enough—not by far.

The entertainment district wasn't for the weak of heart. It was a place of corruption and sin, where the dreamers and the damned thrived. My place was with the dreamers, unwavering in my resolve to see my ambitions through—even if, in the end, it left me no better than the damned.

Chapter One

Krissy

Whoever said hard work and perseverance paved the way to success was a damn liar. And while I wouldn't be where I am today without it, apparently, begging on your hands and knees after a long night out will do all the same. Wearing down Tory was the easy part; it was the fact that I had to wait until the next morning for her to follow through on her promise that took more patience than I was capable of. I slept like the dead despite the anticipation of what tomorrow would bring, only to wake up when the mouthwatering aroma of frybread flooded our tiny apartment.

With the grace of a drunken slob, nowhere near fully recovered, I stumbled to the bathroom to rush through my morning routine. My tangled blonde curls made an awkward crunching sound as I brushed away the remnants of last night's hairspray. Between the mess of hair atop my head, the smeared mascara highlighting the bags under my eyes, and the love bite sitting atop my breast, I wasn't exactly presentable. All of it could be fixed later; what took priority was getting a taste of the first batch cooling off before Lyra could.

It was difficult to make out behind closed doors, but there

was an audible gasp down the hall. A second later, all hell broke loose. Already fighting a terrible headache, concentrating near the bridge of my nose, it worsened as the apartment came to life. The fire alarm wailed, splitting my eardrums in one deafening blow. I didn't think, nor did I hesitate as I sprinted out of the bathroom with a toothbrush still hanging out of my mouth to investigate. Tory was waving a dish towel near the smoke detector while Lyra gawked at her phone.

One look at the stove and all my dreams were shattered. The delicious remains of her cooking lay burned to a crisp at the bottom of the pan. I fought back a choking noise as I watched the black puck sizzle in the oil.

"Was he alone?" Tory shouted over the relentless beeping.

"I don't know," Lyra said, frantically scrolling through her phone.

I spit into the kitchen sink, then turned toward the girls. "What the hell is going on?"

The smoky haze surrounding us seemed to weigh as thick as the unspoken tension lingering in the air. Since Tory moved in after the two became a couple, there have been plenty of times I've had to step in and defuse a situation in order to make living together bearable. Unlike times in the past, the way they stared at one another spoke to something entirely different.

There was a long pause that followed.

Lyra's eyes dropped to her screen. "Hoffman died in a car crash."

"You're kidding me!"

She jumped to her feet, shoving the phone in my face, nearly blinding me in the process. One after another, news articles flashed on the screen with headlines ranging from *Eccentric owner of the beloved Lotte Theater dies at the age of 62* to *Aiden Hoffman dies in a head-on collision; two bodies accounted for at this time.* The articles were grim, each accompanied by an image of Samantha's foreign sports car that made me sick to my stomach. If it weren't for the red exterior mingling in the mix, it would be hard to tell where one car started and the other ended. There was only so much I could read before prying my eyes away and snatching the phone out of her hands. Lyra didn't object as I flipped through her contacts until I found what I was looking for. The drawn-out ringback tone muffled in my ears as the uneven beating of my heart overpowered all else.

"Who are you calling?"

"Jennifer, if she would just answer–" On the other line, the soft voice of our costume designer bled through. "Hello! Was Samantha in the car with him? Is she alive?"

It hardly mattered what strained relationship any of us had with Samantha; waiting for confirmation of her safety was daunting. The images spoke for themselves; it was hard to imagine anyone could survive a collision like that, but Lyra and Tory pressed up close in hopes of hearing good news.

"I'm at the hospital right now. Samantha is alive, but it doesn't look pretty," she finally answered. "It's hard seeing her lying in bed like this, hooked up to all these machines and tubes. The doctors say it's a miracle she walked away with so few substantial injuries." She cleared her throat. "I don't think they'll keep her long, but the police want to question her about what happened last night."

"Do you want us to come down to the hospital, so you aren't alone?" Tory asked.

Her pin-straight hair still had a little wave to it after sleeping on her curls, and I could have sworn there was a hint of shimmer on her high cheekbones. It wasn't very often Tory let me play dress up with her, but last night was one of those rare times when she let me style her from head to toe. Even Daniel let me put a dash of highlighter on the bridge of his nose before drunkenly swiping it away and cursing me for potentially ruining any chance he had of taking someone home from the club.

"I appreciate the offer, but I'm okay," she assured us. "Lyra and Krissy, you guys should head to work earlier than usual. Malik needs to speak to everyone before call time." We argued back and forth several times before she hung up on us, and we collectively agreed that going to work instead of the hospital was the right thing to do. Unlike us, Tory had the day off from her nine-to-five office job and decided to visit Jennifer like the kind soul she was.

In the hope of not being late for a second time this week, Lyra and I scrambled to collect our things. Every so often, I could catch a glimpse of my roommate over my shoulder as she frantically stuffed her belongings in her dance bag. A troublesome look washed over her beautiful hazel eyes. They seemed to stand out more than usual in contrast to her rich, dark skin and the pink athletic clothes that hugged her curvy figure.

"I know you weren't close with him, but are you okay?" An innocent question that hit too close to home. Those stunning eyes of hers seemed to flare with something resembling a mix of grief and anger, the two emotions fighting for dominance one over the other.

In the years I had known Lyra, she had never been one to suppress her emotions, always speaking proudly of who she was and how she felt. It was part of the reason the confidence she wore so visibly made people gravitate toward her. Once upon a time, before she started dancing, she was offered a modeling gig for a local fashion magazine because of that very same confidence and drop-dead gorgeous looks everyone adored. Although I wasn't a part of her life during that time, she loves to tell the story of how she rejected the offer to chase her true passion. Dancing.

I never blamed her for it. I was right there beside her, chasing the very same dream.

"Yeah, it's just a lot to take in right now."

"I get it," I said grimly, tossing my bag over my shoulder. "Come on, I don't want to be late. Malik already hates me as it is."

The walk was short. Only a few blocks away from the theater, it was part of the reason we picked it in the first place. Normally, a quick commute was perfect for rolling out of bed and stumbling to work on time, but today that walk gave me little time to reflect on the events that had transpired. A small collection of bouquets, prayer candles, and stuffed animals came into view, lining the entrance of the old building, forcing me to confront everything all at once. Little trinkets and tokens of grief popped up out of nowhere overnight. Hoffman seemed to have touched more lives than I expected. After two and a half years of working under his roof, I couldn't say the same. Unlike those who were in mourning, you wouldn't catch me leaving behind trash in the streets for a man who gave little to his people.

Lyra and I paused. We were both thinking the same thing, but I was the only one who had the courage to say it aloud. "Well, this ought to be fun," I mumbled, tiptoeing toward the entrance, careful not to trip over the items blocking our path.

———

Murmuring filtered all around us, soft conversations of what-ifs. Rumors were spiraling out of control. A few rows back, I overheard someone already spreading the false narrative that Samantha was behind the wheel and heavily intoxicated at the time of the crash. Samantha wasn't the brightest, but even that story was pushing it.

Malik was uncharacteristically late. Twenty minutes rolled

by, and I felt myself sink into my chair to admire The Lotte from my position near the stage. Jokingly, I always referred to this place as the Great Depression-era bootleg Moulin Rouge. Originally a small theater built after World War I, it was renovated into a luxury cabaret with the same classic art deco style from its primordial glory. It was more of a home to me than any shitty apartment I could afford or even the place I grew up in downtown. The Lotte was far from perfect, and I always resented Mr. Hoffman for never seeing its true potential.

"Thank you for all coming early on such short notice," Malik announced in a booming voice, taking center stage to address the fifty or so of us in the audience. "With a heavy heart, I must inform you all that Mr. Hoffman passed away earlier this morning. Aiden and Samantha were involved in a head-on collision upstate, and unfortunately, he was not wearing his seatbelt at the time of the crash. I was told he died quickly and did not suffer. The police officers who arrived on the scene first believe that the other vehicle involved in the crash turned at the last second, sparing Samantha in the passenger seat. She is currently at the hospital and expected to make a full recovery in time."

Well, there goes that rumor.

"I understand this news is unexpected and tragic. As a reminder, our insurance does cover mental health if you feel the need to speak to a professional about this or anything else. Find me after this meeting, and I will give you the number of a great local psychiatrist who is covered," he said, standing tall despite the little wobble I noticed in his knees. "Lastly, I need to inform you of all the legal matters regarding this building. I've been on the phone with Hoffman's lawyers all morning, and it turns out he did not declare a beneficiary in his will. It has–"

The sentence was cut off by the low murmur of the crowd.

My head whipped around so roughly that it strained the

muscles of my neck. "He didn't write Samantha into his will?" I whispered to Lyra.

"Yes, yes, I know," Malik tried to call back the attention of the crowd. "The fact that Mr. Hoffman does not have any living relatives, nor did he include a bequest in his will, everything will go to the bank. They plan to sell the theater at market value sooner than expected, given the competition within the district."

"When does it go on sale?" someone called out. "Are we still going to have our jobs?"

Malik scratched at his beard, contemplating whether he should withhold information or not. "Saturday. At midnight," he reluctantly answered, followed by an eruption from the crowd. "A lot is riding on this performance—we will most likely have a full house filled with potential buyers."

Lyra leaned in, the minty smell of her gum invading my senses. "Great, we get to replace one shitty boss with another."

"Samantha isn't even here! Who will headline for us?" another shouted.

Malik pinched the bridge of his nose. The poor man was wound up so tight, it had been years since I saw him looking like he wasn't seconds from having an aneurysm due to work-related stress. I can't imagine this was the life he had dreamt of when he immigrated from Turkey all those years ago, but damn was he a sensual theater manager, nonetheless.

Using his native tongue, Malik shouted, quieting the crowd. We had all been cursed out in Turkish plenty of times to know he wasn't keeping it family-friendly either. "Obviously, with Samantha in the hospital, we need to put something together last minute. A lot is riding on this—I need ideas, people!"

The window of grief had closed, and while many of the employees were still struggling to comprehend the loss, the show had to go on. The golden rule of show business that we all seemed to willingly follow without question. If Hoffman were here today, he'd be standing center stage screaming at us to do the same.

"We can use Thursday night's act," one of the background dancers said from a few rows ahead. "It's a solid routine and draws a decent crowd for a weekday."

"Hmm, not bad." Malik hummed, chewing over the idea, but not completely sold yet.

The young dancer was prepared to defend her idea, just as someone else screamed out their idea, then another. Each of them was worse than the last. She shrank into herself, giving Lyra the opportunity to finally speak. "I mean this in the nicest way possible, but those are all terrible ideas. That performance will come off mediocre and bland compared to what we need."

"Then what do you suggest?" he snipped a hint of defensiveness in his tone.

She shrugged. "Krissy could replace Samantha. She has a kick-ass routine that will have every man and woman breaking down the door to see it. Granted, I've only ever seen it while we were both drunk off our asses dancing around our living room, but I stand behind Krissy one hundred percent."

"I second that!" Daniel shouted from a row behind. "I was also drunk, but damn was it good."

It all happened so fast, one second I was brainstorming ideas, and the next I was on my feet, ready to back up Lyra and Daniel's claim. It didn't take an idiot to see the opportunity being delivered to me on a silver platter, but it took more than simply recognizing it to take it for myself. While it was above me to get down to my knees and beg Malik for this chance, I knew it would take some convincing for an opportunity I've surely earned over the years.

"The routine is nearly perfect," I avowed, drawing the attention of every eye in the building. Friends, peers, and rivals alike all watched me from afar, unsure if what I was offering was enough. In time, they would find out for themselves. "You've seen me on stage plenty of times, you know what I'm capable of."

"Performing on a Tuesday night when the crowd is three times your age is very different compared to a Saturday that could make it or break it for us," Malik warned me, raking his fingers through his thick brown hair. "I don't know…"

"At least watch the performance first before you make a decision," Daniel said.

"One chance, please," I begged, knowing only one chance was needed.

"Please," Lyra said, exaggerating her vowels. The warmth of her hand reached mine where our fingers interlocked. She gave me a little squeeze, and I gave her one right back as we waited for a response that never seemed like it would come.

"Fine," Malik cursed. "Be on stage in thirty minutes, and for everyone else, get back to work." With an unofficial audition set in place and all announcements concluded, the room dispersed, everyone returning to their positions with rumors still spreading like wildfire.

Containing my excitement any longer felt impossible, so when enough people were gone, I finally caved and squealed like an idiot. Lyra did the same before leaping up and throwing her arms around me. "I could kiss you right now. Thanks for backing me up."

"Hey, I helped too," Daniel called out, but we both ignored him.

"Tory might be a little jealous, but you could try," she teased.

Hope was for the dreamers. Each of us had our own wild fantasies of where this path would take us, and in this line of business, sometimes those paths crossed. For our little group, the success of one of us meant a setback for another. If I were given an opportunity to rise within the theater, it meant Daniel and Lyra couldn't. Even so, the two of them stuck their neck out for me to support a cause they saw as true, knowing that it was all I ever wanted. People like that were rare to come by, and while my circle was small, those who were in it were golden. Their sacrifice wouldn't go unnoticed, and I couldn't help recognizing how blessed I felt to have people near me who cared enough to try.

Dreamers were delusional with their heads in the clouds. Constantly searching for something that felt just out of reach. For two and a half years, I'd given this place my heart and soul, performing for a crowd that seemed nearly as delusional but for an entirely different reason. Nearly three years of being passed over and disregarded because Hoffman favored those who gave him more than an opening act. Well, Hoffman wasn't here anymore, and now felt as good a time as ever. I wasn't letting this opportunity slip through my fingers. Not now, not ever.

Lyra playfully shoved me and sent me stumbling toward the dressing rooms with a smile stretching ear to ear. "Now, get your ass backstage and get ready to prove him wrong."

Chapter Two

Krissy

To pinpoint the exact time my infatuation with theater started would be nearly impossible, but if I had to guess, I would say it happened around the time my mother started making me watch musicals, so I wouldn't bug her while she studied for nursing school. Then came the countless self-productions I choreographed for an audience of stuffed animals as I twirled about that stuffy apartment, careful not to disturb her work. No matter how little time she had, my mother always made it a priority to join the audience at some point in the night—an adoring crowd to spark my lifelong infatuation with theater.

From a young age, I realized my hotheaded personality and craving for attention could be directed toward something productive instead of being a self-righteous bitch who thought they were God's gift to planet Earth. Theater and dance gave me everything I needed while still keeping me humble. Despite that modesty, I knew my place on a stage and so did every instructor who crossed my path. Malik and Hoffman were the only ones whose opinions of me weren't as celebrated—all that did was light a fire under my ass and make me crave that success more.

Far too stubborn for my own good, there'd been plenty of times when I'd had my resume typed up and ready to be shipped off to the dozens of companies within the district that would have actually appreciated my talent, but when it came to hitting the send button, I could never do it. Something was holding me back, and although it took a while for me to realize what the setback was, it was apparent now that I needed to conquer this obstacle and prove my worth before moving on to the next.

After years of busting my ass, I had earned myself a role as a background dancer on Friday nights and a lead on Tuesdays. Every routine I'd performed was a perfectly curated show by Malik and our choreographers. Never had I been given an opportunity to show my true potential as a performer on this stage, and damn, was I ready for it.

Taking center stage, I breathed through the excitement pumping through my veins, which gave me the extra kick to push forward. Malik's stone-cold expression in the crowd meant nothing compared to Lyra and Daniel acting like my own personal cheerleaders, leaning up against the back bar. They'd both watched me give this performance a hundred times, but having them here for one last time felt monumental.

"Ready?"

"Yup."

Malik cued the music, and the space came to life. With a theater like this, my music was carefully curated to fit the rich historical atmosphere of the building that had been standing in the city for over a century. Every external fear drained away as my body swayed to the rhythm, consuming me. The routine was so ingrained into my muscles that I didn't have to think twice or doubt a single step. I let myself get carried away by the music, embodying the performance with not only my body but my voice. Samantha was notorious for lip syncing on stage—you'd never catch me dead on stage faking any aspect of who I was when I stepped under those lights.

There was nothing outside of this moment. It was a singular stretch of time that I never wanted to end. And like all good things, it eventually did, thrusting me back into reality. The track cut and silence stretched to every corner of the room. No one dared to speak as Malik exchanged a strange glance with Asha, our choreographer, at his side. I stood there panting in short, labored breaths, growing impatient as the silence continued for what felt like a lifetime.

"So?"

"Krissy, respectfully, this is one of the most high-end cabarets in this city, not a strip club." Malik finally spoke, folding his hands in his lap.

"Last time I checked, my tits weren't out when I was dancing, unless you think that would bring in more money...so please enlighten me, how did my performance resemble anything close to a strip show?" I asked indifferently with my hand on my hip.

"It's just a bit much," Malik added.

"No," I corrected. "You're just too traditional."

"I thought it was sexy," Asha applauded.

The Lotte was stuck in the past. The only reason we had regular clientele was because of the historical charm of the place. People loved to be wined and dined in a place their great-grandparents patronized, but at the end of the day, it wasn't paying the bills like it used to.

"What other option do you have?" I warned.

"None," he laughed.

"Exactly. We both know a little sex appeal is needed in this sad place," I responded, waving my hand toward the empty space. "Make the smart choice, Malik, not because you have no one else to turn to, but because you know you loved every moment of it. You're just afraid to admit it."

"She has a point," Asha said, giving Malik a sideways glance. The pause that came next seemed to drag on forever.

"You need background dancers," Malik snapped after a deep sigh. "Teach them the moves with Asha, find an outfit more fitting for the song, and then we'll have a show. But I swear if you mess this up, Davis–"

"You won't regret this."

Chapter Three

Erick

Expecting the reputation to precede her, I was pleasantly surprised when I finally stepped through the threshold after a lifetime of pining for this moment. A childhood of stories and a shoebox full of old photos, I thought I had The Lotte all figured out, but that couldn't be further from the truth.

While the lobby had its charm, nothing compared to stepping into the theater. My gaze followed the expanding room until it landed on the stage, far too large for a traditional cabaret. Originally built for intimate operas in the early twentieth century, it was gutted and renovated into a lounge while still holding its historical allure. A new addition had been added to the stage that extended a catwalk out toward the sea of tables that people were beginning to fill in anticipation of what tonight promised—myself included.

Lola, Antonio, and Damon followed closely behind as I took my time walking to our booth on the outskirts of the dining area —a last-minute reservation after word got around to my people about Mr. Hoffman's untimely death.

With a pointed look, they made their way to the booth

without me even having to waste my breath. I needed space to process this all on my own account, and after years of working for me, they seemed to understand without question. Time and space would surely help, but a little alcohol wouldn't hurt either.

Rather than going to the bar, my eyes locked on an empty table toward the back, smack in the middle of the stage. The opening act was minutes away from starting, so I plopped down in the seat, tossed the tiny paper reserved sign aside, and basked in the ambiance of the space. I managed five solid minutes of peace and quiet before a tiny figure appeared at my side.

"Excuse me, sir, I believe there has been a mistake," a posh voice said. "I reserved this table for myself, and only left for a moment to go to the restroom."

"I don't see a reservation sign," I retorted, not even bothering to turn toward the man.

The scoff that followed made me imagine I might have been the first person to tell him no in his privileged life. And the tailored suit and gold signet ring on his weathered hands confirmed it. Fancy clothes and jewelry to give the illusion of power and wealth when in reality he didn't have a backbone to speak for, and that's why he went lunging for the first worker that passed by instead of confronting me himself.

"Ma'am, excuse me. Ma'am," he called out with a wobbly voice. "This man stole my table and refuses to get up. Can you please call security?"

A young black woman with a dancer's body approached.

"Sir, can I please see your–" Her eyes slightly widened. "Apologies, Mr. Destler." The waitress beckoned over a coworker and directed his attention to the customer, nearly fuming at this point, so red in the face he looked like a tomato. "Can you please show this man to his seat, table sixty-three?"

"Of course," he said, gesturing in the opposite direction. "Please follow me this way, sir."

"This is ridiculous. I've been a customer for a decade. I demand to speak to Malik."

Neither of us spoke for a long while, waiting for his voice to be drowned out amongst the hushed conversations and distant laughter. Once he was gone, she leaned in close, and the comforting smell of cocoa butter washed over me.

"My name is Myisha; I'll be your waitress for the evening. Is there anything I can get you, Mr. Destler? Sorry again for the mix-up."

"I'll take a Manhattan for myself, and do you see that booth over there?" She nodded, finding the table I was pointing at. "Make sure they are taken care of."

"Yes, of course," she cooed, gladly accepting the money I slipped into her soft hands.

Halfway through my cocktail, the opening act finished with a decent performance that only teased the audience for what was to come next. While most people came in anticipation to witness Samantha Wilson's five-year reign finally come to an end, others, like myself, were here for an entirely different reason. It wasn't difficult to pick out the men and women in the crowd who were constantly checking their watches in anticipation for a once in a lifetime opportunity that tonight presented.

With two hours till midnight, the air seemed to ignite with energy.

Myisha, my waitress, brought me a second drink just as the jazz band kicked into rhythm and the curtains peeled back to reveal ten shadowy figures draped in low lighting. The lengthy intro of *And All That Jazz* echoed off the theater walls as every person in the building craned their neck to get a look at the slender figure striding toward the edge of the stage. With the familiarity of a lover, the figure caressed each dancer she passed, gracing her touch upon men and women alike. As the music hit its crescendo, a spotlight sparked to life directly above her, draping her in golden twinkling lights. The light served as her cue to start singing, and all it took was a few lines before I caught myself craning my neck to get a better look, too. With the voice of an angel, she captivated her audience with ease. An angel that hit every beat with the sway of her hips—that was what truly piqued my interest.

Krissy Davis, the last-minute replacement for Samantha Wilson, her name twinkling in the marquee lights. Clothed in a tight dress crafted of small crystals that gleamed as bright as her confidence, she looked like she was plucked right out of the play itself and dropped here for one magical night. With each overly seductive twist and turn, her long, dirty blonde curls stuck to her tanned skin. The longer I watched, the harder I grew until it was nearly painful watching her brush up against other men on stage. She was the essence of sex, and knowing she was a package deal with owning The Lotte made me somehow crave it more.

With feline grace, she leaped from the catwalk onto the nearest table, snagging a champagne flute from an unsuspecting bystander, and drained it in a second flat, making me wish it was her lips wrapped around my drink instead. Despite having every eye on her in the damn place, I swear for a split second while she crawled on that table, her eyes locked with mine.

One more hour.

Sixty more minutes were all that separated me from finally having all I've ever wanted, and sitting here torturing myself until then felt like too much to handle. Before I knew what I was doing, I was up and searching for Myisha, who was chatting up her coworkers in the back near the bar. The conversation quickly died off as they noticed me approaching.

Placing my hand on her back, I leaned in close and said, "Sweetheart, do you mind introducing me to your boss? He and I need to talk."

What difference did sixty minutes make when I already knew how tonight would end?

"I'm not sure," she said, dragging her bottom lip between her teeth.

"Just a quick conversation. That's it." I spoke low against the shell of her ear, sliding my hand down her spine. The further south my hand traveled, the more apparent it became that she was close to caving in. A sharp breath in. The subtle lean into my touch. Those dark brown eyes locked with me. Normally, I would have caved for that type of beauty as well, but tonight wasn't about being greedy.

"Fine. Only for you," she rasped.

Glancing over my shoulder, I found Lola, Antonio, and Damon pushing to their feet. They all gave the stage one more passing glance just as I did before we began following Myisha through the employee-only door and down a narrow hallway. Every few feet, there was a door lining the path, and we continued walking until she abruptly stopped in front of one with the nameplate reading Malik Aziz on the wood.

"Mr. Aziz should be back soon. If you wait here, it shouldn't be long," she said. "And hopefully by the time your meeting is over, I'll be done with my shift."

"Thank you, Myisha," I mumbled to the swooning waitress. It wasn't beneath me to use such lewd methods to get what I wanted—if anything, it made things easier. "Let's hope."

"*Yeah*, let's hope," Antonio echoed close to my ear in a taunting tone after Myisha was long gone. All it took was one shove before he was clutching his arm and moving to the corner of the room to pout. "Asshole."

"Play stupid games, win stupid prizes."

Patience had never been my strong suit, though it was always something I was working on–tonight was one of those rare exceptions when I didn't even make an effort to try. We waited for quite some time, hearing the music slow at the end of each song before kicking back into place with the beginning of another. Just as the next began, the door swung open, and to Mr. Aziz's surprise, he found he wasn't alone. By the look on his face, I'd say he recognized me almost as instantly as Myisha did – the white scar cutting down the side of my face against my light brown skin was a dead giveaway, whether they knew me personally or not.

"Mr. Aziz, have a seat." I pointed to the seat opposite me.

"Mr. Destler, what do–"

"Call me Erick," I insisted with a lazy smile.

"Erick," he corrected himself, nearly stumbling over the word. "What can I help you with?"

Turning toward Damon, I signed for him to get the cheap booze Malik kept in his excuse of an office. "We're celebrating my purchase of the theater," I announced with an overly excited tone unusual for me, but it felt right at the moment. Shoving the tumbler toward Malik, he paled like a ghost. "What's the matter?"

"The theater has already been sold."

I checked my watch, then propped my elbow on the desk and laughed. "Seeing that it's only eleven twenty, I don't see how that can be right. The theater doesn't go on sale until midnight."

"We had a buyer who expressed interest," he muttered, glancing down at the tumbler.

"Well, I'll pay double."

He sank into his chair and began to ramble like a coward. "Even if I wanted you to, the paperwork has already been signed and sent to the bank. It's out of my control. I am truly sor–"

Cutting him off before he could embarrass himself any more

than he already had. "How disappointing," I sighed, knowing this added yet another hoop to jump through to get what I wanted. The roadblock wasn't impossible to overcome, just an annoyance I'd have to manage. "Tell me, who is the lucky bastard?"

"I can't–"

"Malik," I tsked. "I was having a wonderful night before this, so I'm feeling a little more generous than usual. I'll give you one last chance to tell me."

With my patience growing razor thin, I gave him a minute to collect his thoughts. News of the ownership wouldn't be a secret for long, but I needed to know who'd purchased the theater before then. The seconds ticked by, one after another, until I was certain he wouldn't give me the name, even if I let him have the full sixty of them.

I whistled for Lola and Antonio, Damon following their lead.

All it took was one tug of his collar before he flopped on the floor like a fish and cowered for what he knew was coming next. Despite his pleading cries, Malik took the beating rather well as I scoured the office for any scrap of information regarding the new owner. Something that could have been easily avoided had he just done as he was told. Surely keeping secrets wasn't worth being relentlessly kicked from all angles—three against one was hardly a fair fight, but he had a choice and made the wrong one at the end of the day.

It didn't take long to find a signed document amongst the stacks of paper on his desk naming Patrick Martin as the new owner.

"Hmm…interesting," I said under my breath, handing the paperwork over to Lola. Ms. Choi was one of the few employees I added to my team after I assumed my role a few years back who hadn't previously worked for my father. Driven and eager, she quickly climbed the ranks with ease, earning herself a position amongst my inner circle. On the outside, the young Korean American appeared harmless, using her beauty and soft feminine features to trick her prey—but looks were deceiving. "Find what you can about this guy."

"On it."

"Thanks for the help, Malik. I look forward to working with you in the future," I said before leaving the manager curled up in a ball, bleeding profusely on the worn-out carpet. "And please let Mr. Martin know he should be expecting an offer from me shortly."

Coming here tonight with certain expectations made leaving empty-handed sting worse than it should have, but it was the unexpected performance of a lifetime that had me thinking about a certain angel clothed in nothing but crystals the entire way back. And even when I stomped into my office and threw myself on the couch, the only thing I could think of was that voice of hers.

Chapter Four

Krissy

Backstage the bottles were already popping. Rumors of an eager buyer purchasing the theater were spreading fast and we were all just waiting for Malik to make the official announcement, but that didn't stop us from getting a jump start on the celebrating. Daniel took the liberty of pouring me a hefty serving of champagne as we swayed our hips to the muffled sound of the band off in the distance. The Lotte would remain open with live music until two in the morning, but my job was done for the night, and I'd be damned if I didn't celebrate for all I'd done on that stage. Buyer or not, we were getting hammered tonight, I earned that much.

Having recently showered and scrubbed away the grime of the night, Daniel wrapped his arms around my shoulder and pulled me in close, a few drops of water fell from his short brown hair and landed on mine. I might have complemented him on his appearance had I already known the comment would have gone right to his head. The gray slacks brought out his light brown eyes just as much as the green short-sleeve button-down did for his muscular arms. Daniel had too big of an ego for his own good, and there was no need to feed into it.

"Drink up, bitch," he cheered, tipping up the bottom of the flute.

"I agree with Daniel for once. Finish your drink already, we're celebrating tonight!" Lyra appeared at my side with a drink in each hand. "I'm so goddamn proud of you."

I didn't have the heart to explain to them that I'd only been temporarily given the role in Samantha's absence—a slight technicality. While Malik wouldn't have entrusted me with such an important night if I hadn't earned his trust on stage, now that I was here, it was about maintaining the role long after Samantha returned and proving to them all this was where I belonged.

"Amen," I rejoiced, slightly lifting my glass in salute and then downing the champagne in two gulps. The bubbles seemed to go straight to my head, and I laughed through the warm, fuzzy feeling snaking through my body. Tonight felt like the best type of drug—addictive, overpowering, and like my whole body was riding that high—a high I never wanted to come down from.

"I couldn't have done it without you two," I admitted. "Thanks again for everything."

"You can thank us by coming out tonight," Daniel said, holding back a smirk. "I have a friend who works at a place nearby, and he said he can get us in."

"Ahh, where at?" I loved Daniel to death, like the brother I never wanted, but he made it a habit to surround himself with weird people outside of our little friend group. Dive bars were fun, but I didn't want to spend my special night with those strange friends of his in a sketchy part of the district.

A sharp whistle drew everyone's attention toward the other side of the room where Asha was standing, but not alone. A soft hiss traveled across the room, silencing the eager partygoers as they all turned in her direction.

She was biracial, with a Mexican mother and a black father. She made the blonde man look pale in comparison, but in reality, he had a light tan for someone of his ethnicity. There was something about his boyish good looks that felt familiar, but the longer I stared at him, the harder it became to pin down why that was.

"Where's Malik?" someone called out.

"Malik is feeling a little under the weather. He'll come to celebrate soon," she announced. "With that being said, I get the honor of introducing you all to the wonderful new owners of The Lotte. Everyone, please give a warm welcome to Mr. Patrick Martin."

An eruption of cheers and clapping overwhelmed the space.

Patrick stepped forward, his smile gleaming as he waved his hand. The moment he spoke, it hit me—I knew this man.

"Thank you. Thank you. It's my pleasure to be here today and have the opportunity to take The Lotte under my wing. My business partner and sister, Josephine Martin, sends her regards for not being able to make it tonight, but she hopes to meet you all soon. I look forward to getting to know all of you and seeing what astounding things we can do for this company. If you ever need anything, please don't be shy."

The booze began to flow like the Nile River backstage. Dancers, singers, and production crew alike started to drink and dance the night away. Feeling slightly too sober for the occasion, I sucked down another drink before approaching Patrick on a whim amongst the dozen or so others who were trying to impress the new boss. Those blue eyes found mine before I could fully part through the crowd to reach him.

"Miss Krissy Davis. I was hoping I'd be able to speak to you tonight," he greeted me with a bright white smile and an extended hand. "I'm Patrick, and it's a pleasure to meet you."

"Actually, we've met before," I laughed, shaking his hand regardless, feeling a sharp tingle low in my gut as we touched.

"Sorry, you might have to refresh my memory."

"Junior year, RSU. You were roommates with Jackson, right?"

Running his hand over his freshly shaved face, he chuckled. "Christ, that's why I thought I recognized you. I figured I'd watched you perform here before when I came with my family. Turns out it's because you're the girl who broke Jackson's heart— I swear that poor guy locked himself in his room for two weeks coping with the heartache."

Relationships came and went, especially during my college years, with very few of them leaving their mark. Hearing that name again felt like nails being dragged down my spine, and it took much more effort than I was willing to admit to keeping my composure while speaking about the eight-month romance once more. As difficult as it was to recall that portion of my life, I still had a vivid memory of Jackson introducing me to his gorgeous roommates after a lousy first date that he insisted would get better if I allowed him to take me home.

In the months that passed, our paths rarely crossed besides the occasional house party or a quick hello in passing as Jackson dragged me to his bedroom. Needless to say, each time we spoke it was a breath of fresh air compared to the people my ex-boyfriend usually surrounded himself with. Toward the end of the semester, I remember Patrick packing up his belongings, boasting about some study abroad program in Europe he'd been accepted to through the university. By the time he'd returned to the States, I'd already broken things off with Jackson and had no reason to befriend him while I swore to detest men altogether.

"I promise you, he deserved it."

"Can't say I blame him for being so upset after losing someone like you."

"God, that feels like so long ago." I sipped my drink, fighting back the blushing feeling washing over my cheeks. Since the years that have passed, he'd grown his hair out, letting it flow loose and wild. Besides that, not much had changed—still handsome as the day I met him.

"A lifetime ago," he agreed. "Looks like we will be seeing each other much more now."

Lifting my glass in the air, he followed suit. "Congrats on snagging this beauty. The Lotte needs someone like you to keep the lights on."

"Congrats to you too." *Clink.* "Seems I have a star in my theater, and I plan to have you on that stage more often, Miss Davis."

Hoping to keep this unbelievable night going, I decided to push my luck. "My friends and I are actually going to go celebrate after this by going to a bar around the block. If you want, you can come with us; you're more than welcome to join," I offered, praying I could get this man drunk on the dance floor with me. It was both our nights to celebrate. Shouldn't we both indulge?

"I would in a heartbeat if I didn't have some business to take care of. I promised Josephine, my sister, that I would stop by her apartment," he explained, fiddling with his glass. "How about we save the drink I would have bought you tonight for another time? How does that sound?"

"I'm holding you to that drink, Patrick. It was good seeing you again," I said, leaving his presence for the company of my friends. The two of them watched me stride toward them with a mischievous look gleaming in their eyes.

"Already trying to get into the boss's pants? Turns out you and Samantha have more in common than you thought," Lyra jokingly mumbled into her cup.

"Shut up! Patrick and I have known each other since college. I was just saying hi."

"Sure," Daniel hummed.

"Tory is on her way backstage right now. As soon as she's here, we'll head out."

Clothed in a short black two-piece set and five-inch heels to complete the look, I was nearly freezing as I walked through the crisp September night. Daniel insisted we didn't need to waste our money on a cab because the club was just around the block, only a quick, sketchy walk through a dark alley to get there. I would have fronted the twelve bucks for the whole group if it meant I wouldn't have to wander around Republic City, practically begging to be robbed or jumped while wearing the borrowed designer top and mini skirt with a subtle slit down the thigh.

Turns out Daniel undersold just how close the club truly was—his definition of around the block meant the building directly behind us. The majority of the buildings in the city were long rectangular structures with two or more businesses housed within, each storefront facing a different block, one in front, and another in the back.

The alley between buildings dumped us out right at the end of the queue, where a handful of people waited under the red neon light shaped into the name of the venue: Don Juan. I'd heard stories of the club but never had a chance to test it out myself. It was the type of establishment you'd need a miracle to get into without knowing someone within. Exclusive was fine, but a place that was impossible to get into wasn't the type I liked to visit.

"Stay here, just in case. I'm going to see if my friend is manning the door."

With a thick brick wall separating us from the speakers within, the muffled music was just loud enough to feel the vibration of the bass from where we stood. Daniel had disappeared amongst the crowd, and the longer we waited for him to return, the more I realized I couldn't feel my toes. Using the hardly audible music as my guide, I swayed my hips to the rhythm in hopes of keeping warm in the meantime.

Five minutes passed, and the line didn't move an inch.

"Where the hell is he?" I cursed under my breath.

A few more minutes dragged by before I noticed Daniel's tall figure parting the crowd. His already thinned lips were locked in a tight line, eyes narrowed. "I don't know where he is, but I just texted him. Let's wait here until he texts back."

"I don't know how much more I can wait. I'm freezing."

"I promise, it won't be long," he assured us.

It wasn't like us to give in to Daniel's whirlwind ideas so easily, but Lyra, Tory, and I all seemed to have some unspoken agreement that we would give it some more time before we kicked it to the curb. With our patience growing thin, toes nearly purple, I finally caved after ten more minutes.

"Ah," I groaned. "This is stupid. Let's just go back to The Lotte. They're all probably drunk without us by now. Plus, I don't think I can feel my toes anymore."

"I second that," Lyra and Tory said in unison. The two girls looked nearly as cold as I did. Lyra wore a deep red cocktail dress that covered up as little as my outfit did, and with box braids that hung low on her back, her scalp was hardly protected from the wind chill. Tory, on the other hand, was wearing a devastatingly beautiful two-piece jumpsuit and coat that Lyra kept wrapping herself in for body warmth.

Daniel sighed. "Are you sure? Tonight was supposed to be special. We drink at the theater every weekend."

"I appreciate the gesture, but I promise I'd rather be drunk with our friends than lose a toe tonight," I said, and then kissed his icy cheek. "Okay, let's get the hell out of here."

Daniel, bless his heart, was trying his best, and although I appreciated the sentiment, it wasn't worth standing out in the cold all night just in the hopes of getting into the club. We had places to be and accomplishments to celebrate, so with that being said, we got moving and set our sights on returning to the theater.

Retracing our steps through the dingy alleyway back home, we spotted a shadowy figure leaning up against the wall. The soft glow of his cigarette was the only source of light illuminating his face on this cloudy night. Besides Tory, who grew up on a reservation out west, we were all raised near the city and knew well enough to keep our eyes forward and heads down.

"Hey," he called out.

Eyes forward. Head down.

"Hey," he repeated in a thick Italian American accent. Refusing to acknowledge him, I kept walking until we'd nearly passed him. "Aren't you the girl who performed tonight at The Lotte? Davis, right?"

"Yes," I said in a steady tone, unsure where this was going, but calling me by name was enough to stop me in my tracks.

"I was just there a few hours ago watching you perform—great show! What are you doing out here in the cold? Shouldn't you be out celebrating?" Shrouded in shadows, my eyes had adjusted enough to see his inky black hair styled with gel and the subtle curve of his once broken nose. Something about his care-free style, with just enough effort to put into getting ready, made him look devilishly handsome but clearly trouble.

"That was the plan for the night, but we couldn't get in," I answered, gesturing toward the club. Out of the corner of my eye, I could see my friends tense up, confused why I was making small talk with this stranger in an alley...and honestly, I wasn't sure either.

"Don Juan?"

I nodded.

"Lucky for you all, I know the owner, and I don't think he would mind if I let you in," he bragged. "You and your friends can come in through the back entrance. I'll make sure a star like you is taken care of tonight." With a quick flick of his wrist, he unlocked a side door to the building and gestured for us to follow. Shrugging my shoulders, I led the way for the group. If being the star of The Lotte meant I could potentially receive special treatment from time to time, I was more than prepared to abuse that privilege on occasion.

"If we get murdered, I'm going to come back and haunt you," Lyra whispered.

"Loosen up, Lyra. And if you get murdered, I'm probably getting killed too. Ghosts can't haunt ghosts."

"I hate you sometimes."

I blew her a kiss and pushed forward.

Our new friend, or potential murderer, led us through the back of the house until we reached a large metal door. On the other side was the luxurious chaos that was Don Juan, one of the most exclusive nightclubs in Republic City. The dance floor sat in the center of the room, sunken into the floor with a swarm of people seductively dancing to the rhythm of music the DJ on the raised platform was mixing. On the outskirts of the dance floor were booths and seating areas where people drank, smoked, and hooked up in the low lighting. We were directed to the enormous bar, where four bartenders were scrambling to fulfill all the orders for the busy night. One of them saw us approaching and dropped what he was doing instantaneously.

"Hey, Ryan!" he shouted and pointed toward us. "Make sure you take care of this group. Their first round is on the house." The bartender gave him a thumbs-up and got to work on pouring the four shots.

Before he could walk away, I grabbed his arm and shouted over the music. "Thank you."

"Enjoy your night, Krissy." He smiled and pulled away. Standing there for a moment, I watched him disappear into the crowd before my eyes pulled up towards the balcony on the second floor overlooking the entire club. It was far too dark to make anything out on the balcony, but I could have sworn someone, or something, were watching me. That weird tingling sensation electrified my nerves as I strained my eyes to see what it was.

"Krissy. Get your ass over here," Tory called, breaking me from my trance.

"Coming!" Daniel grabbed two shots off the bar top and pretended to take mine when he saw me not moving fast enough. "Don't you dare, Daniel, or I will smack you upside the head."

"I wouldn't dare drink without the great Krissy Davis in our presence. And with that being said, this one's for you," he said, handing over the mystery shot.

"To Krissy," they shouted.

"To me," I cheered myself, letting the smooth taste of tequila hit the back of my throat.

Chapter Five

Patrick

The Martin family comes from a long line of musicians. My family tree was filled with generations of talented instrumentalists who played for adoring fans in packed Parisian opera houses and were personally invited to perform in Versailles during a time when the monarchy was still alive and well in France. When fame and glory weren't enough of a thrill as they had once been, my ancestors packed up their lives and sailed across the Atlantic Ocean, seeking something entirely different.

I wasn't quite sure what they were looking for in the new world, but they must have found it because they set their roots down in Republic City and never looked back.

Jazz had taken the country by storm, and for my great-grandfather, the first of the Martin children to be born on American soil, it was love at first sight with the rich harmonies and syncopated rhythms. From what I'd been told he lived a long and fulfilling life as a trumpeter performing during the Roaring Twenties and died peacefully in his sleep next to his beloved wife long before my father was ever born—which might have been a blessing in disguise, for had he known his own kin would break generations of Martin tradition, he might have rolled over dead from the news alone.

My father didn't have a musical bone in his body and refused to even try when his parents suggested putting him in classes. Despite that innate flaw, he was an avid connoisseur of the art and heavily invested the money he'd earned in finance into the thing he loved from afar. The Martin family may not personally own any of the businesses in the entertainment district, but their presence was known.

Well, until now.

Purchasing The Lotte was a risky business venture and a massive financial undertaking that Josephine had ensured me would be worth it in the long run, though she had more to gain from this than I did. When she'd received word that our offer had been accepted for the theater, thanks to her fiancé's connection at the bank, my sister sent me across town to introduce myself, scope the property, and then report back with my initial thoughts on the place.

And boy, did I have some thoughts about The Lotte.

Backstage was a riot with dancers drinking their weight in champagne and flirting with whoever was within arm's reach. It took a few tries to break away from the crowd, but eventually, I managed to leave behind the managers and crew eager to make a good first impression and found a quiet corner to call Josephine and check in with her.

I pulled out my phone to find she'd already texted me.

Josephine: Dinner turned into drinks. Won't be home until tomorrow. Talk to you then.

I dialed her number before I could think twice about it.

"You are joking, right?" I said as a way of greeting.

"I told you I was busy," she answered, battling the music in the background.

"Josephine," I rasped. "I—we had plans. You explicitly told

me to come over tonight so we could discuss the theater and now..." I shut my eyes. "You have no idea what I gave up tonight for you to just bail on me."

Clothed in the most tantalizing dress I'd ever seen with thousands of individual crystals sewn onto it and a matching garter, Krissy Davis had walked back into my life looking like a dream. It was hard to forget a face like hers, and the moment she took center stage, all the hopeless pining I'd done in college came rushing back all at once. I didn't even want to think about what the night could have been had I said yes to her offer to join her for drinks. Mulling over what-ifs and fantasizing about each possibility wasn't doing any good, nor was it keeping my mind sharp.

"Whatever it was, I'm sure you'll be fine," she sighed, her voice becoming sharper through the speaker. The obnoxious sound of the bass in the background was growing more distant as she was likely walking away from the booth to have a more private conversation. "You're being a bit dramatic."

"It's the principle of the matter. You told me—"

"Don't speak of principles when you have no concept," she interjected, a bite to her tone. "Might I remind you that you wouldn't have a job if it weren't for me? Or that this might be your last opportunity to be in father's good grace?"

"That was a misunderstanding."

"No. No, it wasn't. Accept what happened last summer already and move on. I'm going out of my way to give you this opportunity. The least you can do for me is do your job and do it well. I'm relying on you to help me before the wedding," she reluctantly said.

Her words sliced deep.

Failure is perceived to be the learning block of success. One cannot exist without the other—or that's what we've been told. Regarding all that had happened last summer, I was inclined to think differently. What lesson could I have possibly learned by mishandling millions in investments? What possible benefit could come from sullying my name in the financial district, making my father regret ever employing me, and begging my dear sister for one last chance to redeem myself?

For all that she has done for me throughout our childhood, I owe her far more than running the theater on her behalf. I reminded myself that despite my failures, she was the only one who cared to take me under her wing when no one else would. I reminded myself that I wouldn't be where I am today without her love and support.

The theater was never mine to begin with, but with some twist of fate, here I was. And I was determined to make something out of it in order to repay–

Nearby, the distant sound of hissing came into earshot. Each was as pained as the last.

"Josephine, I have to go. I'll speak to you tomorrow," I said before hanging up the phone and following the strange sound.

Down the hall and to the left, I found the source of the noise behind closed doors. Malik sat on a worn couch with sunken cushions and tears in the corner. Each hiss was followed by a mumbled phrase I didn't recognize that could have resembled either a curse or a prayer. Given the way Asha tended to the wounds on his forehead, it could have been either one. The manager was swollen in all the wrong places, making his slender face appear inflated and grotesque with splashes of crimson that Asha hadn't yet tended to. The man looked like he'd been to hell and back, and by the way he clutched his rib in a white-knuckle grip, it was clear his injuries weren't purely facial. It had only been hours since we last met to sign the papers, but I hardly recognized him now.

"What the heck happened?" I asked, wide-eyed and suppressing the urge to wince at the sight of all the blood.

"Close the door behind you before someone sees us," Malik rasped.

As the lock clicked in place, I whirled around searching for an answer that Malik and Asha seemed reluctant to answer as they stared at one another. Some kind of silent communication passed between them.

"Someone needs to speak."

She blurted out, "Malik was attacked by someone."

"Asha," he warned.

"No," she shut her eyes and took a deep breath, "if you are going to refuse to go to the hospital or report the attack, then the least I can do is tell Patrick. He deserves to know. Especially if what you say is true about the theater."

"I already told you that calling the police won't do any good. What's done is done."

Ownership would come with a price. A never-ending list of responsibilities that would test the strongest-willed of us all. I'd witnessed it countless times as my father shared that vulnerable part of his life with me, grooming me for an ascension that would never come. Whether I was prepared or not, from that first signature until forever more, the theater was now my responsibility. And it was my burden to protect those beneath me.

I stepped forward, ignoring the rolling sensation in my lower gut. "Malik, protecting whoever harmed you will only do more harm than good. This person doesn't deserve your discretion, and as owner of the theater, I have a right to know what happened on my property."

"Very well, you'll find out sooner or later." The manager looked me dead in the eyes and said, "Destler paid me a visit after the show. He sends his regards and promises you'll be hearing from him shortly for an offer on the building."

"Is this some sick way of sending a message?"

"No," he gestured to his split lip, "this was for refusing to give up your name or the fact that you were in the building when he was looking for you. Who's to say what he's truly capable of? You have a target on your back, Mr. Martin. I suggest considering what that means for you before declining his offer."

I had lots to consider, but it had nothing to do with giving up my theater.

Chapter Six

Erick

Fallen from the grace of God, an angel would have to willingly clip their wings as Satan compelled them to, in order to be stripped of divine fate. Free of corruption and sin, she stumbled into my domain with her wings intact, but watching her from my vantage point high above, I could tell she wasn't as completely pure as she looked.

I reminded myself that even Lucifer himself was once an angel.

Antonio leaned against the railing next to me, his face draped in a collection of colorful lights bouncing around the club. "I figured you wouldn't mind if I let Miss Davis and her friends skip the line."

"What? Do you want a pat on the back for doing your job?"

"A *thank you* every so often would be nice," he teased. There weren't many people I let speak to me like that, Antonio being the rare exception.

"I can thank you by making you scrub toilets for a week," I retorted, not in the mood for his usual smugness. "Leave me alone," Antonio grumbled to himself as he pushed off the railing, making sure to warn Lola about my *exceptionally* pissy mood tonight as he walked away.

The night had started like none other, and the longer it seemed to drag on, the more sour my mood turned. My only saving grace was the tall blonde who stumbled into my club looking as stunning as she did on stage, but even that didn't completely solve my problems.

Plucking the joint from behind my ear, I switched to something more fitting for my *pissy* mood and sparked it to life. Alcohol clearly wasn't doing the trick, so I switched vices for the night. The crude tightness of my lungs burned the longer I held it, only releasing it when I felt like the organ might collapse any second now. A thin trail of smoke danced through my line of sight as freely as Krissy did below. Without the confines of her routine, she moved more sensually than before, grinding up against her drunken friends with the brightest smile painting her lips. Once again, in a crowded room, she had my full attention and kept me wishing I had hers.

Focus, Erick.

As time passed by, the red glow of my joint slowly smothered itself out. I tossed the roach in the ashtray to my side, and when I glanced up again, I found that Krissy's group had shrunk in size. The man she originally arrived with was long gone—he'd run off with the girl he was flirting with all night and dragged her off to the darkest corner of the club. As for her other friends, the young black girl was looking green in the gills, hauling her girlfriend to the restrooms before she could make a mess of my club.

Part of me wished she would, so I could thank Antonio properly.

The absence of her friends didn't seem to bother her. Krissy carried on, dancing alone without a care in the world, only needing herself and the music to enjoy her night.

It wasn't long until someone capitalized on the opportunity, swooping in to try their luck without her friends to keep the creeps at bay. Throughout the night, she'd captured the attention of dozens of men and women alike, and why wouldn't she? Women like Krissy did so effortlessly by simply existing. And like the leeches they were, they planned to take advantage of her being alone. A lengthy white man about as wide as my left thigh approached my little angel first and leaned down to whisper something in her ear. Krissy mimicked the actions by rising to her tippy toes, shouting loud enough for him to hear over the pounding bass. The longer the interaction went on, the more painful my grip on the railing became.

His hand brushed her hip, and she instantly stepped back, but he didn't seem to read the message because he advanced forward again, subtly ignoring her shift in body language.

Seeing red, I pushed off the railing and made my way toward the stairs.

Security was typically good at reading the room and spotting handsy men before they became a problem. With no one in sight to help her, I took it upon myself to handle the situation before it could escalate any further.

Pushing through the throng of drunken idiots, I broke through only to find Krissy nowhere near the dance floor where I'd last spotted her. Instead, she was leaning forward, elbows propped up on the bar, sipping a colorful drink nearly halfway gone. The creep wasn't bugging her anymore, but he clearly wasn't gone for good. He'd found a table to sit at and watch her from afar like a predator looking for its next meal.

The somber look in her beautiful blue eyes made me pause. Slightly dilated and wide. A far cry from the smiling woman I saw dancing earlier, an echo of her former self. My original plan was to come down here looking for trouble, but seeing her like this, I decided to push that aside and focus on her well-being instead.

Ryan already had a Manhattan poured for me by the time I reached the bar. Leaning my back against the counter, an arm's length away from her, I took slow sips of my drink and reminded myself why I keep him employed and paid well. Ryan knew his way around a bar.

"Is that perv in the red shirt still staring at me?" Like the sweetest honey, her voice drips from her lips, raspy and low, leaving me nearly as stunned as I was when I heard her first sing. Not expecting her to be the first to speak, I paused for a moment, pretending to search for the asshole. Using that borrowed time, I collected my thoughts and steeled my nerves.

"I don't think he's stopped staring at you all night," I pointed out.

She groaned, and the noise went straight to my cock. "That's what I was afraid of…I lied and told him I had a boyfriend when he insisted we should drink and dance together, but that rarely does the trick, huh? He insisted that because my boyfriend wasn't here, we could still have a good night together. Why are men such trash…no offense, unless you're one of those types of guys, then I take it back."

I huffed out a laugh, loving her boldness. "Unfortunately, boys will always assume someone's fair game unless they see your arm wrapped around said guy, and even then…" I trailed off.

Wrapping her full red lips around the crystal, she took a long sip. "Usually, my friends beat off any creeps trying to get within ten feet of me, but they all ran off. Do you think talking to you now will be enough? Maybe he'll think we're together."

The warmth of my whiskey mingled with my high, making me feel just as bold. "I doubt it. He won't think that unless he sees my tongue down your throat, and even then, he seems pretty persistent." Turning toward the bar, I was just about to shout for Ryan to radio for security when her little hand wrapped around my forearm.

"Not that I'm totally against an incredibly attractive man shoving his tongue down my throat, maybe we should start off with a dance first?" she suggested with a gentle smile.

Leaning in close enough to feel the warmth radiating off her body, I heard her breath hitch. "If you're planning to just use me to ward off creepy men, then I'd rather just call security for that. So, tell me, Krissy, are you just using me, or is this the little excuse you came up with to get me to dance with you?"

Tilting her head to the side, her lips brushed up against the shell of my ear, instantly making my arm break out in goosebumps. "Maybe a little of both, but mostly just finding any excuse to be close to you," Krissy admitted, low and seductive. The DJ transitioned one song into the next, giving her the perfect opportunity to drag me by the hand to the dance floor, completely unaware of my little name slip-up.

We reached the center of the crowd, in perfect view of our *little* friend watching from where he still sat. Krissy stopped dead in her tracks, hooked her hand around my neck, and pulled herself close. It's my hand nudging her on the small of her back that pressed us flush with each other. Letting the music guide us, I lost myself in our proximity, the intoxicating smell of her perfume, and the weight of her body grinding against mine. Being the greedy bastard I was, I spun her around, so her ass pressed up against my erection, wanting her to know exactly what she was doing to me.

"Is this close enough for you?" I mumbled, nuzzling into her neck.

Krissy moved her hips selfishly and spoke barely loud enough for me to hear over the bass. "No, not at all."

"Don't tempt me." I was rewarded with a groaned-out moan as I nibbled the sensitive spot on her neck and let my hands roam freely, exploring whatever forbidden fruit I could. If her wings aren't clipped now, I plan to do it myself, nail them to my wall so I stare at them forever knowing I did that to her. "We could really make him jealous if you wanted."

"Don't tempt me," she retorted. Nothing about what was happening was about making him jealous, and we both knew that, but neither of us was willing to admit that completely yet.

One song bleeds into another, then another. Neither one of us was willing to pull apart from where we were connected until I was slick with sweat and ready to drag her to the nearest secluded part of the club. Having her like this was all I could have asked for after how the night was going, but it wasn't enough. I needed more.

Krissy began to slump in my arms, her movements turning sloppier as my mouth trailed a line of kisses from her exposed shoulder to her jaw. The taste of her skin was the sweetest drug that promised I would surely be an addict. Reaching her jaw, she turned, lips parted. Inches apart from one another, all I had to do was lean in a little closer, and I knew I would be a goner. Just as I worked up the courage to close the gap, a hand landed on my shoulder. "Erick, you need to see this," Antonio shouted.

"Handle it yourself. Leave." Antonio doesn't waste his breath repeating himself. It's the look in his eyes that told me this wasn't something he could do on his own, forcing me to make a difficult decision. "Give me a minute. I'll be right back," I told Krissy, wanting to kick myself for leaving her like this. With a sluggish nod, she moved to the outskirts of the dance floor and found a seat while Antonio pulled me aside and began rambling on about something I couldn't make out over the music and my own thoughts. Over his shoulder, I watched her slump in the chair and ask the nearest woman for the time, and she obliged, flashing her home screen toward her. With the harsh glow of the screen illuminating her face, she looked far drunker than she should be after what she had over the course of the last two or so hours.

"Erick," he called. "Get your head out of your ass. I'm talking to you."

"Make it quick, or I swear to God."

Opting to show instead of tell, he shoved his phone in my face. The soft black and white glow of the club's surveillance footage played with the time stamp about forty minutes ago in the corner. Through the tiny screen, I relived Krissy dancing alone and being approached by the man from earlier. What the cameras captured that I couldn't see from my vantage point was him slipping something into her drink as he leaned in to speak to her. The powder dissolved almost instantly, and Krissy proceeded to nervously chug it when he finally backed off.

With few suppliers in the city, I had a hunch I knew where this came from.

"Find that fucker and bring him to me." I shoved the phone in his chest and rushed back to Krissy, who now had her face nestled in her hands. "Krissy, look at me. Are you okay?"

"No," she mumbled into her hands. "I feel–I feel really drunk and dizzy. It got way worse when I sat down." It had been long enough since she ingested whatever the hell he put in her drink for it to start taking full effect. No wonder he was standing off to the side watching her like prey. He was playing the waiting game for this exact moment. "How do you know my name? I just met you. I—I don't even know your name."

"You headlined tonight at The Lotte. I make it my business to know exceptional people," I explained, crouching down so I was at eye level with her. "Someone slipped something into your drink, and whatever drug it was has worked its way through your system. Don't worry, I'm going to take care of you. Now let's find you some water and a place to rest."

She slurred a string of curses.

"It's alright. I got you." I pulled her up and began to guide her back toward the stairway leading to the balcony. The closer we got, the harder it became for her to keep herself upright; it was as if her head was made of bricks and every which way she moved, the heaviness weighed her down. As delicately as I could, I hoisted her in my arms and carried her the rest of the way, but instead of rising to the perch, we descended the stairs into the depths of hell. With Krissy limp in my arms, I struggled to press the code on the keypad and unlock the steel door.

Although I compared it to hell, this place was the closest thing to a safe haven I had. The soft white lighting flickered to life, illuminating the hidden lounge beneath the club only my closest confidants and living family members knew about. It was nearly as large as the club above, still as pristine as the day it was built in secret during the early twentieth century.

Bypassing the tables and chairs haphazardly spread throughout the space, I entered my office door to the right of the bar. Krissy moaned something that I couldn't make out as we passed the threshold—the poor thing could barely keep her eyes open as the weight of them lulled her into sleep, seconds from giving in. As stunning as she looked cradled in my arms, her lips slightly parted, I lowered her down to the couch. There wasn't much I could do for her besides give her a place to rest, water, and time to work the drugs out of her system.

"Drink this," I encouraged, bringing the rim of the glass to her lips. Nearly too far gone now, she sipped the water slowly, not even bothering to open her eyes. "Good girl, keep drinking."

"Don't do that," she slurred, turning away from me and burying her face between the back pillow and the top cushion.

"Do what? Make you drink water?"

"No. Don't call me that," she slurred into the pillow, then continued mumbling to herself. I only caught bits and pieces, and I could have sworn she mentioned something about liking the term of endearment too much coming from my lips, but in her drug-induced state, I couldn't say for certain.

"Get some rest, little angel," I whispered, smoothing out her hair.

Countless times I've sat in a stuffy church being told God works in mysterious ways, punishing sinners for their wrongdoings if they don't repent. At a young and naïve age, I waited patiently for God to take justice upon the sinners in my life, and when that time never came, I learned two things that became pivotal moments in my upbringing. One, there was no such thing as God. And two, I would take it upon myself to enforce that justice if need be.

Damon shoved the sinner to his knees for judgment. Attempting to collect himself after the fall, he peered up at me, pathetically. Weak. Feeble. Puny. None of them quite described the shell of a man before me.

"What the hell do you want?" He bit out, trying to disguise the tremble in his voice.

Damon tossed me his wallet, and I quickly plucked out his ID. "You tell me," I said, scanning over the card. "Jeffrey H. Stevenson, who lives at 567 West Keiser Way, apartment 213. What the hell are you doing in my club, drugging my clientele?"

"I didn't do shit," he responded defensively. Too quick for my taste.

My hand was around his throat in the blink of an eye. Jeffery choked on what little air I provided him as I began to squeeze, constricting his windpipe. "There's nothing I hate more than a liar. So, let's try again," I suggested. "Why the fuck did you think you had any right coming here tonight to drug people's drinks?" When he didn't answer, I dug my nails into the flesh right below his jaw and forced him to turn his head to the right. "Do you see her? Do you even remember slipping something into her drink, or was she just one of the dozens of girls you did that to?" Krissy lay unconscious, riding out the effects of the drugs in her system. "Let me guess, you tried your luck with the prettiest girl you could find, and when that didn't work, you figured by drugging her you might still have a chance. So, you sat back and waited for her to start feeling it so you could swoop in and take her back to your place and have a little fun?"

Jeffery attempted to look away, but I didn't let him. "Stop," he pleaded. "No, man."

The longer he stared at her, the more he trembled under my touch. He began to shake so violently that it rattled his bones. After the shaking came the sniffles and tears, but they weren't the tears of someone ready to repent—they were for fear of being caught.

"Were you going to hurt her, Jeffrey?" I screamed in his ear. "Answer me, you piece of shit!"

"Yes," he sobbed.

My fist collided with Jeffery's nose, instantly breaking it with a spray of blood that soaked the rug beneath my feet. He'd been knocked out in the first blow, but that didn't stop me from continuing just so I could have the pleasure of hearing the various snaps and breaks his body could make. Every touch of rage I'd been holding onto came pouring out as I beat Jeffrey mere feet away from the woman he attempted to harm. Damon let me have my fun for a while before peeling me off the lifeless body so badly mangled he didn't resemble anything close to his driver's license photo.

The fucker was still breathing, and that in itself was too much mercy for my liking.

Having been in this exact situation plenty of times, Damon removed the body from my office, leaving a trail of blood in his wake. The beating was my mercy; death would eventually be his payment for preying on the weak – a type of weakness that would never exist if he didn't use dirty tricks to blindside his prey. Deep down, I knew if Krissy was of sound mind, she would have no problem handling him—she seemed like she could hold her own, but while she slept off whatever was in her system, I'll be there to protect her.

Chapter Seven

Krissy

Regret filled every crevice of my body. Caught somewhere between consciousness and slumber, I began to notice the pounding in my skull, the tightness of my limbs, and the swirling in my gut. The worst part of making poor decisions was having to live with them the next morning—though I'd learned a trick or two for dealing with such inconveniences after four years at RCU.

Prying open my heavy eyes, expecting to be in my apartment, I found myself in a strange place with my whole world tilted on its side. An arrangement of furniture with an Art Deco flair was perfectly placed throughout the space, along with a billiards table and replica paintings on the wall that looked as if they also originated from the turn of the century. For a split second, I thought I woke up in the wrong decade, then shook off the strange thought when I realized how stupid that sounded.

To my side was a small table just out of reach. Atop it was a glass of water and a bottle of Ibuprofen, and although I had no recollection of how I ended up here, I took a leap of faith and reached for it in hopes of easing the splitting headache hammering the right side of my skull. I willed myself to move when every instinct was telling me to stay put. The tips of my fingers barely grazed the cup before my world spun around me.

It all happened so fast—one moment I was lying on the couch, and the next, I wasn't.

"Mother fucker," I cursed, landing with a thud only to miss the explosion of glass flying in all directions.

While attempting to collect myself off the floor, the door across the room unlocked with a sharp click. That's when the daunting realization hit me that I wasn't alone. The term fight or flight gets tossed around a lot, but unless you're in that type of situation, you'll never understand how action dictates your fear, and you move without thinking twice—I lunged for the largest shard of glass and tucked it out of sight.

Basking in the light of the bathroom, he emerged as a shadowy figure filling most of the door frame. It only took one step into the office for me to realize his eyes had found mine long before I even knew he was staring. The softness in his brown eyes didn't match the white jagged scar stretching from above his right eyebrow to his cheek—it seemed to glow in contrast to his light brown skin. His features were fierce yet stunning, and what fragments of the night I did remember didn't do justice to the beautiful biracial man standing across the room from me—but beauty did not equate trust.

"Are you okay?" he asked in a husky voice. When I failed to answer, he took a step forward; only then did I find it in myself to stand.

"No, yeah, I'm fine. I just fell," I said in a clipped tone.

"You should probably sit down."

"No," I retorted, crossing my arms. A million questions circled around in my head begging to be answered, but I blurted out the first one that could make its way out. "I'm good. I'd prefer it if you told me where the hell I am and what happened last night. Waking up in a strange place after a night out isn't always a good sign."

"What do you remember? Maybe I can fill in the gaps," he suggested, stepping away from the threshold, eating away at the space in the room on his walk to the wet bar.

"Dodging my questions isn't a good sign either. Where am I?" I repeated, studying the room again, trying to pull from the deepest corners of my memory to explain how I got here. "I don't even remember leaving the building. Are we still at the club?"

He nodded. "Yes, we're beneath the club in my office. Now answer my question."

The night was a blur, only fragments of a celebration gone wrong. "Not much—I remember drinking and dancing alone after my friends ditched me, then being approached by you at the bar. Besides that, I don't remember anything, which is weird —really weird considering I only had three cocktails and a shot...." The number of drinks I consumed in no way correlated with the way I was feeling now; it simply did not add up. My relationship with alcohol had been a long-standing one since high school, and we knew each other well enough to know something was amiss.

The man hummed his disappointment at all I could recall. The noise churned my stomach. "You were drugged last night," he admitted so casually I thought it was a joke at first, but the longer he held my stare, the more it settled in that he was indeed telling the truth. "But not by me."

"I don't believe you."

He took a long sip of his whiskey before placing it down and moving toward the laptop at his desk. With a few clicks of a button, he had surveillance footage pulled up in order to clear his name. Like a frightened deer, I remained frozen in place, watching the computer screen from afar, only taking one cautious step forward to see better. The timestamp in the corner of the screen flew by as the gaps in my memory played out before me. One moment, I was savoring my time alone—the next, a man was murmuring sweet nothings in my ear to keep me distracted while he slipped something in my tequila sunrise.

The footage skipped several minutes, to me flirting at the bar before dragging the man before me to the dance floor for what felt like a lifetime of sensual dancing that truthfully was getting me a little hot and bothered watching it now. That feeling quickly washed away as I watched the progression of my drug-induced state begin to take over, becoming so sedated that I needed to be carried away by my dance partner.

"Don't worry, he learned his lesson," he vaguely explained as the video concluded.

In an attempt to avoid his piercing brown eyes filled with such passion, I dropped my gaze to my bare feet, heels long forgotten and lost. Near my toes were hundreds of little splatter marks equivalent to a Jackson Pollock painting all over the rug. Blood. It was blood. That strange, overwhelming sensation kicked back in–through the relentless drumming in my ear, I tried to assess the situation without landing myself on the five o'clock news like all the other girls who were murdered or kidnapped. There was no way I'd be another statistic.

"What kind of lesson?"

"The type where they never get an opportunity to hurt anyone ever again."

The drumming worsened, playing to the rhythm of my panicked state —one step back, then another. I found myself rambling on and on to keep him distracted as I continued putting distance between us. "Well, this has been a lot of fun. Thank you for saving me from that creep. I owe you one," I laughed nervously. The next step had my back flush against the door–the only exit in the room. Jiggling the doorknob behind my back, I found it locked. "Umm...the door is locked." He didn't budge, hardly even blinking as he watched me intently. "Okay, this isn't funny. Open the door so I can go home."

Rounding the desk, he approached. I stood so firmly against the wood as he did, I could feel each individual vertebra grinding against it. The shard of glass tucked into the waistband of my skirt sat so securely against the small of my back, I was scared that if I moved the wrong way, I'd slice the skin open. I found myself holding my breath as he closed the distance between us. My lungs screamed in protest, waiting for the last possible second to release it, and when I did, it wheezed out. If he heard it, he didn't make it known; instead, he reached out for the door-knob to my right side.

"Locking it was only a precaution..." Time seemed to slow as we both watched his hand hover over the metal, then retreat back to his side. "But now that I think of it, you being here does present some possibilities that may work in my favor."

"If you wanted me for my body, you should have just done it while I was unconscious so I wouldn't have had to remember something so terrible," I blurted out. The surveillance footage was proof enough that his intentions were purely sexual. The way we scorned each other's bodies was enough to know that at some point in the night, I wanted that too, but now there was nothing sensual about the way he stared down at me with preda-tory intent.

He leaned close enough that the rich scent of his cologne stung my nostrils. I couldn't pick apart the exact scent, but it smelled refreshing like a cool breeze. "Inevitably, that time will come, but I want you willing and begging on your knees for me to fuck you when it does. I don't need to resort to cruel methods to get what I want—unlike our little friend last night," he whispered. "No, I think I might keep you here. You have something else I want, Krissy."

I let him ramble on, hardly comprehending a word of it as the drumming overpowered each sentence he uttered. In slow, steady movements, I inched my hand behind my back and reached for my ticket out of here. When I finally got the glass between my fingers, I moved fast.

But so did he.

Anticipating my sloppy attack, he had me pinned to the door by my neck and wrist before I could get close enough to strike. Both hands continued to tighten until the shard of glass slipped out of my hand, shattering into a hundred pieces below, a few tiny fragments nicking my bare feet.

Brains against brawn—I thought I could outsmart him at his own game, but all it left me with was fighting for each labored breath at his mercy. He shook his head as if he was attempting to filter out his anger, but the tightness in my jaw and increasing pressure on my wrist told me enough to know he was losing that battle. His large hands swallowed my slender neck, but the grip was never tight enough to hurt me. "I'm going to give you one last chance...When I open this door, take the tunnel on the left connecting the club to The Lotte and leave."

The door disappeared from behind, and the hand that was once pinning me had now moved to stabilize my hips to ensure I wouldn't fall back. I inched away, not wanting to give him my back in case he changed his mind about letting me go. The office opened up into a massive expanse of a room adorned with a similar Art Deco flair, but much more lavish than the other one. It was as if the space was plucked right out of a history textbook and brought to the modern world. I might have stopped to admire it more if the circumstances had been different.

As promised, a poorly lit concrete tunnel broke off from the main room. I had finally given him my back and was itching to glance over my shoulder one last time, but I already knew what I would see if I did. I could feel his eyes scorning my flesh with an intensity that was both confusing and terrifying. The situation as a whole was just that—a goddamn mess—this man took it upon himself to save me during my darkest moments, but acted as my damnation when I woke up dazed and confused. I didn't know what to make of it all besides the need to run as far and fast as I could.

I stepped into the darkness of the tunnel without a second glance, not wanting to give him that satisfaction.

By the grace of whatever heavenly being was watching over me, the tunnel did in fact lead me back to the theater. At the end was a short wooden ladder with a trap door that spat me out backstage. It took me a few shoves of my shoulder to get the boxes off the hidden passage and crawl out from the depths of hell. With another stroke of luck, I found an old dance bag and practice shoes I'd accidentally left last week near my vanity that made walking home far less humiliating than if I'd been forced to wear my outfit from last night.

Somehow, I managed to make it home without fainting from dehydration and got about halfway to the fridge before I was nearly tackled by my roommates.

"Where the hell were you, Krissy?" Lyra shrieked, leaping off the couch. "We were seconds away from calling the cops."

"One second you were on the dance floor, the next you were gone." Daniel nervously paced within the confines of our tiny kitchen. "We couldn't find you anywhere."

"Don't you dare give us that bullshit, Daniel. You were off flirting with anyone who looked in your direction. *You* should have been with her," Lyra said, wagging her finger at him.

"You wouldn't be blaming me if you didn't have your head in the toilet all night."

Rubbing my temple, I tried to ease the tension building up there. "Guys! Guys, I'm fine," I shouted, making my head feel like it was about to split open. The relentless shouting stopped, but everyone gave me a weary look as I guzzled down half a water bottle and moaned with relief. "Tory, do you still have my wallet and phone?" Sluggishly, she rummaged through her purse and handed over my belongings. At the beginning of the night, I pawned them off on her instead of taking a purse of my own—one of the many mistakes I made last night. A few weekends ago, my favorite purse was stolen, and replacing everything cost me a pretty penny, so in hopes of not having yet another purse stolen or lost, I left mine at home. "Thanks," I mumbled, scrolling through the dozens of missed texts and calls.

"Where were you?" Lyra repeated. "We couldn't find you anywhere, and when we asked security to check the surveillance footage, they refused. I swear if that asshole wasn't twice my size, I would have punched him in the face for telling me no."

"I got sick, and one of the managers of the club let me rest in his office until I felt better," I vaguely explained, leaving out the worst bits to save them the heart attack that would surely follow. Lyra would have a conniption if she knew I'd been drugged and inadvertently saved by a man who stored me in his underground office, all while threatening to keep me there. There was no need to stress everyone out any more than they already were; I was alive and safe, that was all that mattered.

"A manager?" Daniel questioned. "What's their name?"

"Shit, I don't know, we didn't exchange names or shake hands," I huffed out, then returned to sipping my water. "He was a tall biracial man, too good-looking for his own good."

"That doesn't sound like any of the managers my buddy works with."

"Large white scar cutting across his face," I added. The three of them exchanged a look that was unsettling to watch. "Does anyone want to fill me in here?"

He snapped his eyes shut and huffed out a long breath. "Krissy, please tell me you didn't sleep with one of the district owners."

Chapter Eight

Krissy

We argued for several minutes about my night spent with the owner while I battled arguably one of the worst headaches I'd ever had. Tory was more than prepared to drag me out the door to get me to take a sexual assault evidence kit from the hospital, but I talked her out of it after a long-winded conversation. There were gaps in my memory, but I knew enough of the night to know it wasn't necessary.

Calming their nerves wasn't an easy task, but I somehow managed to convince them I was okay with just enough time to run off and take a quick nap before work. It wasn't nearly as much sleep as I needed; yet, I handled the lack of sleep and violent hangover with a sense of grace that surprised me.

From the audience's perspective, I gave a show-stopping performance—a mere perfect match to the night prior, but, as I stepped off that stage, I couldn't help but feel like I was mindlessly chasing a high. Never quite reaching that euphoric feeling of dancing center stage that I'd hoped for. The worst part of all was that I couldn't even blame it on the hangover anymore; the truth was that I was distracted, replaying what little I remembered from the club over and over again until the image of Erick Destler had burrowed itself deep into my mind.

Working in the industry as long as I had, I was well aware of the names of the people who had the district wrapped around their fingers. As influential as their power may be, it was as if they were phantoms; their presence was known but rarely seen unless summoned. And having only worked at The Lotte throughout my entire career, it made running into another owner that much more unlikely.

"You were amazing tonight," a voice startled me. I slapped my hand against my heart and released a shaky breath as I turned to find Patrick standing behind me. "Sorry if I scared you."

"Just a little," I laughed. "You snuck up on me, Patrick."

"Apologies."

"Really, it's okay."

"How was the party last night?" Crossing his arms, he leaned against the nearest wall, trying his best to keep his eyes up. Outfits like this left little to the imagination, and I could see him visibly struggling not to let his gaze travel southward. A black corset draped in shimmering beading and fishnet stockings was nothing out of the ordinary for this company and was frankly empowering as hell to wear while dancing for a crowd, but standing before Patrick like this made me feel more exposed than normal.

"It was fun—would have been better if you didn't have stupid responsibilities to tend to," I said, not fully convincing myself of the words coming out of my mouth. "You know you promised me there would be a next time?"

"I know," he answered with a boyish smirk. "Can I take you out tomorrow for dinner to make up for it? You aren't on the schedule for Monday...unless you already have plans."

Perhaps going out with the new owner of the theater wasn't in good taste, but...there was no harm in catching up with an old friend, even if I was well aware there was nothing friendly about the way he watched me.

"What time?"

"How about six at Lure Steakhouse?"

"Okay, I guess that will make up for you ditching us last night," I teased, placing a hand on my hip. Patrick lost the good fight; his gaze inevitably traveled with the movement, and I felt victorious because of it.

"It's a date then. Text me your address, and I'll pick you up around six." Patrick rattled off a series of numbers that I saved in my contacts with another tiny victory to put under my belt. "Oh, and Krissy, I left a little gift for you in your new dressing room. I hope you like it."

"Thank you, Patrick." I blushed like an idiot, not even bothering to hide it. "See you tomorrow."

Earlier today, Jennifer had boxed up all of Samantha's things and replaced them with mine. Admittedly, it felt a little dirty to impose on Samantha's dressing room before she'd even been released from the hospital, but Jen had reassured me it was only part of the business. Despite the twinge of guilt, it was hard not to marvel at the small nameplate that now hung near the doorframe. Miss Davis. Nine small black letters that meant more to me than the world.

One step closer to my long journey ahead.

"Holy shit," I gasped. "I could get used to this."

If seeing the nameplate for myself felt like a dream, the sight of my dressing room filled to the brim with gifted bouquets felt like the closest thing to heaven. Dozens of beautifully colorful flowers spread all across the room, nearly making it impossible to see my own stuff amongst them. Between a vase of sunflowers and a bustle of forget-me-nots, I found a tiny wooden box with intricate golden designs painted onto the surface, all tied up with a beautiful black silk ribbon on the vanity. The style resembled something that looked like it was straight from the Rococo era, with the elegance only a queen would possess.

I was floating on cloud nine as I reached for the only gift that mattered.

Tossing the ribbon aside, I eagerly flipped open the top of the box and–

My heart sank.

Inside the box was something even my worst nightmares couldn't conjure up. Placed delicately at the bottom of the box was a severed finger, still caked with dried blood. I didn't need any further confirmation to know exactly who this came from, but the tiny note taped onto the inside of the lid did so anyway. Written in elegant cursive handwriting, the message read: *I reassure you, he learned his lesson.*

To my surprise, I didn't scream, didn't run, didn't throw up despite my stomach violently churning. I remained frozen in place, staring at the severed digit...wishing there was more to relish in. Men who think they can take advantage of women deserve far worse fates than this. A finger simply wasn't enough, and although I didn't know much about the man who gifted me this act of vengeance, I knew deep down he realized that too.

As promised, a knock lightly tapped against our apartment door at exactly six o'clock. "Coming," I shouted, still frantically collecting myself. Late per usual. Clad in a borrowed outfit from Tory, I shoved on a pair of nude heels to match the salmon-colored dress with a gorgeous scoop neckline that accentuated my subtle curves and full breasts. There was no way I'd ever make enough to afford a meal at Lure Steakhouse on my own, but I could at least dress the part.

"Hi," I huffed out, swinging the door open to find Patrick standing there, hands in his pockets, and a smile that lit up the hallway. Dressed in a gray designer suit perfectly tailored to his figure, the fabric highlighted his height and lean frame. His sandy blonde hair was styled in a way that looked effortlessly wavy, with just enough length to yank on. "Sorry, I was running a bit late."

"It's okay. Are you ready now?"

"Yes, let's get moving," I urged, stepping out of the apartment.

Lyra shouted from behind, "Have fun, you two, curfew is at ten, little lady." I heard Patrick choke out a laugh alongside Lyra and Tory, who were getting a kick out of embarrassing me.

"What am I, a nun? At least midnight?"

"Eleven-thirty, take it or leave it," she playfully retorted.

"Fine." I rolled my eyes and locked the door.

"I didn't know you still lived with your parents. Should we go back so I can introduce myself to your old man?" Patrick said, playing along with the joke.

"If you want to make a stop at the cemetery on the way to the restaurant, you can meet both my parents," I suggested casually.

Patrick cursed. "I'm sorry, I didn't know, or I wouldn't have joked about it."

I raised my hand to stop his nervous rambling before he could embarrass himself any more than he already had. "What's the point of having two dead parents if you can't use them as a punchline every so often? Everyone copes with death in different ways, and I just so happen to use humor as mine. Plus, it's been so long since it happened." *Liar.*

"If you say so, Krissy," he responded, yanking at his collar with a weary look in his eyes.

I've been wined and dined in the past, but never like this. Arriving at the restaurant in his white Mercedes, we made quite an entrance that continued to impress as the night played out. He spared no expense in filling our table with the finest foreign wine and gourmet food that he didn't even bother glancing at the price tag when he ordered, but I sure as hell did out of curiosity.

It didn't take someone with half a brain to know this was clearly a date, and no matter how much Samantha and Hoffman crossed my mind, amongst other terrible finger-shaped thoughts, I couldn't bring myself to care. The role had been mine long before Patrick stepped back into my life, and favoritism would never be at play if I had anything to do with it. This was solely about two friends reconnecting in a coincidental way.

And I'd be damned if Patrick wasn't making quite the first impression.

If there were a list of the qualifications of a perfect gentleman, Patrick would tick off all the boxes. I was treated with far more respect than I had been in an excruciatingly long time. The night was filled with laughter, reminiscing about our time in college, and staring into each other's eyes like horny teenagers.

It was nearly perfect.

And even after experiencing a date only a romance author could conjure up, something still lingered deep in the back of my mind, slowly eating away at that happiness. No matter how much I laughed or smiled at Patrick's stories and vice versa, my mind continued to return to that tiny box now hidden beneath my bed, locked in a sandwich bag.

The box taunted me in my sleep, wanting something more

from me that I didn't quite understand. Possibly because the gift from a member of the Destler family felt more like a warning than a gift. It had inevitably become more of a distraction than Patrick's hand resting on my knee under the table.

"Have a good night, sir." The waitress dropped off the check and turned to tend to her other tables. Of course, when I offered to pay or at least leave the tip, he flat-out refused—not that I could afford the tab anyway, but I still offered to be nice. Patrick shoved his card back into his wallet and then left a hefty tip that the waitress would surely be gawking at later.

"Thank you again for all this. I'm pretty sure this place has forever ruined steak for me."

"Stars like you deserve the world. I just hope it made up for missing the celebration the other night. It nearly killed me to say no to you."

I tilted my head, a strand of curls breaking free. "Have you seen backstage after a show? There will be plenty of opportunities to celebrate in the future, and I understand that you already had plans with your sister. It's no big deal. I promise."

"It wasn't ideal, but I'm sure you're right."

"Did everything go well with your sister?" I asked, noticing the subtle shift in body language.

Patrick blew out a breath. "Apparently, owning a business with your sister isn't as glamorous as everyone makes it out to be. We might have pissed off some other owners by *stealing* the theater away from them—there's already been an offer made to purchase it from us, and it hasn't even been forty-eight hours yet."

"I hope you said no."

"Rejected every last one." He ran his tongue over his front teeth, then bit back a smile. "You don't want me to leave, do you?" I rolled my eyes as the waitress collected the check and bid us a good night. Patrick cleared his throat. "Well, if that's the case, I don't live too far from here. Do you want dessert and coffee?"

"As much as I would love to, I have a curfew at eleven-thirty, remember?" I joked, bumping him with my shoulder. "How about we save that for date number two? I teach a dance class early in the morning and should probably get some good rest beforehand."

"Adults or children?"

"Neither. Teenage girls," I answered, and he grimaced. "I know. I know. Despite what anyone thinks about working with a bunch of hormonal teens, I really enjoy teaching the class. It gives them an outlet, and it wasn't so long ago that I was an angry teen who needed dance more than anything to get through the day."

On top of it being additional income in a city where it nearly costs an arm and a leg to live comfortably, the studio allowed me to give back in a way I hadn't realized would mean so much to me when Asha first introduced me to the group about six months ago. It was only one day a week and rarely interfered with my work at the theater.

"That's very kind of you to help those girls, Krissy," he said, hands in his pockets. "If there's anything the studio needs, I can speak to my father about donating, or I have connections in the district that could help too."

"Connections?"

"Yeah, I know all kinds of people around the city, just one of the many perks of working for my father after college. You wouldn't believe the people you meet working in finance. Some better than others."

I dragged my teeth over my bottom lip. "You have no idea how much that would mean to the studio. Maybe we can talk about it next time you decide to ruin food for me."

"Next time it is."

Autumn was by far my favorite season, with longer nights, dropping temperatures, and the holidays quickly approaching. I begged Patrick earlier to opt out of using valet so we could enjoy a brisk walk down the street before it became too cold to do so anymore. Amongst all the other reasons, it was also an excuse to walk by his side, clutching him for warmth—and he didn't seem to mind either.

"Hold up, my strap is slipping."

Patrick leaned against the passenger's side door and watched me struggle to fix my heel. He snorted as I hopped around on one foot like an idiot. "A little help would be nice." He kicked off the car and offered me a hand for stability.

"Now I think I understand why Jackson was so heartbroken over you," he pointed out.

"And why's that?"

Patrick's eyes dragged over my body twice before finding the words. "I've only spent one night with you, and I couldn't imagine losing your interest. I'd be just as heartbroken as he was."

With two feet firmly on the ground, I felt like I was floating. He hadn't removed his hand yet; it seemed to be the only thing keeping me grounded and an invitation all wrapped in one.

"Well, it was a hell of a night, Patrick."

I stepped forward, accepting that invitation, bringing myself close enough that the tips of our shoes touched. His hand seemed to tighten in response, leaving me eager to return the favor. I ran the tip of my nail up the length of his suit jacket, the pop of red tracing a path until I stopped at his collar, waiting to see who would take the leap first. I wasn't above making the first move, but seeing how nervous he looked staring down at me, I wanted to give him the chance to take it for himself.

"Have I told you how beautiful you look tonight?"

"Twice now, I believe."

"Good," was all he said before finally taking the leap. Trapped in an entanglement of limbs and lips, Patrick kissed me with a sense of passion absent from my life. Bathed in moonlight and lust, we kissed one another up against his car until my head was spinning and everything outside of this moment ceased to exist.

At least for some time.

Chapter Nine

Krissy

A part of me knew I should have tossed it out the moment it came into my possession or even burned the evidence and forgotten about it altogether. It was my first Thursday night off in years, and I was spending it staring at the ceiling, contemplating what to do with it instead of enjoying the freedom. I hadn't touched it since I shoved it under my bed a few days ago and prayed the smell wouldn't leak through the plastic.

It was out of sight, but definitely not out of mind. The damn thing had a chokehold on me, and there was only one true solution I could think of to save my sanity. Leaving all rational thought behind, I threw on a satin emerald-green dress and black heels, touched up my makeup, and dug out a purse from my messy closet that was large enough to fit the stupid box.

I found myself rushing out the door before I could reconsider.

"I know I promised to hang out with you guys tonight, but I have to leave. I already ordered a pizza as an apology, and it should be here in about twenty minutes," I said, popping my head into the living room.

"Look who's all dressed up." Tory pursed her lips in my direction. "What is this, date number three?"

My relationship with Tory and Lyra was usually pretty transparent; we didn't keep secrets from one another, but some things were better left unspoken. I needed to do this on my own without getting them involved for their protection and my well-being. So, letting them believe I was seeing Patrick tonight was the right choice, not the smart one.

In actuality, Patrick and I had our third date planned for some time next week—he'd earned it with flying colors after the second. Patrick had invited me over to his place, and we spent nearly the whole night watching old scary movies and eating snacks on his couch. Part of me loved it even more than the first date, and I sure as hell wasn't complaining when neither of us caught the end of the movie.

"I'll be back late tonight."

"Have you guys slept together yet?" Lyra asked bluntly.

I sighed. "No, not yet."

"You should have done it after the first date. I would have," she suggested.

"Lyra, you're a lesbian. I highly doubt you would have had sex with Patrick, let alone any man who makes a move on you."

"The man is filthy rich. If switching teams meant I could live comfortably, I'd fake it," she jokingly admitted, and Tory punched her in the arm. "I'm kidding. I love you, Tory."

"Bye," I cut in.

"Use a condom," was the last thing I heard before slamming the door.

Waving down the first cab that passed by, I hopped in and plopped the purse in my lap. Through the foggy window, I watched the street number ascend, and with each passing block, the weight of the purse felt much heavier resting on my thighs than it did when I first placed it there. Five minutes later, the driver pulled off along the curb, and I considered telling him to circle the block one last time, but I tossed him the cash before I could. Suddenly, I found myself stepping out onto the sidewalk with far less confidence than I had when I formed this stupid plan.

It's a busy club with people everywhere. You'll be fine.

Like the night before, dozens of eager people waited out in the cold for their chance to party at Don Juan. Men clothed in their finest outfits clutched onto their freezing cold girlfriends who wore dresses more fitting for a cool summer night.

I don't even make it ten steps alongside the queue before something burning hot hits the top of my foot. A discharged cigarette bounced off me and landed on the disgusting sidewalk. I bit back a scream as my flesh singed and looked up to find the owner of the cigarette chatting up his friends, not a care in the world.

"Excuse me, sir, were you done with this?" I asked in a fake timid voice, picking up the butt and shoving it in his face, giving him no choice but to notice me. He gave me a quick glance laced with disgust and then returned to his conversation. I took the soft glow of the dying cigarette and dropped it down his colorful dress shirt, then shoved him in the chest, making sure the embers and ash crumbled into a hundred pieces against his skin. "Don't litter, asshole."

"Fuckin' bitch," he hissed, trying to grab me from across the velvet rope. I stepped out of the path of his grimy hands and made my way toward the front of the line. One of his more reasonable friends yanked him back and reminded the group that leaving meant they lost their place altogether.

"Back of the line, blondie," someone shouted as I approached the large double doors.

"Line starts back there," a bouncer said in a dry tone, pointing in that direction.

"I need to speak to Mr. Destler right now," I demanded, then sat back and watched her try her best not to smile like she thought I was full of shit. The taller man to her side looked me up and down twice, like he was thinking the same thing. "Tell him Krissy Davis is waiting outside. Go ahead, I'll wait, radio it in," I challenged with a smug look.

"Davis, you said?"

"Yes."

"Give us a minute," she replied. The bouncer stepped to the side, speaking quietly into her earpiece. It took a few minutes, but she returned, eating her own words. "Down the hallway and toward the left of the bar, you'll find another bouncer manning a door. They're expecting you, Miss Davis."

"Hey," the litterbug shouted. "Why does she get to go in before us? She just assaulted me." Throwing up both hands nice and high, I flipped him off before disappearing into the club.

Even early on a Thursday night, the club was packed. Pushing through the crowd, I rammed my shoulder into a few people by accident just to get through to the other side. Following the bouncer's directions, I ended up down a narrow, dimly lit hallway with a lone employee guarding an open archway with yet another velvet rope blocking my path.

"Mr. Destler is upstairs," he informed me.

Passing through the threshold, I found myself on a landing with two paths on either side. One crawled up to an inevitable confrontation, and the other descended a path I vaguely remembered, with no clear connection.

"Miss Davis," he prompted me to move when he noticed me lingering, trying to piece together the memory. "Mr. Destler is waiting."

Choosing the unfamiliar path, I climbed up to a large balcony overlooking the club, complete with a private bar and lounge. It had room for at least thirty people, but only three occupied the space. Erick Destler, even with his back turned toward me, lounging in a booth, overwhelmed the balcony with his presence alone. Cautiously, I approached, rounding the table, and found a seat directly across from him.

"I was surprised, to say the least, when I heard you were outside my club," he said after plucking the joint from his full lips. Erick was wearing a pair of tight black slacks, matching dress shoes that glowed red under the club lights, and a white button-up rolled up to his elbows that accentuated the black ink etched into his skin. The tattoo designs were too hard to make out in the dim lighting.

"I'm not here to make small talk, Mr. Destler."

He huffed out a laugh. "I'd say we know each other well enough now, call me Erick," he insisted. "Tell me then, why are you here?"

That was a loaded question with a few possible answers, but instead of verbalizing any of them, I dropped the wooden box on the table and shoved it toward him. Erick leaned forward, examining the intricate designs with the tip of his finger. "Don't bother, it's not in there. I'm not stupid enough to bring my only form of collateral with me."

"Smart girl," he said with a proud smile. "Did you not like my gift? Or should I bring you the whole body next time?"

"Here's the thing, I don't care that you saved me the other night. You're going to leave me alone, or I will take the finger to the cops and explain everything. Is that understood, *Mr. Destler?*" I asked, keeping my poker face intact.

"No, you won't," he countered in a cold tone.

"What?"

"I know a bluff when I see one, and I don't appreciate being lied to yet again," he answered, puffing out a long trail of smoke before proceeding to take another hit. "Do you want to know how I know you are lying?" He paused for a moment. "If you really wanted me to leave you alone, you would have already taken the finger to the police and reported it. But no, you threw on your shortest dress, did your makeup, and dragged yourself all the way down here to try to blackmail me. Too bad that won't work out quite as you planned."

A chill ran down my spine.

"You think you have me all figured out, but I promise you don't."

"Oh, you think I don't know you?" Erick chuckled. "I know enough to know you grew up in Republic City for most of your childhood, got your bachelor's in dance and a minor in theatre from RSU, and that you're currently living at Riverside Apartment Complex with two friends in unit 4065."

My skin heated, and I found myself praying he couldn't see the discoloration in my cheeks from where he sat.

"All of those things that you can easily find online," I managed to say, barely concealing the shakiness in my voice and the tremble in my hand. From what I'd heard, owners in the district feed on others' weaknesses, and I refused to give any man like that exactly what they want.

Rising to my feet, I rounded the table and stepped out in front of him between his spread legs and plucked the joint right from his lips, then placed it between mine. Taking a long drag, I slowly puffed it out in his direction, the smoke curling around the contours of his face. A series of coughs bubbled deep within my lungs, and it took everything I had not to give in. I couldn't remember the last time I smoked, perhaps in college.

"And frankly, it's creepy that you took the time to research all that if you ask me. Now, I'll be going, thanks for your time," I deadpanned.

"It's all part of the job," he said. "Interestingly enough, I did just learn something new about watching you tremble in your seat back there."

In a flash, Erick kicked out my foot, and I went tumbling forward, only managing to catch myself by placing my knee between his thighs and my hands on either side of the top cushion, now dangerously close to him. His calloused hand grabbed the underside of my knee and pulled me closer, so my bare skin was pressed up against his slacks, tight with a visible erection. "Even when you were nearly shaking in your boots trying to play the fake tough girl act, I could see you rubbing your thighs together. It was subtle, but I noticed. Tell me, does fear excite you?"

The joint slipped from my cherry-red lips and landed ember side down on his forearm. Erick didn't flinch; instead, he groaned, making the sounds from deep within his chest. And I unconsciously felt overcome with the urge to rub my legs together just to feel the friction of pleasure between my burning thighs.

Staying here in the position set off every internal bell, whistle, and alarm in my head. I was moments from giving in and ignoring them all when his thumb brushed the side of my knee, urging me to do so already. And because he wanted it just as bad, I knew it was too dangerous to indulge. I pulled away and rushed toward the exit to escape every bad idea racing through my head.

Dialing the right number took a few tries, but when I did, Patrick answered on the third ring. "Hello," he shouted on the other line, battling the terribly loud music in the background.

"Will you be home soon?" I asked, making my final descent down the stairs and shoving my way through the people occupying the lounge below.

"No, I'm at my soon-to-be brother-in-law's bachelor party. Is everything okay?"

Of course not. A creep who sent me a finger knows my address, and I don't want to be alone right now or ever.

"Yeah, but Lyra and Tory got into a pretty bad fight, and I don't want to be at the apartment right now." Rounding the last corner toward the exit of the club, I made the mistake of peering over my shoulder. The soft amber glow of the joint was all I saw near the railing of the balcony, and that in itself was enough to continue lying to Patrick and beg for somewhere safe to sleep tonight. "I need somewhere to go until things cool off."

Waiting for a cab, a slight breeze cut across my bare skin.

"I won't be back in town until early tomorrow morning. If you want, you can go to my place, use the keypad on the garage door, and wait for me to get home."

"Are you sure, Patrick? I feel weird staying there while you're gone."

"Krissy, make yourself at home. Please," he drunkenly insisted.

"Okay. I'll text you when I get there."

Chapter Ten

Erick

That slightest hint of hesitation was enough to answer a lifetime of questions. Although she wasn't ready to admit her fascination, she lingered for but a fraction of a second, and that alone was telling enough. Krissy Davis would return to me, maybe not tomorrow, or the next, but in time, she would come crawling back.

Patience was a censorious trait, one that would pay off for both of us in the long run.

The atmosphere of the club seemed to shift; whatever charm the place held left along with her, so I journeyed down to my office and locked the door behind me to escape her absence. The joint, stained red by her lips, had long died out by the time I sat down, but the part of me that yearned for her told me to keep it between my lips because of the lingering taste of her on the paper.

I'd give up everything to have a real thing.

She needed time. And I needed patience. Patience would reward me in the end, but it didn't mean I had to suffer until that day came. Pulling out my phone, I opened the surveillance app and rewound the footage until I had a still frame of Krissy hovering over me, back arched, lips parted, looking like my sweetest temptation. My salvation. Her simultaneous damnation.

One image let my mind succumb, twisting my imagination into my filthiest desires. Allowing me to fantasize about what would have happened had she dropped all defenses and finished what we started all those days ago. What fire might consume us both if we dared to ignite each other? What sweet seductions might lie between us when our bodies become one? I stared at that image until I felt like a weaker man, one who would gladly fall to his knees to worship her body for the work of art it was. If only she knew of all the ways I planned to please her, maybe she would—

Someone knocked on the door. "What?" I screamed out in frustration.

"Martin responded to our counteroffer," Lola shouted back, her words muffled behind the thick wood. The moment had already been ruined, so I reluctantly let her in along with Damon, who was trailing closely behind after cleaning up.

"And?"

"What do you think?" she tossed over her shoulder, strutting past me. "He rejected the damn offer without even looking at it. Can't say I'm surprised. He didn't even blink when I gave him our original offer. While we were waiting for him to get back to us, I compiled all I could find on our *beloved* new owner." Lola set down a thick stack of paper on my desk before sinking into the couch next to Damon. "Twenty-nine-year-old pretty boy who bought the theater with his trust fund, along with another family member. Lives twenty minutes outside of the city. His father has heavy ties within the district but doesn't favor one over the other from what I can tell—invests with Blanchet amongst other owners, but Patrick doesn't from what I can tell."

I cursed under my breath.

"Are we certain he isn't associated with Blanchet?"

"Nothing from my intel would suggest it."

In an industry that thrived on opposition, rivalries amid the district owners were far worse than any competition you'd find onstage. It was a small blessing that Patrick didn't have any political ties wrapped up in the district, but it also meant he had no allies to protect him. If he planned to reject my offer, not once, but twice, then perhaps it was time we spoke in person.

"Find Antonio. We're all going for a drive."

A gorgeous reddish-brown Victorian home sat on Martin's property that climbed up three stories into the darkness of the night. One lonesome light shone behind the curtain on the second floor, giving us enough invitation to join. Without the congestion of the city, homes were far more spread out in neighborhoods like these, which ensured we had the privacy we needed for what fun we had in store.

Under the cover of darkness, we each slipped on our masks and stepped out of the beater car we used for this type of discreet work. With a family legacy to uphold and an instantly recognizable scar that could pick me out of any lineup, we always chose the safest route for work like this. With a variety of masks to choose from, Lola and Antonio wore slips that covered the bottom half of their faces, while Damon wore a beat-up hockey mask he'd found at a second-hand shop downtown. I, on the other hand, wore a handcrafted mask I purchased for a costume party a few years ago that resembled a weathered skull, covering my face from the base of my hairline to the top of my lip.

Damon dismantled the surveillance while Lola got to work

picking the lock on the back porch. The lock clicked open with hardly any effort, and we entered once Damon gave us the signal that we were all clear. Draped in moonlight bleeding in through the stained glass, I scanned the back entrance for any signs of life. My eyes were instantly drawn to the darkest corners of the room where the light didn't quite reach, but I found nothing unusual in the home. The interior matched the exterior's historical flair with a few modern amenities scattered about. It had a type of charm that seemed lacking in this day and age.

Leading the pack, gun drawn, I walked us toward the switchback staircase and took two steps at a time, careful not to agitate the old wood and ruin our element of surprise. With a free hand, I traced the lengths of the railing with the soft leather of my gloves, making me revel in it all. Nothing compared to the thrill of the hunt when they didn't even know someone was lurking in the shadows. Usually, by the time they learned the truth, it was already too late.

Reaching the landing, the upstairs hallway broke off into two paths, one on either side of us. I picked the right side first, knowing the lamp in the window was somewhere in that direction. We funneled through the tight space, quietly searching each room we passed, turning up empty each and every time. By the time we reached the last door, I was seething with the realization that Patrick might not be here.

"Let's try the other side of the house," I whispered.

The creak of old wood snapped my attention toward the stairs. A slender shadow ascended to the second floor, fidgeting with something in its hand, completely unaware of what lurked down the hall. The figure was far too small to belong to a male, and for a split second, I considered the fact that we might have made a grave mistake in our intel. But as I strained my eyes to get a better look at the shadow, my heart lodged itself in my throat, so much so that I wasn't sure I could breathe properly. The unmistakable silhouette of Krissy Davis stood before me, wearing nothing more than an oversized t-shirt, the hem hitting halfway down her beautifully tanned thighs.

The mind can be a cynical bastard, so much so that it loves nothing more than to play tricks on us all. Creating distant whispers that were never spoken or figures that can't quite take shape. Krissy abruptly stopped, her back to us. For a long moment, she stood there in uncomfortable silence, seeming to work up the courage to figure out whether her mind was being as cynical as she'd hoped.

Unfortunately for her, there were no tricks to be played.

A sliver of moonlight cut across her face as she dared a half step back. Bathed in the cool glow, I could see her eyes widen. Trying not to make any sudden movements, she examined the group, her eyes darting between the four of us, frantically assessing her odds. But as her gaze lowered to the gun at my side, she found herself counting the steps separating her from the landing.

Freedom was calling her name; all she had to do was reach the stairs before I did.

"Krissy." Stepping out of the shadows, the presence of darkness still enveloped me. Bathed in all black besides the bone white mask I bore on my face, I silently communicated that any hope of escaping would fail. By the second step, she had read the message loud and clear. Krissy tossed the remote from her hand, hitting me square in my chest, then raced down the hall in the opposite direction.

I sprinted after her, chasing her down the short path. With mere seconds separating us, she used that to her advantage by barricading herself in the first room she stumbled across. The wood splintered and groaned in protest as I rammed my shoulder into the door, over and over again, until the sounds of her muffled cries were drowned out amongst the relentless banging. I gave it one more good hit before two hinges snapped clean off the doorframe. My intent was never to scare my little angel, but she left me with no choice when she went running.

I entered the room to find Krissy hysterically trying to pry open the window with a sob caught in her throat. "No! Help!" she shrieked, clawing her perfectly manicured nails at the wood. "Help, please!"

Without a soul to hear, those pleading cries meant absolutely nothing as I dragged her away from the window, one arm wrapped firmly around her waist and the other snuffing out her cries. "Shhh, we wouldn't want anyone to know we were here, now do we?" I mumbled low against the shell of her ear.

Krissy was a danger to herself and the integrity of this job. While my aim was never to harm her, there were necessary precautions I had to take in order to prevent the situation from escalating any further. I drew us closer toward the broken door as she kicked and thrashed within my hold.

"Krissy, you need to calm—"

She managed to wedge her leg between mine, offsetting my next step. All our momentum sent us tumbling forward through the threshold, and in a desperate attempt to catch myself, I relinquished part of my hold, but my efforts were for nothing. I heard the resounding crack before I could register what had happened. It wasn't until I landed hard on my ass that I realized Krissy now lay limp in my arms, a trickle of blood dripping down the side of her beautiful face.

She was knocked out cold.

Nothing about today was ideal. What started off as a hopeful endeavor had quickly turned into a shit show, one that had me dressing wounds and tending to an unconscious Krissy once again. Unlike the last time—when she woke up within my care and nearly took out my eye with a shard of glass—what little trust I had for the dancer was replaced with weariness and suspicion. As a fighter and a potential flight risk, I had to ensure she wouldn't be a danger to my people or herself, which led me to the only logical conclusion as we patiently waited for Patrick to return. He wasn't expected back anytime soon, but I didn't get where I am today by assuming anything. So, we holed ourselves in the basement and played the waiting game.

While I stood in the shadows monitoring her every breath, she sat in the center of the dingy concrete room, strapped to a chair. As I mentioned, the situation wasn't ideal, but for those rare moments I had to go upstairs to check on Lola and the boys, I needed to be confident that when I returned, I would find her right where I left her.

Waiting gave me something I wasn't used to wielding—the gift of time allowed me to sit with my own thoughts and ponder a few lingering questions that needed to be resolved. By the time I noticed her slowly starting to wake up, I had answered three of them. One: for whatever reason, Krissy was in *his* house, and I was livid about it. Two: Krissy had somehow snared me in her trap despite being in my life for hardly any time; whether it was purely lascivious or not, it had still happened. And three: despite not having any interest in a partner since I broke off my engagement years ago, I was prepared for the trials and tribulations that came with exploring my infatuation with the young dancer.

Krissy slowly gained consciousness, attempting to spread her wings, only to realize her arms and legs were tightly restrained. It was subtle, but the way her nostrils flared, and her chest heaved, she was beginning to panic internally. Careful not to make a noise, she pulled at the ropes searching for any weaknesses, and began assessing her situation. The blood from her rosy cheeks seemed to drain instantly with the realization that there were none, and why would there be? I tied them myself.

"Krissy," I tsked, circling the outskirts of the room. "Poor little Krissy. Look at you."

Suddenly, we were back in the hallway, fear twinkling in her stunning blue eyes. There was no use in hiding behind a mask or even lurking in the shadows. It was my voice that gave me away. She didn't need to see the grotesque scar branding me as a Destler to know who stood mere feet away. Little did she know, I was the least of her worries.

"Did you follow me here from the club?" she asked with a wobbly voice and a stiffness in her limbs that looked uncomfortable against the restraints.

"How does your head feel?"

"Did you follow me here from the club?" she asked again.

"As much as I wish it did, the world doesn't revolve around you," I responded. "I came here to pay the new owner of The Lotte a visit after he declined my offer for the theater, so you can imagine my surprise when I found you roaming around his house half-naked and alone." Krissy winced, only provoking me further. "Which leaves the question...why are you in Patrick Martin's home? Are you sleeping with your boss, Krissy?" The messages I found in her phone were enough to suggest they weren't, but seeing the constant flirting between the two felt like someone had stabbed a blade between my ribs and twisted it. "You have enough talent not to have to resort to sleeping your way to the top. I hope you know that."

"It's none of your business if I am or not," she spat, searching for my voice in the darkness. "But for the record, we are just friends." The stiffness in her tone echoed her defensive nature, answering a few more of my questions almost instantly.

"If you were only friends, you wouldn't be wearing his old college t-shirt and nothing else," I pointed out, pulling at her sleeve possessively. "Men like Patrick, who are used to getting what they want, may think differently if they find a beautiful half-naked woman in their house." I resisted the urge to rip the damn thing off and clothe her properly.

"We're friends," she repeated.

"Yeah, just *friends.*"

If there was ever to be trust between us, that right had to be earned, not taken. I was well aware that her perspective of the Destler name was stained after our last few interactions, but she needed to learn that those preconceived notions weren't necessarily true. I needed to assure her that she was safe. I made one final loop around her chair before stepping into the dim lighting to do just that.

"If I untie you, Krissy, will you behave?" I asked, squatting before her, hand hovering over the rope. "Or will you try to stab me with a shard of glass like the last time?"

She nodded innocently, carefully studying my every move.

"Hmm. Let's see—" The instant I unbound one ankle from another, she kicked out with the force of a madman, aiming directly between my legs. Krissy was quick, but not quick enough. "At this point, you should know better," I warned, yanking her ankle to the side so her legs were spread wide open for me. The hem of the shirt slightly rose as I did, covering up just enough to tease what I might find if she dared to spread her legs wider. "As pretty as you look all tied up like this, I hope you know I don't enjoy this."

"I doubt that, asshole. This is all some sick game to you. Following me here. Chasing me through the house. Hurting me. Tying me up like this."

Our eyes met. "Like I already told you," I hissed. "I came here to pay Patrick a visit, so you can imagine my surprise when

I found you strutting around like you owned the place. As for the injury, you did that to yourself. None of that would have happened if you'd let me explain myself."

"And tying me up?"

"A precaution. Especially after last time." I shrugged. "So, let's try this again, Krissy. Can you be good while I untie you?"

I traced my thumb over her ankle in lazy circles, waiting for a response.

"I guess you'll just have to find out," she said with a straight face.

A challenge if I'd ever heard one.

"After our little dance the other night, there's lots I'd like to find out when it comes to you, Miss Davis."

"Clearly a lapse in my judgment letting you get that close to me."

"Clearly," I echoed. My greedy hands bypassed the ropes completely and traced a path starting from her ankle up the smooth skin of her tanned leg, relishing every inch I gained. I studied her carefully, watching the way her body reacted to my touch and searching for any sign to stop. "So, tell me, will you be good if I untie you?" I whispered, noticing the rise of her heaving chest as I grew closer, the way her nipples hardened against the fabric of that damned shirt. Brushing my thumb over the sensitive inner part of her thigh, I pulled back, knowing I had her hooked.

"Why did you—" She paused, realizing just how needy she sounded for more.

I rose, struggling to conceal my own desire and curiosity. All I could do to keep from touching her was to wrap my hand around the back of the chair and lean forward to stabilize myself, savoring our proximity instead. "I think you must have really hit your head hard, little angel, if you're letting me get so close to you. Or was it just another 'lapse in your judgment?'"

She stared up at me, completely dumbstruck.

"You have two choices. I either take you home right now or you come back to my apartment," I offered. "Pick." It took her several moments to register what I was saying. The question eventually snapped her out of her thought and brought her whirling back to reality. I'd be lying to myself if I didn't admit it hurt a little to see that look of innocence turn to one of shame for what she'd almost let me do to her body.

"Are you going to hurt him?" Refusing to meet my gaze, she stared down at my polished dress shoes. "You came here to hurt Patrick for not signing off on your offer, right?"

"That will depend solely on Patrick and his actions," I answered truthfully.

She grimaced like it might pain her to say what would pass her lips next. "Please don't hurt him. He's done nothing wrong besides purchasing the theater, and frankly, he cares for us more than the last owner ever did."

"Based on what I've seen, he isn't as innocent as you believe him to be." There were rules to follow, and Patrick had made his choice to bend them the moment he stole the theater away before it went on the market. If he didn't plan to play by the rules, then neither did I. "Am I taking you home or—"

"Let me talk to him," she blurted out, startled by the words coming out of her mouth. "Give me time, I can figure something out. Maybe—maybe I can convince him to accept, so no one gets hurt."

"I don't want to waste my time on a lost cause."

"Please, give me a chance," she choked out. And something cracked in my chest.

If only she knew the truth—if only she knew the man who hid behind his scars. For Krissy, simply explaining myself and my character would never be enough; she needed to see it unfold before her very eyes to understand I wasn't who she perceived me to be. What chance did we stand if she thought of me as her damnation rather than her salvation?

I mulled over the idea for a long moment, and despite every reason not to, I found myself giving in so easily. "Don't make me regret this."

Chapter Eleven

Patrick

The surveillance system was down. I'd restarted my app several times, thinking it was a mistake, before I realized something was terribly wrong. All rational thought had flown out the window when I ditched the bachelor party that went to hell and started driving frantically, trying to call Krissy with no luck. I was prepared to give it two more tries, and after that, I was set on calling the police.

"Hello?" Krissy's beautiful, raspy voice bled through my car's speakers, and I felt like I could finally breathe for the first time in the fifteen minutes since checking up on her.

"Holy shit, Krissy," I shouted without meaning to. "I thought you were dead. My surveillance cameras were down, and when they came back on, I couldn't find you anywhere. I was seconds away from calling the cops."

"Patrick," she cooed, "I'm okay. Everything's fine."

"Good. Are you still at my house? I'm about twenty minutes outside of town."

"You're not driving, right? You've been drinking," she squealed.

"My sister's fiancé had gotten into a fight at the bar a few hours ago. I had to sober up in order to deal with that bullshit. I promise you, I'm okay to drive." My grip on the steering wheel tightened as I recalled the hellish night. I loved my sister enough to have intervened despite not being much of a fighter myself. I was lucky to make it out with only a few scrapes and bruises, but it served as a firm reminder to never get on my future brother-in-law's bad side. "Where are you?"

"I'm home now."

"I'm coming over."

"Patrick, it's nearly three in the morning," Krissy interjected, but it was too late. I had already made up my mind. "Are you sure?"

"Stay up a little longer. I'll be there soon." She didn't fight me on it. Instead, she reminded me of the address I already had programmed in my phone and begged me to drive carefully. Despite that, I found myself driving a little faster, eager to reach the woman who had been on my mind all night. I'd somehow won her over in multiple ways, and I intended to keep it that way. Jackson was a fool for ever losing her. I wouldn't be so absent-minded.

Chapter Twelve

Krissy

The apartment was dead silent. Even with the warning text from Patrick, I still flinched when a soft knock came from the door. Erick had given me his word that no harm would come to Patrick as long as I followed through on my part, and as much as I wished I could believe him, I was grateful Patrick was here so I could ensure his safety as much as mine.

I didn't want to be alone tonight, nor did I want to be alone with my thoughts. The last thing I wanted to do was unpack how easily I nearly gave in to my own desires to someone who never deserved it in the first place.

"Hey, I–"

I yanked Patrick into the apartment and deadbolted the lock before he could finish his sentence, then stamped my lips against his to deflect the string of questions I already knew were coming. "It's good to see you too," he chuckled against my lips. "What happened to your head?"

"Oh. I hit my head earlier when I was getting boxes out of storage at the studio. What's that?" I asked, pointing to the plastic bag in his hand. It took everything not to think of the blood-soaked band-aid on my forehead or the splitting headache that came with it.

"I picked up some food in case you were hungry. There aren't many options in the middle of the night, so hopefully this Mexican food is good. I brought some for Tory and Lyra, too. Have they kissed and made up yet?" Patrick whispered the last part, craning his neck down the empty hall.

Kissed and made up? Oh, yeah.

Lies were a tricky thing; they were always convenient in the moment, but a burden to remember if you wrapped yourself in enough of them.

"Thanks, I'm starving. Lyra and Tory worked it out a few hours ago," I lied, adding to the web of lies I'd woven. "Come on, let's go to my room so we don't wake them up. The last time I accidentally woke up Tory, I was drunkenly making ramen in the kitchen, and she threw a pillow at my face and then cursed me out in her native language."

I guided Patrick through the quaint two-bedroom apartment toward my room in the back. Behind the privacy of my locked door, I felt safe enough to let out a little sigh of relief and finally took a moment to take in the gorgeous man before me, still clothed from head to toe in designer, all dressed up for his big night out, which was partially ruined by me. Something about the warm smile and bag full of burritos told me there wasn't anywhere else he'd rather be, and sensing that was comforting beyond reason.

"Besides the fight, how was the bachelor party?" I asked, sitting on the edge of the bed. "And by the way, you look good all dressed up like this."

"Thank you." Patrick found a seat next to me and rummaged around in the plastic bag until he found a tinfoil-wrapped burrito to hand over. I had no idea what kind it was, but at this point, I couldn't care less; I was starving. "Charles loves the eccentric things in life and surrounds himself with like-minded people, so the night was lavish to say the least. Before the fight, we were all having a great time hanging out at one of the nicest gentlemen's clubs upstate," he turned red in the face and began stuttering over his words, "—not that I was paying for any dances myself—only drinking and smoking cigars."

"Patrick, we aren't a couple. If you did get a lap dance tonight, I wouldn't give a shit," I explained after swallowing a delicious bite of food that left me nearly drooling for the next.

Patrick shifted uncomfortably atop the duvet cover.

"About that…"

Oh, no.

I stopped him before he could embarrass himself. "Patrick, look…I know we've gone on a couple of great dates, but I should have been more upfront about my intentions behind them. Right now, I don't want anything serious, and I'm not sure when I will, if ever. I love hanging out with you, and I'd like to see where things go, but I want to be as transparent as possible, so you don't get your hopes crushed. I can already see wedding bells in your eyes, and that terrifies me."

"Wedding bells?" he choked out a nervous laugh.

"You know the look a guy gives you when he's already planning out your future before you've gotten close enough to know each other's favorite color or type of movies," I explained, using my hands for dramatics. "You know, stuff like that."

"Blue. Documentaries," he blurted out. "Blue is my favorite color, and war documentaries are my favorite types of movies to watch. Now you know."

"Patrick, I'm being serious," I groaned. "I don't know what I want, and I don't want you to get screwed over because I don't want a relationship at the moment."

He took the liberty of taking both of our meals and placing them on my nightstand so we could focus our attention on the conversation. When he returned, Patrick placed his hand atop mine. "Well—thank you for being honest with me, but before you interrupted me, I was going to tell you how much I've been enjoying our time together and wish it were something more. I'll admit it stings a little hearing you say that, but it's okay to not know what you want out of whatever this is between us yet, and I hope you know I'll be by your side while you figure it out."

My hand cupped his clean-shaven cheek. "Are you sure?"

"One hundred percent."

Patience and understanding weren't traits men my age usually handled with such grace—or maybe it was just the men I picked in general. Patrick was willing to give me the space I needed to make those tough decisions for myself, and somehow, knowing that made me crave him more. For a second, I let myself indulge in what that might look like if I decided on something serious. Would he be the final puzzle piece to complete a seemingly perfect life—a rising career, friends who cherished me, and a dependable boyfriend to tie it altogether?

It seemed good in theory, but again, something was holding me back that I couldn't quite put a name to. At the very least, I could rest easy knowing I had time to figure it out.

Swinging my leg around, I moved to straddle his lap. Patrick sucked in a sharp breath before wrapping his arms around me, drawing me closer to capture my lips. There was so much left unspoken—I had said my piece and was done with it—but poor Patrick let that kiss speak for everything he couldn't vocalize. I attempted to deepen the kiss to keep it purely sexual, except he didn't allow it, maintaining his slower pace and controlling the tempo for both of us. In an act of rebellion, I rocked my hips to my own tempo, grinding against his noticeable erection.

Patrick flipped me onto my back, crawling atop to admire the view.

"You are the most beautiful woman I've ever seen. You take

my breath away every time I see you," he said in a low tone. The compliment went straight to my head, making the throbbing between my thighs nearly unbearable.

Taking his time, Patrick stripped off my tank top and cotton pajama shorts to reveal my lacy pink panties and nothing else. Not giving him a chance to remove them, I reached between us and fumbled over his belt buckle until I finally managed to sink my hand below his waistband. Thanks to our second date, we weren't crossing any line we hadn't already stumbled over while curled up on his couch, leaving me wondering if tonight, of all nights, was the right one to take it further with Patrick.

Using the beads of precum as lubrication, I stroked his cock in leisurely movements, starting from the base of his shaft to the very tip, where I focused my attention. "Jesus Christ," he mumbled, lowering his forehead to mine, completely at my mercy. "I'll cum too quickly if you keep doing that."

"I don't see the problem," I teased.

"It is for me," he explained, between kisses. "I'd like to last long enough to do more than just get a hand job." Forcing himself to break away, he stripped out of his clothing with a sense of urgency that wasn't there earlier, making a mess of my room with everything scattered about. It wasn't until he reached his pants that he began to slow his pace, not forgetting to fish out the condom he conveniently had in his pocket.

Kneeling completely naked before me, he huffed out a laugh at the sight of me propping up on my elbows to get a better look at him in all his glory.

Patrick palmed his cock, stroking it a few times.

He slowed his pace. "You take my breath away."

Patrick rolled on the condom and lightly pushed me back flat against the mattress. Starting at my neck, he left a trail of kisses between my breasts and down my stomach, until he reached the waistband of my panties. All sense of urgency was suddenly gone as Patrick took his sweet time sliding the fabric down my thighs, drinking me in every step of the way.

The scent of latex filled the room as Patrick lined himself up between my thighs and parted the folds with the tip of his cock. "God, you have no idea how many times I've imagined being with you," he mumbled against the skin of my neck.

"Aren't you going to ask?" I moaned.

"Ask what?" He pushed in a little further.

"For my consent."

Patrick pulled away; eyes wide, mouth slightly parted. "Shit —sorry, I assumed we were on the same page. Do you want this?"

Raking my nails down his back and pulling him back in, I mumbled against his lips. "Yes, I want you inside of me. Now. Please."

I allowed myself to be consumed by his gentle touch, savoring the panted moans and overwhelming sensation of our bodies joining as one. It was nearly four in the morning when he slipped from under the covers and into the adjoining bathroom. The soothing sounds of the running shower were lulling me to sleep, promising an end to arguably one of the worst days of my life. As shitty as it started, I couldn't help but smile at the thought of how it ended. Patrick climbed back into bed, wrapping his arm around my waist, and that stupid cheeky smile of mine seemed to double.

"Sage green and musicals," was all I said before drifting off to sleep.

Chapter Thirteen

Krissy

Lyra and Tory came rushing out of their bedroom with the same energy and excitement as a golden retriever, eager to see what was happening in the kitchen.

"Morning," I grumbled, still rubbing the sleep away from my eyes.

"Morning," they said in unison.

"I didn't even know you were home. I figured you were staying the night at Patrick's place," Lyra said, preparing some cinnamon oatmeal for her partner while Tory ogled what I was making. "Speaking of last night, how was the date? Did you guys have sex yet?"

"Good." I yawned. Seeing her opportunity, Tory reached for the second glass when she thought I wasn't looking. Because of her slow reflexes and bad timing, she only managed to get halfway there before I swatted her hand away with the spatula, sending her stumbling back, cursing up a storm as she rubbed at the red mark. "Hey, that's not for you."

"Holy shit, is he here? Like right now? You two for sure slept together last night, I can see it in your eyes," Lyra whisper-yelled.

Admittedly, I'd had a little bit of a dry spell. There were plenty of opportunities, but no one worthwhile to bring home. While I was perfectly content with waiting for someone good to stumble into my life, last night felt like finally scratching an annoying itch that was just out of reach. As exciting as that was, the girls seemed more ecstatic than I was.

"I see it too. She has that 'I just fucked my boss' glow to her skin,'" Tory said right as Patrick stepped out of the bedroom. Suddenly, all eyes were on him, and he started to turn a shade of soft pink. Patrick cleared his throat, then took a moment to collect his thoughts while he finished buttoning up his shirt before addressing us.

Hearing her phrase it that way made my skin crawl. Tory was only trying to tease me, but they both knew my situation well enough to know it in no way resembled what Samantha and Hoffman had. I wasn't with Patrick for the sole reason of achieving my goals, nor did I need to sleep my way to the top to earn that right.

"Technically, I'm in charge of Malik, who's *your* boss, so I'm not sure if it counts because you're not my subordinate," he pointed out. "Good morning, ladies. If you're feeling hungry later, there's some Mexican food in the fridge for you both."

"Thank you," was all I heard as Tory beelined it to the fridge.

"Good morning." Patrick awkwardly approached, unsure how to greet me after the night we shared. He settled on kissing the top of my head, which felt more intimate than anything else. As much as I enjoyed our night together, I felt more than adamant about sticking with my decision about where we stood.

"You seem like you either drink tea or hot coffee in the morning—neither of which I have. I hope this is fine." I handed over the iced latte.

"Thank you," he mumbled between sips. "I prefer matcha

over anything else, but this tastes good too. God knows I need caffeine after last night." Lyra snorted from her side of the kitchen, and we both chose to ignore her as if it hadn't happened. "I was thinking...if you'd like a ride to work, I'd just need to stop by my place real fast to freshen up."

"No," I blurted out too quickly, then steadied my tone. "No... it makes no sense for you to travel more than an hour there and back when we're already in the city. I have a pack of toothbrushes here; you can have one if you like." The second it came out of my mouth, I realized my mistake as Patrick's eyes lit up. In my defense, I only offered it to protect him in case any of Destler's little minions were camped out waiting for him, ready to break their promise, but he took it as me implying something more idyllic and romantic—not sure how romantic a toothbrush can be, but Hollywood makes it seem more intimate than moving in together sometimes.

"Do you have a blue one?"

I snorted. "Let's go check."

Upon entering the theater, Patrick and I attracted a few wandering eyes. By the look on my coworkers' faces, you'd assume I'd walked into work completely naked, not shoulder to shoulder with the owner of the place. I was no stranger to working with overdramatic people, given that I'd practically grown up on a stage. Although I hardly gave a shit what anyone thought about the matter, I was more than prepared to shut down any rumors right away.

It took two coworkers mentioning it before anyone dared to ask me again.

Patrick and I had gone our separate ways for the day. The hours seemed to fly by as I worked my way down the laundry list of things I had to do before showtime. Every so often, our paths would cross, and my stomach would do that silly thing that made me feel like I was sixteen again, stealing moments with my crush backstage. It was a hell of a way to go about the day, but knowing at any moment I could stumble across Patrick made it that much better.

———

With about two hours until showtime, the theater had come alive with excitement and chatter. I locked myself in my dressing room, ignoring it all to finish the last few things on my preshow list. I managed about twenty minutes of peace and quiet before someone knocked. I couldn't help feeling a little disappointed as Malik stepped in and locked the door behind him.

"Hey, kid."

"What's up, Malik?" Our eyes briefly met through the vanity mirror before returning to the makeup sprawled across the table —big and bold, just like the show tonight.

"Saw you and Patrick walking into work together," he pointed out, making himself at home by plopping down on the old leather sofa behind me. It was originally placed on the other side of the room, but was quickly moved when I discovered the tunnel running along the path of the theater conveniently spat out here in my dressing room. A false sense of security, if you will.

"I didn't know saving the environment by carpooling was a crime," I said with a straight face, and Malik bit back a laugh. "Yeah, we did, and what's the point?" The theater manager wasn't much for gossiping, and he didn't seem to bat an eye when Samantha started sleeping with Hoffman, so why did this require a private conversation of all things?

"It's none of my business, but you two seem like a cute

couple." A compliment from Malik was like rain in a desert, rare, but when it did come, it was like a flash flood—all at once and a miracle that it ever happened.

"We aren't a couple," I corrected him. "Patrick and I were hanging out last night. It got late, and he crashed at my place."

Malik didn't respond at first, prompting me to meet his gaze once more.

"Was that before or after you visited Don Juan?"

My brush nearly slipped out of my hand. "How do you know that?"

"You remember my cousin, Ömar, right? He called me last night, telling me about the wild night his friend had. I guess a *sexy blonde* threw a lit cigarette down his shirt, which looked strikingly similar to my lead act. Weird, huh?"

"And?"

Malik rose. "And? Why were you at Don Juan last night?"

"Again, that's none of your business. You aren't my dad, Malik."

"Who the hell do you think beat the shit out of me a few weeks ago?"

Rumors had spread like wildfire. I'd heard a few whispers in passing about how he'd ended up nearly so badly beaten that night, he should have been hospitalized. Stubborn as an old goat, he refused and insisted on working through the pain. There had been speculation about who hurt Malik, but amongst the more outlandish ideas, I thought the one involving the Destler name was by far the most unbelievable.

I couldn't say I was surprised.

"Mr. Destler wants this theater. He's already taken extreme measures to make that abundantly clear, and then you go about being stupid enough to willingly walk into his club. I already lost Sam. I don't need to lose you, too."

Hearing his name sent a shiver down my spine. I'd yet to

figure out what my next move was regarding our deal, but I knew time wasn't on my side.

"I'm so glad to know you only care about my well-being when the theater is at risk. You wouldn't want to lose your moneymaker, would you?" I said coldly and returned to my work.

"Krissy—I'm being serious."

"Why does Destler want this place anyway?"

Malik scratched the back of his neck. "I can't say for certain, but I'm going to assume it has something to do with the original owner of the theater. When the bank had the deed signed and notarized for Mr. Martin, I saw documentation mentioning someone named William Destler. I guess after he immigrated here in 1919, he built the theater a few years later, along with some other jazz clubs in the district."

"Sounds like you did your research."

"A few quick Google searches and I had a few answers to some lingering questions—but I'm serious, Krissy. Be careful."

If Erick's family was the one to build the theater, it made sense why he might want to return the property to its rightful owner; however, I couldn't help thinking there was more to the story. There was a feverish need to possess the theater that didn't feel like it could be wholly explained by family pride, especially when he practically winced each time I called him by his last name.

What more could he possibly want with the theater that he wasn't saying?

The question stuck with me for the rest of the night. It made me stare at the most minute details of the theater while on stage that I would normally overlook, hoping for an answer. By the time the curtains closed, I turned up with nothing other than the obvious family connection.

Curiosity was a dangerous game, one that had never steered

me in the right direction before. That became apparent when I returned to my dressing room to find a single rose tied with a black ribbon waiting for me on my vanity. Whether it was a warning or something entirely different, I wasn't sure, but I was curious to find out.

Chapter Fourteen

Krissy

A month came and went without hardly noticing the lapse in time. Between teaching dance classes, weekend shows, and countless dates with Patrick, I had been so engrossed in my own schedule that I failed to notice it was nearing the end of October. The only true indicator that time had passed was the bundle of dried roses tucked away in a drawer like my dirty little secret.

One for each show.

It started as a nuisance. A not-so-subtle reminder of the deal we struck and my failure to get anywhere with Patrick. In the week that passed, I'd learned two important things about the new owner of the theater: he was determined to see things through and took great pride in the progress he'd made in improving business. It was a blessing as much as it was a curse, and as more time passed, I knew nothing good would come from his stubbornness.

I began to expect a rose after each performance, hiding away for whatever reason instead of tossing them in the trash where they rightfully belonged. The threat was clear, and I never imagined it could be worse until I found my vanity empty one night.

My time was nearly up, and I was no closer than I was when I begged for mercy.

———

The following day, my vanity was empty again.

And the same thing the day after.

———

Snow had just started to stick on the ground when Malik was looking to spruce up the weekend shows to draw a bigger crowd during the holiday season. He had turned to me for innovative ideas, seeing how well the last time turned out. It took about a solid two weeks before I was confident enough to present what Asha and I had painstakingly worked on. Countless hours were spent in front of a mirror practicing while Patrick sat in the corner of the studio with a laptop balancing on his thigh—supportive as always but nearly just as overworked running a business without his sister's help. Her absence was understandable given that she was planning the final touches of her wedding, but the less time she carved out for the theater, the more stressed Patrick grew.

Opting for a modern soundtrack with older vibes, the song boomed through the speakers as I took center stage. Moving fluidly to the beat that quickly captivated my audience of three. Patrick was gawking at me before I even began singing, and Asha was subtly bobbing her head to the trance-like rhythm. It was one of the four songs I had in my arsenal, so it was only a matter of convincing Malik they were weekend-worthy acts and that my position at the top was secured.

As quickly as the song began, it was over. I threw everything I had into those three minutes of pure sexual energy that dripped sophisticated fun for our growing clientele to drool over.

Patrick was up on his feet, whistling his applause. "Beau travail!"

"What do you think?" I called out to Malik, searching for his expression past the bright light. The light designer noticed me struggling, so he cut the lights, revealing Malik's unreadable mask, staring back at me.

"It's too modern," he pointed out.

"I wouldn't necessarily call the early two thousands modern at this point, but whatever you think, Grandpa," Asha sarcastically said. "We'll make sure from here on out that every song we perform is old enough for a social security check and a plot picked out at the cemetery."

Patrick was at my side, kissing my temple before I even noticed him approach. My attention was zeroed in on Malik as he fought internally with what I presented to the group. If there was one thing he hated most of all, it was being proven wrong.

Everyone in the room knew it, but the old bastard just hadn't come to terms with it yet.

"I don't care what he thinks, you're performing that next weekend. I'll veto his vote," Patrick mumbled close to my ear.

"If anything, I'll just perform it for you in the bedroom," I whispered low enough to keep our audience from eavesdropping.

"Perhaps both then."

The sound of clapping rattled off the theater's acoustics in slow intervals. It took everyone a moment to find the source nestled up against the back bar. A bushel of wild red curls was the first thing I noticed as Samantha revealed herself from the shadows of the mezzanine. "Seems a little hypocritical, doesn't it?" she shouted.

"You've got to be fucking kidding me," I mumbled under my breath.

"Samantha, go back home," Asha warned.

She ignored her, stepping toward the sea of tables and chairs that separated us. "You fuck the owner of The Lotte and get praised for it, but when *I* did it, I was labeled a gold-digging whore who had to spread her legs to get any type of actual recognition in this business," she seethed. "Yet what do I have to show for all those years I dedicated to this place and Aiden, the man I will reassure you, I *actually* loved? Wait—don't answer. Nothing. Nothing is the right answer. Absolutely nothing...besides thousands of dollars in medical debt, a failed career, and a dead fiancé."

A run-in with Samantha was inevitable, and I was surprised it took her this long to pay us a visit. As tragic as her story was, her little tantrum was uncalled for and as unprofessional as you could imagine, but when had she ever been professional, to begin with?

"Samantha, you're only embarrassing yourself by causing a scene like this," I shouted. "Leave before you make things worse."

Asha scrambled out of her seat and rushed toward the back of the theater. All the while, Patrick possessively pulled me to his side when he noticed me stepping toward the challenge. The dancer was no real threat to either of us, but he still felt the need to do so as she screamed in our direction, nearly hysterical at this point. There was an emptiness embedded in her dark green eyes that spoke to the absence of empathy and spirit she once had.

Trauma can rip away the purest parts of us with ease and leave us a shell of our former selves. It took me years to see the life return to my own eyes after their death, and it took me even longer to sit in a car without panicking. Samantha's pain was fresh, manifesting itself in violence and denial that we all inevitably have to overcome with time and healing. That pain never truly goes away, but with patience, it ached a little less with each day that ticked by.

"Don't tell me what to do," she screeched at the top of her lungs, her vocal cords so overly strained they shook with the last syllable. Asha approached, careful not to spook her as Malik watched everything like a deer in headlights. "I don't need some attention-seeking whore to tell me what to do. You should just cut off the middleman and start working at the strip club already because by the time I fully recover, that will be the only place in town that will hire you with a show like that."

I saw red. It was the second time she'd called me a whore, and I wasn't going to let there be a third. I was stomping toward the stairs before I knew what I was doing, fist clenched, and jaw so compacted my teeth ached. Malik and Patrick were right on my heels, but before they could stop me, I already had Samantha's hair wrapped around my fist, holding her in place as I punched her in the face.

Before my father passed away, he used to take me hunting despite how much I hated the act. He used it as an opportunity to connect on a deeper level and teach little life lessons that I didn't quite appreciate at the time. Of all the lessons he ingrained in me, the one I held the closest to my heart was not letting anyone walk over me. Although he didn't realize it at the time, that virtue would continue to protect his daughter in an industry that was determined to break her long after he was gone.

With no remorse, I kept swinging down on her, completely hellbent on making her suffer. Samantha was wailing for me to stop—it's funny how the people with the biggest mouths are never willing to back it up at the end of the day.

An arm wrapped around my waist and yanked back before I could land the final blow.

"Let go of me!" I protested, trying to squirm out of his hold.

"Stop struggling, Krissy," Patrick gritted out as he dragged me backstage toward my dressing room. The poor guy was holding on for dear life, and I nearly escaped a few times, but he held on strong, only releasing me until we were behind closed doors. "Cut it out! You need to relax."

"Don't tell me to relax, Patrick," I snarled. "You had no right dragging me away like that."

Patrick took three long strides, breaking the distance between us. Forcing me to meet his gaze, his hand lightly cupping my cheek. "Yes, I did. This isn't like *you*. You can't just go around beating up injured women like that, Krissy. She isn't even fully recovered yet. You should have been the bigger person in that situation."

"Bigger person," I mocked under my breath, then scoffed. "If being the bigger person means I let people walk all over me, then that's the last thing I want. You clearly don't know me if you assume I'd turn the other cheek."

"The Krissy I know is kind, cares for her friends, teaches dance classes to underprivileged children during her spare time —you can be the bigger person if you choose to be. You are making a choice right now not to be."

I ducked out of his grasp, the glimmer of hope draining from his wide eyes. "The Krissy you know is only part of who I am. I don't need some man to swoop into my life and think he can change the parts of me he finds less than desirable. Especially one that isn't even my boyfriend," I warned. Indecisive as ever, I'd gotten no closer to zeroing in on my intention toward Patrick, and that was abundantly clear to one of us. The other was trapped in his own delusions.

"Krissy," he called out low and submissive, attempting to reach for my trembling hand, still burning from the anger boiling beneath my skin. "Change can be good. You shouldn't fear bettering yourself."

"Do you want me to change for myself, or is it because I don't fit your perfect standards of a woman you should be with?" The silence was confirmation enough. "Patrick—please just leave. I need to cool off, and you aren't helping."

The warmth of his hand skimmed my fingertips before retreating to his side in defeat. "Don't shut me out again."

"I'm not shutting you out. I just need space. Give me space." A simple request that I felt like I'd repeated on an endless loop. While Patrick was caring and compassionate, his presence felt smothering at times. I'd written off the clingy behavior as the reason I hadn't committed yet, but that was just another silly lie I told myself as I attempted to figure out how to protect him.

He sighed, frowning down at me. "Take your time, Krissy— just please don't forget about the business meeting with my sister and Malik tomorrow—"

Patrick's entire body went stiff, eyes fixed over my shoulder. "What?"

I had no one else but myself to blame for the mess on my vanity. Scattered amongst the cosmetics and hairpins, I caught a glimpse of the rose I could have sworn I put in the drawer before venturing onstage. The room was thick with lingering tension, and the air surrounding us only worsened as I prepared for a fight I knew was coming.

"Seriously?" Patrick shoved past me, roughly nudging me to the left.

"Oh my gosh, Patrick," I groaned, raking my fingers through my curls, nearly delusional and utterly exhausted. "I cannot keep having the same argument over and over again. I will go insane. I don't know who the hell sent me the flower. Please, just drop it already."

Erick's little gift did not come without its repercussions,

causing distrust in an already rocky foundation, so much so that I'd been forced to hide the bundle of dried flowers to keep the peace between us a little longer.

When he didn't answer, I turned to find Patrick tracing his thumb over the thorn, transfixed by its horror or beauty, I wasn't sure. The rose was a vibrant shade of red, with petals blooming outward—nothing like the crumbling mess stuffed in my vanity drawer. In lieu of a black ribbon, a scrap of paper had been fashioned to the stem with a thin string. The elegant cursive writing was barely visible from my vantage point, and no matter how much I willed my legs to move, I couldn't bring myself to step forward and face what awaited me after failing to fulfill my end of the bargain.

"Krissy," he breathed. Time stood still for but a moment as our eyes met through the mirror before rushing back into place like a dam caving under the pressure of a raging river. I was vaguely aware of Patrick stumbling about the room searching for his phone, and he rambled on about Samantha and the police, but it all melted together as the river raged on. I stepped forward, testing my legs as if it was my first time walking, and when I didn't collapse under the weight of my own body, I dared another.

I sucked in a sharp breath, feeling the blood drain from my limbs in one fatal blow.

Time was fleeting, his patience along with it. Whatever mercy he'd spared on my behalf only extended so far. Written upon the tag was a death wish, one signed and hand-delivered by the devil himself for my failure to comply. My failure to find a way out before it was too late.

Don't mistake my absence for safety. The day of reckoning has come.

Chapter Fifteen

Patrick

Rivalries are bred from competition; enemies are forged from something much more sinister. Samantha hadn't been in the right headspace when she trekked all the way down to the theater and made her threats clear. What didn't sit right with me was the extreme measures she took to make her cruel intention known. I was more than prepared to call the authorities after finding the rose in Krissy's dressing room, but after mulling over it with Malik and Asha, we decided otherwise—at least for some time while Jennifer tracked her down and attempted to have a civil conversation about what had happened before moving forward.

In the meantime, there wasn't much to do but wait, which made going about the rest of the day and the next agonizing. Krissy and I had reservations we couldn't cancel, no matter how tense things were between us or the situation at hand. As they say in the theater: the show must go on.

In true Martin fashion, Josephine strolled into the restaurant fashionably early and noticeably alone. "Where's Charles?"

"Hello to you too, Patrick," she groaned, kissing each cheek as a way of greeting. "Charlie thought it was best to sit this one out. I hope you can understand, given our situation. However, I could ask you the same thing. Where's your little date?"

I didn't like it one bit, but I understood why the two of them made the choice to rarely be seen together in public, and the uproar it might cause if they did.

Josephine and I slid into the booth, my sweaty palms sticking against the rich leather as I shifted uncomfortably back into position. While there wasn't much of a gap in age between us, personality-wise, we were polar opposites. Always had been. Always will be. Being in the presence of my older sister often set me on edge, but it was nothing compared to what tonight promised.

"Krissy teaches a dance class downtown," I glanced at my watch, "the lesson should have already wrapped up by now. She'll be here soon."

With a quick skim of her menu, she drew her attention elsewhere, typing on her phone as she spoke. "Hmm, she has a second job? Do we not pay her enough at the theater?"

Charitable living wasn't in my family's vocabulary, nor would they ever understand Krissy's reasoning for helping those children. For someone like Josephine, that was especially true. She valued money above all else, so much so that she'd gone as far as to secure a fiancé who could financially support her lifestyle, going against our father's wishes. I wasn't there when Charles asked our father for his blessing, but from what I heard, it left their friendship in ruins.

"She's paid well enough. Though it's none of your business, she teaches on the side to help her community. Krissy has a big heart," I explained, knowing it would go in one ear and out the other. "I'm sure you'll love her as much as I do."

The waiter interrupted our conversation, and as predictable as always, she ordered the wine, and I ordered a whiskey sour. An awkward sense of silence followed, stretching well after he had returned with our drinks in hand. Josephine scrunched her nose with the first sip of her Sauvignon Blanc, then cleared her throat. "While we still lack an audience, I must ask, have you made any progress with the theater? I doubt I need to remind you how important this is to Charlie and me."

There was much to discuss when it came to the theater, but there was no use in bothering her with the rose fiasco until it was resolved.

"We've had a seven percent growth in profit since we purchased the theater. Reviews and word of mouth are driving in new clientele from all over, and we're planning on introducing some new acts this month for the holidays," I explained, puffing out my chest a little more than usual. "A few connections I made at the firm last summer have agreed to invest, including one of my buddies."

"If I gave a damn about that, I would have asked. Try again, Patrick, this time tell me what I want to hear," she said, swirling her wine about.

I sighed, feeling slightly cut down. As much as I cherished my sister, we often didn't value the same things when it came to our joint business venture. I viewed the theater as an opportunity to not only aid my sister but also make a space of my own that I could be proud of. I'd grown to love the work I'd done at The Lotte. "I'm still searching, but I have reason to believe some documents I found in the storage will lead me in the right direction."

"So, in other words, you have nothing to show for your time owning the stupid place?" Josephine set down her glass and leaned forward. Under the intimate soft lights hanging above the booth, her gown seemed to shimmer. "Perhaps this is your sign to eliminate any distractions preventing you from doing what you've been told."

"She isn't a distraction."

"Prove me wrong then," Josephine insisted. "I'm assuming the blonde in the tight red dress coming our way is her? Let's see if you can have your cake and eat it too." With the poise of a snake, she took one last sip of her wine before snapping her mask back in place. As easily as it cracked, it was fixed. Bringing back the version of my sister everyone knew and loved, and by the way Krissy gleamed, she was falling for it, too. "Krissy, I assume? Hello, darling."

"It's nice to finally meet you. Sorry, I'm late, one of my students' parents was running late, and I had to wait until she was picked up," she explained, finding her place next to me in the booth. Our legs brushed up against each other, and my heart fluttered in response.

"It's alright." I kissed her temple. Still longing for her touch, I placed my hand on her knee and relished in the smooth warmth of her proximity. That fluttering feeling deep within my chest, relentless as ever.

"We're all here now, and that's all that matters." My sister waved her off. "Although I will warn you, pick what you want for dinner fast. Patrick gets grumpy when he's hungry." Josephine wore many masks. Growing up with her, I've seen them all grow and evolve into a well-polished tool she used to her advantage. My biggest hope for this dinner was for her to realize those masks weren't needed around Krissy, and the two of them could form a friendship without them. I was sure of it.

"That's where you're wrong. I'm only grumpy because I'm around you," I teased.

We both shared a laugh, and I couldn't help but notice Krissy wasn't joining in.

"Shouldn't we wait for Malik to order?"

"Do you mean Charles?" Josephine asked, running her fingers through her short blonde hair, slicked back into a bob. While we shared similar color, I inherited the bouncy curls from my mother's side. A stark contrast to her pin-straight hair. Additionally, she was gifted my father's hooked nose that gave her an unconventional beauty contrary to modern standards. As subjective and inaccurate as they are, she was always beautiful in my eyes. "Something came up, and my fiancé had to cancel last minute. He sends his regards."

Krissy turned to me, a puzzled look on her face. "You told me Malik was coming."

"No, sweetheart. I told you dinner was going to be with Josephine and Charles. You must have misheard me. A simple mistake."

Beneath my hand, her leg tensed up and remained that way for quite some time as we went back and forth on the matter. The discussion came to its natural end when the waiter returned, prepared to take our orders.

Dinner was almost like a dream. Two of the most important women in my life, excluding my mother, of course, laughed and shared stories over wine and handmade pasta. As the liquor flowed through my sister, I noticed her mask slowly starting to slip. From a drunken snort to a silly anecdote about nearly burning down the Christmas tree when we were nine and eleven years old, I found fragments of my sister below the fabrication she wore.

As much as the evening was everything I ever imagined, one thing remained. Haunting me despite all the laughter and cheers. The tension in Krissy's leg never relaxed, making me question what the matter was. Letting what-ifs and speculation ruin the night wasn't worth the effort, so I pushed forward, trying to ease whatever tension consumed her.

Perhaps the rose still had her shook up.

"Gosh, I wish Charlie were here. He gets terribly jealous when he doesn't get to drink the wine I charge to his card. Plus, he's always the life of the party," Josephine drunkenly said, leaning her head back against the cushion. "You'd enjoy his company, Krissy."

"I guess we'll have to find another night that works around his schedule," I suggested.

"I'm always up for good food and drinks."

"Well, if not soon, then at the rehearsal dinner," Josephine declared.

"Rehearsal dinner?" Krissy mumbled under her breath. "I didn't know I was invited."

I squeezed her knee. "Of course, you're my plus one. The rehearsal dinner is a week from now. Charles and Josephine rented out the entire theater for the evening, then the wedding will be the following day at Union Chapel."

Krissy jerked her knee away under the table with a smile still gleaming toward my sister. To the untrained eye, it appeared nothing was amiss, but for the life of me, I couldn't pin the sudden change. What the hell had just happened?

"What color dress are you going to wear, Krissy?"

"I'm not sure yet, it looks like I'm going shopping tomorrow."

The check finally came when our bellies were full, and our eyes were heavy. We waited a bit longer, chit-chatting about the excitement of the upcoming week, but eventually, one of Charles' men swung around and picked up Josephine in front of the building. We said our goodbyes, then we were off, walking shoulder to shoulder toward the valet. I stopped at the counter to get my keys, and when I turned back around, I realized Krissy wasn't where I left her. Instead, she was making her way toward the sidewalk, arms crossed to shield herself from the wind chill.

"Krissy," I called out, snatching the key from the valet and sprinting after her. "Krissy, what are you doing?" Yanking her back by the inside of her elbow, I forced her to face me. "What are you doing? It's freezing out here."

"Fuck off, Patrick," she deadpanned and yanked her arm back.

"Goddamn it," I muttered under my breath. Instead of chasing after her, I jogged back to my car and used it to close the distance between us. Those long legs of hers were able to make it half a block down before I pulled up alongside her on the curb and began shouting from the open passenger-side window. "Sweetheart, it is freezing outside. Please get in the car. We can talk about whatever's going on."

"I'm done talking. You've done enough of that."

Creeping slowly alongside her on the busy street, we drew a few onlookers, curious as to what was going on. To no surprise, Krissy couldn't care less how many people were staring or whispering to others. Because why the hell would she? She wasn't the one being painted as the villain in this scenario. No, they were all whispering about me and my inability to tame her. Beneath the cover of night, my face burned red hot, and the longer it took to wrangle her in, the more unbearable it became.

"Get in the car. Please." Shifting into park, I ran around the car and crowded her against the side of a bodega. "Sweetheart, it's a forty-minute walk to your apartment from here. You'll get mugged or freeze half to death before you make it home. Please get in the car."

She stared up at me for a long second, weighing out her options.

"I'm only getting into that stupid car because I feel like I'm going to lose a toe," was all I heard as she stomped past me and slammed the door shut, making me wince a little. Inside the car, the tension was as thick as the snow blanketing the city; even the soft rock music playing through the speakers did nothing to alleviate it.

"Krissy–"

"No," she interjected. "Save it."

"How can I make things better, if I don't even know what's the matter?"

Illuminated in the soft red glow of the brake lights ahead, she peered out the window, refusing to face me as she spoke. "Playing dumb makes you look pathetic, but we can start with the fact you lied about Malik."

"We've already talked about this. It was only always supposed to be Josephine and Charles. Malik's name never left my lips."

"Stop trying to gaslight me, Patrick. You told me Malik was going because you knew I would never agree to this family meets the girlfriend bullshit. What are you going to do next? Trick me into spending Christmas morning with you and your parents? Should I buy matching PJs for us, or will you? Speaking of outfits, when were you going to tell me I was your plus one for this wedding? Huh?" Krissy rambled on with a hardness in her tone that cut deep enough to feel myself bleeding out in front of her.

"Why are you scared to be part of my life? Are you embarrassed to be seen with me, or is it just your commitment issues flaring up again?" I snapped. Out of the corner of my eye, I saw her head whirl around.

"Sounds like you're the one *mishearing* things now. No, commitment issues here, not from me, no, this was a test run, and I needed time to see whether I wanted something more with you. Turns out you failed miserably, Patrick. Congratulations," she bit out with an overly fake smile.

The streetlights blurred ahead. One instant, my perfectly curated life felt indestructible; the next, it felt like it was slipping through my fingers. Each attempt I made to collect the pieces only made them slip further. No matter how hard I tried to hold on, I knew she was trying to wash her hands of me. She was slipping from me the quickest.

I won't lose you. I won't let you slip away.

"Did you hear me? I'm done," she reiterated.

"Krissy, you should consider what this means for you," I suggested in a dry tone, surprisingly calm compared to my erratic heartbeat thumping in my chest and the tears brimming in my eyes.

"You should have turned down that block," she said, pointing at the windows. I ignored her and kept driving. "Patrick."

"It would be a shame if you lost your role at The Lotte. You've worked so hard to be where you are today. It would be a tragedy to lose everything over something as silly as this."

She gasped, choking on the thick air around us. "Are you threatening to fire me if I leave you?"

My silence was enough of an answer.

"You act like The Lotte is my only option. I won't have any trouble finding work in this city with my resume. Good try though."

The car rolled to a stop at a red light, giving me a chance to give her my full attention. "You misunderstand, sweetheart," I started. "I hate to break it to you, but the reputation you've gained in the city among the entertainment district has stained your career. Everyone thinks you've slept your way to the top. None of the other theaters would dare hire you because of it. You'd be lucky if you were even considered by the local strip club, and even then, with my connections in the city, I'd make sure they knew better than to steal you away from me. Your place is on stage at The Lotte, by my side, the sooner you realize that the better."

The connections I'd made in the financial district had been beneficial over the years, along with the people I've met through Charles. Making a seemingly large city feel smaller with each business partner I met. Each of them knew my relationship with Krissy and my intention to keep her performing at The Lotte and nowhere else. Republic City was a dangerous place; shielding her from that world had always been my top priority. None of that could be achieved if Krissy weren't by my side.

"So, you're blackmailing me?"

"No, I'm protecting you from yourself. You are making hasty decisions you're going to regret in the future." I reached out to rest my hand on the place where the hem of her dress met mid-thigh. She flinched, but allowed it after thinking better of it. "What we have is special. We can't toss that away after one or two fights. I'll prove that to you, Krissy, give me a chance."

Several minutes of silence passed by as we turned into my neighborhood. Krissy had yet to respond, remaining frozen beneath my touch as she stared out the window, a stoic expression etched into her face like a marble statue. From the time we had shared together in our romantic bliss, I've learned Krissy needs to process things on her own accord, so I gave her what time I could until we pulled into the driveway.

"Sweetheart, are you ready to come inside?"

"Okay," she mumbled, leaving me behind in the car to make her way toward the house.

Chapter Sixteen

Krissy

I fucked Patrick as if it was our last time—because it was.

Giving him a false sense of security. Hope. The final say in the argument he thought he'd won. That was only the first step. The next would come at a price I was more than willing to pay. The fragility of a man's ego is astounding. They find themselves so entitled and with an over-inflated sense of privilege that they can easily justify extorting and coercing someone into staying with them just because they simply want it to be true. Patrick was more naive than I thought if he thinks I'd roll over for him and play the submissive girlfriend he wished I was as he robbed me blind of everything I'd worked so hard for.

As I watched him peacefully sleep next to me, I plotted my next move.

Chapter Seventeen

Erick

Krissy hadn't followed through on her promises, and it was only a matter of time before I sought her and made good on mine. I'd exercised far more patience than I was usually capable of, but my generosity was growing incredibly thin.

Exhausted from discussing our plan of attack, the four of us lounged on the balcony overlooking the empty dance floor. It would be mere hours until the space was filled with swarms of individuals looking to forget the woes of the outside world. A safe haven for those who dared to enter. While work had tirelessly consumed my life, the confines of the club had always brought me the same type of protection as those who patron it, though I rarely indulged in the fun—not since *that* night. Taking advantage of the peace and quiet, Damon, Lola, and I played cards while Antonio mindlessly scrolled through his phone. After a few pathetic rounds and a far emptier wallet than when he started, he opted to sit this one out.

"Are you sure you don't want to play, Antonio?" Lola called out, a smug grin painting her red lips. She wasn't much for conversation unless she was either robbing us blind or finding a way to get under Antonio's skin. Today she seemed to be doing both and damn well, I might add. "This time I'll make sure to go easier on you."

Antonio scoffed. "I learned my lesson the hard way. I'm not trying to lose enough to pay off your rent again. And don't you even dare." He pointed at Damon who was just about to sign something and join in on all the fun, but the glare on his face was enough to make him back off, laughing to himself as he returned to his poker hand.

"No need to be a dick about it. We're all just having a little fun," I glanced down at my watch, "but it is nearly the end of the month. Lola *does* need to cash in a check for her landlord."

The calm before the storm was always bliss. It's what came next that brought hardships worth enduring. So, I soaked up what little normalcy I could with the people I surrounded myself with in hopes of having more of these moments in the future.

"Ha. Ha. I'm so glad I can be the butt of every joke for you guys. Wait till–"

Buzz. All of our phones went off at the same moment—never a good sign.

"...the hell?"

Antonio being the first to see the surveillance notification was already sprinting toward the exit, gun drawn. I fumbled my phone a couple of times chasing after him with adrenaline pumping through my icy veins. I was hot on his trail when I managed to open my phone and read the notification that pinged at the top. Two clicks later, what I found staring back at me left my heart lodged in my throat, hardly leaving enough room for air to pass through in order to properly breathe.

"Antonio, stop!" I shouted, taking multiple steps at a time, risking tripping over my own two feet. "Back down! Back down!" Within seconds of opening the door, I managed to catch up and yank him back by his collar. "Are you fucking deaf? I said back down."

"Someone triggered the alarm in the tunnel," he snapped back.

Leaning forward, the smell of his cheap cologne burned my nostril. "If I have to tell you to back down one more time, I'm going to snap your pretty little neck." Antonio nodded and scurried off to Damon and Lola at the top of the stairs gawking down at us. A gun at each of their hips. "Don't follow me. I'll call if you're needed."

Damon signed his understanding and Lola gave a stern nod.

It was strange. There are moments in our lives when we don't quite understand the implication of what they will mean for us. And then there are others, where before we even enter them, we are fully aware of what they promise. Crossing that threshold, I had no idea what having her here meant for me, I just had the foresight to know it was a blessing regardless of why. Had I still been a religious man, seeing Krissy leaning over the bar top, peering over her shoulder when she realized she wasn't alone anymore would have been an answer to a prayer. A light in the dark. A shred of hope in a damned world.

Wearing a pair of blue jeans and a knitted sweater, she looked more domesticated than anything I'd ever seen her wear before, but then again, I was thoroughly convinced she could be wearing rags and would still be the most stunning creature on this planet.

"It's a speakeasy, isn't it? I didn't have much time to admire it last time I was here," she said, her raspy voice surrounding me with the warmth of her presence. "I would tell you it's amazing, but I think you already know that. Plus, it feels like a bit of an understatement."

I approached slowly, finding a seat several feet away from her.

"My great-grandfather built it during the height of prohibition," I explained. Krissy's eyes wandered around the room admiring the attention to detail. "It took a few years of restoration to get it back to its original glory, but I like to think it was worth the time and money."

"I would agree."

"As much as I would love to talk about my family legacy or what's left of it. Aren't you the one that said she didn't have time for small talk?" Something about her was off, it was like the light had been sucked right out of her soul and I was dying to peel back those layers and find out why.

"You're using my own words against me, Mr. Destler–"

"Erick," I interjected, leaning back in my chair, arms crossed. Krissy pulled out a chair and sat directly across from me. The expression painted on her face read as impassive, but it was clear she was masking her true intentions.

"Okay, *Erick*," she grumbled. "I'll jump straight to the point. You and I both know you're targeting Patrick Martin because of his little business venture. Whatever you have planned, I want in."

My scoff echoed louder than I intended. "Why the sudden change of heart?"

"It's none of your business. All you need to know is I want retribution."

Propping myself up by my elbows, I leaned forward, stealing more of her attention.

"For me to agree to this, I need to know why." A whirlwind of theories smacked me upside the head, each one leading me down a darker path until my fists were clenched so tight that my nails left little crescent shapes indentations in the palm of my hand. "Did he hurt you?"

Krissy's gaze flickered down to my hands, noticing my pent-up aggression. "Yes, but not in the way you're thinking. Nothing physical," she assured me, then let out a sigh she must have been holding in for a while. "Patrick is blackmailing me into a relationship. He won't let me leave willingly without ruining my career. I need your help."

Being the lovesick bastard I was, I'd already made my decision before she could even finish. My little angel could ask anything, and I would blindly agree if it meant she would be safe and happy. Though it made it easier that we both had the same target in our crosshairs.

"I warned you about him," I reminded her.

Being so close to her once more was intoxicating. Although it had been a month since the night in the basement, what little I saw her did not do justice to being in her presence like this. From the shadows of the mezzanine, closed off to the public, I'd watched countless performances and left a rose as my appreciation. A small token of my praise that was far from what she truly deserved in exchange.

"What's done is done. Are you going to help me or not?" What time had passed had undeniably changed her. She no longer spoke with an empty sense of confidence like before. If she still feared me, she didn't show it, perhaps her time with Patrick was enough to push those notions aside.

Or she feared him more than she ever did me.

"It depends on what you have in mind," I told her. "I imagine you wouldn't have come all this way empty-handed." Krissy smiled for the first time and my heart kicked out of place at the sight of it. I found myself smiling along as she whipped out a bundle of loose pages from her back pocket and deposited them on the table that divides us. Chicken scratch filled every corner of the pages, carefully outlining her plan in excruciating detail.

"You want the theater. I want my freedom and revenge. I have a way both of us can walk away from this happy," Krissy began to explain. "Patrick and I are attending a rehearsal dinner next week at The Lotte. You and I are going to stage my own kidnapping mid-event, then demand ransom in exchange for the transfer of ownership. After I'm released, you'll possess the only leverage Patrick holds over my head. I'll be free, and Patrick will pay the price. However, my only stipulations are that you must promise to keep me employed after and allow me to earn my role in earnest and make sure Patrick doesn't go after my friends when I'm gone."

I was beaming with pride but held it back until the time was right.

"What's stopping me from going to the theater right now and blowing his brains out? Much quicker and less messy, if you ask me," I suggested, only to test her wit and find holes in her perfectly orchestrated plan.

Krissy took a moment, searching the room for an answer, perhaps for theatrics. "If Patrick is killed, his sister would have full ownership rights. If you killed her, it would be passed down to her soon-to-be husband. Which leads us down a messy chain of people you'd need to kill for the property to be eventually seized by the bank. And on top of that, based on the nature of Patrick and my *friendship*, the police will label me a suspect which will have a more detrimental effect on my reputation even after I'm cleared as innocent. The kidnapping is clean and easy."

"He could go to the police," I pointed out.

"If you threaten him with my life, he won't. Patrick is a nonconfrontational man unless provoked, if you give him the simplest route out, he will take it—no questions asked."

"Patrick doesn't have full ownership of the theater. How will he convince his sister to agree?"

The question stumped her for a moment before she elegantly ran through her solution piece by piece. Everything I threw her way was perfectly dodged. Through meticulous planning, Krissy and I were able to devise a seal-proof plan that left me far more impressed by her devious thinking than I had previously thought. Our plan was cruel and unforgiving, and based on what he did to her, Patrick deserved everything that was coming to him.

If all went well, we would both end up with what we wanted. In one week's time, all would be put into motion. Krissy would be free, and at this point, that's all that matters to me.

Chapter Eighteen

Krissy

Four more days. That was all that separated me from freedom. Until then, I forced myself to smile at my gilded cage and reminded myself it would all be over soon. Besides the lack of physical intimacy between us, on the outside, nothing seemed amiss. I kept the façade firmly in place and if had I not craved his downfall so badly, I might have felt bad that he fell for it all so easily. Frankly, what I had in store was child's play compared to what he deserved. There was no room for empathy or guilt when his betrayal cut deeper than any heartbreak, any loss of love.

Patrick deserved no mercy.

Erick and I both agreed our arrangement promised an uncertain future. It could take hours—days—or even weeks until Patrick agreed to our terms. Mentally, I prepared myself for an indefinite amount of time away from my loved ones knowing I had to keep the secret to myself. News of my kidnapping would likely reach them within hours of the event, but no matter how much I knew it would kill them to believe it was true, I couldn't risk any loose ends by telling them our plan. Lyra and Tory were a liability, but in time, they would understand when the storm finally blew over. Although I had no idea when the next time I would see them, I made the effort to get everyone together one last time, if not for their benefit, then mine.

Feeling as if this was our last hurrah, I spared no expense to make the night a memorable one by pulling a few strings and managing to book a reservation at one of the most up-and-coming burlesque shows in the district—The Velvet Rope.

Patrons swarmed the small lounge, buzzing with excitement. For a midweek show, the crowd was rowdy, Daniel, Lyra, and I weren't helping the cause as we whistled and hollered in anticipation of the curtains being drawn back. And neither was the array of colorful drinks already halfway gone sprawled across our table—and while I was placing blame, I guess the pills we took back at the apartment weren't helping either.

Between the alcohol, drugs, good ambiance, and even better company, it was almost enough to forget the worries of the outside world just beyond these walls. Almost, but not quite.

Soft music played within the lounge, draped in dark sensual lighting. Nearly every seat in the house was taken, except a few couples mingling about or slowly making their way toward their reservation. With three raised levels all facing the main stage in a half circle, our table was toward the back, smack in the middle—the best I could do on short notice.

"I think we'll hit our two-drink minimum before the show even starts," Tory pointed out while sucking down a frozen margarita. "Give me two more minutes and I'll do it."

"I didn't bust my ass working all weekend to not exceed the drink minimum ten times over," Lyra joked, waving her hands flamboyantly about before a light suddenly caught her attention. "Daniel! Get off your phone, it's family time."

Daniel had been secretly gawking at his phone for the last few minutes with the assumption that none of us would notice the harsh glow of the screen illuminating his torso. While Lyra called him out for disrespecting our quality time together, I lunged for the damn thing.

"You're still texting that girl you met at Don Juan?"

"Give it back! I wasn't done reading." Like a sinner in church, he panicked, nearly clawing my eyes out trying to get it back. I leaned out of his reach, arms stretched far above my head while simultaneously trying to read the texts aloud to mortify him. With no siblings or living relatives, these assholes were the next best things, and I loved to torment each and every one of them.

"You're being such a baby—oh—holy shit." In pursuit of embarrassing Daniel, I had conveniently stumbled across a conversation that felt well worth my time to read compared to his terrible flirting and hopeless romance. There had been rumors and whispers as to why Jennifer had been gone all day yesterday, but it looked like little Daniel was hiding some information from us.

"Let me see," Lyra demanded.

The phone was ripped from my hand before I could finish. I was ready to tackle him to the floor to get it back, but Daniel just scrolled to the top and cleared his throat. "Before you so rudely took my cell phone, I was asking Jennifer what happened with the Samantha debacle. She said the surveillance footage showed Samantha entering the lobby and going directly to the stage. Unless she had someone helping her, there's no way she could have put the rose in Krissy's room."

"I think we're all well aware I'm not a Samantha fan, but I'm kind of glad she didn't do it," Lyra admitted. "With that being said, the creep that left you that rose is still out there, and maybe you should be more careful until they figure out who it was."

"I'm not sure why we keep ruling out the secret admirer theory?" Tory asked. Choking on a laugh, I washed it down with my Moscow mule. "Or it could be the type of secret admirer that becomes so obsessed with their target, they murder them in the dead of night?"

Daniel groaned, slouching in his chair. "Can we *not* have this discussion right now? Thinking about my friends getting murdered isn't exactly keeping my buzz alive and well."

"Then what do you suggest we talk about, *Daniel?*" I hissed his name.

"How about we talk about you and Patrick?" he suggested with a shrug. After years of knowing one another, he was just as nosy as the day we met in our intro to dance freshman year of college—if not worse now. "How are you guys? Have you finally made things official or are you still being a wimp about it?"

I took a long and slow sip before answering. Ethically lying was always on the table for me if necessary for survival or to protect someone I cared for. This meant there was never a need for lying within this group, secrets were a rarity amongst people I trusted, but to keep the ruse going it was one of those rare times I had to bend the rules a little in order to protect them.

"Yeah, Krissy," Tory taunted. "Spit it out."

"Well, I've already been invited to some family functions, so I guess you could say things are moving along...."

"Mrs. Krissy Martin. It's got a nice ring to it," Tory mumbled to herself. I punched her square in the arm to shut her up before the conversation could escalate to baby talk and dying old together. "Ouch! It was a compliment."

"Have you found a dress for the rehearsal dinner and wedding yet?" Lyra asked, just as invested as the rest of them.

"No," I groaned, toying with the ends of my curled hair. "Do you want to go shopping tomorrow after work?"

"Wait—let me guess what you are going to say." Tory softened her voice and changed her mannerisms to mimic Lyra's tone. "*Of course, unless I'm too hungover to function. In that case, you go without me but pick up a breakfast sandwich from the corner store on your way home, so I don't die."*

In retrospect, it wasn't that funny, but with all of us drunk and looking for a good time, we howled in laughter, drawing a few judgmental eyes in our direction, but none of us gave a shit. That was the beauty of being together: we always had something to laugh about and someone to make fun of.

Lyra leaned over and kissed her partner on the cheek. "It's like you stole the words right out of my mouth, baby."

Gradually the music coming from the speakers grew louder, the light in the back of the house dimmed, and the show began. A foursome of performers tumbled their way to center stage, each of them contorting their bodies in nearly impossible ways. Two of them wore hardly anything, giving the audience a very lewd opening act. I loved every moment of it.

Amongst the repeated cheers and whistles, I felt the slight vibration of my phone that I first mistook for the bass of the speakers. Beneath the tablecloth, I switched my phone to night mode and attempted to read the notification without blinding anyone nearby.

"Hey! Why does she get to be on her phone?" Daniel complained, but neither Tory or Lyra acknowledged him while they watched the show in awe.

Patrick: How's the girl's night out so far?

Krissy: Good. I'm about two drinks deep.

Krissy: And I'd hardly call it a true "girl's night out" with Daniel here.

Between messages, I set my phone down in my lap and enjoyed the show. Keeping the illusion alive was important, but I wouldn't give up my time with my friends to accomplish it. A few numbers passed by before my phone vibrated again.

Patrick: Fun.

Krissy: Are you going to tell me what's wrong or do I have to guess?

Patrick: No. Have fun with Daniel on your girl's night out.

Biting my tongue went against everything I believed in. I could feel every muscle tighten in my body, holding back from lashing out at his idiotic jealousy. Instead of playing the innocent loving girlfriend that reassured his ego that everything was fine, I ignored it altogether as the drinks took their effect, making it easier to sit back and enjoy myself without worrying about Patrick.

My phone buzzed again, and where it rested on the bare skin of my thigh seemed to itch. The longer the notification went unread, the more the distraction of the show lessened over time. I finally caved when I reasoned with myself that all it would take was just one look before I could return to my carefree attitude and not allow Patrick to ruin my night out.

Making sure my friends weren't looking, I peered under the table and tapped the screen.

Unknown: Should I expect you to walk around in nothing more than an oversized t-shirt or will you bring actual clothing with you?

The strange message didn't register at first. I stared down at the screen for several seconds until I could piece it together.

Krissy: Don't consider yourself that lucky. I'll be fully clothed the entire time.

Unknown: I doubt that...

Tory gave me a strange look when I scoffed louder than I intended.

Krissy: Are you calling me a liar?

Unknown: All I'm saying is, if history repeats itself, you'll be begging me to touch you again. And in order to do that I need to strip–

"Holy shit, stop flirting with Patrick," Tory groaned close to my ear, catching quick glimpses of the conversation. "We get it you guys are all cute and in love. This is family night, remember?"

Luckily, in Tory's drunken state, she missed the name at the top of the screen. Feeling a prickle of embarrassment, I stuffed my phone in my purse and pretended none of it had happened.

"Don't worry, I remember."

"Do you think if I stretched every day, I could do that to my body too?" Tory asked as we funneled out of the theater with the crowd. We all shot down her hopes and dreams collectively with a few comments and laughs. Tory was about as athletic as a rock; you could skip it and not much else.

The last forty-five minutes had flown by, filled with extraordinary dancing, comedic acts, and a classy touch of sex appeal that allowed me to not only enjoy time with my friends but also gave me some ideas to incorporate into our show—with more clothes on, of course. Malik would no doubt hate anything I brought to the table but knowing that only made me want to do it more.

"I'll prove you guys wrong."

"Whatever you say, Tor," I giggled. The laughter quickly died as I pulled out my phone to find an absurd amount of unread text messages on my screen. All from Patrick.

Patrick: Krissy? Please answer me.

Patrick: Are Lyra and Tory even with you? Don't lie to me...

Patrick: I don't trust Daniel. I've seen the way he looks at you. If he had the chance, he would steal you away from me in a heartbeat. He won't.

Patrick: Right?

Patrick: Please text me back. I'm sorry.

Patrick: Sweetheart. Are you okay?

I cringed within myself watching all the red flags unfold themselves in front of me. Patrick was setting the groundwork for the beginnings of a deeply toxic relationship. Frankly, if I didn't have someone like Erick I could turn to, I wouldn't know how to leave this relationship with what Patrick held over my head. I counted my blessings, knowing this would end one way or another.

The autumn breeze smacked me in the face upon exiting the building. We turned right and walked toward the nearest subway station full of conversation, and reminiscing about the night. Amongst the tiny snowflakes littering the street in a white blanket, the Mercedes nearly blended in. My eyes instantly locked on the vehicle, and I told myself I was just being paranoid, since plenty of people owned that model of car, but when the driver's side door swung open, it confirmed my worst nightmare. Patrick stepped out, throwing on a coat with the grace of a God, and waved us down as he buttoned it up.

"Hey, no boyfriends on family night," Tory said. For a couple of misfits like ourselves, our little found family was everything, and Patrick being here threatened its very fabric.

"What are you doing here, babe?" I greeted him with a quick peck on the cheek.

"I remembered you telling me the show was going to end around eleven." *No, I didn't.* "And I was already in town to see Josephine, so, I figured you'd all need a ride home."

"Don't mind if I do," Lyra cooed. "There's no way I'm going to turn away a ride home in this fancy-ass car. This sure beats sitting next to some piss on the subway."

Lyra and Tory were already barreling toward the car when Patrick turned to address Daniel who was silently standing at my side. "The Mercedes only seats four. I'm sure you don't mind,

Daniel. It saves the girls the trouble of walking around in the city at night, if you care about their safety you'd understand."

"Patrick," I snarled. "This isn't necessary."

The two men glared at each other for what felt like a lifetime but in actuality, it was only a few heated seconds.

"You understand, right?" he asked again, letting his charm mask his pent-up rage.

"Text me when you guys get home. I'll catch you later, Krissy," Daniel mumbled.

"Daniel, don't leave. I'll go with you. It's dangerous to be out alone." Patrick blocked me from chasing after him and dragged me back toward the car by my inner elbow, digging in his nails not enough to hurt, but enough to serve as a warning.

"Where's Daniel going?" Lyra asked, watching him disappear amongst the flock of people through the tinted windows. "One of us can just sit on his lap. We could have made it work."

"Daniel being the good man he is, offered to let you girls drive home comfortably. I respect that." Patrick buckled himself into his seat and pointed to the passenger side floor mat where a tiny white package sat at my feet. "That's for you, sweetheart."

"Um, thank you." Using the passing streetlamps as light, I carefully opened the present and pretended I wasn't sick to my stomach. Tossing the lid to the side, I found a simple gold necklace with a circular pendant hanging from the delicate chain, the circumference of the pendant encrusted in diamonds. "It–it's beautiful."

"That's the cutest thing I've ever seen." Tory leaned forward to get a better look.

"I figured you could wear it this weekend," Patrick suggested with a triumphant smile like he wasn't trying to buy his apology with sparkly things.

"Now I just need a dress to match."

Four more days. Four more days. Four more fucking days.

Chapter Nineteen

Krissy

The Lotte was bathed in hundreds of twinkling lights and floral arrangements that looked far more fitting for an actual wedding than a rehearsal dinner. I guess when money wasn't quite a problem as it was for the average person, the price tag of a single dinner doesn't matter at the end of the day. It left me wondering how they'll manage to outdo themselves tomorrow. Luckily for me, I won't be around to see it.

Patrick trailed me along to mingle with the few guests invited to such an exclusive event. Being the businessman he was, he made it his mission to speak to every last one and spend an exceptionally long time introducing me to distant cousins and posh aunts and uncles that seemed unimpressed by making my acquaintance. The first half of the night was filled with so much small talk that it left my facial muscles aching from all the smiling. Each conversation was as painful as the last, and even more so when all I could focus on was the clock behind the bar taunting me.

I'd endured a full week of pretending for the sake of the plan, but somehow the last few hours were the most unbearable. Seconds felt like minutes, minutes felt like hours, hours felt like days. On the outside, I handled the pressure with nothing but grace—but internally, I was so desperately trying to claw my way free. To seek the light in the darkest moments. To escape him.

In one of those rare moments of peace between conversations, Patrick stepped forward and pushed a strand of hair behind my ear. "You look amazing tonight."

Shopping with Lyra had been nothing more than a headache, but at the last minute, I managed to find a black silk gown that stopped just above my knees on my own while walking home one evening. The pipe corset was what drew my attention to the display in the window, but it was the way it pushed and lifted my breasts that had me charging my card soon after. It was an outfit fit for a widow attending a funeral rather than a rehearsal dinner, but in my mind, it was all the same. "Remind me to get you a pair of earrings to match this necklace."

"A good boyfriend would do it on his own accord," I countered.

"Hearing you say that is the sweetest goddamn thing you've ever said," he said, leaning in close to whisper near my ear. The undeniable sting of bile rose in my throat. "Say it again, sweetheart."

I pulled back, tilting my head up so I could glare up at him through long lashes. A string of curses and vile names sat on the tips of my tongue, but they never found their way out. "Buy me the earrings first, and then we can talk about indulging your little fantasies."

He hummed his approval and subtly pressed his erection up against my hip bone, knowing we had an audience even in the dark corners of the room. "As much as I wish we could sneak away to have a few minutes alone, we still need to say hi to Josephine and Charles. Your sister is waving us over," I said while running my hand over his lapel.

"I hate when you're right," he sighed. By the small of my

back, Patrick led us toward the couple, nearly looking as lavish as the décor surrounding them. Dressed head-to-toe in outfits that looked like they had been plucked right off the runway and tossed on them.

Josephine lit up when she saw us coming and urged her fiancé to stand and introduce himself. It only took one dinner with Patrick's sister to know she was the fakest bitch I'd ever met. Some things tend to run in the family, I guess.

"Ah, is this the girlfriend I've heard so much about?" Charles said with a heavy French accent. With piercing blue eyes that had about two more decades of wisdom embedded in them compared to his fiancée, though he was still incredibly handsome with salt and pepper hair and strong facial features. From what little Patrick had told me about the Martin family drama, Charles' age played a factor in why only his mother was in attendance tonight.

"Pleasure to meet you. I am Charles Blanchet." By way of greeting, he kissed my cheek, leaving the skin a little itchy from the prickle of his short beard.

"The pleasure is all mine," I said, attempting to keep my composure at the mention of his last name. If he was the same Blanchet I was thinking of, his family owned the Republic Opera House and two of the most prestigious ballet studios in the state. A fact that Patrick failed to mention when speaking so fondly about his future brother-in-law over the weeks.

"Krissy is the woman who has stolen my little brother's heart," she emphasized, noticeably already drunk. She must have a lot of trust in herself to drink red wine while wearing a long white gown like that, I thought to myself.

"Maybe in time she'll be joining the family too." Charles chuckled, causing the rest of the group to follow suit.

The comment felt like a million tiny needles being embedded in my skin all at once, but it was nothing compared to Patrick squeezing my hand to reinforce the idea. Something tense wafted in the air, eating away at the space between us so fiercely that I could feel the sensation down to my bones. Charles plucked a cigarette from his jacket and sparked it to life, all the while studying my reaction as if it were all a test I hadn't prepared for. The lighter cast a strange orange glow across his features, and all so suddenly, I knew he could sense how uncomfortable this conversation was making me feel. That's when I glanced back at the clock.

Five more minutes.

"Not sure my brother can swing much better."

"Only if I'm lucky enough," I offered, feeding into the narrative they were spinning. "If you will all excuse me, I need to be on stage soon. I'll be right back, sweetheart."

"Good luck," he whispered back.

As a gift to the couple, Patrick suggested I could perform a few songs to liven up the evening. The seemingly kind gesture would have been just that if I wasn't aware of Patrick's intention to claim me as much as the property the theater sat on. With hidden intentions of our own, Erick and I planned to use the performance to our advantage.

With three minutes left, I circled the stairs to the raised platform. Despite taking this very stage hundreds, maybe thousands of times before, no performance felt as paramount as this. The moment I moved into position behind the standing mic, the background music faded into the track I'd selected especially for the festivities. My voice stretched to every inch of the theater, filling the space with soft jazz music perfect for the ambiance. People still went about mingling and eating while I performed— only about half the room had given me a passing glance.

The clock struck seven, and I mentally prepared myself for what that meant.

Here we go.

The song kept playing, and I continued to sing as I watched the clock tick by with each second. One minute rolled by, then the next, with no sign of Erick. My voice remained in pitch, but with the more time that passed, the more it threatened to flatten out. There wasn't much I knew about the man who claimed the Destler legacy, but punctuality was something he seemed to heavily reinforce when we originally smoothed out the plan. Even going as far as to hound me about every detail down to the very second in preparation for this evening—something was terribly wrong.

Just beyond the blinding stage lights, I could vaguely make out the silhouette of Patrick watching me. It was abundantly clear I'd made a grave mistake, that I had put my faith in a man who wasn't coming. How could I step off this stage and face Patrick? What the hell was I going to do?

The end of the third song quickly approached, and I fought back the tears. Very rarely did I ever cry, but putting my trust in a miscreant felt so childish looking back at it now. Why would he help me if he could get everything he wanted without the risk?

Erick Destler wasn't coming, and I'd already convinced myself it was true.

The song faded into nothing, and I took a bow amidst the applause and whistles. The noise was nothing more than a ringing in my ear, a soft, low buzzing that seemed to drown out the world and reminded me of what awaited me at the end of the stairs. Had I not felt so foolish, I might have pitied him.

People in the audience sang their praise while others gasped and pointed past me, seeing something the others didn't. The spotlight above faded to black, and the look of horror etched upon their faces became clear. I was about to glance over my shoulder and check when I was suddenly yanked back. I'd never been so grateful to feel the cold touch of a gun pressed to my temple.

He came.

While most of the audience shuddered, there was a handful of individuals who had guns drawn and aimed our way in the blink of an eye. I'd never seen anything like it—it was like a movie, something you'd seen a million times on the silver screen but never imagined you'd be part of.

"What the hell," Erick cursed under his breath.

"Stop. Stop," a voice desperately called out from the shadows. Patrick sprinted toward the stage, pausing on the first step. "No one shoot. Please," he pleaded for my safety with tears in his eyes, arms extended outward like he was handling a dangerous animal that could attack at any moment.

Forcing out fake tears, I mouthed the words help me.

"Let's talk this out," he suggested with a shaky voice.

"Shoot him and get it over with," someone shouted.

"Yeah. Do it already!"

Others in the crowd chimed in, overwhelming the already tense situation with heightened stakes. With a room full of trigger-happy assholes and a masked assailant, that meant one wrong move and the night would likely end in bloodshed. A terrible hiccup in our plan that neither of us anticipated.

"We need to leave," Erick whispered, holding me tighter.

The floor below my feet suddenly disappeared. A neat little trick seldom used when it was originally built, along with the rest of the theater, and with so many years passing since its creation, hardly anyone knew of its whereabouts, given the changeover of ownership and lack of use. I heard someone shout the beginning of my name and not much else as shots rang out above, narrowly missing us by mere inches.

The drop couldn't have been more than six feet, but as the

world around me changed in a split second, it felt much higher. The strange sensation of free-falling lifted my stomach before smacking hard onto the crash pad. Positioned as such, Erick took most of the impact as I landed atop him. That didn't stop him from recovering fast and scanning my body for any visible injuries. A bullet wound, or possibly a broken bone. There wasn't a scratch on us. We were both on our feet and sprinting within seconds of his assessment. Safety was no longer guaranteed, so we chased after it, praying we could make it to the tunnels in time.

"Stop, please!" Someone followed after us, jumping into the path of danger by plummeting into the unknown.

That's the thing about luck, fleeting in nature, it was bound to run out eventually. While luck had brought us this far without a bullet to the skull, it was a far cry from assuming we'd make it to the exit before Patrick could catch up. We pushed forward regardless, firing a few warning shots to slow him down. A part of me thought I would be able to breathe more easily once the large metal door was shut, but as his fist collided with the glass a second later, I couldn't bring myself to do it. The relentless pounding of his fist and the muffled sound of his cries followed us all the way down the path where safety was promised.

It wasn't until we crawled into the tunnel that both of us could stop and catch our breath. In that slight moment of peace, my back slammed against the concrete walls, and I allowed myself to savor the cool touch before Erick ripped off his skeleton mask and tossed it down the length of the tunnel. Suddenly startled, I couldn't hide the involuntary flinch of my limbs.

"What the fuck was that? I thought it was a rehearsal dinner, not a goddamn NRA convention," Erick shouted, throwing his hands up.

"I didn't know," I mumbled, pressing my spine firmly against the concrete. "It was just a rehearsal dinner. I already told you."

"Krissy, who's Patrick's sister marrying?"

"Charles."

Erick crowded me against the wall, sucking up all the oxygen and leaving me with none.

"Charles who?"

"Blanchet."

The name incited something deep within him, unlocking a fury long dormant. In a flash, Erick had me by the shoulders, fingers grinding against my bones. I stifled a scream, not fully understanding the degree to which his anger resisted. Even if I screamed, would anyone hear me down here?

I'd made plenty of mistakes, but was asking for his help one of them? I held my breath waiting for confirmation.

"Do you know who the hell Charles Blanchet is? Clearly, you don't, because none of this would have happened if you did. We wouldn't be in this mess. If I'd known...."

"He's an owner, is he not?"

He scoffed. "You have much to learn, little angel."

"I—I didn't know who Josephine was marrying until tonight. I promise."

A tear slipped free, and then something softened in his expression as he watched it. A long pause followed, and as he noticed another tear about to fall, he raised his bruised knuckle to wipe it away, but I flinched.

"You could have been hurt. I would have never put you in harm's way had I known," Erick said, finally breaking the silence. Only then did I meet his gaze, a little surprised at what I had just heard. "Come on. I think we both need a drink."

Leaving me pinned against the wall, Erick led the way into the depths of hell. Plucking his mask and the duffle bag I'd stashed down here days prior off the floor. I wasn't sure how the hell I'd gotten myself into this mess, nor how I would get out of it; the only thing I seemed certain of was that Erick was right. I desperately needed a drink.

Chapter Twenty

Patrick

*G*od help us all. Through these dark times, I turn to you. Guide me to the light.

There wasn't a trace of her. Krissy was gone, and there was nothing I could do to stop it. I'd sworn to protect her, and when the challenge arose, I'd failed her miserably. It all happened so fast. One moment, she was singing like an angel for the swooning crowd, and the next, every gun in the building was drawn and pointed at the masked man holding her hostage. I wasn't quite sure what was worse, the split second of uncertainty between the time I heard the shots and didn't know if she was okay, or the sight of her being dragged away from the small glass panel, feeling as hopeless as ever.

Willing party guests scoured every corner of the theater with the same vigor as a SWAT team, even going as far as to check it twice before coming to the awful conclusion that neither of them was in the theater anymore. Somehow escaping, despite the increased security posted around the theater—it simply did not add up.

"I'm calling the cops," I announced, unlocking my phone as I paced the halls backstage. I hadn't sat still once since the attack, and it was unlikely, I would be able to until I had answers. Sensing my erratic disposition, Charles approached with a surprisingly calm demeanor and gently lowered the phone before I could.

"Patrick—brother, I'm going to be frank with you. You aren't calling the cops." He continued, cutting me off when I opened my mouth to protest. "Come, let's speak where it is more private."

He directed my sister and me to the closest room so this conversation could continue without an audience, which conveniently happened to be Krissy's dressing room. The lingering scent of her fresh perfume smacked me like a wall upon entering, and I struggled to fight back tears with those not-so-gentle reminders of her surrounding me. Charles crossed his arms and leaned up against the vanity where she kept the bottle of perfume I loved so much; it was one of those rare gifts she adored just as much as I did when she used it.

Lord, keep me strong.

"Given the nature of my line of work, it's best not to have the cops sniffing around where they aren't wanted. And because we're practically family now, I can assure you, my men and I will handle this. Best in the business, right, mon chaton?"

"Yes, my love," Josephine confirmed, painfully unamused by the night's festivities.

"A few days ago, someone left Krissy a threatening message." I forced myself to look at my sister. "I know I should have told you, but we couldn't prove it was the person we suspected, and I didn't want to bother you with rumors and petty rivalries. I would have come to you had I known the threats were earnest." I turned to Charles. "Are you positive you can handle this? Because if not, the next place I'm going to is the police station."

Charles pushed off the vanity like the question had deeply insulted him. "No cops," he said coldly, clasping his hand on my shoulder. "Write down the names of those you believe to have left the message, even the person you mentioned before. You have my word; things will be handled accordingly."

Searching for my sister's reaction to all of this, I sought out her reflection in the mirror, finding something else entirely. Tucked in the frame of the vanity mirror was a small envelope addressed to me in elegant cursive handwriting. I lunged for it, scrambling to open it with shaky hands as Charles and Josephine curiously watched over my shoulder. Breathing down my neck to catch a glimpse of the short but haunting message left for me.

Miss Davis will remain in my possession until further notice. If you wish to gain back her freedom, the price for her life is the deed to The Lotte.

Life for property. It was as simple as that in the eyes of the sender. If I didn't call the number below and agree to pay the horrifying ransom, it would mean forfeiting Krissy's precious life for a scrap of property that was as much mine as Krissy was.

The note crumbled beneath my trembling fingers as realization slowly crept in.

"There's something else I didn't tell you," I said in a hushed tone. They glared at me with unreadable masks, warning me to tread lightly. As I mustered up the last of my courage, I spoke of the anonymous offers made on the theater and the persistent nature of the sender. The confession did not come without its questions, and after I answered every last one of them, the room fell uncomfortably silent.

"This should have been brought to our attention weeks ago. While you were pointing your finger at washed-up dancers, it seems as if we have a real crisis on our hands." Charles crossed his arms and smoothed his tongue on the inside of his cheek. "If my suspicions are correct, and this is an owner taking extreme measures to get what they want, then we must proceed with caution."

"But Krissy could be –"

"I will not draw blood before it is necessary, boy," he snapped. "Especially if it's Destler."

"Speaking of Destler," Josephine said suddenly, drawing both of our attention to where she lounged on the sofa. "I hope you don't mind me spoiling your wedding gift early, but after you proposed, my mother and I went searching for our families' portraits in storage so we might get them framed for the ceremony. She thought it would be lovely to have them present in spirit; however, when we were searching, I stumbled across old love letters between our great-grandparents. We thought nothing of it besides the romantic nature of the notes until we skimmed over a portion where he was speaking about his music career. Turns out our beloved great-grandfather was rather lively during the prohibition era, playing till dawn in unruly speakeasies throughout the district.

"In one of their correspondences, he begged her to watch him perform, vaguely describing the location of the speakeasy. An underground venue with entrances only accessible through a quaint little opera house or a jazz club in the heart of the entertainment district. A jazz club that I later learned was converted into a club," she smirked. "It's only a matter of finding the theater entrance, which Patrick has been tirelessly searching for weeks now."

"Ah, so the rumors are true." Charles plucked the cigarette from her lips and kissed her with such passion that it felt awkward to be in the same room while it was happening. "I don't deserve you, mon chaton, merci. Je vous aime."

"Whether or not Destler is to blame for her disappearance, we now possess the means to finally topple his reign."

Chapter Twenty-One

Erick

My belief in the divine faded years ago. I had nothing left to put my faith in, but as silly as it may sound, I felt as if my mother had been watching over me tonight. What hell had we brought upon ourselves by stepping into a lion's den looking for a fight? Ignorance and unintentionally gambling with life meant our odds were low, but somehow, by chancing death, we made it out on the other side alive. Had I known—had my people discovered this information sooner while digging around in Martin's affairs, I would never have played with fate like that. I would have never put Krissy in harm's way.

There would be hell to pay for the missed intel.

Fully aware that Krissy was following me from afar, I led us out of the humid tunnel and into my office, where I tossed her duffel bag on the leather couch in desperate need of something to wash down the vexation. A little weed was my normal vice, but tonight called for something much stronger.

Moments later, the soft clicking of her heels trailed behind. As I poured whiskey into the tumbler, I couldn't help closing my eyes and basking in the freshness of her perfume that soon followed. That familiar scent enveloped me in the understanding and comfort of knowing she was safe. Knowing that tonight could have taken a turn for the worse and somehow, we'd both made it out alive, and I would do anything in my power to keep things as they are, despite what obstacles we'd have to overcome.

I welcomed the smokiness of the whiskey burning my throat as I tossed back the drink and then poured another to settle my nerves.

"Until I can ensure your safety, you'll stay here in my office. I'll personally take you to the safe house once things have cooled off," I explained, turning to offer her a tumbler with a hefty pour. Standing in the doorframe with her arms tucked in close to her chest, she looked fragile, like a soldier plagued with shell shock returning home from war. "Take it," I insisted, "it will help."

Krissy studied the drink, tilting her head to the side like she was running through all the possibilities of what could happen from accepting a drink from a criminal like me. If my actions regarding the kidnapping weren't telling enough, I'd make her learn one way or another. I was the least of her worries, and the sooner she learned that, the better. Eventually, she took it, tossing it back without flinching. Two finger-widths of whiskey gone in a second flat, and after what we both endured, I think she needed more.

"Do you want me to find you a cot, or are you okay with sleeping on the couch?"

She finally spoke. "The couch is fine."

"I'll let you get settled in then. Blankets and food will be sent down soon."

Leaving her like this was wrong, I understood that, but what had come to light regarding our situation needed to be addressed as soon as possible. What other choice did I have? Blanchet's involvement meant this wasn't going to be a simple operation that would resolve itself in a few days' time. This was no longer a silly dispute between sweet Krissy and a disgruntled man, too proud to set her free. No, this was a ticking time bomb, a means for war generations in the making. Charles may not know for certain it was me behind the mask, but I needed to prepare security before his suspicions led him to my doorstep.

Lola, Damon, and Antonio rose to attention as I ascended the last few steps to the landing of the third-floor balcony.

"How did it go, boss?" Lola asked.

"Antonio, we need more men posted outside of the building. After you ensure security is sound, go downstairs and bring Krissy some blankets and food," I said to my cousin, then turned to Damon, signing for him to reach out to our connection at the station and make sure nothing had been reported to the police. "And Lola, take a seat for me. We need to have a conversation about the intel you provided me."

Upon further investigation, we discovered that Josephine and Charles' union wasn't common knowledge. It was a whirlwind romance that started off as nothing more than an innocent friendship and slowly evolved into a scandal in the making. It was no secret that the Martin family invested heavily in the Republic Opera House, but what was kept well out of the public's eyes was that, despite their partnership, Charles had gone behind his friend's back and ignored his objections to the marriage—a critical piece of intel we missed in our initial search. Had the circumstances been different, I might have assumed Lola was withholding information because her loyalties lay elsewhere. And although I believe it was a harmless mistake on her behalf, it didn't mean I wasn't watching her more closely.

I flopped down into the armchair, utterly exhausted.

"Have you heard back from Damon yet?" Antonio asked,

leaning up against the balcony railing, looking nearly as rough as I felt. It had been hours since we had a moment to rest.

"I haven't even had a chance to check my phone," I said, pulling it out from my back pocket and scanning through the dozen or so unread notifications until I spotted his name. "Damon said there hasn't been anything reported yet, but Officer Mattson will keep him updated if anything changes."

"Charles is involved in too much shady shit to get anyone besides his people involved," Antonio said, stating the obvious. While the Blanchet family might own some of the most prestigious houses in the district, that didn't mean Charles wasn't tangled up in a whole mess of illegal activity. As much as he despised my family for *sullying* the district with our unruly nightlife and overstepping our boundaries for generations, he was just as much at fault for bringing trouble to this part of town, employing people to sell drugs on his behalf backstage.

For someone who preached virtue, he was the furthest thing from it.

Vying over property and profit was only the beginning of why the Blanchets and Destlers loathed one another. As if it were a living beast, the feud had evolved and grown into a wicked thing that stemmed from events that took place long before our time. Today, as Blanchet's empire flourishes, he relies heavily on the district's nightlife to sell his products, but with strict rules in each of my clubs and programs I personally funded for rehabilitation centers and affordable medical treatment, I've been stepping on his toes ever since I assumed my role.

"What did you end up bringing Krissy for dinner? Did she like it?" I asked, running a hand over my face, seconds away from falling asleep in this very spot. It wouldn't be the first time I crashed here after a long day, and it wouldn't be the last. The club was closed for the night, so if I did, I might actually get a decent night's sleep.

"Well—she enjoyed the blankets I brought her," he choked out.

My eyes snapped open.

"Did you forget the food?"

Antonio's confession was like a shot of espresso in my veins. I was up in a flash, grabbing him by the shoulders and snarling down at him as his eyes bulged out of his head. He became painfully aware of how easy it would be for me to push him over the edge and began to beg for forgiveness with cloudy eyes. "I—I forgot. I'm sorry. I knew security was a top priority, and I was trying to ensure all of us were safe here at the club, so when I went downstairs to help her, I totally forgot about the food and only brought the blanket. It slipped my mind. I fucked up. I can go get something right now," he began to ramble.

"That was *three* hours ago when I asked you to do that," I fumed, my jaw painfully tight. "You're lucky we're family, or you'd be lying on the dance floor right now with a broken spine." At a quick glance, a stranger would probably have no idea that we were related if they saw us walking together down the street. While my genetics were a perfect blend of my mother's Italian roots and my father's African heritage, Antonio heavily resembled his Mediterranean ancestors. And although I couldn't let my cousin get away with everything, being the overly confident dip-shit he was, he got away with plenty more than the rest of them. "Forget it," I bit out. "I'll do it myself."

Not knowing exactly what to get Krissy, I opted for the best takeout restaurant open this late at night and something that would be filling enough to last her until morning. The takeout bag rustled around as the styrofoam containers shifted with each step. It was about ten-thirty at night, and there was a good chance Krissy was already fast asleep on the couch; in that case, she'd wake up to a nice surprise waiting for her on the side table.

"The hell–" I mumbled to myself, walking into the speakeasy.

Krissy was sprawled out on the bar, staring up at the light fixtures with a half-empty bottle clutched against her chest. Her knees were bent, causing her black gown to pool at her hips. With those gorgeous, long legs and dirty blonde hair slipping off the mahogany wood, she looked like the subject of a Rococo-era painting. I would spend a lifetime learning how to paint if it meant I could capture this moment forever and the beauty entangled with it.

"Krissy?"

"Hmm," she moaned lazily, tilting her head to the side and slightly up, elongating her neck in a way that made me want to bury my face in the column and praise her for all her bravery today.

"Are you drunk?"

"Well, I was hungry and bored, so I decided to fix one of those problems on my own. No thanks to you." If the glossy look washing over her usually vibrant blue eyes wasn't evidence enough, the way she pushed herself up into a sitting position on the bar was sloppy. She was drunk and glaring me down without an ounce of fear in her heart. Whether it was because of the ridiculous amount of liquor coursing through her system or the fact that she'd finally come to her senses after months of denying herself, Krissy didn't look at me in the same way she used to. Instead, she was sizing me up as I approached, her gaze falling to my rolled-up sleeves where the seemingly endless art spread up my forearm to disappear beneath my clothes and reappearing near my collar. "What's that?" She pointed to the takeout while subtly licking her lips, hoping I would give her the answer she was looking for.

"An apology," I admitted. Krissy was now in my care—a guest in my home, she should be treated as such. "I sent one of my people to do something I should have personally done myself. I hope you like Indian food." She didn't object as I placed the bag down beside her and fished out the takeout, handing her some butter chicken and plastic utensils as I did the same for my chicken biryani.

"Maybe you should surround yourself with better people, or I'm expecting too much from a bunch of criminals," she said, sitting crossed-legged on the bar, dress pooling in her lap like an angel with drunken words that outlined her crude and honest personality.

Finishing my first bite, I turned to look her dead in the eye. "If you knew half the things the other owners were doing in this city, you would label me a saint. I only do what is necessary to survive and keep them from destroying this place brick by brick. If you can't see who the real criminals are, then perhaps, you're more blind to the truth than I thought," my tone was dry and stern, "and for my employees, I have the best working for me, but there isn't much I can do about idiot family members I take under my wing as a favor."

Saying the last bit felt like there was a thick coat of ash sitting on my tongue, making me choke on my own words. All my people have done recently is mess up in catastrophic ways. I remind myself it was only a fluke, and normally, they were employees I could always rely on without hesitation or doubt.

We ate in silence for quite some time. Krissy scooped rice from the container in her lap, me an arm's length away, sitting at the barstool facing the opposite direction of her spaced-out gaze. Unlike the excitable drunk, she was the first time we met, tonight had unlocked something deep within her that allowed her demons to fester and grow. There was a sense of familiarity, having been in the exact same position too many times to count, but with no one by my side to ease those demons away. Too much loss and heartache for so few years. If you allowed it to, all that pain and suffering would grab you by the talons and drag you down. That's why having some kind of anchor was important, someone who could keep you from sinking into those emotions further. I tried to provide Krissy with something I never had myself.

So, I remained at her side, offering her what comfort I could. Every so often, I could sense her gaze lingering on me before retreating back a moment later. I carried on like I didn't notice the five times it happened.

"You don't scare me anymore. You know that, right?" she blurted out, trying her best to hide the slight slur to her words.

"Are you sure about that?" I retorted. "Say that again when you are sober, and I might believe you."

She sighed; the scent of her breath hit me like a wall—an explosion of spices mixed with the sting of whiskey. "Today made me realize what I am truly scared of, and it's *not* you."

"If I don't, then tell me what does."

"Dying," she plainly admitted, letting the alcohol fuel the conversation. Her fear was completely valid. We were within mere inches of death tonight, with every gun in the building pointed directly at us. Even with Patrick pleading with the guests not to shoot, it didn't mean a rogue bullet or a bad shot couldn't have ended our night a lot differently. "And the fact that Patrick is so manipulative, he is willing to crush the people around him to get what he wants. It just turned out I crave making his suffering more than his actions scare me—so I guess dying takes the lead then."

"He'll more than suffer," was all I offered as reassurance.

"Let's hope. I'd prefer not to waste my time faking my own

kidnapping for nothing," Krissy mumbled to herself while I was within earshot with enough conviction to slice into my heart. This wasn't for nothing, and I'd prove that to her time and time again. "I have to pee," she suddenly said, then tossed her food to the side with no regard, a few pieces of chicken nearly spilling out. I underestimated just how drunk she was until I watched her struggle to get down from the bar. I was up on my feet in a flash, my arms wrapped around her back, gently lowering her to the ground.

"I got you."

"Oh."

With Krissy in my arms, she slowly slid down until her bare feet hit the floor. Every painful second, I endured her body pressed against mine, I felt myself begging to give in to temptation. A selfish part of me wanted to take from her what we both deserved, and something about those wide eyes glaring up at me told me she wanted it just as badly as I did. Deep down, I knew all of that could wait, that I wanted her to lust over me with sober eyes and without a heavy heart. I reminded myself to be patient and that our time would come, but that didn't stop me from tracing my finger down her hip as I slowly retraced my hand back to my side. She lingered for a moment before finally walking to my office.

Krissy stirred behind the closed door. I tried to give her space, but my meal was nearly finished when I realized she had been in the restroom for far too long. I waited an additional few minutes before I ventured into the office to make sure she was okay. That's when I found her, passed out on the couch, still wearing her evening clothes, wrapped in a blanket. Her painted lips were slightly open as she slept peacefully after a day gone to hell. She deserved the rest, and I didn't dare wake her as I placed a bottle of water and ibuprofen within arm's reach and found my place in the stiff armchair at her side.

Chapter Twenty-Two

Krissy

I t was a dreamless sleep. The kind that if you didn't wake the next morning, you wouldn't have known any differ- ence between a good night's rest and a peaceful passing. When I did wake up, I had no recollection of tucking myself into bed or even ending up in Erick's office. The only memories of the night were a stiff headache, tightening around my brows, and the gown clinging to my sweaty skin.

Besides the harsh glow of the computer monitor illuminating the back wall, the rest of the office was shrouded in darkness. With no access to my cell phone for tracking purposes or a window to check, I had no concept of time or how long I'd been asleep underground like this. Careful not to aggravate my headache, I slowly got up in hopes of finding out, but stopped short when I found Erick resting in the armchair beside me. Blending into the darkness so seamlessly, like something about his presence insisted he belonged there. Fast asleep and completely unaware that I was staring, I selfishly took my time studying him from head to toe. From the jagged scar cutting down his face that gave him a hauntingly beautiful appearance to the soft rise and fall of his chest with each breath, to the way he bundled himself in his tattooed arms to keep warm. Saying I wasn't attracted to this man would be a goddamned lie, I made that abundantly clear the first night we met when I asked him to dance—and a few times since. I reminded myself I could admire him all I like, but knowing what I know now, I had no business getting wrapped up with a man like that. Erick Destler was trouble, and lusting for him wasn't going to help my current situation.

Desire was natural; acting on it wasn't.

I shook off the feeling and forced myself to get up. With each step, the silk gown felt awkward and sticky against the dried sweat on my skin. It was driving me insane, so much so that after checking the time on the computer, I took my bag into the bathroom and planned to do something about it despite feeling absolutely terrible. At the very least, it was a problem I could fix on my own, unlike the others.

The bathroom was fairly simple in spite of the rest of the office, equipped with a sleek modern shower and all the toiletries someone might need if they planned to spend a good amount of time working down here. Clearly updated compared to the rest of the building to fit Erick's needs.

I hopped into the shower, insisting the water be ice cold in hopes of cooling down my feverish skin. I could have stayed like that for hours, trapped beneath the shower head, so focused on the temperature rather than my mistakes. It was my own pocket of isolation where the world couldn't bleed through. I switched the faucet, and the drastic change was like a shock to my system. Inevitably, my mind began to wander, lulling me into unwanted thoughts and anxious tendencies that were better to avoid altogether, but once it started, it couldn't stop.

Death seemed to cross my mind more than anything else. Coming back in waves that overpowered me with crippling fear and thoughts of what could have been. The possibility of leaving behind the people I love and the kind of emotional damage I would have inflicted at the cost of carelessness. After losing both of my parents at such a young age, the grief devastated me. Ripped me apart and left me questioning everything I knew. I wouldn't even wish that level of pain upon my worst enemies, let alone the people I care for.

"Stop that," I mumbled to myself, forehead pressed against the cool tile. Memories of body bags, grinding metal, and flashing lights came at me all at once. Those paralyzing memories dug their claws in deeper as I scoured my mind for anything else to latch on to. I braced both hands on the tile and began panting as I found myself once more wrapped in a blanket and sitting on the curb while the officer spoke to me. Not a single word registered as my gaze transfixed on the blood staining the asphalt. "Stop," I repeated, crumbling down to my knees, knocking over a shampoo bottle in the process.

One moment, I was fighting back the tears, heaving on the floor, the next, I was reaching for a lifeline. That silly shampoo bottle became my last chance of releasing myself from my haunting past, pulling me back to reality. I read the label three times through, working to regulate my breathing, even going as far as to imagine Erick lathering his hair as I popped open the top and sniffed the earthy scent of the shampoo. As stupid as it felt to rely on such methods, it did its job and continued to do so as I refused to let go of the memories of Erick. I rose back up to my feet to finish up before it could happen all over again.

By some stroke of luck, the armchair was vacant. With no way of knowing how much he might have heard while I was showering, it was better off this way. Erick was gone, but not without leaving a note in his wake, explaining that he had business to tend to and would send down breakfast within the hour.

While Erick had agreed to take care of my basic needs while

I was under his care, that didn't mean he was responsible for keeping me entertained. I stared down at the note for quite some time, unsure how I might spend the day. Boredom was my worst enemy, and I tended to avoid it like the plague because with boredom came troubling thoughts and with troubling thoughts came the torrential spiraling that followed. Normally, my days would be jam-packed, shuffling about the city from dance class to work to clubbing with my friend. There was hardly a moment to breathe, let alone to think. And with Patrick showing no signs of giving in anytime soon, I would have to figure out how to keep those troubling thoughts at bay.

Just as Erick had promised, a breakfast sandwich was left for me outside the door. A delicious croissant sliced in half and loaded with different meats and cheeses that kept me full until lunch was delivered hours later. Unlike breakfast, a black man, as big as he was tall, entered the office to hand deliver the meal.

"Hi, what's for lunch?" I asked, sounding far more excited than I intended. He hardly gave me a passing glance as he set it down and turned to leave. Completely ignoring me altogether. "Wait! Do you want to play pool? I'm sure Erick wouldn't care if you took a twenty-minute break." Then he was gone, leaving me standing there like an idiot. "Asshole," I mumbled to myself.

I wasn't fit for isolation. I did all I could to fill the time, but it still didn't feel like enough. There was a reason I thrived in environments where there were people to talk with and things to do. I convinced myself that was the reason why I was struggling to hide my excitement as Erick returned for dinner with a bottle of wine in his hand.

The burst of excitement was sadly short-lived. He stumbled into the speakeasy wearing his emotions like he wore his clothes —dark and too many for my liking. From the hollowed-out look in his usually deep brown eyes to the top few buttons of his shirt undone to the way he sluggishly walked toward me, he appeared exhausted and did nothing to hide it.

"You look like hell."

Expecting some kind of kickback for the comment, instead, Erick huffed out a lazy laugh and gestured for me to follow toward the main seating area. "I feel like hell," he responded, pulling out dinnerware from behind the bar and starting to plate each dish family style. The meal consisted of authentic stone-fire pizza with sauces so runny that it pooled in the middle, Prosciutto di Parma so thinly cut that it was making my mouth water, gnocchi topped off with fresh parmesan and basil, and tortellini tossed in a fine vodka sauce with tiny chunks of sausage. "And starving," he added.

"Yeah, I can tell." There was no way in hell just the two of us could finish all of this. "It looks like you're feeding a small army."

"I didn't know what you wanted, so I got a little of every- thing," he admitted, plopping into the seat with a thud. "Come and eat before it gets cold." He didn't have to ask me twice before I scooped up a little of each dish in order to get the full experience. One bite was enough to tell that everything was handmade from scratch by someone who put their heart and soul into cooking authentic Italian food.

"God, where did you get this?"

Erick lowered his fork and met my gaze. "My aunt owns a bistro uptown. It used to be a family business, but now she runs it on her own."

"Is she the one with the son you hired, or is that another idiot relative?"

"Yeah, Antonio is her idiot son," he answered. "It seems like every year our family tree is shrinking little by little. When that happens, you tend to keep those who are still around close by, even if they're total screw-ups. I love him nonetheless."

"So, is your hiring criteria idiot family members and silent assholes?"

"Silent assholes?"

"You know." I waved my hand flamboyantly. "The tall black guy who looked like he could crush me with his big thumb. Did you tell all your employees they can't interact with me, or does he just like to play into the whole intimidation factor?"

Erick nearly snorted out his wine, laughing hysterically as he coughed away the tightness in his chest. Leaving me sitting there, awkwardly waiting for an explanation.

"Damon is partially deaf," he explained with lingering laughter in his tone. My eyes were nearly as wide as my mouth, realizing my mistake. "Damon had a work-related accident years before my father took him in. After he lost his hearing, he had trouble finding work, but stumbled across Don Juan when they were hiring a doorman. It didn't take long before he worked his way up and eventually joined the ranks when I took over. So, if he was ignoring you, he wasn't doing it intentionally."

"That explains a lot," I mumbled, and then took a sip of the fine-aged wine. "Now I feel like the asshole."

"Probably because you are," he smirked with boyish charm.

"Ah, watch it," I warned, a little too flirty for my own good. "Only I can say that."

Erick leaned forward to join in. "I'll do whatever I want when it comes to you, Krissy." Flirting was all good and fun, but if I continued feeding into this conversation, I wasn't quite sure I could trust myself around him. There was a long pause that followed. Sensing that he had overstepped some kind of line, he leaned back and stepped down. "Speaking of assholes," he finally said, wiping his mouth with a napkin and then tossing it onto the empty plate. "Martin still hasn't messaged the burner phone. Knowing what we know now, I don't expect he will anytime soon. Every step he takes is going to be perfectly orchestrated by his brother-in-law, so I figured we could send him a little something to get the ball rolling," he suggested.

"What do you have in mind?"

"Go put on the dress you were wearing last night."

The black gown, a tainted souvenir forever associated with the memory of that night, clung to my skin. The fabric was still stained with sweat, tears, and spilled whiskey. The greatest shame was the fact that I would probably never wear the dress again, despite how stunning it looked and the pretty penny it cost.

Erick returned with his arms full of the props we needed to make this look believable. A Polaroid camera, handcuffs, and a silk scarf, to name a few. I lightened the load by taking a few from his hands and followed him out of the depths of hell into the empty club, a few hours away from being opened to the public. The most obvious and safest choice would be to close Don Juan indefinitely, but closing the hottest club in the city would draw too much attention and project blame. So, it wasn't even an option. All Erick could do was increase security, let fewer people in, and hope for the best.

Running on borrowed time, Erick led us to a storage room at the back of the house. We worked silently, moving the boxes of napkins, wristbands, and coasters from one side of the room to the other until we had an empty corner that gave away nothing of our location.

"Are you sure this will work?" I asked, dropping the last box. I was out of my element, but I knew a decent plan when I heard one. Blanchet and Patrick needed a kick in the ass, and we were going to have a little fun doing it.

"Do you doubt me?"

"No." I grinned.

"Good, now stop wasting time—turn around and put your arms behind your back."

"Okay, officer," I teased and followed as instructed. The reverberation of his footsteps clicking against the concrete grew louder as he approached from behind. It wasn't until the third or fourth step that I realized I'd stopped breathing altogether. I was just about to peer over my shoulder to see why he was taking so long when he lightly gripped the inside of my wrist and began lightly stroking it as he fumbled with the handcuffs in the other hand.

"Tell me if it's too tight." A series of metallic clicks followed, locking me in place. "How's that?"

"Could be tighter," I jokingly said.

Erick huffed out a laugh, the warmth of his breath brushing up against the back of my neck, making my arm break out in goosebumps. He seemed to instantly notice, running his thumb over them before tightening the cuff with one final click. I fought back the urge to hiss as the cool metal bit into my skin. "As you wish," he mumbled. "For this to look believable, you need to act the part of a kidnapped victim. Can you cry on demand?"

Searching deep within, I picked apart and forced myself to relive the most traumatic thing I could conjure up. For that brief moment, I allowed those troubling thoughts to win, and as I glanced over my shoulder, I showed him just how convincing I could be. A single tear spilled free. "Perfect." The praise went straight to my head, making my stomach somersault as a result. "Now go cower in the corner and keep crying until your makeup smears."

Ever so gently, I lowered myself to the floor, back pressed against the frigid wall as I tucked my knees into my chest and lightly sobbed. It all came so easily, the acting, the crying, like there was some part of me still suppressing the horrors from the night before. Erick ate it up, reaching for the camera to capture the moment.

"This looks pretty damn believable," he said, smiling down at the image. With one final shake of the photo, he showed me his work. The photo was hauntingly beautiful; if I didn't know better and saw it on a true crime documentary, I would think it was real. "We need more. We'll give him a few more days, and if we haven't heard anything by then, I'll send them out."

Like an artist locked in his studio, Erick got to work creating his art. Putting me into a series of twisted positions that displayed the fabricated danger I was in. I was nothing more than his little plaything to make his vision come to fruition, and I ate up every moment of it. Having fun with my time outside of the office and the chance to have company with another—even if it was him.

"We're almost done—bend over the table," he demanded, pointing to the small rectangular table that had once been used for the club, then slipped on his skeleton mask—that *damned* mask. The product of my nightmares, salvation, and lust-infused dreams. As tired as he was, the second he put it on, the life seemed to come back to his eyes, highlighting the deep brown of his irises and little flecks of black scattered about.

He was the personification of death. Terrifying and beautiful.

Bending forward, the edge of the table cut into my hips. Face down, arms tied back, I didn't realize how vulnerable I was in this position until it was too late. Erick didn't stop until his body was firmly pressed up against my lower half.

"What are you–" Erick took a fistful of my hair and pulled me back, our bodies melting as one. We both shifted forward despite there being no room to do so, and his erection pressed firmly against my ass as the edge of the table rubbed up against the aching between my thighs, only worsening the situation. Erick yanked again, forcing my head back until it was parallel with his, exposing my throat to him. My breath hitched, and he groaned in response.

"That's not very believable," he whispered against the shell of my ear. "If I didn't know better, I'd say you were enjoying this, little angel."

"No," I said in a tone that wasn't half believable.

"One more photo, little angel, then I'll reward you for all your hard work." Erick set down the camera and wrapped his arms around my waist. "One more," he repeated. Slowly, his hand began to rise, tracing a path up my stomach, between my breasts, and around my neck with enough pressure for there to be pleasure instead of pain. My eyes rolled back, completely under his spell. Utterly lost, with no power to return. "Can you do that for me?"

"You aren't making this any easier," I said, hardly loud enough for it to be considered a whisper.

"I never do." He slightly tightened his grip with one hand, then reached for the camera with the other. "Here's your time to shine, Krissy. Make it look believable." I only had a split second to react, and as the camera flashed, I took the opportunity to jolt forward, pretending to show signs of a struggle. My scalp ached where Erick still had hold of me, but as quickly as it started, it was over. He released his grip but kept me caged up against the table with his body as he set out the photos, one by one, for me to admire. Seven perfectly wicked pictures.

"What do you think?"

Only seven. I could have sworn there was another flash...

"Perfect," I snipped, shimmying out of his hold and beelining it for the exit with a burning between my thighs and a prickle of shame in my heart. "Send them out."

Chapter Twenty-Three

Patrick

I thought I knew the effects of suffering on the soul until nearly two days had passed without her. Forty-five hours to be exact. With hundreds of thousands of people going missing every year, there is extensive research stating that the first seventy-two hours are the most critical in any case. With each passing breath, bringing us closer to that seventy-two-hour mark, I felt more hopeless than the last. Although this was still a matter of life and death, it seemed like our situation had one dividing factor among the endless cases of people disappearing without a trace. I had witnessed the abduction and caught a glimpse of her captor and knew his terms and conditions regarding the price for her life. There was hope, after all.

If that last forty-five hours hadn't been enough of a punishment, my phone was constantly ringing. Flooded with endless texts and calls from friends, family members who witnessed the attack, and concerned employees who caught wind that something was amiss. Lyra and Tory were relentless in their questioning, calling me at all hours of the night, demanding answers, and making me question why I had ever given them my number in the first place. The few that were in attendance that night were the only ones that knew the truth, and with their relationship with the Blanchet family, it was going to stay that way. For her closest friends and roommates, there was no hiding the fact that she was missing. I'd convinced them to keep things quiet in the meantime, but it was up to me to do damage control and reassure them that everything was going to be okay. As Charles had said, the more they knew, the more of a liability they'd become.

And liabilities had to be dealt with.

Walking through her apartment complex stirred up old memories of sneaking around in the dead of the night and enveloping myself in everything about her. When I was with her, I felt the most at home. Felt the most like myself, and had there been more time I would have told her how I truly felt. I fought back tears of frustration as I exited the elevator and found her apartment. All it took was one knock before Lyra swung the door open so aggressively that it nearly snapped off the hinges.

"About time you finally showed up," she said in a clipped tone.

I pushed past her, taking all but three steps into the apartment before realizing Tory and Lyra weren't alone. Daniel was sitting in the living room, arms crossed, watching me like a dog. Just beneath my skin, I could feel my blood begin to boil at the sight of him sitting here in her apartment like he owned the place. Staking a claim in her well-being like he gave a damn. Following my gut hadn't led me astray yet, and when it came to Daniel, I'd had a weird feeling about him since the day we met.

"Patrick," Lyra shouted, joining us in the living room. "It's time you gave us some damn answers. It's been days, and we're scared shitless."

"We're calling the cops," Tory announced.

"No, you are not," I barked with a sharpness in my tone that had both of them straightening in their seats. "I already told you once, and I'm not going to tell you again—no cops."

"Krissy was *kidnapped*! Someone took her against her will and is doing God knows what with her as we speak. You're her boyfriend, how can you sit back and do nothing? When someone gets kidnapped, normal people call the police!" Lyra's voice boomed off the walls.

"Seems a little suspicious," Daniel mumbled, holding my stare.

"And what are you suggesting?"

"I've seen my fair share of true crime documentaries. It's usually the boyfriend, you know," he pointed out with a smug attitude that had me moving before I knew what I was doing. Daniel's shirt was balled up in my fist, and Lyra shoved me before I could wipe the smile right off his face.

"Back up," Lyra screamed, "and start talking."

The whole situation had me on edge and acting irrationally. Stress wasn't something I handled with grace, but had come in abundance lately. I ran both hands over my face, releasing a shaky breath, then smoothed back the rogue strands of hair shaken loose from my little outburst.

"Tell us what happened, or we're calling them right now," Tory warned again.

"Fine," I snapped. "We have reason to believe the party responsible for her kidnapping is the Destler family, but we aren't certain yet." Before any of them could bombard me with more questions, I continued. "It's likely they targeted her because of her relationship with my family and the business she's conducted with Charles Blanchet. If the cops haven't been able to stop the Destler family after more than a century in this city, then they're useless to us now. My brother-in-law has given me his word that he will handle this himself and get her home safely without relying on the assistance of the police. I love her just as much as you guys do, I promise you, this is the only way."

"Charles Blanchet," Tory choked out, shaking her head. "What kind of *business* did she have with him? Was she planning on leaving The Lotte for Republic Opera?"

"Buying drugs," I said without a hint of dishonesty in my voice. "Krissy met Charles a few weeks ago, and when she found out who he was, she jumped at the opportunity." Krissy was a party girl through and through. It was a likely excuse that her roommates seemed to believe without hesitation, which made convincing them to stay out of this even easier than I thought it would be.

The room was silent for a long moment as they mulled over the idea.

"You've got to be kidding me." Lyra flopped onto the couch, pulling at her braids. "So, what I'm hearing is that you would rather protect your brother-in-law by not contacting the police, even though he's the one selling drugs? Sounds like you care more about him than Krissy."

"How my brother-in-law lives his life is none of my business. The same can be said for Krissy, but that doesn't change the fact that she still made the choice to buy from him. If the cops start searching for evidence regarding her disappearance, what happens if they accidentally find a surveillance tape or transcripts that she was purchasing drugs from him? Forgive me for looking out for the people I care for. And don't even get me started on the exams the hospital will conduct if the police actually do their job and find her. Along with a rape kit, they'll likely test her for any drugs in her system, and that in itself is enough evidence to convict. The situation is grim, I understand that, but this option is our best chance of getting her home safely."

"She could just lie and say the guy who kidnapped her forced her to."

"Are you willing to risk everything for the hope that they might believe her?"

Lyra didn't seem to like my answer, but it was enough to shut her up and make her consider the consequences.

"If it really is the Destler family, do you think it has anything to do with the night she spent with Erick Destler?" Daniel asked, and the girls shrugged.

The moment the question left his lips, I felt a lump rise in my throat, blocking my airways and preventing me from speaking. It took four tries before I could choke out a response. "Kris—Krissy would never."

The three of them exchanged a look.

"The night the theater was sold, we all went out to celebrate at Don Juan. Krissy got sick and spent the night in his office while she recovered," Tory answered.

"Did she have sex with him?"

"God no—well—actually I don't know. She said she didn't, but..." Tory trailed off.

"Do I have your word that you won't contact the cops?" I quickly changed the subject, knowing if I didn't right that second, I'd begin spiraling.

Lyra and Tory stared at one another for a while, communicating without words.

"Yes, but don't you dare think it's because we want to protect you and your stupid family. You get Krissy back, or, so help me God, I'll sell out your entire family then find a way to blame you for the drugs," Lyra threatened.

"Noted."

Everlasting. Relentless. The sound of the ringing buried itself deep within my skull, and if I had to listen to her voicemail greeting one more time, I'd shatter my phone against the passenger side door and turn this car around and keep driving until I was outside of Don Juan. It would be a mistake to go—I know that, but I couldn't think straight, and Josephine wasn't making the situation any better.

I needed answers from her—and Krissy.

Stop, don't think that. Krissy would never. She knows better than to sleep with—

"Hello? Hello. Josephine?"

"Yes, hello," she said casually, the distant sound of music playing in the background.

"You've been ignoring my calls."

My sister sighed. "Patrick, I'm on my honeymoon and the service here is terrible." Charles spared no expense in whisking his new bride away to a private island after their ceremony. I'd done everything besides get down on my hands and knees and beg them to postpone the wedding. Josephine, stubborn in her own way, had refused to move the ceremony, which was understandable given that everything was nonrefundable, but I was a little surprised and hurt when she refused to reschedule their trip to help me.

"I still don't understand how you can be sipping drinks on a stupid beach while people are in danger. You and Charles promised me this would be handled," I bit out, blinking enough times to clear my vision.

"And it will be."

"Being nine thousand miles away isn't handling it," I shouted. "Do something. Please do something, or I will." My grip on the steering wheel tightened, and tears began to spill free. "Please," I begged in a voice I didn't recognize.

There was a long pause.

We were loved. There was no denying that. Growing up in our household, I never questioned whether or not my parents loved me. However, as a child, it was incredibly difficult to understand why my mother and father were so absent from my life. Looking back at it now, I can fully comprehend just how hard my parents worked to provide my sister and me with everything they could to better our lives, but when you're just a child, you notice the obvious. And the thing that was the most apparent to me was that Josephine was always there. She practically raised me within that empty house, and I truly believe it was the reason why our relationship was so strong.

Which is why it hurt so much when she finally spoke.

"Patrick, listen closely," she said. "Charles is handling this situation, and if you step on his toes, losing Krissy will be the least of your worries. He's given you his word, and that should be enough. You're letting your emotions and your dick get the best of you. This isn't just some random criminal off the streets. This is a Destler, and this will be handled accordingly. Do you understand?"

Part of me wanted to resent her for sounding so much like our father.

"She could be hurt. This can't wait. There must be something he can do now."

One second, I was speaking to my sister, and the next, the phone was handed off to Charles.

"Frère? Bonjour." Charles' thick accent bled through the line.

"Frère, please tell me there is something we can do—something I can do," I pleaded, not caring who heard the agony in my voice as I walked through the lobby of the theater.

"Your sister tells me you're worried about your friend. I gave you my word, and in my family, that means something. I assure you, my people are investigating and following Destler right now. Once we have confirmed it's him, we'll plan our attack.

Nothing happens until then," he warned. "In the meantime, you need to leave us alone while we're on holiday. Oui?"

"Oui," I echoed. "Tell her I–"

He hangs up before I can finish my thought.

Within the confines of my office and away from wandering eyes, I let out several shaky breaths, managing to somehow pull myself from the void. If Charles was to be trusted, his men were currently following Destler and actively searching for her. Knowing that was the only thing keeping me afloat. It didn't feel like enough, but it was something...

The envelope instantly caught my attention. Amongst the stacks of applications neatly arranged on my desk, there was no missing it. The strange letter only had one thing written on it in elegant black ink: Motherfucker. I was hesitant to even reach for it, but when I did, its contents came spilling out.

Had I not already been sitting down, I could have crumbled to my knees.

Seven photos stared back at me. Each one encapsulated my worst fear. I foolishly had prayed that her captor would take mercy, but that hope was gone, along with my sanity. I had failed her and continued to fail her every step since. There would be hell to pay. Not only for the people who have hurt her, but for my own failures. There was a price for everything, and suddenly it didn't matter whose feet I stepped on if it meant waking up from this nightmare once and for all.

I picked up my phone and dialed before I could talk myself out of it. It rang three times before the line connected. "Did you run out of investors for your theater already?" a familiar voice asked as a way of greeting. "You must be desperate if you're calling me for money."

The entertainment and financial districts were not without their differences, but at the root of their existence, they were nothing more than different masks hiding the same beast. Forged on the backs of those who have come before, the two districts were designed to allow the most cutthroat amongst us to thrive in a city determined to wear us down. While I may not have been successful downtown working with my father, the connections I made there could save me from others.

"Jonathan, I have a favor to ask..."

Chapter Twenty-Four

Krissy

By the third day, I'd developed something of a routine, a sense of normalcy for a situation that was anything but. It was all fine and good until the fifth day rolled around and I found myself terribly dreading it all. There wasn't much excitement in predictability, but each time the large metal door pinged open at seven o'clock exactly, Erick brought the promise of something fun and unique with him every time. I never quite knew what to expect; he kept me on my toes. Maybe I was just desperate for a break from my mundane routine, but something about that hour or so we spent together was always the highlight of my day.

Neither one of us had addressed what had happened the other day in the shadows of the storage room during our little photoshoot. The way he carried on with light conversation made it feel like it had all been a figment of my imagination. Something I dreamt up during another lonely night. And while the entire thing felt like a dream, the way the memory seared itself into my mind, I knew it wasn't.

The door swung open. Damon and Antonio stumbled in during one of my games of solitaire, sprawled out on the table below. Apparently, delivering the products I'd requested hours ago was now a two-man job—or at least it was when it came to Antonio.

"Took you long enough," I said, placing the seven of spades down.

"Don't get your panties in a twist," he playfully said, a hint of his accent licking each word. Even looking at him now, I still had a hard time wrapping my head around the fact that he and Erick were related. From the inky black hair, strong Roman nose, and olive skin tone, he looked the furthest thing from being related by blood. The only similarity between the two men was the symmetric beauty in their facial structure and their long, thick lashes.

Damon set down the bag, careful not to disrupt the game. Drawing from the deepest corners of my mind, I individually signed each letter to spell out the word thank you. Instead of American Sign Language, I opted for Spanish in high school to fulfill my foreign language credit. Although there was one summer during dance camp many years ago when a counselor taught the girls in my bunk how to sign the alphabet for fun.

His eyes widened, and his expression softened. It was the type of change that, if you weren't looking hard enough, you would have missed it.

"Like this," he said, his voice raw as if he hadn't spoken in quite some time, and from what Erick had mentioned, he wasn't much for conversation even before the accident. Damon lifted an open palm to his chin and tipped it down, then gestured for me to follow his lead, teaching me the proper way to sign my appreciation. After a few practice runs, he nodded in approval and pointed his thumb to his chest with an open palm.

"The big guy likes you," Antonio interjected, taking a seat across the table.

"How can you tell?"

"That stupid smile on his face." He gestured toward Damon, lounging in a booth. His expression was as stout as his personality, though he looked a little more relaxed than he normally did while scrolling through his phone.

"I'd hardly call that a smile," I snorted.

"It's as close as you'll get to the real deal," he countered, collecting the cards off the table and then shuffling them with the grace and skill of a Vegas dealer. He gloated a bit with his showmanship before he equally divided the deck into two stacks.

"You sure your boss won't mind you guys dicking around on company time?"

"Nah, don't worry about Erick. The worst that will happen to me is a slap on the wrist, plus we deserve a little break. That fucker has been working us like dogs cleaning up the mess he created," he said, shoving a stack toward me.

"What are we playing?"

"War."

"Really? What am I, ten?"

"Take it or leave it."

"Fine." Beggars can't be choosers, I guess.

Antonio and I flipped through the deck, locked in a heated match that was neck and neck for the majority of the game. With a stroke of luck, my discard pile began to grow as I collected more and more of his lower suit cards. Gloating about an early victory, I teased him, "I figured being related to Erick meant you'd be more of a challenge to beat."

He scoffed. "Sweetheart, I'm a Donati, not a Destler—he gets his cunningness and winning personality from his daddy's side." Then he paused to look at his card. "And his mediocre good looks."

Calling him mediocre felt criminal, even if it was a joke.

"Were you two close growing up?"

He bit the inside of his cheek, calculating his words as he

shuffled the deck for the next round. "Mama was never a fan of her brother-in-law or the family business. She practically beat my aunt when she found out. So, for most of my childhood, our relationship strictly revolved around spending time together during the holidays or the occasional family dinner. It wasn't until his mother died and he started living off and on with his grandfather that we got closer. Now the asshole can't get rid of me."

Antonio's story answered one question and unintentionally prompted several more.

"I'm sure your mom is proud that you followed in your cousin's footsteps," I teased. "You say you're a Donati, but you sure as hell act like a Destler."

Before we could start the rematch, he flung the instruction card at Damon's stomach to draw his attention away from his phone. The two of them rapid-fired a conversation with signs that looked as fluid as water, then turned back to the game.

"My mama nearly wrung out my neck when she found out I was wrapped up in the district. After I paid off all of her debt and bought her one of those designer bags she was ranting and raving about, she quickly learned to turn the other cheek," he explained, placing down his first card. An eight of hearts, superior to my two of spades. "You know, there are plenty of things to talk about besides Erick and my family, unless the thought of him is the only thing rattling around in that pretty little head of yours. You talk about him an awful lot – just something I've noticed over the last few days. Even," he pointed over his shoulder, "Damon agrees with me."

"He can barely hear our conversations."

"Well, I told him so..." he laughed. "You got a little crush on my cousin, huh?"

"Maybe I'll do your mother a favor and wring out your neck for her," I said. "And no, I don't have a *crush* on Erick. The man is just helping me get what I want, nothing more. I'm using him. And God forbid I ask you a simple question about your family, next time I'll make sure to ask your political opinions or something stupid like the last time you cried."

"It'll be right now if you don't get your ass upstairs." Erick's voice boomed through the speakeasy. The threat read loud and clear as Antonio and Damon jumped to their feet.

Unwilling to turn and face him, I mumbled to myself, eyes closed. "Of course, he heard that."

"Coming, cugino," he chorused. In passing, Antonio patted my head twice. "Have fun."

"Vaffanculo," I hissed. I wasn't fluent in any language other than English, but I knew a handful of curse words for moments like this. The two men disappeared upstairs, leaving me to face a temperamental Erick all on my own. We'd been so preoccupied with our game and the rare chance of company, none of us noticed the time getting dangerously close to seven o'clock. Which was a damn shame because I knew Erick had stumbled in mid-conversation, but with no way of knowing how much he heard, I was left awkwardly watching him plate the ramen and sake, wondering if it was worth bringing up.

"I didn't—"

He interjected, "You don't need to explain yourself. Now eat before it gets cold."

The smell of it alone was enough to make my mouth water, but it was nothing compared to the sight of the bowl he placed before me. With dark, steaming broth surrounded by a collection of veggies and a hard-boiled egg, I couldn't pick up my chopsticks fast enough to dig in. It only took a few bites for me to instantly regret being so excited in the first place. Whatever weird tension lingered between us became abundantly clear when the sound of us slurping our noodles was the only thing that filled the room as we struggled to make conversation.

"Any good news?"

"Nothing yet," he said between bites. "Patrick has, without a doubt, seen the photos by now, but I haven't heard a peep from him." Blanchet was throwing a wrench in our plan. Patrick would have given in by now if it weren't for him. Weak men tend to bend for whoever has control, and right now, we have none.

"Do you think I can go to the safe house soon? No offense, but living in your office isn't exactly glamorous," I admitted, keeping my tone lighthearted. "I do appreciate the unlimited drinks, though."

"Some of those bottles are twice as old as our combined age, watch it, Davis," he warned with a tone that didn't quite reflect his dreary mood. "Blanchet still has his lackeys following me around town, waiting for confirmation that it was me who took you before acting. It isn't smart to relocate you from the club just yet. You'll be safe here in the meantime."

"Maybe Damon or Antonio could sneak me out if they're only following you."

"They have the place being watched twenty-four seven—good try though."

Growing more and more restless with each passing day, I wasn't sure how much more of this I could take before I finally snapped. Only time would tell.

Chapter Twenty-Five

Krissy

If I concentrated hard enough, I could feel the slight vibration of the bass as I lay restless on the couch. It was a Saturday night—the club upstairs was alive and well with dozens of drunken idiots having a much better time than I was. Erick had left hours ago, tending to his business, leaving me drowning in my own thoughts, utterly alone and pissed off. I understood his reasoning for keeping me here, but I felt myself withering away with each passing breath. Faking my own kidnapping was supposed to be a liberating sense of freedom and a path to achieve my goals at The Lotte, but I couldn't help feeling like it was turning into my own personal hell. At this point, it felt like a game of wits, and I was losing terribly. Maybe if I skipped town, changed my name, and somehow managed to smuggle my roommates with me, I could escape this all. Yup, that would solve all my problems.

The bass shook the foundation of the building with such force, the glass of water rippled in response. I threw a pillow over my face to drown out my scream. It was calling to me like a siren, and it took every ounce of strength not to cave into its tantalizing coercion.

Anything I did to distract myself failed miserably. Reading only made me tired. Playing pool or cards reminded me how alone I was. Drinking the alcohol behind the bar only made me think of Erick. Thinking about him made me replay the last time we spoke, and the lingering guilt that followed. Reminiscing about old times made me angry for keeping my friends in the dark and forced me to imagine the pain I was putting them through. And sleeping was pointless. I felt like there was no scenario in which things played in my favor—except one.

"Fuck it," I mumbled, giving in too easily but too bored to care. In a split second, I was on my feet, digging through my duffel bag searching for something suitable for the occasion. Not quite sure how to properly pack for something like this, the only thing I could find was the dress I wore the night of the rehearsal dinner. All it took was a quick wash in the sink, a blow-dry, and a snip of the hem, and I had something that resembled a cocktail dress. "Good enough," I said, admiring myself in the bathroom mirror. The hack job was far from perfect. The hem of the dress sat mid-thigh in choppy lines, but under the dim lighting of the club, it wouldn't be noticeable.

Finishing the look, I slipped on a pair of heels and made for the exit. As meticulous as Erick was regarding security protocol, it was a little surprising to find that the door was only locked on one side. Keeping that in mind, I made a mental note to prop open the door so I could return without anyone noticing. I snuck out of the speakeasy without a problem and started to ascend toward the music calling my name.

On the second landing was an archway leading into the club, with a man stationed beyond the velvet rope to turn away any wandering guests. Knowing there would be no way around the bouncer without causing alarm, I walked back to the bar and grabbed a tumbler off the shelf, and sent it flying. Glass shattered against the wall leading up to the third floor, and to no surprise, the bouncer chased after the sound, abandoning his post and giving me a small window of opportunity to sneak by undetected.

The club was the best type of chaos, a cheap thrill that felt like it had been injected right into my veins, making me feel more alive than I had in quite some time. A sea of people partied and danced within the safety of Don Juan's walls. The very place that had once been described as an unbreakable fortress, and while my safety was guaranteed under Erick's protection and the increased security surrounding the building, it didn't mean I shouldn't take precautions for my little night out.

To my right, there was a bachelorette party all wearing an array of colorful wigs while they drank and laughed, celebrating their blushing bride. All of them were participating in the fun except one member of the group, who looked green around the gills. While a few of her fellow bridesmaids were distracted helping her sober up, I snatched the lilac-colored wig still in its packaging right under their noses. All it took was a little adjusting in the bathroom mirror, and there wasn't a hint of blonde that could be found. With a newfound confidence, I journeyed toward the bar, drawing far more attention than I intended. One of the many onlookers followed after me, a nearly middle aged Mexican man who on any given day could have attracted my attention based solely on his silver fox good looks, but I wasn't interested—not now.

"What are you drinking?" he shouted over the music.

"Whatever you're having." With no wallet, I had no other choice but to flirt my way into a few drinks.

"Two shots of tequila," he ordered, and like magic, two shots appeared before us.

"So, where are you from?" he asked with a sly grin. I answered by slamming the shot glass down on the bar and quickly thanking him for the drink before venturing off toward the dance floor. There was only so much small talk I could stomach before the free alcohol simply wasn't worth it anymore, and by the look of a gleam in his eye, he wanted something much more from me than a little friendly conversation.

By the time I reached the first step leading down to the sunken dance floor, someone had grabbed me by the elbow. I spun around, expecting the old fox to either beg me to stay or demand payment for my drink, but instead, I was met with someone completely different.

"Princess, you'd better go back downstairs before this turns into an unnecessary mess." Antonio glared down at me with an inflection in his tone that mimicked his normal playfulness with a just hint of threat embedded in it.

"Thanks for the suggestion, but respectfully fuck off, Antonio," I gleamed. We stayed like that for several long seconds, holding each other's gaze and waiting for the other to give in, then it dawned on me that if he had any real power to force me back downstairs, then he would have done it by now. "Have fun explaining this to your boss."

I jerked out of his hold and left. Antonio found a place leaning up against the railing and watched me like a hawk as I wiggled my way through the crowd, finding the perfect spot to dance. It felt like ages since the last time I stretched my legs and moved so freely; it was an opportunity I wasn't planning on letting him or anyone else ruin.

Letting the rhythm guide me, I danced for my own pleasure, completely unbothered by the crowded space. I wasn't sure how many songs came and went; each one trapped me in its clutches until I felt drunk off the music alone. I was so lost in the moment that I didn't think to look up at Antonio until it was too late. His attention wasn't focused on me anymore; instead, he stared off into the distance, slowly tracing a path toward me. Following his line of sight, I watched the crowd part one person at a time until Erick came into view.

One moment I'm dancing, then the next I'm being hauled away.

"Erick–"

Beyond the stairs leading up to the main level of the club were four private alcoves reserved for VIP guests willing to shell out thousands of dollars for bottle service. Fashioned with pristine white couches, a small rectangular glass table, velvet privacy curtains, and enough room to mingle, the space wasn't quite worth the price, but people still paid the hefty price for the privilege. Erick lightly shoved me into a vacant alcove, and I went stumbling forward, tripping on my own two feet, running into the nearest wall just out of view behind the curtain.

"You're lucky Antonio texted me," he snarled, the veins in his neck clearly visible under the muted light from the club filtering in. "You're begging for a death wish, aren't you?"

Refusing to give in to his fear tactic, I barked back, "You're the one who told me I was safe here, unless you were just lying to me."

"This is a club, it's not impenetrable. You're going back downstairs right this minute."

"Make me," I said, exaggerating each syllable nice and slow. Erick was keeping his distance, but his glare kept me pinned against the wall, waiting to see if he'd take the bait.

"Do I really need to remind you that we laid out these rules long before we ever set this plan in motion? All you have to do is follow them. Follow the damn rules, Krissy, or I'll make you regret ever making a deal with me in the first place."

"Yeah, we created rules for a situation that no longer exists. Everything," I gestured with my hand, "has gone to shit. If you want to hold me accountable for your bullshit made-up rules, then go ahead, but I don't regret a thing. I was going absolutely crazy being cooped up in that office."

"You're too stubborn for your own good. Do you really want to go down this path?"

"Last time I checked, I had a reward to cash in," I rebutted. "Don't I deserve my reward first before your silly little punishment?"

Those soft brown eyes of his hardened in response.

"I think you're a spoiled brat who's used to getting her way. So, no, I don't think you deserve it, nor are you taking any of this seriously." Erick leaned in, his breath mingling with mine. His gaze fell to the neckline of my makeshift dress and kept traveling down until he reached the hem, where he seemed to drink in the sight of my bare thighs, toned after years of dance.

"I'm going dancing." I shoved him in the chest. "You're welcome to watch...if you're into that kind of stuff."

Of all the decisions I'd made tonight—all the stupid and selfish decisions, I couldn't bring myself to regret a single one until I dared to lay a hand on Erick. That might have been the most reckless of all. A foolish mistake that had me pinned against the wall a second later, hands restrained at the level of my neck. It all happened so fast, one moment I was making my way toward the exit, and the next, I was succumbing to my own weakness. While his nails dug into my flesh, the most punishing of all was our proximity, the weight of his body leaning into me, and the heat of his breath along the column of my exposed neck.

He slightly loosened his grip, but he kept me firmly in place by shock alone. "I'm sure you'd love it if I pulled up a front-row seat and watched you dance from dusk to dawn," Erick mumbled close to my ear, "but simply watching isn't enough for me anymore, Krissy. Nor is letting you get away with whatever you want just because you're being a little brat. We are heading downstairs, and I don't want to hear you complain about it again."

I forced myself to face him so that I might address his arrogance. Our lips barely grazed in a feather of a touch. It was merely an accident, but I couldn't help noticing Erick's entire body stiffen atop me.

"What's the matter?" I breathed.

Tucked away behind the thick velvet curtains, the outside world dulled to a mere whisper. Nothing beyond it held any meaning—the relentless drumming of the bass faded into obscurity, the chatter of conversation drowning out amongst the thumping of my heart, or even the orchestra of lights trickling into the alcove that didn't quite feel as enticing as they once had. It all meant nothing as every sense connected to our proximity was set ablaze, threatening to burn me alive as I waited for an answer I wasn't sure would ever come.

"You drive me absolutely insane," he whispered against my lips. It wasn't enough to be considered a kiss, but the way it stole my breath away...

I didn't think to ask what he meant by that before closing the distance between us.

While there had once been hesitation and resistance, it had been quickly replaced with suffocating desire. If I were a flame, then Erick was my twin, burning as hot and bright as I was. The taste of him was indescribable, but somehow, I knew—I knew it was meant for me—a drug that I desperately needed more of. Each of us fought for dominance, neither of us willing to give the other control. Erick pushed his tongue past my lips, and that was all it took for me to sag within his hold and allow him to devour me completely.

Our tongues moved in perfectly sloppy movements, hungry for all that we'd starved ourselves of. Erick deepened the kiss as he pinned my wrists higher, bracketing them with one hand so he might explore with the other. While every kiss felt like a plea, a desperate, ravenous one that neither of us could get enough of, each touch was much gentler. From the swells of my breasts, past the curves of my hips toward the apex of my thighs, it was as if he was savoring, memorizing the shape of my body. And had I not been restrained, I would have been just as greedy with my own hands.

His lips left mine, and I thought for a moment, I might die without them.

"Erick," I groaned, struggling to break free, but his grip tightened.

"Krissy," he breathed against my neck, his lips trailing along my collarbone before inching upward, kiss by kiss, until I was panting for him. His touch was the sweetest kind of temptation, a longing for release that left me trembling as his hand stilled between my thighs. My fingers itched to reach down, to guide him to our imminent damnation, but then Erick's nails dug into my flesh, and he whispered, "May I touch you?"

My response was right there, poised on the tip of my tongue, but when I opened my mouth, nothing came out. I tried again, ready to be stroked by the fire consuming us, but instead, the words that came tumbling weren't fuel to add to our burning desire. They were an echo of all that had come before.

"I—I didn't mean what I said," I stammered. "What I said earlier... about using you."

Erick slightly pulled away, eyes searching.

The timing was all wrong—his hands were still scorching my flesh, his lips a breath away, and yet, even with him invading my every sense and luring me toward release, I couldn't bring myself to give in when the weight of my words from earlier still lingered between us. I couldn't move forward without him understanding that this wasn't about using him.

Erick wasn't a tool; he was my salvation.

"I didn't–"

Someone screamed, and Erick pulled back further. "The hell was that?"

"Someone is probably just drunk–"

There was another scream before a deep boom rattled the foundation of the century-old building. My whole world went crashing on its side. In the blink of an eye, Erick had us on the floor, his large frame shielding me from debris funneling into the alcove. Spilling out in endless columns of white dust that coated my lips and solidified in my lungs. I knew I was screaming, but no matter how much I shrieked, there wasn't a hint of the noise amongst the relentless buzzing echoing deep within my eardrums. Eyes shut to keep out the dust, lungs burning with each breath, I wheezed. The buzzing festered and grew, isolating me from the outside world where I knew the screams of the injured and dying lay just beyond the velvet curtains. When the foundation finally stopped shaking, I counted down from ten and forced my eyes open, finding a sea of white blanketing the room, a thick layer of dust still lingering in the air. Erick blended in seamlessly, a muted version of his former self. I knew he was talking to me, but I couldn't make out a word.

"I can't hear you." I pointed to my ears.

Erick tried again, but with no luck. Lip reading was never my strong suit, but by some rare stroke of luck, I caught the last word and pieced the rest together. I nodded, letting him know I was fine. That confirmation was enough for him to drag me to my feet and send us sprinting toward the glowing green exit sign, hardly visible near the bar. The only thing separating us from our only exit was a mob of people running around in a state of tumult. People pushed and fought their way toward safety. It was a struggle just to keep from separating amidst the chaos, but somehow, we managed to do so without being trampled, not stopping until the crisp air of the outside world hit my flushed cheeks. There was still a ringing in my ear, but I was beginning to make out more sounds amongst it.

"–car–structure down–street," Erick explained, leading us through the alley toward the busy street lined with patrons of Don Juan, blanketed in white. The city street looked like a war zone with people bleeding and wandering helplessly, looking for their loved ones. The faint sound of sirens wailed in the distance.

Erick was hellbent on leaving the scene. While he dragged me away, I searched amongst the crowd for any sign of Antonio or Damon. Each face I scanned gave me no indication of what had happened to his cousin after leaving us back on the dance floor. With the amount of blood spilling on the streets, it was easy to assume the worst. Off in the distance, across the street, a head of blonde hair caught my attention. I blinked once, then twice, to ensure I wasn't seeing things. Patrick lurked in the shadows, watching the patrons funnel out of the entrance—no, he wasn't watching, he was searching.

Searching for us.

"We need to go," I urged, not entirely sure if he'd seen us. "Now."

The silence was so loud as we drove further away. Even the rumbling of the restored 1960s muscle car couldn't save me from drowning in it. Each time I thought about breaking the silence, it never transpired; there was nothing to say after that.

We were alive. Erick's hand resting on my thigh was a reminder of that.

Before authorities could make it on the scene, Erick and I were speeding out of the entertainment district, selfishly leaving the chaos behind. It was several minutes later when he turned into a driveway, dipping into the underground parking. A security guard sitting in his booth gave Erick a lazy salute and raised the parking arm to let us pass.

The warmth of his hand left my thigh, snapping me back to reality as Erick whipped around the hood of the car to open the passenger side door, dragging me to my feet with a look that told me he also knew words couldn't fix this. All he could offer was the comfort of his touch and presence until the initial shock wore off.

"Morning, Mr. Destler," said the receptionist working the graveyard shift in the lobby. "Oh–gosh! Mr. Destler, are you okay?" If our appearance wasn't evident enough, maybe it was the void of nothingness in our eyes. It wasn't quite shell shock, but what we had experienced felt strikingly similar to a war zone.

"We're fine," he said in passing, not giving them a chance to question further.

I managed to catch a glimpse of the building as we were driving by, but I wasn't aware of how massive the skyscraper was until we stepped into the elevator. Nearly a hundred twinkling red lights represented each level. Despite the sheer size, the ride was fairly quick, dropping us off two floors from the tippy top. A structure of this size should have housed at least ten or more apartments, but there were only four doors down the narrow hallway, one of which Erick had a key to.

A small, dark foyer fed into an expansive space where the kitchen and living room blended into one with ceilings nearly two stories tall, making enough room for the loft that overlooked it all. As we passed through the kitchen toward the stairs, we attracted the attention of a furry friend that went scampering after us. The loft was simple; a king-size bed to the right with a walk-in closet just past it and an adjoining bathroom that he dragged me into first.

Like I was made of glass and might shatter any second, he urged me to sit on the edge of the tub as he started up the shower, testing the temperature until the room was thick with steam. Erick stripped down to his boxer briefs. The inky black patterns etched into his skin were on full display. In light of everything that had happened, now wasn't the time to admire the art covering his body, but something about counting those roses and searching for the blossoms was the distraction I needed not to crumble. Amongst the hodgepodge of art spread out across his flesh was a full sleeve sprouting roses from the back of his right hand to the last vine creeping up his neck. Lower down, beneath each kneecap, was a pair of olive branches supporting the joints. Opposite his heavily inked right side was a depiction of the Fallen Angel by Alexandre Cabanel on his ribs with such accuracy, it looked like it had been plucked right from the canvas.

"We need to clean you up," he said softly, reaching for the hem of my dress.

I gasped, reality suddenly smacking me in the face. "Antonio. We need to go–"

Erick cupped either side of my face, forcing me to look at him. "My cousin is okay. He went outside for a smoke right before and just missed the explosion. He's fine," he repeated. "Now let's get you out of these clothes and cleaned up, little angel."

I nodded, giving my consent.

There was nothing sexual about the act. Erick stripped me bare, tossing my dress alongside the boxers in the pile on the floor, then pulling us both under the showerhead. The fresh, clean water slid down our bodies, collecting all the dust and grime and washing it away at our feet. While most of the water was a strange, murky white color, there were pockets of red that pooled around my toes. I silently scanned Erick, trying not to raise the alarm, but only found a few bumps and bruises, which meant the blood was coming from me, though I didn't feel it.

Plucking one of the bottles from the niche, he carefully massaged the shampoo into my scalp, cleaning any evidence of the night. While he worked, I traced the fallen angel branded over his rib, repeating the motion over and over again to keep myself grounded. Erick tilted my head back, rinsing the shampoo from my hair. Our eyes met. I hadn't realized I was avoiding them until now.

And that's when I knew I couldn't hold it in any longer. Sucking in a sharp breath, my bottom lip began to tremble. Erick pulled me into his chest just as a sob caught in my throat.

"I know," he whispered, then kissed the top of my head.

The tears eventually subsided–my emotions still ablaze. After any evidence of the night was scrubbed away, Erick clothed me in an oversized t-shirt and joined me in bed. With an unspoken agreement, I wrapped myself in his arms and welcomed an end to a day carved from hell.

Chapter Twenty-Six

Erick

Had the structural damage of the building been more severe, it would have been easy to assume this was nothing more than a threat—a violent promise that would have called for immediate retribution. But that wasn't the case. This was a trick, a dirty ploy to lure Krissy and me out of the club. A trick he wasn't even man enough to do himself.

Patrick assumed I'd pull my bargaining chip from the rubble of the building if it meant saving her and protecting my endeavors. While it was a good idea in theory, luckily, he was foolish enough to keep his attention turned toward the people funneling out of the entrance and missed us as we slipped out of the alleyway. Amongst the chaos, Blanchet's men, who had been following me for days, were also completely unaware we had already gone. Disguised in a thick coat of dust and a lilac wig that kept Krissy's identity partially hidden, she was unrecognizable. At the end of the day, he helped me accomplish what I couldn't before. Krissy was now safe in the comfort of my apartment. Originally, she was to stay in a safe house until a deal was struck, but seeing how much had changed already, it was a necessary precaution.

"How many?" I sighed, gripping the railing that was still warm to the touch. The century-old building was still standing strong, dust and debris littering every surface in a sea of white ash. Don Juan would live to see another day, but it would be a miracle if everyone from last night made it out unscathed.

"Twelve in the hospital with severe injuries and burns. Two confirmed dead—trampled amongst the panic," my cousin reported with a straight face. The son of a bitch was lucky to be alive; he would have been in the heart of the explosion if his nicotine addiction hadn't ironically saved his life. There was no way he was going to kick the nasty habit now—I could already picture him boasting about this the next time I nagged him to quit.

"Damn it," I said under my breath, raising a shaky hand to run through my hair. "Lola." With the feminine grace of a killer, she stalked forward. "Reach out to the families and make sure all medical and funeral expenses are covered." All those who were injured wouldn't bear the overpriced medical expenses for my mistakes—sadly for the dead, it was too late for apologies.

William Destler, my great-grandfather, was surely rolling over in his grave. He established the club as a safe haven for people during a time in history not as forgiving as our own. It had been passed down through our bloodline—a Destler legacy, if you will. Excluding his own son's failures, this was a huge stain on that legacy.

"I'm on it," she responded. Antonio and I watched her slip out of the building, weaving through first responders assessing the damage, with Damon in tow.

"How is she?" he asked in a dry tone.

"Fine," was all I said. It had nearly killed me to pry myself away from her early in the morning and leave with nothing more than a lousy letter explaining my whereabouts. Twice now, I'd put Krissy in the path of danger. This time, she crumbled in my arms—a mere shell of the confident woman I'd grown to respect and admire. She was still the strong-willed, beautiful, stubborn woman who had captured my heart the first night I saw her perform, but being forced to face death once more had taken its toll. Seeing that side of her was difficult to witness, knowing that if I hadn't acted so foolishly, agreeing to this deal without knowing the true extent of what I was getting us involved in, she wouldn't be hurting like this. I offered what comfort I could until I had to leave, but it would never be enough when people were relying on me to act fast and make the party responsible atone for their actions.

"I tried to stop her–"

I interjected. "I don't want to hear it. You had clear instructions not to touch her, and you followed them. There was no way you could have gotten her downstairs without doing so. She's safe, and that is all that matters."

"Still...she shouldn't have been on the floor when it happened."

"What did I just say?"

"Just accept my apology so we can move on from this conversation already," he said, glaring over my shoulder. "Prepare yourself, Officer asshole is coming this way."

The warning only gave me three seconds to mentally prepare.

"Boys," Sanderson Miller said, clasping my shoulder. The cheap scent of his cologne hit me before he did. Every time I smelled it, I couldn't help but think maybe it was a lousy trick to keep the people distracted from his balding head and pale skin. His efforts were for nothing; I noticed them all, including a few of his other flaws. Neither of us could stand to be in his company, but when a relationship is profitable, you tend to turn a blind eye.

"What do you want?" I snapped.

"No need to be so rude."

"I've been standing here for two seconds, and you're already wasting my time, Miller."

"Fine, I'll get right to the point," Miller said. "This explosion is drawing a lot of attention from RCPD. There's only so much I can do without painting a target on my back, and I'm not in the business of cleaning up your messes without proper compensation. And seeing that this is a pretty big mess, well...I think you know where I'm going with this."

The club was swimming with cops, and it was only a matter of time before they started digging around in places they shouldn't have during a routine inspection. The last thing I needed was for them to find something incriminating.

"You'll get double what I normally pay you if you make this disappear."

I'd pay triple if he'd leave sooner. Miller had once had a mighty and long-standing relationship with my father when he ran the business, and that alliance would transfer over to me as long as I kept paying him for his work. He'd been sweeping the Destler name under the rug long before I was even in diapers. As much as I loathed him, decades of loyalty didn't go unnoticed.

"And...you'll willingly hand over the surveillance footage as evidence. It's easier to convince them there's something to search back at the station than within the walls of your club," he proposed. "We'll do our part to find who did this, but I figure you already know. If I could give you some advice, boy, deal with this issue sooner rather than later. I don't need the people of this city suffering because of some bullshit hissy fit between owners."

Miller and I shook on it. RCPD still had a job to do, and handing over the footage after I personally examined it was the least I could do to keep them from searching where they weren't wanted.

"I never imagined Blanchet would take things so far," Antonio said once we were alone.

"This wasn't Blanchet," I explained. "He wouldn't be this careless or lazy. No, this was Patrick trying to scare us. If he wants to play dirty, then so be it, but he'll have no one else but himself to blame when all of this is through."

Walking into my apartment, the fumes hit me like a wall.

Once I stepped past the threshold, there was no turning back. The pungent scent of toxins hung heavy in the air, covering the entire foyer in a gray haze. I followed the smoke, springing into the unknown without hesitation, knowing Krissy and Ghost were in danger.

The sink was set ablaze, dancing with orange and yellow flames that consumed the black heap lying in the basin. Krissy stood in front of the sink, completely mesmerized by the spectacle. The more the flames fed, the more the fumes swallowed, eating up every pocket of clean air and replacing it with a foul scent that couldn't be healthy to breathe in. The smoke detector started blaring just as both of us were thrown into a coughing fit, our lungs protesting with each gasp of air. I doused the flames and shoved Krissy outside onto the balcony before going back in for a second time to find Ghost cowering in a corner upstairs, too frightened to even let me hold her.

"What the hell were you doing? Trying to poison yourself and my cat?" I snapped.

Krissy coughed into her hand and then pointed at the large glass windows separating us from the kitchen. "That stupid dress is a bad omen. I nearly died twice wearing it. I had to get rid of it and the wig."

Ghost, completely unbothered by the shouting, found a

sliver of sunlight to bathe in. It hadn't snowed in days, and although it was cold outside, it was bearable if you weren't standing in the shadows of the overhang.

"Did it ever occur to you to toss the damn thing out instead?"

"Burning it was the only way to *truly* get rid of it," she explained, becoming uncharacteristically embarrassed midway through the sentence. While her voice stayed steady, the look on her face spoke volumes. "I had it under control. The fire was isolated to the sink."

"If you are going to stay at my house, promise me you won't set any more fires. I've had enough near-death experiences in the last week to fill a lifetime. I don't need to add immolation to the list because you're getting superstitious for no reason."

"Call it superstitious all you like, but the facts don't lie. That damn thing deserved to be burned to ash, no matter how good it looked on me."

I shucked off my jacket and offered it to her. If she was cold, she showed no sign of it, but I knew better. Clothed in nothing more than the t-shirt I lent her last night, she was simply just being stubborn as usual.

"That's being a little overdramatic. It's hardly that cold right now."

"Dramatic?" I raised an eyebrow. "And that coming from the girl who almost started a kitchen fire because she thought a piece of fabric had something against her."

She snatched it away, and I couldn't help but smile. The initial frustration and shock of walking into the mess she created hadn't fully worn off, but the more time that passed, the more I was able to steady my fear, knowing that they were both safe now. I found a seat and waited for the rest to pass as Krissy padded to the balcony's edge and peered over. The selfish side of me loved the sight of her wearing my clothes without a lick of makeup on, looking angelic with the city as her backdrop. The view alone was part of the reason I'd purchased the real estate. During the summer months, I could sit out here for hours, watching the city breathe with life.

"You seem surprisingly yourself today, given what's happened," I pointed out.

"After the night we staged the kidnapping, I learned that nothing good comes from sitting around and sulking. Wishing things could have been different didn't change the past, nor did it solve any of the problems ahead. This time, I'm just pissed off and ready to get this over with. I'm ready for him to pay for not just hurting me and ruining my career, but harming others who didn't deserve to be caught in the crossfire. Last night only confirmed that I made the right decision when it came to leaving Patrick the way I did. There was no reality in which I could have left him without a fight or being destroyed in the process," she explained, wrapping herself tighter with the jacket.

I couldn't say I condoned Krissy starting a fire in my kitchen, but a part of me was grateful ashes were all that remained. While she made grand professions claiming to have moved on and wanted nothing more than blood in exchange for Patrick's actions, I could see the hurt in her eyes. Something resembling fear lingered there as she masked it with rage and vengeance. And while all three could be true at the same time, I was learning there was more fear in her heart than she let on. It wasn't my place to judge, question, or even pressure her to talk about it. The least I could do was accept that burning those physical reminders could help lessen the mental obstacles weighing heavily on her heart.

"I think it's time we talked about what happened last night."

She nodded, urging me to speak.

The stoic look etched onto her beautiful face didn't falter as I explained what I had learned this morning in heavy detail, refusing to leave a single thing out. She hardly even blinked as I broke down the death toll, the number of individuals injured, and the damage done to the building. The situation was grim, and there wasn't a reality in which I would ever hide that from her. There were questions, of course, and I answered each and every one as honestly as I could, despite not having all the answers myself.

"Am I safe here?"

Of all the questions, that one cut the deepest. I was on my feet in the blink of an eye, closing the space between us. It took everything not to give in to my natural instinct to wrap her in my arms like I had last night, but I resisted the urge and instead tipped her chin up so she would meet my gaze and heed my words. "Of course, you are. No one knows you're here besides my inner circle and a few men I have stationed around the complex. And for the employees who saw you walking into the complex with me last night, I already know where their loyalties lie–"

"You said the same thing about Don Juan."

"And you would have been safe if you stayed below the club as I told you to. Sometimes I think you're more trouble than you're worth."

"I might be trouble," she peered up at me through her long lashes, "but I think I'm growing on you, Erick."

I scoffed, trying and miserably failing not to smile down at her in a way that would have shown my hand too early. "As much as it pains me to admit it, I think that might be true."

She smiled back like she knew that I was lying through my teeth. Krissy had more than grown on me, but admitting that would come in time.

It took another twenty minutes before the apartment was safe enough to enter. Even then, every fan was spinning, and every door was cracked open in hopes of aerating the place properly. The apartment was only one of the many problems that awaited us. While I was no stranger to the trials and tribulations that seemed to follow me with each turn, things didn't feel as daunting as they once had. Through that perpetual darkness that resided within, I couldn't help but notice the littlest light bleeding in with each smile, each snarky comment, and each time she made me laugh.

Things were grim, but they didn't seem so bad with her by my side.

Chapter Twenty-Seven

Patrick

Those who are willing to sacrifice hope, sacrifice themselves in the end. Giving up the hope of rescuing Krissy meant destroying everything I'd built and everything that could be. Clinging to hope meant taking risks that could very well land me in an early grave, but in her darkest moments, Krissy needed me to be the light guiding her home. She needed her savior to take calculated risks and gamble on suspicions that kept drawing me back toward the club when she was too weak to do so. I'd spent hours studying those Polaroid images and based on what I found, I'd determined every risk would be warranted.

Barely visible in the corner of one of the images was a box of napkins from a distributor that sold to the theater. All it took was one phone call to our warehouse representative to discover their only other clientele in the city besides us was a senior citizen home and Don Juan. With my next phone call, I was forming a plan, seeking out help from less-than-favorable people who played in trickery and knew tactics to draw attention in crowded rooms. While their expertise came with a hefty price and their work didn't quite pan out as I'd imagined, the destruction they had left behind sent a message to Destler that I was a force to be reckoned with.

The images had told me one secret. I kept searching them over and over again, praying I'd find another. It took everything to pry my eyes away from them as the door leading into my office swung open with a resounding thud. Josephine stomped her way into the cramped space with her husband in tow, long before they were expected to return to the States. I stood up to greet the newlyweds, but the warm welcome was cut short. All it took was two long strides before she was on me, the blistering sting of her palm against my cheek.

"What the hell is wrong with you?" she shouted, shaking out the pain in her hand.

Charles carelessly flicked his cigarette on the floor as he entered behind.

"Mon amour, stand back." He gently shoved his wife to the side in order to get his turn. His solid fist connected with my jaw, and I struggled to stay upright but inevitably fell to my knees, gawking up at the blurry figures that watched me crumble onto the floor. The worst was likely over, but I feared I might black out if the dizziness didn't subside. "I don't give a damn who you are. You don't get to disobey me."

"I don't know what you are talking about," I said.

Charles ruthlessly kicked me in the gut while I was down. Every nerve ending in my body was set ablaze as the pain rippled through each limb. I choked out in agony, begging him to stop in a voice I did not recognize.

"Don't you dare lie to me. I don't care that you are family. I'll gut you like a fish," he growled. "Did you attack Don Juan?"

"No more secrets, Patrick," Josephine added.

I glared up at my sister, nails digging into the wood flooring for stability as I attempted to rise. "At least I did something instead of sitting on my ass on some tropical beach," I said, flecks of blood spraying out with each word. The comment earned me two more kicks before my sister pried him away from inflicting a third.

"This is your final warning, boy," he snarled. "Mess with me or my business again, and you won't live to see Krissy freed."

The Blanchet family had always had close ties with the Martins. Our father had much success in the late eighties working with Charles in perfectly legal and profitable business ventures. Although our family was well aware of the much darker side of Blanchet's business, our parents never seemed to mind as long as they benefited in other ways. I had heard whispers of his cruel nature but had never witnessed it for myself. Any time I interacted with him, he was all charm and wit. It wasn't until the night of his bachelor party, when he nearly beat a man to death, that I truly recognized the cynical side of him that he hid so well in plain sight.

Charles had said his piece and was nearly content. Not without kicking me one last time before storming out of the room. I had the haunting suspicion he had taken mercy on me, that a few bruised ribs and a lashing on the tongue were nothing compared to his wrath. While Charles' warning had been brutal and swift, what my sister said next was stolid and terribly agonizing. A betrayal months in the making.

Josephine squatted before me, brushing her finger across the swollen skin of my jaw. I jerked away, not wanting her fake sympathy.

"I warned you," she reminded me. "You brought this upon yourself, and you're lucky that I had time to calm him down before he came, but if you cross Charlie again, there is nothing I can do for you. Nor will I stop him. If you stand any chance of repairing this damage, find the tunnel entrance before it's too late."

"I know, I will."

It was a silly lie I kept repeating to myself with no intention of following through. For once in my godforsaken life, I was leaving her shadow and basking in the glory of carving my own path. I'd already proven I could accomplish more in an afternoon than in all the days Charles had promised to rescue Krissy. While this whole situation was a mess, I had learned the true intentions of those who claimed to be the closest. Josephine had picked sides long ago, and knowing her loyalties lay elsewhere was the only wake-up call I needed.

While blood may bind us, it is love that divides us in more ways than one.

Chapter Twenty-Eight

Krissy

Erick's apartment was a breath of fresh air. Who knew being kidnapped—even if it's fake—wasn't half as bad when you had natural lighting, plenty of space to roam about, and all the amenities to live comfortably for an indefinite amount of time? As devastating as the attack was, there were positives that came from the unfortunate situation. I desperately latched onto that optimism and counted my blessings that we were both safe between the walls of his home.

That glimmer of optimism seemed to be all I had when my heart ached for the friends I left behind and the goals I put on standby to escape the situation that seemed to be getting progressively worse with each breath. I held onto that glimmer tight instead of worrying myself with what-ifs and damning thoughts.

Buoyancy seemed hard to come by in light of everything that transpired, but with a little time, I began to feel more like myself with Ghost to keep me company, never leaving my side while Erick dealt with his business throughout the day. Erick and I had slipped into a little routine over the course of the week; unlike before, I was given the freedoms I only dreamt of. In Erick's absence, he had men stationed both inside and outside of the apartment, which meant I had plenty of time to make quick friends. Most of them were hesitant at first, not sure if their boss would approve, but it didn't take long before I had them playing cards with me, sharing jokes, and watching me while I performed little shows on the piano.

Things weren't ideal, but it was a hell of a lot better than before.

While there were breaks in the days, little exciting moments that broke up the mundane, there were a few things that never changed—nor did I want them to. Erick would stumble into the apartment, nearly too exhausted to stand, and dismiss the interior guards to take their place after a long day's work. Erick rarely spoke about how he was combating a potential attack from Charles or another from Patrick. Nor did I ask.

The loft apartment only had one bedroom, and since the first night we slept here, there had been an unspoken agreement that we would share the space. Each night we would crawl into bed, taking our separate sides, and by the time we woke up, we were an entanglement of limbs, curled up against one another and reluctant to pry ourselves away. It would have been easy to look too much into it, but seeing that this was all temporary, I tried not to.

Ghost purred, leaning harder into my palm as I stroked her soft gray fur. She'd curled herself into a tight ball on my lap, demanding more attention like she couldn't get enough of it. Never having a pet of my own while growing up in the city, it didn't take long for me to grow attached—the same went for her. Erick had silly rules about what furniture she could and couldn't jump on, but lucky for us, what he didn't know wouldn't hurt—

She jumped down the second she heard the door groan open, saving us both a lecture.

Like the changing of the guards, Richard rose to his feet, moving to his post out of the apartment as Erick stepped in. The two men greeted one another with a subtle nod and nothing more. Erick strolled into the apartment with his forearms lined with bags, clearly too stubborn to make two trips. The groceries landed on the counter with a thud, and a few apples sprang free, rolling on the marble a few feet before he caught them.

"What did you buy?" I called out from the living room, craning my neck to catch a glimpse.

"Come here, little angel." With the softness of a request but the inflection of a demand, I listened, closing the distance between us as my stomach flipped in response. The nickname meant nothing in the grand scheme of things, but I swore each time I heard it lately, my body reacted as such. "I hope you're hungry."

"I'm starved," I answered, hopping on the counter, prepared to watch an artist at work. "Do you need any help making dinner?"

He shook his head and got to work washing, preparing, and cutting all the vegetables before placing them in neat little piles. Between the onions, chiles, garlic, ginger, bell pepper, carrots, and tomatoes, the kitchen counter was a sea of vibrant colors. It dawned on me a few times to ask what he was making, but something about trying to guess was so much more fun.

The sound of sizzling oil had Ghost cautiously enter the kitchen to investigate. Once she was close enough, she scrunched her little nose up in the air, smelling the explosion of spices that danced all about. It didn't seem to matter to her what Erick was making; she brushed herself up against his legs, begging for scraps.

"My great-grandfather brought this recipe with him when he immigrated from Durban, South Africa, after the devastation of the Spanish Flu and post-World War hardships. It's been passed down through my family since."

"What's it called?" I asked, swinging my legs out.

"Chakalaka," he answered, removing the pan from the heat and adding beans, thyme, and more spices to the mix. "My dad tried to teach my mother how to make it—I love her to death, but it was terrible." He laughed, lost in his own memories before returning to reality once more. "God, I'd give anything to be able to sit around the table with her and eat her terrible chakalaka again."

I considered asking about his family, but thought better of it.

"It looks amazing." My heart beat a little harder when Erick smiled in response.

The orange heap of veggies and beans was dished up in two bowls and garnished with a dash of leafy greens. Erick slid the bowl over to me, not daring to take a bite until I'd gone first—yet another part of our silly little routine. At first, I used to find it strange when he watched like that, but now I've grown to expect it, offering my brutally honest opinion after each dish. It didn't matter if he'd made it or it was takeout, I always gave a sincere review.

All it took was one bite, and I was hooked. The traditional African dish was an explosion of flavors that screamed the type of comfort and familiarity I wasn't accustomed to. And somehow knowing it came from Erick's hands made it that much more special.

Erick leaned over the island and began digging into his meal with a smile that told me he already knew. The kitchen was decently sized for an apartment in the city, with plenty of counter space to choose from. He'd conveniently picked the space closest to me so that anytime he lifted his spoon to eat, he would brush up against my side.

"So, are you going to tell me or just keep me guessing forever?"

I studied him for a moment, not quite sure what he was talking about.

"Are you going to tell me what I should be telling you, or are you going to keep *me* guessing forever?"

With a devilish smirk plastered across his face, he glared up at me sitting on top of the island and playfully jabbed me with his elbow. "We've shared too many meals to count now, and even after all of that time, you still haven't told me which one was your favorite."

"You're kidding." I paused, the truth hitting me upside the head. "Was this your terrible way of learning what my favorite food was?" He nodded. "Why didn't you just ask like a normal human being?"

"This way was so much more fun," he said. "If I had to guess based solely on the cute little moans you make when you take your first bite, I would say your favorites have been the Italian food from my aunt's bistro and the breakfast bagel from the other day. Am I right?"

I scoffed. "You're insane, and the fact that you're right makes you that much more insufferable. Should I tell you my favorite movie before you make me watch every movie ever produced?"

Erick abandoned his food, breaking the distance between us so he could part my legs and stand between them. Atop the counter, Erick and I were now eye level, but with his hand engulfing my thighs, yanking them forward to bring me closer to the edge, I felt so much smaller than him in that moment. "If it meant I could get to know you better, then I would pluck every flower, watch every movie, and even travel to every continent to learn everything there was about you, Krissy."

I wasn't entirely sure I was breathing properly.

"Typically, men don't jump through so many hoops just to

get between my legs." In such close proximity, I couldn't help but place my hand on his shoulder, my thumb idly circling the spot above his collarbone. "I'll save you the trouble. Poppies. *Chicago*. And North America only by default because I haven't traveled much."

Erick leaned in, his breath mingling with mine. "Then let me make my intentions perfectly clear. If all I wanted from you was a good fuck, I would already have you tied up in my bed panting my name."

I jolted back. "You can't be serious?"

"Dead serious," he breathed. "I'll admit the more superficial things about you were what caught my attention at first. With the type of energy you demand on stage, how could I not? It was the day you snuck into the tunnel with plans of vengeance and fire in your heart that I knew it was the woman behind the glitter and limelight that really had me hooked. Beautiful, radiant Krissy, with a stubbornness as terrible as a mule and a spirit as bright as the star she is." His eyes traced over my features, noting the stiffness in my posture and visible avoidance in my gaze. "Is it so hard to believe that someone would want more from you than just your body?"

I forced myself to take one deep breath in, then another. By the third, I felt my lungs constricting and my chest tightening. I searched for the words but could only focus on the lack of oxygen and the sensation of the room closing in on me slowly but surely. Jumping off the counter, I shoved him aside, trying to escape before the walls could fully close in. With more distance came more oxygen. It took a moment to breathe properly, but once there was space between us, it was a bit more manageable.

"You know I broke things off with Patrick because he wanted something more and I didn't," I reminded him as a way of warning. "It's the reason we're in this mess, to begin with."

"Krissy," he sighed, pushing off the counter. "The reason

we're in this mess is because some prissy asshole couldn't take no for an answer and resorted to blackmailing you to keep you as his little pet." Erick circled the island, threatening to ruin any progress I'd made. "I make my intentions clear so you know what to expect from me, but I would never force you into something just because I wish it to be true. Patrick and I are not the same."

I scoffed, arms crossed. "You wouldn't be the first man to make that promise to me. 'Oh, Krissy, I *swear* I'm different from other guys. Give me a chance.' It's always the ones who beg the most that hurt you the worst."

Jackson, junior year of college, had practically begged on his knees for another chance after burning me once. Foolishly, I'd fallen for the trick and lived in romantic bliss for all but two weeks before he slipped back into his old ways—criticizing my dreams, belittling me for every choice I made, prioritizing drinking with his friends instead of going to shows he promised to attend, and using me for my body instead of having a meaningful relationship.

"You date boys instead of men, what did you expect would happen?" The only thing I could think to do was groan in response. "You know, it's really funny, Krissy. You love to bitch and moan, but when it comes down to it, you can't deny there's something more between us. If you truly resented the idea, you would've had no trouble voicing it, but instead, you roll your eyes and avoid it, hoping it will go away so you don't have to acknowledge it." He paused, stopping so we stood shoulder to shoulder but facing the opposite direction. For a second, his finger flexed out, wrapping itself around my own. "Take your time, little angel, but make sure you find me when you are ready to admit it."

Erick stepped forward, breaking our connection.

"But I hardly know you," I called out before he could disappear onto the balcony, an unlit joint now between his lips.

"Roses. Europe. And it's too hard just to pick one, but I love sad movies," he mumbled, his back turned to me. "As I said, find me when you are ready."

Erick and I had been through hell and back, yet the man I watched on the balcony was still a mystery to me. I knew bits and pieces without fully understanding his story or who he was. Those gut-wrenching confessions and declarations hit closer to home than I had realized. I wanted nothing more than to do what I was best at. Avoid and ignore. It would be so easy to turn away, finish my dinner, and act like we'd never had the conversation in the first place, but I knew there was no going back once I took that first step.

The spacious apartment was impressive on its own, but it was nothing compared to the large panels of glass that separated the living space from the balcony, stretching up into a partial skylight where the ceiling met glass. The closest comparison was that of a greenhouse, letting in ample light and opening up the space, giving me a clear view of Erick leaning up against the railing. The wind caught hold of his smoke, carrying it southbound in a thinning cloud to eventually disappear into nothing.

"Can I have some?" I asked, joining him along the edge. "My back still hurts a little from when you tackled me onto the floor—it's the least you can do."

"I think you're downplaying that whole situation a bit. I wouldn't necessarily call shielding you from an explosion with my own body a little tackle," he said, handing over the joint.

"Thank you for that...I mean it."

"You're welcome, little angel," he responded. "Next time, you can return the favor."

"Let's hope there isn't a next time," I said before taking the joint between my lips and sucking in. The familiar burn of smoke expanded and contracted my lungs, giving me life while simultaneously taking it away with each breath. The ruinous sensation wasn't enough to steel my nerves, but at the very least, it wasn't making it worse.

"Let's hope."

Another deep breath in, and I was ready to fill the silence that followed.

"Hmm...so roses are your favorite flower? Seems a bit cliché if you ask me. You're either a die-hard romantic, or it's the only flower you know," I teased.

"That's a story for another time," he suggested. I couldn't help feeling like I'd hit something of a soft spot by bringing up the flower. I intended to make light conversation, not completely derail the entire thing while he stared off into the skyline, silent as ever. It took him several long minutes, and a few passes back and forth for him to collect his thoughts while he watched the glistening high rises sprawled out across the city, nearly as unmoving as him. "But I am curious, did you like the roses I sent you?"

My brows furrowed. "I thought those were a warning to remind me to convince Patrick to sell you the theater."

He stared at me for a long moment, those deep brown eyes of his struggling to suppress the myriad of emotions fighting for dominance. "Krissy," he started, then peered off into the distance, "those roses weren't a warning, besides the last one—but that wasn't meant for you."

"Oh." *Oh.*

A long silence followed as I mulled over the implication of that gesture and what it truly meant outside the context I'd automatically assigned to it, along with what that meant for Erick's character. All those weeks of fearing the unknown, when in reality it was much more innocent than I thought.

"The first night I saw you at the theater, you performed a number from the musical *Chicago*," he said, finally breaking the silence, "of all the movies in the world, why is that one your favorite?"

"It's a funny story, actually. I–" Erick's hand lightly brushed mine as I passed along the joint, making me instantly lose my train of thought. "Well, growing up, my parents didn't have much money, which meant they were constantly working to make ends meet. If my mom wasn't working, then she was at home with me, studying for nursing school on the side, barely managing to juggle it all. At eight years old, I was a complete brat if you could imagine that–" Erick huffed out a laugh, and I lightly punched him in the arm before continuing, "Oh, hush. Trying to study with a wild child running around the apartment wasn't exactly working for her, so my mother would throw on different movies in hopes of getting some peace and quiet. Little did she know *Chicago* wasn't remotely anything an eight-year-old should be watching, but God did I love it. I watched that stupid movie so many times I nearly memorized every dance number. After that, my mom realized it was worth scraping together some extra money to put me in classes. That went on for another year or so before I was put into foster care, then I had to find other ways to get lessons."

Once I realized the direction I was headed, I found a natural stopping point and forced my attention elsewhere, hoping it would help lessen the lump forming in my throat. In Erick's words, that was a story for another time.

"Yeah, that's definitely not a movie for kids," he noted. "But in all seriousness, it sounds like your parents loved you very much. Most people don't go so far as to support their children even when they are struggling themselves."

I was one of the lucky ones, blessed with loving parents who would have burnt down the world if it meant building me a new one from the ashes. It wasn't always something I shared with those who were closest to me, but I was constantly thinking of them and the hole in my heart they left behind. What emptiness would they have filled if they were still with me today? What would my life have been like if I had never had to step foot into foster care? If they were still alive, how could I thank them for everything they'd sacrificed to ensure I was happy and healthy?

I was well aware I'd done little to recognize my own grief, nor had I worked to repair what was broken. Standing here next to Erick, I realized that was the last thing I wanted to do. Especially with him. So, I did what I did best and changed the topic, shifting the attention away from me.

"Very lucky," I agreed in a chipped tone. "I never pegged you as the sad movie type."

"I'm full of surprises, Krissy, all you have to do is ask." Sucking in the last of the smoke, Erick smothered the roach, then gave me his full undivided attention. "They aren't the type of movies I can watch all the time, but every once in a while is fine." Erick cleared his throat. "I have an arsenal of movies that would have you bawling your pretty little eyes out within the first twenty minutes."

"I rarely cry." I pursed my lips. "I doubt I would."

"We'll see about that."

Erick abandoned me again, seeking the warmth of the apartment. Peering through the window, I could see him shuffling about the room just past the glare. Collecting different things and placing them in the living room for safekeeping. First, it was a bunch of fuzzy blankets that he draped over the couch and floor, then it was a massive bowl of popcorn topped with butter, and lastly, an expensive bottle of wine uncorked and ready to drink. It took him ten minutes to set up the room, but when he was done, the place looked like a dream. It was the kind of gesture that had my heart betraying me.

"Come put your money where your mouth is," he taunted, patting down the empty space on the couch. I obliged, curling up next to him and wrapping myself in one of the blankets. Ghost saw the opportunity and took it, jumping into my lap before Erick could protest. "I'll show you my favorite movie as long as you promise to do the same."

Chapter Twenty-Nine

Erick

Krissy put on her best performance yet. Somehow holding on until the bitter end, but inevitably letting her emotions get the best of her. As the credits rolled, so did the tears. Even with wet cheeks, swollen eyes, and an attempt to hide it all, I couldn't help but admire her beauty. It was the type of beauty that couldn't be bought or fabricated, something that resided within. For reasons I could not understand, Krissy constantly had her guard up, only lowering it for those she trusted to reveal a compassionate spirit that longed for closeness and making everyone feel welcome in her presence in exchange for her respect.

I'd caught glimpses of it—moments when I'd stumble into the apartment to find my men roaring with laughter or utterly captivated by her enchanting music. I saw it months ago, when she didn't know I was watching from the shadows of the mezzanine, or when her laughter echoed from her dressing room down the tunnel. I saw it when she sat with Damon, patiently practicing sign language so she could better communicate with him.

Krissy rewarded those she deemed worthy, which only made me crave that level of intimacy from her even more.

Truthfully, I wasn't sure I'd earned it yet.

Patience would be the price, and opening up to her the burden. But some people were worth every bit of the pain that came with it.

The movie had ended, and I had stolen an hour and a half of her time. Curled up in a mess of blankets, every moment of it meant more to me than she could ever comprehend with her guard still firmly in place. It was getting late, so I threw on something mindless to watch, mostly for background noise. Krissy started to doze off between commercial breaks, eventually falling asleep with her head resting against my shoulder. I let myself savor the proximity for a few minutes before attempting to scoop her up in my arms and take her upstairs so she could sleep more comfortably on the bed.

She jerked awake, rubbing her eyes frantically to wipe the sleep away.

"I'm up. I'm up," she persisted, her voice raspier than it normally was.

"You were asleep before I moved you—don't lie."

Like a child, she pouted her lips. "I don't want to go to bed."

"Get ready for bed. We can stay up a little longer, only if you promise to lie down in bed."

"Fine," she groaned, rising to her feet with a stretch.

Ghost trailed after her, looking nearly as tired as Krissy. In my line of work, I never imagined there would be enough time to adopt, nor did I care to have a pet, but as fate would have it, when a malnourished kitten nearly on the brink of death comes begging for food, you tend to find the time in your busy schedule. Three years later, Ghost was as healthy as can be and a vital part of my life. Ghost began to fill a hole in my heart that formed well before my mother passed away. It wasn't enough, but it was healing, nonetheless. The first few years were tough, filled with long nights trying to gain her trust with food and attention, but my patience was eventually rewarded. Yet it took all but three days before she and Krissy were nearly inseparable—not that I was complaining.

As I cleaned up, I could hear her movement in the bathroom upstairs, stomping around far too loudly. Once the living room was presentable, I snagged the half-drunken bottle of wine and brought it upstairs with me to find out what all the commotion was about. I stopped short, finding Krissy dancing about the bathroom as she washed her face. In all her glory, she moved so freely, swaying her hips and twirling about without knowing what lurked in the shadows.

"I thought you were tired?"

Her head jerked toward the door, slightly jumping with surprise.

"I thought I already told you I wasn't," she said, grabbing the bottle from my hand.

"You talk a big game for a girl who was drooling on my shoulder not ten minutes ago," I teased, snatching the wine from her. Krissy gasped, acting far more wounded than she really was, pretending to clutch the nonexistent pearls. Neither of us had enough to be considered drunk, but with each sip, I brought myself closer to that thin line. For once, after weeks of meticulous planning and stress-induced dreams, I allowed myself to indulge, having fun as I drank with a woman who needed tonight as badly as I did. "Lie down on the bed and tell me you're not tired." I smiled.

"I can't wait to prove you wrong, *Mr. Destler.*"

I leaned forward, my arm propped against the doorframe for support. As I captured her gaze through the mirror, I found myself speaking with little consideration of the consequences. "I thought we already talked about this. Don't call me by my last name unless you're prepared to call yourself Mrs. Destler."

Krissy looked like she'd seen a ghost, turning her attention back to the dozens of tiny bottles of moisturizer and creams she applied to her face daily.

Maybe I was closer to that line than I'd thought. The wine was clearly stirring this conversation, taking me into uncharted territory that I would never vocalize if I were sober. As the words left my lips, I knew there would be no recovering from that, not that I fully regretted saying it in the first place. I took one final gulp of wine and left the bathroom to get ready for bed myself, not without sneaking one final look over my shoulder before disappearing completely. Her cheeks were bright red, and no matter how much product she rubbed on her skin, there didn't seem to be any way to lessen it. Krissy Davis was blushing, and I couldn't believe my eyes. A woman like her could have any man groveling at her feet, begging for her attention as they threw every praise and complaint her way without her even breaking a smile, but I had made her blush, and I felt a weird sense of pride for it.

Neither of us addressed the comment as we slipped into bed. Krissy wore nothing more than a thin tank top and matching pajama shorts that left little to the imagination, but who was I to speak? I wore a pair of gray sweatpants that did the same.

Krissy flipped over on the mattress so she was facing me, then pointed to the pillow. "See. Not tired."

"Is that so?" I huffed out a laugh. "Then what do you suggest we do until you are tired?"

Krissy chewed on her bottom lip while trying to decide, undeniably more playful and animated after a night of drinking, despite how tired she looked. "How about," she paused like she wasn't quite sure of her response, "I get to ask you a question, and you have to answer it no matter what, and in exchange, you get to do the same? As childish as it may sound, it would be nice to know the man I'm sharing a bed with a little better."

My little angel wanted to play a dangerous game, and who was I to deny her?

Patience would be the price, and opening up to her the burden.

I nodded, urging her to go first.

"Remember, you made a promise to answer no matter what," she reminded me.

"I know. I know. Do you not trust me?"

"Sort of," she answered honestly.

"You have my word, but if that isn't enough, we can always shake on it."

More than distance separated us. What boundaries or obstacles kept us apart didn't feel nearly as daunting as they should have been. Krissy leaned in slightly, hesitating to move any further. Time stilled as she watched me through those long, dark lashes of hers. "Shaking is too professional," she whispered, taking that final leap. Although we'd only kissed once before, I'd dreamt about doing it hundreds of times since meeting her. I had imagined what type of blessing it would be to have her in such a way that desire and infatuation didn't consume either of us like a fire set ablaze. To imagine what it would be like to hold her in my arms and taste her without urgency. To imagine that closeness and care.

"Far too professional," I mumbled against her lips.

Her lips brushed mine. There was a moment of hesitation—a moment of longing that spoke to the embers of desire that sparked to life. I allowed myself to indulge for but a heartbeat before forcing myself to pull away, knowing that if I didn't, I'd be lost to her completely.

"Okay. Hmm...this is going to be fun."

"Ask your questions already, or I will," I warned, making myself comfortable on my side of the mattress.

"Fine. Why won't you tell me about the story behind the roses?"

"Because that story is difficult to talk about. There are open wounds I'm still slowly working through."

"But–"

I clasped my hand over her mouth. "Your question was asking me to explain *why* I wouldn't tell you about the roses, not the actual story behind it. Wording is everything, little angel." I smiled. "That was your one question, so now it's my turn."

Krissy had set the tone, reaching for answers unobtainable by most. While I had challenged her to take risks and explore treacherous waters, she'd attempted to ask the most difficult questions right out of the gate. If she had every intention of learning the man behind the mask, I had no problem treading with her.

"I've been thinking a lot about what you said at dinner." Her eyebrows rose. "I understand not wanting to be with a piece of shit like Patrick, but you've made comments here and there about commitment as a whole. What is it about being in a relationship that terrifies you so much? Why wouldn't you want to be with someone if they made you happy?"

"That was two questions," she said, clearly deflecting.

"What about being in a relationship terrifies you so much?" I restated.

She sighed, closing her eyes to collect herself. "Have you ever been burned while cooking before?" I nodded. "The first time is always a mistake. Something you do by accident and swear it will never happen again. You promise yourself you'll be careful next time. When it inevitably happens again, you blame the stove, the pan, or anything but yourself. Because how could it ever be your fault? You wouldn't purposely harm yourself?" She smiled, but it didn't reach her eyes. "One day, there's a kitchen fire, everything is burnt to a crisp—there one moment, and gone the next. Cooking used to be the only thing that brought you joy, but without a kitchen, it doesn't seem worth it to try to rebuild or find a new house with a shiny one, because inevitably everything will burn down just like the last time—you'll just hurt yourself again." Krissy paused. "This game isn't as fun as I thought it would be. I didn't realize this would turn into a little therapy session right off the bat. I'm not even sure if that made sense, but it's the only way I can explain it."

"Your heart is only trying to protect itself, that's understandable," I assured her.

She danced around the metaphor, careful to tread lightly. The fire could have been a number of things, but I had my suspicions based on how little she spoke about her family; I suspected it had something to do with them. I wasn't one to push. I knew the rest would come on her own accord, not some silly game where I forced her to speak on matters she wasn't ready for.

"I guess," she rasped. "Alright, my turn again. *Why* are roses your favorite flower?"

Years of therapy had paved the path to acceptance, but I wasn't lying when I told Krissy it was an ongoing journey. Part of me knew living with that type of grief would always linger well after.

"Get comfortable. This is a long story," I warned her, and she tucked herself more firmly under the covers. "Growing up, my dad was absent for most of my life. Working for my grandfather meant he spent more time managing their businesses in the district than he did with his own wife and kid, and anytime he did come home, he was a drunk piece of shit that neither of us deserved to be around. My mother was a saint. The only constant and reliable part of my life that I never imagined I'd be without one day. My mother and father both agreed to keep it a secret at first, that it would be best to hide the truth until I was old enough to comprehend the severity of the situation, but over time, it became harder and harder to lie about the frequent hospital visits and strange breathing treatments.

"It wasn't until my mom was in the last ten years of her life expectancy that she told me she had Cystic Fibrosis, a life-threatening disorder that damages the lungs, making the fluid in them thick and difficult to breathe. Nowadays, the life expectancy is about fifty to sixty years, but—but back then it was much shorter with limited research, funding, and technology. She fought for as long as she could before those lungs of hers gave out." I cleared my throat. "After her funeral, my grandfather started to care for me while my father took a more prominent role in the Destler family business."

Krissy was glued to my every word, hardly breathing as I spoke.

"Cystic Fibrosis can be a pretty tricky word for a kid to say. I can't remember the full story, but there was this little kid a few years ago who couldn't pronounce it, so they started calling it sixty-five roses instead, and it just stuck with the community. Now roses are heavily associated with the disorder, and I tattooed them all over my arm as a reminder of the woman who sacrificed everything to make me the man I am today."

Ever so gently, as if they were real, she reached out and traced her finger over a rose, leaving a trail of goosebumps along my skin. From the back of my hand to the side of my neck was a tangled-up mess of roses and vines consuming the entire right side of my body. It took countless hours to complete, but the pain was nothing compared to seeing her rest so peacefully under the soft glow of the prayer candles, clothed in the same lilac dress she wore on Sundays while still breathing. While my mother was deeply religious, there was something twisted about knowing she was buried in that same dress. Something that once represented vibrancy and life, while we sang and laughed in the pews only weeks before. I didn't remember much from that day, but I'll never forget that damn dress.

"It's beautiful. She would have loved it."

I didn't have the heart to tell her that my Catholic Italian mother would have had a conniption if she'd seen what I'd done to my body. The woman hated tattoos with a passion. The same could be said for my father if he were still alive, but for an entirely different reason. With nothing on my body to represent my South African heritage, he would have bitched and moaned until I did something about it.

"I'd like to think so too."

We took turns questioning one another until it was well past midnight. Neither of us would quit until she could barely keep her eyes open, and I was brimming with a wealth of knowledge. From the most minute details, such as the way she took her coffee to the events leading to the fatal car crash that took her parents, I knew countless things about Krissy that I memorized to heart and cataloged for later. While the wine had done its job, making it easier to speak so freely, I'll admit it was incredibly difficult to open old wounds that I assumed were closed, and by the way Krissy stumbled over some of her stories, I knew she felt the same.

"It's getting late," I mumbled, glancing over at the clock on the nightstand. "You get one more question. Make it count."

Krissy sucked air between her teeth, attempting to think of one. "How did you get that scar across your face?" The second she uttered the words, a phantom pain sliced down my cheek, making me slightly wince. She, of course, noticed. "You don't have to answer if you don't want to, as you said, it's getting late."

Krissy wasn't the type to falter, and neither was I. Very few knew the story behind the scar cutting down my face in jagged, uneven lines, and even fewer knew why they never healed properly. Being so young when the accident happened, I thought the disfigurement was a death sentence, something that would haunt me throughout my adult years. That was until I learned it could be a tool, a way to intimidate others. And while living with the scar didn't bother me like I imagined it would, the reason they were there in the first place wasn't that simple.

Before she could argue, I pulled her onto my side of the bed, tucking her in against my chest. If she could hear how erratic my heart was, she didn't make it known; instead, she nestled herself closer.

"My grandfather was many things, but a good person was not one of them." And part of the reason we were in this mess to begin with. "There wasn't much he valued in life, but religion was above all, despite his loss of morals. Nothing spoke truer to the type of man he was than drinking his weight in liquor and gambling away his savings on a Saturday just to turn around and repent his sins on Sunday. When my mother died, I spent every Sunday of my childhood in a stuffy church being forced to pray to a God I no longer believed in. My grandfather would shove me to my knees and make me pray while reminding me that God works in mysterious ways and her death was all part of his plan." I paused. "The religious trauma surrounding all of that is an entirely different story altogether but...there was one Sunday in particular, I decided to ditch with Antonio when I was thirteen and full of stupid ideas.

"As you can imagine, he was beyond pissed when we came home. It was so long ago, I don't remember who started screaming first, but things got pretty heated, then I said some foolish things that I probably shouldn't have about him and the church." An image of his bright red face flashed in my mind. "He beat me for what I said. It was nothing I hadn't seen before, and if things had stopped there, I would have left with only a few cuts and bruises, but later in the night, when he got drunk, things turned dark. I used to tell myself what he did was more about his failure than my own, but after so many years, I think he was just a sadist.

"He got blacked-out drunk, smashed a bottle of gin, and took a shard of glass with him to my bedroom, and used it to make me *repent* for my sins. While I should have been rushed to the hospital immediately, he made me recite prayers at my bedside with blood gushing down my face. I was lucky I didn't lose an eye.

"The theater might be the last true connection I have with my mother, but deep down, I think the only reason I ever wanted it so badly was to spite my grandfather for losing it in the first place and what hell he forced me to endure. I wanted to succeed where he'd failed."

Something wet dripped down my side. A soft sniffle followed.

"Krissy, look at me. Are you crying?"

"No." She sniffled again.

Ever so gently, I tipped her chin upward, forcing her to meet my gaze. "You know," I said softly, "for someone who claims they don't cry, you've done it a lot lately."

"I can't help it." She choked out a laugh.

"Don't cry, little angel, it happened a long time ago. I don't cry about it anymore, and neither should you." I couldn't even remember the last time I cried. Had it been months, maybe years? There wasn't a single tear worth shedding for the past that shaped me into the man I am today. Every obstacle, every heartache had brought me here to this moment, and although I didn't believe in divine fate, I knew this was where I was meant to be. Wrapped in Krissy's arms, tackling a future filled with unknowns and the hope of something more profound that didn't rely on our collective trauma to define who we were or what we could become.

"You were only a child, Erick. Someone should have been

looking after you. Someone should have stopped him." She started to ramble, speaking far too quickly to keep up. "What did your dad do when he found out?"

I leaned in to kiss her forehead. "That was your last question, remember? Get some rest, little angel."

There would be more questions to come—I knew that, but for now, both of us were too exhausted to argue in circles to keep the conversation going. Krissy thanked me for the movie night and then nestled herself in more closely before the soft sound of her breathing filled the room moments later. Leaving me staring up at the ceiling, restless as ever, considering how I would answer that question the next time it was inevitably asked. How I would explain that my father took the word of my abuser over his own son. It was only ever spoken about once, and then everyone magically forgot about it despite the physical reminder I wore. Or how I refused to attend either of their funerals, let alone mourn the loss.

For some, death is an end, and for others it is a beginning. I was gifted a business nearly in shambles and built an empire from its ashes. I built something my great-grandfather would have been proud of—something I was proud of.

Sleep didn't come easily that night. I felt myself drifting for hours until I was startled awake, pulled from the restless dream. It took a few moments to realize where the noise was coming from before I reached over to the nightstand, careful not to wake Krissy. Ghost perked up as I flipped open the burner phone and blanketed the room in a harsh white glow.

Unknown: We both have something the other person wants. I think it's time we met.

Chapter Thirty

Erick

It was likely a trap. The thought had crossed my mind more often than not. Making the exchange should have been his first move, a quick and painless end to the terror of that night, but foolishly, he thought he could have it all, the theater and the girl. Selfish as ever, he took matters into his own hands, drawing first blood and inevitably starting something he didn't have the means to finish. He'd failed miserably, and he was likely paying for it on Blanchet's behalf.

Good, he could rot in hell for all I cared, I thought to myself.

Given Patrick's nature and that persistent need to possess both Krissy and The Lotte, I knew answering his text would only bring trouble. And so did Antonio, but I answered, nonetheless. There was blood on Patrick's hands, and there would be no reality in which he could wipe them clean without atoning for what he'd done.

For a delicate matter of business, we handled it as such, meeting well before dawn to discuss and argue over the various possibilities and what line of defense we would take. With no way of knowing what Patrick's true motives were, the four of us devised a plan that forced him out of the district and into neutral territory. A billiards club on the Upper East Side of town that wasn't run by any partial owner worth noting and was easily motivated to turn a blind eye.

We had set the stage—it was only a matter of getting Patrick to hit his mark.

The location was secure and searched twice over for good measure. That didn't stop me from worrying. It seemed to be all I did lately. Suddenly, jobs didn't feel as thrilling and carefree as they once did. There were things—precious things—at stake now, and one wrong move meant losing it all.

The place was the epitome of a dive bar in desperate need of a remodel and a visit from the health inspector, but who was I to judge when the owner was taking bribes and looking the other way for us? A dozen or so pool tables lined the middle sections of the room, with high tables scattered about. No one played besides a young couple that occasionally laughed louder than the rock music playing in the background, drawing a few judgmental eyes in their direction. Toward the entrance was a bar that over-looked it all, plastered with an array of different stickers that made the dingy wood pop with color. A few older gentlemen sat drinking their beers in silence. Most of the space was bathed in red and blue neon lights, but where the light didn't touch was a set of booths with just enough privacy to make this work. For a Thursday evening, the place was moderately busy at first glance, but from the customers to the waitress flirting her way into a bigger tip, all of them were my employees. Every last one of them.

Patrick was playing a dangerous game. The price for arro-gance was walking into a bar unarmed, defenseless, and completely surrounded on all fronts. It took one look to know he'd wholeheartedly believed there was no way to trace him back to the scene of the crime, and he was nothing more than a help-less man longing for the safety of the woman he claimed to love.

He was certain there was no possible way I could have identified Elijah Parson, a lowlife criminal who did dirty work for a living, from the surveillance footage alone, and then pieced together his connection to Jonathan Winkler, who conveniently had ties with Martin investments. And there was absolutely no way I could have captured him a week earlier for questioning, only to inevitably discover how he had executed the attack on the club by infiltrating a morning delivery and hiding an explosive device in one of the kegs.

Patrick stumbled into the bar, looking characteristically out of place. Our eyes instantly met, as if he could sense me lurking in the shadows. I held his gaze for as long as I could before deliberately lowering it to the mask resting upon the table. Patrick swallowed the lump in his throat before walking toward the booth, failing to hide his fear.

"Mr. Destler." His voice was steady, despite the way he carried himself. "I'd say I'm surprised, but I had my suspicions. Oh, you don't have to." Damon rose to his feet and began patting down his suit, searching for anything that would warrant an attack or setup. Once he was cleared, Patrick slipped into the booth, acting as if he'd just been violated. "That was hardly necessary, Mr. Destler. I'm not foolish enough to break the terms of our agreement."

There were names for men like him, terribly offensive and accurate names that encompassed everything he was and more, but the only one that came to mind was abuser. Abuse in any form was unacceptable, yet without any bruises or physical signs, it was hard to prove that it ever happened in the first place. Krissy had too much pride to admit it, but with what little she had shared with me about her time dating Patrick, I knew enough to know all the signs were pointing toward an emotionally abusive relationship. The excessive jealousy. The lying. The blackmailing. The manipulation to keep her tethered to him.

Shit—I've seen it for myself. A few months ago, there was a hold-up, and it took me longer than usual to sneak backstage after one of Krissy's spectacular performances. I barely had enough time to place the rose on the vanity and slip into the shadows before the door to the dressing room swung open. Krissy and Patrick walked in, both completely oblivious to the fact that they weren't alone. They spoke freely, keeping the conversation light, making plans for the following weekend. Anytime Krissy would suggest something, Patrick would insist they do it alone, excluding the people she clearly cared for. There were countless excuses, but all were isolation tactics he was guilting her into believing. At the time, I didn't think much of it, especially when the conversation was so nonchalant. Things took a turn for the worse when Patrick noticed Krissy smiling down at the gift I'd left behind and placing it with the others in her vanity drawer. It took everything not to lunge for him when he started throwing out false accusations and screaming at her for keeping such sentiment.

If given the chance, I would have done things differently. I would have paid him no mercy, struck him down before there was anything he could hang above her head. I clenched my fist at my side, resisting the urge to reach over the table and snap his pretty little neck. Unfortunately, killing him wouldn't do us any good; it would only mean his sister, a Blanchet, would have sole ownership of the theater, and we would only solve one problem to inevitably spark countless more.

"You have two minutes—that's it," I deadpanned, not even sure I could last that long in his presence. Something about his arrogance reminded me of my grandfather, and that made me feel sick to my stomach.

He sighed, shifting uncomfortably on the leather seat. "I understand the theater is your price; however, I am not the only partner who has a stake in the property. If it were only me, the damn thing would have been signed off weeks ago, and none of us would have been in this mess to begin with. Convincing my sister will take time, but if you can release Krissy immediately, I will make it happen. We both walk away happy."

Miss Davis will remain in my possession until further notice. If you wish to gain back her freedom, the price for her life is the deed to The Lotte. The deal had once been cut and dry. My intentions were nothing more than to gain back territory that was once lost, now—well, now things weren't quite that simple.

A hundred years ago, my great-grandfather immigrated to the States with only clothes on his back and the change in his pocket. He grew an empire from nothing and made a name for himself as a young black man during troubling times. From my understanding, the theater and jazz club were only a fraction of the buildings he owned in the district, most of them apartments and businesses he rented to other black entrepreneurs, but these ones in particular were built with a tunnel connecting them to evade prohibition laws and keep his affair with Rosita Blanchet a secret. Marjan Blanchet grew suspicious of his wife and had her followed. With enough evidence to confirm his worst fears, he tipped off the police, not only exposing the illegal operation but catching her in the act. Rosita was forced into isolation by her husband and never permitted to see her true love again. Sparking a century-long feud that seemed ever-changing.

Both The Lotte and Don Juan remained in my family's possession until my grandfather gambled away the property rights. While the theater was a historical part of our legacy, it was also a connection to my mother that I longed for. In the late eighties, my mother was a waitress, serving tables just to make ends meet. From what I was told, my mother and father fell in love rather quickly. Her memory was fleeting, hardly a whisper of what it once was after so many years. Much of her belongings were tossed out after her funeral, and what little I remember of her was tainted by my grandfather's failures.

So, yes, the theater meant the world to me, but at the end of the day, it was just a building.

"I don't see a reality in which we both walk away from this happy," I said, my voice breaking the taut silence hanging between us.

Patrick stared blankly, his mouth opening as if to protest. "The deal was the theater—"

"The theater," I interjected, "is merely one piece in all of this, but what of the others?"

Patrick hesitated, caught off guard. He opened his mouth again, then closed it, retreating into silence. I didn't waste another breath on him. Instead, I pulled a folder from beneath the table and spread its contents between us. Photos, documents, offshore bank records—it was all there, merely another piece in the web of lies he was so tangled up in.

"Tell me, Patrick, what do you know of Elijah Parson?"

He hadn't been terribly difficult to locate, nor was getting a confession out of him. Wearing him down over the week until he admitted his accomplices took an immense amount of patience. The proof lay before us, a testament to his willpower. Despite how strong he was, every stubborn spirit has its weakness.

Patrick schooled his features, but his eyes betrayed him. "I've never seen this man before."

"Interesting. And while that may be true, that doesn't hide the fact that this man," I tapped the image of Elijah, gagged and beaten beyond recognition, "has an overseas bank account you've been funneling money into, Patrick. Those deposits—*your deposits*—showed up days before the attack. You may not have ever seen this man, but you sure as hell know his name."

"That—"

"Our time is short," I snapped, glancing at my watch. "So, I suggest you let me finish."

Patrick fell silent, his lips pressed into a thin line.

"Whether or not you admit to knowing this man doesn't matter. It doesn't change the fact that I have these records at my disposal. And with a little convincing, I could have a written confession from him in no time. With that being said, there is a way to make this mess disappear..."

Patrick's jaw clenched. "What do you want?"

I leaned back, folding my hands. "I'll agree to release Krissy with one exception. Sign over the theater, I'll release her unharmed as promised, the records will never see the light of day, and Elijah Parson will take the fall for everything. But..." I paused, letting the silence hang between us like a guillotine poised to fall at any second. "You agree to never see Krissy again."

Patrick's fists clenched and unclenched, a battle waging behind his eyes.

"If you truly cared for her," I said softly, "this wouldn't even be something to consider."

"Absolutely not," he scoffed. "You can't seriously think you can keep us apart. Krissy would never agree to this either."

There's no reality in which I'd release Krissy without ensuring her safety was guaranteed. Replacing one prison with another was never part of our plan. She deserved more than to live in fear of someone who thought they could stake a claim in something that never belonged to them in the first place.

I kept my expression neutral, letting Patrick stew in his own defiance. "Then the deal is off the table," I said calmly. I checked my watch again and smiled. "And would you look at that—your two minutes are up."

"Wait," he desperately called out as I began to rise to my

feet. "I'm giving you exactly what you want. You can have the theater, it's yours. Have it!"

What a lying piece of shit.

While moments like these were fleeting—a mere speck on a timeline as vast as days numbered. None of them compared to reaching for the Polaroid I had hidden in my suit pocket. With the flick of my wrist, the image went skidding across the table and landed directly in front of him. Giving Patrick a clear view of Krissy bent over a table with her wrist resting on the small of her back, handcuffs biting into her skin.

"Call me when you're ready to be a fucking man. If you cared for her as much as you claimed to, you shouldn't wait long. Pretty little things like her can easily be broken."

Selfishness came in many forms. For Patrick, it meant playing with and manipulating those he cared for when he saw fit. Objectifying them to feel better about himself or fill whatever fundamental piece of his terrible childhood he likely missed. For myself, it meant savoring this moment longer than it was needed. It meant basking in the glory and plotting my next move before the meeting was even over. While selfishness was warranted in some instances, it was a filthy curse that took more than it gave in others.

And in this instance, it gave right back. Something out of the corner of my eye swung out, slamming into my jaw with immense force, rattling the bones beneath my skin. My vision went blurry, and the bar around me turned into an assembly of oddly shaped figures. It took me a few moments to register what had even happened, but when I did, I found Patrick standing before me, looking nearly as stunned as I was that he landed the punch.

All those weeks ago, I swore to Krissy that the integrity of this deal would remain intact. I promised both of us that our patience would be rewarded—that Patrick would suffer in more ways than one. And while I still believed the worst was yet to come, that didn't stop me from yanking him by the collar and swinging back. Breaking every rule and promise I'd made. One moment, I was standing on my own two feet, the next, I was toppling over Patrick, relentless as ever. Too blinded by my own rage to even consider stopping on my own accord. I might have blacked out because by the time Damon managed to drag me away, there was so much more blood than I had realized—his and mine both. Patrick had gotten in a few good swings, and I was now aware of the aching in my ribs and the taste of blood on my lips.

Promises were broken, blood was spilled, and if it wasn't for Damon, I wasn't sure I would have stopped. None of that seemed to matter as I watched Patrick wail in agony on the ground.

I spat at him, blood spraying everywhere. "Krissy would never love a piece of shit like you."

Chapter Thirty-One

Krissy

The apartment was dead silent. Making each note flourish and expand as it echoed off the high ceiling. I mindlessly drummed my fingers over the keys, and it filled me with a type of loneliness I hadn't realized was slowly creeping up on me until now. A longing for something that kept my head above water when it felt nearly impossible to stay afloat in the past.

Theater had given me an outlet, a place to prove my worth, and an opportunity to find a family of my own. I'll admit I'd been avoiding the piano as much as I could, only playing when I had an audience or when I was so desperately bored and trapped between these walls that I had no other choice. It had been years since I last played in earnest. While I took classes when I was younger, there simply wasn't enough money for both dance and piano lessons, so my mother forced me to choose between the two. A decision I never regretted in the slightest until later in life when I told Lyra about it. Her background was in dance, but growing up playing three different instruments, she jumped at the opportunity to teach me. The beginning of our friendship was built on drinking cheap tequila after work and staying up late to perform little shows in her apartment, which blossomed into a nearly inseparable relationship. She asked me to move in soon after that—

I shut my eyes as the aching in my chest worsened. The memory took hold, but it was nothing compared to the guilt of keeping Lyra and the others in the dark, forcing them to worry when in reality I was safe—well, as safe as I could possibly be for now. As much as it hurt to lie to the people I cared for the most in this world, I reminded myself it was for the best. Especially when such powerful families like the Blanchets were heavily involved. There wasn't much I could do for them, but protecting their innocence was enough for now.

Ghost didn't bother waking up when I started playing again. A lullaby with a name long forgotten that took a few tries to get right. Listening to music had always been a way to cope that typically worked for me, a form of grounding or distraction depending on the day. And while the music was helping, it did nothing to keep my thoughts from wandering. I was no longer thinking about the path I'd taken, but the man who walked alongside me every step of the way.

A tortured soul that had been through hell and back. A man longing for love and belonging in a cruel world that had done nothing but try to cut him down. Instead, he rose from the ashes and made a name for himself, becoming a man he could be proud of despite his upbringing. He vowed never to forget where he came from and used it as fuel to better himself in the end. Trauma affected us all differently; for some, it was so debilitating that it echoed in every aspect of our lives, and for others, they could process it accordingly and grow from the experiences that tried so hard to define us. I admired Erick for doing what I couldn't when it came to healing, but by the way he spoke of his mother, I had a feeling there was more to his story.

I thought of Patrick. Of what he confided in me about his

childhood. Both Erick, Patrick, and I shared something in common: neglect. At a young age, we all experienced it in different capacities. With the loss of his mother, Erick was forced into a household that abused him in more ways than one and attempted to shape him into what they saw fit in order to take over the family business. Patrick wanted nothing more than his parents' love and affection, but what he got instead was years of pining for his sister's approval to fill that void. For myself, although we didn't have much growing up, I was loved and cared for. Always cherished by my family, who would have given up anything to put a smile on my face. It wasn't until I was thrown into foster care that I realized I wasn't as loved as I thought. Children much younger than I were adopted every day. Eventually, I aged out of the system and was forced to fend for myself, seeking validation and love from an adoring crowd atop a stage after years of feeling unworthy for simply being myself. As healing as dance was in some aspects of my life, it had also turned into a beast I didn't know how to keep satisfied.

The funny thing was, although we all three shared that common experience, it was what we did after that truly defined who we were. Erick strengthened his empire despite the burdens he inherited, offering a place for misfits and dreamers to seek refuge in a city determined to wear him down. Taking his profits from the handful of clubs he owned in the district, he gave back to the community by providing aid and resources to people in rehabilitation programs or who couldn't afford proper medical care. Although he didn't admit it during our drunk questioning, I had a feeling the reason behind it had something to do with his mother.

I found a scholarship specifically created for orphans and used that opportunity to go to college and finish what my mother couldn't. My degree opened many doors and allowed me to connect with girls at the dance studio with similar backgrounds, giving me a chance to give back in ways I wished someone would have done for me. And Patrick...well, he had taken his trauma and shaped it into a terrible weapon that he used against others. Forcing them to bend to his will and love what empty part he didn't love about himself. I'd nearly fallen for it. How could a man have me questioning my identity, my worth, or even my sanity? How could I have been so stupid not to see it coming?

Don't do that. Don't blame yourself.

There was only one person to blame in all of this.

The front door swung open, hitting the back wall with a resounding thud that shook the entire foyer. I nearly jumped out of my skin as my hand slipped, hitting the wrong key. Ghost leaped from where she was resting at my feet and scurried away to hide while I remained frozen in place, completely mortified at what I was seeing.

"Jesus, you're bleeding." I swung my legs over the bench once I found the strength to move.

Erick was clutching his ribs with bloody knuckles as he made his way to the kitchen. By the way he carried himself, I could tell he was in an immense amount of pain, but that didn't stop him from hiding it in other ways. His face was that of indifference, a perfectly curated mask he constantly wore. Only ever taking it off when we were alone.

"Erick," I barked. "What the hell happened?"

He ignored me, rummaging beneath the kitchen sink, his focus entirely elsewhere.

"Hello? I'm talking to you, Erick."

The longer the question went unanswered, the more it set my nerves on edge. As soon as the white first aid box came into view, I snatched it out of his hand and stepped back, putting myself out of reach.

"Give it back," he snapped, reaching for the kit.

I took another step back. "Tell me what happened first."

"Krissy," he warned, jaw clenched.

"Tell me."

"It's none of your business," he muttered, voice tight.

"I beg to differ."

"Last chance, Krissy."

"Did someone hurt—" The sentence died in my throat as he lunged forward, catching me by surprise. He tossed me over his shoulder, and I let out a shriek. "What the hell, Erick? Put me down!"

Of course, he didn't listen, making his way through the apartment and up the stairs. Each step took its toll, flaring up whatever injury he was hiding. It was a miracle he could even keep himself upright, but by the way he was hissing through his teeth, I knew with time he would weaken.

"You don't get to barge in here and start acting like a dick," I yelled, raising the kit as if to whack him on the back, but thought better of it. "I can't—"

Erick dropped me on the bed, and I bounced a few times before meeting his gaze.

"Drop it," he grumbled. "It's over, and that's all that matters. Now give me the damn first aid kit before I pry it from your hands."

"I'd like to see you try."

Even in a fit of rage, Erick lived for a good challenge.

Before he could strike, I jolted back, scrambling across the sheets with the kit raised high above my head to keep it away from Erick's greedy hands. He didn't waste any time, grabbing me by the ankles and yanking me back to the edge of the bed. Before I could even register what had happened, I was pinned down by his crushing weight, his panting breath hot against my neck.

Time seemed to beat to the rhythm of its own drum, ticking by one second after the other with no sign of him moving. I was about to scream at him to get off of me, but the words died on the tip of my tongue when I turned to find his deep brown eyes burning into me.

"Erick—"

Ever so gently, he pried the kit from my fingers, his gaze never leaving mine.

Something unspoken passed between us, and I was reminded of the last time Erick had me pinned down and helpless. The thrill of being at someone else's mercy. The moment of hesitation before the inevitable happened. The burning desire blossoms into a raging fire. Erick must have felt it too because I could feel the length of him hardening against my thigh.

"I only wanted to make sure you were okay," I said in a soft voice.

"I know," he rasped, his chest rising and falling in quick successions.

A beat passed before he finally pushed himself upright with excruciating effort. He stopped short, looming over me sprawled out across the sheet, my clothes askew from the struggle. His eyes darkened as his gaze swept over my every curve.

I glared up at him. "What?"

"What's your safe word?"

"Excuse me," a nervous giggle bubbled up my throat.

From this angle, the light didn't quite hit the curves of his face. He was shrouded in shadows, and as he hovered over me, I couldn't help noticing how he welcomed that darkness with open arms, becoming the personification of its likeness with that mask tucked firmly in place. For the first time in months, I was utterly terrified of the way he drank me in.

"Tell me your safe word," he demanded, fingers clenching around the kit as if it were the only thing keeping his hands to himself. "Because by the time I finish washing off this blood, if you're still lying here like this, I can't be held responsible for what happens next."

I blinked a few times, slowly registering what he was implying.

"Red," I sputtered, suggesting the first thing that came to mind.

"It's time we finish what we started back in the club, don't you think?"

I nodded; not sure I had any fight left in me.

"Good," was all he said as he turned away.

The moment the door closed, I could finally breathe.

It was odd. The stark contrast between the man who poured his heart out just hours ago, compared to the one splattered with blood and more closed off than ever. Erick's temper was predatory, the type that lurked in the shadows, hiding behind his charming features and devilish smile, but never made itself known until it was too late. I'd never seen him quite this upset, so whatever it was, it must be bad. I'll admit it stung a little to be pushed away when I tried to talk to him, but perhaps communication wasn't what he needed. Maybe he needed something else entirely.

The sound of running water got me moving, fumbling with the straps of my top and flinging my leggings across the room with hardly enough time to prepare myself for what I wanted him to stumble into. Erick wanted me lying in bed, but by the time the door opened, I was elsewhere, kneeling, back arched, heart thrashing against my chest.

Erick circled the bed like a predator stalking its prey. Something about the slow anticipation made the entire thing exhilarating. There was no preparing for what was to come next because when it came to Erick, he lived for moments like this— the thrill of keeping you waiting and utterly powerless. Moments where fear was a method of play instead of something to hang over someone's head. And there was no denying that the sight of him standing at the foot of the bed was exactly that.

I wasn't ready to meet his gaze yet. Instead, my eyes drifted down his body, drawn to the glimpse of soft brown skin and chest hair peeking through his partially unbuttoned shirt. My gaze traveled south, lingered for far too long on the visible erection straining his slacks, making my mind run wild and imagine a night in which we were never interrupted—a night where he followed through on his promises.

Noticing that I was staring, Erick shifted the bright red rope from one hand to the other, forcing me to look away. My breath hitched at the sight and what that meant for me. For us.

"Are you ready, Krissy?"

"I don't think I have a choice," I said playfully.

With his free hand, he skimmed my bottom lip with his thumb, slightly smearing the red lipstick I put on, especially for him.

"You always have a choice. You say the word, and it's all over."

If I was guilty of staring, then it was nothing compared to the way Erick drank me in. Savoring every inch of my bare skin. It took every ounce of restraint not to brush my thumb over my nipple and give in to my body's natural temptation, but I knew better than to succumb just yet.

"You always have a choice when it comes to us, Krissy," he repeated. "Now, turn around."

With my back to him, I shut my eyes and savored the feeling of his touch—the way goosebumps broke out all across my skin as he moved the hair off the back of my neck. Whatever game we were playing was just that—a game and nothing more. A way to indulge in our desire without care for the consequences and what it would mean for us to take this next step. I was content with believing that until Erick broke character for but a moment, placing a kiss on the side of my neck. Even though he couldn't speak about it yet, everything was going to be okay.

He yanked my hands behind my back and bound them together. While there was a sense of uncertainty and fear, I felt cared for and safe in his possession. He took his time wrapping the soft cotton rope around my upper torso, binding my arms firmly in place so they couldn't move. Like an artist at work, he was consumed by his craft, not resting until everything was perfect. While he was careful and delicate with my body in some instances, he was rough in others.

"There's just something about seeing you like this, little angel."

He tightened the rope with enough force to knock me back right into his chest, the friction unbearable where the fabric pressed against my skin.

"How does that feel?" he asked, his breath hot against the shell of my ear.

"I think I might prefer this over the handcuffs."

He huffed out a laugh before placing his hand on the base of my spine. I went tumbling forward with no way to catch myself. It became nearly impossible to breathe; my face pressed into the sheets, the fabric smothering me, leaving me utterly exposed to him.

"I was thinking the same thing."

I shuddered under his touch as he ran his finger between my thighs.

"God," he cursed. "Since the night in the basement when you were strapped to that chair, I've only dreamed what it might be like to take you like this—tied up and defenseless. Yet no matter how many times I've fantasized about it, nothing could have prepared me for this." His hand inched closer, his voice tight with restraint. "You drive me absolutely insane, Krissy."

"I might go crazy if you don't touch me already," I said breathlessly.

"You can complain all you want, Krissy, but that doesn't change the fact that I'm the one in control," he rasped, his finger sliding between my thighs with deliberate slowness.

It had been weeks—nearly a month now—since I'd last been touched like this. One finger was the sweetest relief. Two felt perfect, stealing the breath from my lungs. But three—God, it hurt, hovering on the edge of pain and pleasure, it forced me to surrender completely.

"I have all the control, little angel. If you really want something, speak up. Beg for it."

"Erick," I moaned, hardly recognizing my voice.

"Say it, Krissy. Beg for more."

His pace quickened, ruining me in the process.

"Please," I whimpered as he curled his fingers.

"Beg for me."

From the moment I first met Erick, I had always been acutely aware of the darkness that clung to him. A tether to his soul that bled out for all to see. And while that darkness had once made me falter. But now, it wasn't something I feared—it was something I craved. Something I wasn't sure I could handle another second without being fully consumed by it.

"I need you," I whispered. "Please."

Slowly, the darkness crept up over me, stealing every rational thought as the sound of clothing being removed and tossed aside was all that filled the air. I tried to glance over my shoulder and catch a glimpse, but the way I was positioned made it a lost cause.

The mattress shifted with his weight, and I knew there was no turning back. The darkness would win, and I'd be better off for it. Because when it came to Erick, everything about him stumbling into my life felt intentional—like an answer to a prayer I'd been waiting my entire life to receive.

"I need you, Erick," I moaned, as he positioned himself behind me.

Erick slammed into me without warning, and I knew without question the darkness would never be enough. To have him once meant always longing for more—longing for us. He pulled away, nearly slipping out of me before slamming back down again, the rhythm cruel in its perfection.

He gripped my hips hard enough that they would surely bruise and kept going until I felt myself shatter beneath him. I was so lost in it all, I didn't notice how many times I cried his name, begging for release. Erick reached beneath me and began teasing my clit until I was sobbing into the sheets. My nipples ached, my clit throbbed, and I felt myself clenching around him, trembling on the brink of losing myself completely.

Erick had ruined me and rebuilt me anew.

Waves of pleasure washed over me, relentless in nature. I succumbed to my desire and relished every moment we were connected as one until I was dripping down my thighs and panting into the sheets. There was a moment where I hoped there would be more–that Erick wasn't quite done until he found his own pleasure. That was until he reached for the bedside table and left me completely.

"Tell me your safe word again, little angel."

Something cold and sticky was poured all over me.

"Red," I stuttered.

"Good girl," he whispered, rubbing the tip of his cock through the lube and lining himself up behind me. An entirely different type of fear kicked in. I squirmed and wrestled beneath him, unprepared for what was to come next. "Tell me, Krissy, have you let someone fuck you like this before, or do I get that pleasure for myself?"

I groaned into the sheets. "There's no way in hell I'm letting you do this."

One word could end it all. Three letters, and all of this would be in the past.

Erick yanked at the ropes and forced me to slightly rise off the mattress, pressing me more firmly against his cock. There had been plenty of opportunities to try, none of which I thought seemed worth it, given the people who offered. So, I bided my time, never really seeking out that type of pleasure from any past partners.

He tugged harder. It wasn't quite enough to finally cross that line, but it was enough to make me sweat and consider my options before it was too late.

"We had our little fun, but this—" He leaned down, mumbling against the shell of my ear. "This is for what you did back at the club. I've been dreaming about fucking the brat out of you since."

"That doesn't mean I have to follow through. I say the word, and you stop—that's our deal."

"Then say it. Do it. Say the word, and I won't fuck the brat out of you as you deserve." A beat passed, and I said nothing. "Exactly. That's what I thought. You want this more than you're willing to admit."

And with that silent admission, he did the unthinkable. It was hardly in, and I was already scrunching my face at the unusual sensation. Inch by inch, he filled me so painfully full. The first thrust shocked me. The second one ruined me. And somewhere after the ninth or tenth, I was sobbing in the sheets, crying for him to stop. He'd built me up moments ago to ravage me in the next. And I loved every minute of it. I was helpless, vulnerable, and crawling back to pure bliss.

The sounds that escaped his lips were pure ecstasy to my ears. He groaned with every thrust, whispering words of praise that he thought were drowned out by my cries, but I heard every single one. When he moaned my name, I nearly came again.

"God, you're perfect," Erick murmured, his thrusts becoming frantic, desperation overtaking him. "Do you even realize what you do to me? Do you realize how much I need you?"

I attempted to answer, but all that escaped my lips was a broken moan. My body was set ablaze, every nerve alight with a mix of pain and pleasure so intoxicating it blurred the lines between them. I wouldn't recover from this. I couldn't.

"Look at you," he rasped, his nails digging into the flesh of my hips. "You take me so well, little angel. Like you were made for me."

"Erick," I sobbed, his name spilling from my lips like a prayer.

"Say it again."

"Erick!"

"That's it," he groaned, his thrusts becoming punishingly deep. "Say my name while I ruin you. Fuck, Krissy," he bit out, his rhythm faltering.

With one last thrust, he pulled out completely, and the sudden absence left me reeling. Warmth hit the small of my back as he finished, his body shuddering with the force of his release. He took several long seconds to recover, the weight of what we'd done hanging in the air between us.

"I'll be back, little angel," he finally said, his voice hoarse.

He disappeared, only to return with a wet cloth to clean me up. The ropes that had been strapped so tightly that they left red imprints all over my body came next. Each time he removed a section, he pressed soft kisses to the nearly bruised skin before moving on to the next. The act felt intimate in itself, and all I could do was lie there, savoring it.

Once I was freed, he pulled me under the covers and wrapped me in his arms. We lay there spooning one another for some time before he finally broke the silence.

"Are you okay?"

"Yeah," I choked out, my voice hoarse. "I'm okay, just exhausted."

Beneath the covers, it didn't feel like I was close enough to him, despite there being little room between us. I squirmed into place, settling myself into position.

"You don't seem tired."

I swayed my hips, feeling him harden against me again. "No, I'm absolutely exhausted."

It hadn't occurred to me how starved I was for him. For how long had I denied myself that pleasure and kept Erick inside of my fantasies instead of acting on them. Too many times, I had convinced myself that longing for something I knew was wrong would be a grave mistake. That picking someone else because they were supposed to be safe was what I was meant to do after years of secretly pining for stability and love. I'd tricked myself out of something that was calling to me, and now that I had it, it felt impossible to stop.

It didn't take long to pick up on the hint, lining himself up and slowly pushing in. "I'm so proud of you, Krissy. In every-thing you do and everything you've overcome, but especially tonight," he said in a hushed tone, leaving a trail of kisses starting from my shoulder and leading up my neck. "I'm in awe anytime I'm near you."

"Erick," I moaned out, my voice like honey.

My past was riddled with self-sabotage and isolation when it came to intimacy and relationships. It was always easier to avoid it all than allow myself the possibility of getting hurt. Erick knew enough without needing to say it outright. And although I wasn't ready to face that fear, something about being close to him like this made me hopeful for a future in which all of this wasn't so terrifying.

264

Chapter Thirty-Two

Patrick

A theater without its star was like a candle without a flame. A hopeless sense of purpose, so close to reaching its true potential but coming up short. Without Krissy to assume her role, Malik had been shuffling around between different options with little purchase, each as terrible as the last, forcing us to send out applications to keep the theater doors open and customers happy. I loathed the idea and absolutely despised a reality in which her role was not waiting for her when she returned, which made deciding on behalf of the theater's well-being feel like a betrayal to not only myself but to the future I so desperately craved.

Samantha Wilson would reprise her role as leading lady once more, a decision not made lightly. Fully recovered and hungry for more, Samantha's headshots were among the dozens of other applicants. It was a temporary solution that would create a buzz in the district and likely increase ticket sales based on the scandal alone. Malik had assured me that Samantha was familiar enough with the theater that rehiring her wouldn't deplete our resources and time before inevitably firing her when Krissy returned.

Malik wrapped up the morning meeting with the big announcement, leaving the crowd with more questions than answers. Speculations and rumors were quick to spread, growing at an exponential rate as thoroughly as the rumors of Krissy's disappearance had circulated weeks ago. While very few knew the truth, the masses were under the impression she'd checked herself into a rehab center, and based on her glowing reputation, it wasn't an unlikely story, nor did any of the managers shut down the rumors themselves. Krissy thrived in chaos, giving us a narrative that worked in our favor.

As the rumors spiraled, so did Krissy's beloved friends, borderline harassing me for information about her disappearance. On any given day, I would have done my best to avoid Daniel and Lyra at all costs, but today was the rare exception. I managed to corner Daniel backstage, packing up Krissy's belongings in preparation for Samantha's arrival.

I stopped on the threshold, not daring another step forward, when I noticed how the scent of her perfume no longer lingered as it once had, and anything distinctly hers was being boxed up as if it were a burden, to begin with. I swallowed the lump in my throat before fully entering.

"I told you that I would handle this," I said as a way of greeting. Daniel paused for a beat, his hand hovering over a pair of nude heels he was about to toss in a box already teeming with clothes before continuing to silently work. "Yet you went behind my back and reported her disappearance to the police despite every reason not to."

RCPD received an anonymous report yesterday, and although Charles' connection at the station couldn't reveal who'd called them about Krissy's disappearance, it didn't take much to put the pieces together.

"God forbid, if something bad happens to her, you'll have no one else to blame but yourself. You had no right," I continued.

Daniel diligently worked, sorting through item after item while refusing to even acknowledge my presence. It was as if I was speaking into the ether, my voice dissipating into nothingness, never to be heard again. I knew very little about the people Krissy surrounded herself with, but I was well aware they were an unsavory bunch that liked to announce themselves in any room they were in. Attention-seeking whores that thrived on as much chaos as Krissy did, corrupting her slowly but surely. It wasn't like Daniel not to voice his opinion, which made the silence slightly uncomfortable to stand in.

"I gave you my word that I would bring her back to where she rightfully belongs," I seethed. "Was that not enough for you? Could you not handle one simple task, or are you that dense?"

Daniel slammed a brush down on the vanity, rattling the old wood. The room went eerily still as if it were holding its breath, patiently waiting to see what would happen next.

"And where is it exactly that you think Krissy belongs?" he asked, turning slowly.

"She belongs home. She belongs with me."

"Krissy," he shouted, immediately lowering his voice when he noticed the open door, "doesn't belong anywhere near you, nor is she some prize to be won as you make her out to be. She is a goddamn human being who deserves more than to be disregarded and forgotten about when God knows what is happening to her. For someone who claims to love her, you've shown no remorse in her disappearance, yet the people who actually care for her are so disheveled they can't even bear the thought of packing up her stuff, so I had to come down here and do it for them despite how much it hurts me, too."

Daniel took one big step forward, bringing himself inches from my face. While we were relatively the same height, Daniel had a good half inch on me, and I had to peer up at him to meet his gaze.

"Jealousy is a nasty look on you, Daniel. I guess my suspicions were right."

He leaned in closer. "What a sad, pathetic life you live. It must be so exhausting being so deeply insecure about yourself that you are threatened by anyone and everyone who steps on your toes." Daniel smiled like he knew something I did not. "Play pretend all you like, but we all see through the façade and recognize how ill-fitted you are to run this theater. No one batted an eye when Krissy was still dancing on that stage because her presence overshadowed all of your flaws, but now that she's gone, it's never been clearer—especially after today. Krissy would be so proud."

His every word crawled under my skin, taking root and sprouting into something preternatural. It set my blood ablaze, promising that nothing good would come from the outcome.

"I did what was necessary to keep this theater running," I explained in a clipped tone, resisting the urge to lunge forward and take him by the throat like I wished I had the last time he dared to overstep his boundaries and accused me of the unthinkable.

"Tell that to Krissy when you find her."

Daniel made for the door, and in a fit of rage, I pounced for the nearest object and sent it soaring across the room. Glass shattered against the back wall as the remnants of what used to be a vase exploded into a million pieces. A crack splintered the air for but a second before fading into suffocating silence. The tiny shards of glass scattered across the old sofa and what was left of the water in the vase soaked the cushions and floor below.

"Everything I have done is for our future," I said, heaving with each breath.

He glanced over his shoulder like he had more to say, but instead shook his head and laughed. "Pathetic," Daniel muttered to himself before disappearing down the hallway.

I felt myself crumbling into pieces, trembling under the weight of my own body as I mulled over his every word. This theater was meant to be a blessing—a fresh start with the promise of everything I'd been robbed of from a past that no longer fit my needs. I'd staked my claim in the entertainment district as an act of triumph, branding my name amongst the few who were fortunate enough to call themselves owners, all while aiding my sister's endeavors. I had every right to do as I pleased with my business and had the power to eradicate anyone who stood in my way.

I raked my hands through my hair and let out a shaky breath.

Krissy was merely a piece of that puzzle. The finishing touches on the life I'd rightfully earned for–

The sound of dripping water pulled me from my thoughts.

My gaze swept over the room, coming up short for an answer. It continued in sporadic fits, sounding as if it were coming from inside the room. When I'd had enough of the relentless dripping, I chased after the sound, knowing the broken vase wasn't a viable explanation.

Careful not to slice open my knees on broken glass, I lowered myself to the hardwood flooring and peered under the sofa where the dripping was the loudest. Beneath the cushions was a stream of water that had trickled down from the back wall, wiggling itself between the grooves of the floorboard. The water followed at a slant until it completely disappeared between one of the cracks.

Tracing the tips of my fingers along the floorboard, I noted how distinctively different it was compared to the rest. The edges were worn as if the polish had withered away after decades of misuse. As if the wood had been passed through many hands.

I fell back on my heels, my head whirling as I tried and failed to unlock my phone.

Josephine answered on the third ring. "I already told you. Charlie would handle the report and any backlash from it."

"I found it."

"Excuse me?"

"I found the passageway." A beat passed. "Josephine?"

She laughed, the sound being a cross between utter disbelief and exhausted happiness. "We'll be there in twenty minutes. Don't you dare move a muscle until Charlie and I get to the theater."

When the line went dead, I tipped my head back and laughed myself hoarse.

As fate would have it, we now possessed the means to put an end to this waking nightmare.

And for the first time in weeks, all was not lost.

Krissy would return to me, and I would prevail.

Chapter Thirty-Three

Erick

I was convinced heaven couldn't be found between the pages of scripture or kneeling at an altar, for heaven was here in Krissy's arms. Within her presence. Krissy and I were two storms clashing into one another, two broken souls that found refuge in the most unlikely of places.

When I rushed into the apartment yesterday, I could hardly think straight, let alone make any rational decisions. I acted on impulse, and the moment I saw her pinned beneath me, looking like the most beautiful creature I've ever laid my eyes on, I knew I had to have her. To feel anything besides the overwhelming rage that nearly drove me to my knees and made me question how anyone could harm someone like her. It took every ounce of strength not to turn around and finish what I had started with Patrick, but Krissy reminded me that my place was here with her.

Selfishly, what frustrations I couldn't manage on my own, I took them out on her as a form of distraction. That became abundantly clear the moment I was face-to-face with my own reflection, forced to take a hard look at myself and contemplate my actions. As I scrubbed my hands clean, I knew I'd taken it too far and was prepared to walk out of that bathroom with an apology on my lips. That was until I saw her kneeling at the foot of the bed.

A better man would have picked her clothes up off the floor and told her to dress, but I did no such thing. Her beauty was intoxicating, something that poets and artists could only dream of encapsulating in their work. Krissy took my breath away, and as I approached her, I realized I was shaking. Not from anger as I once did, but something entirely different that was utterly terrifying in the best possible way.

Each time I'd forced her to recite her safe word, I felt as if I was begging her to stop me. For her to say the word and all of this would be over, because if there was a reality in which she didn't want this as badly as I did, then there would be a heartache I likely wouldn't recover from. I needed her to tell me to stop before I lost myself completely to her. Being with Krissy meant more than playing silly games and fulfilling desire; it was the start of something more.

Krissy Davis had my heart, and I couldn't imagine a world in which it was any other way.

Without the responsibility of her busy schedule, Krissy took advantage of the freedom and slept in for most of the day. I didn't dare to wake her up as I got ready to meet with my insurance representative to discuss the aftermath of the explosion; instead, I lightly kissed the top of her head and left.

I could think of about a hundred other places I'd rather be right now than trapped in a cramped office space discussing my business's lengthy insurance policy in exasperated detail. A hundred and one if you count being dead. I was fairly certain I was going to develop early signs of arthritis if I was forced to sign another document. As dreadful as the entire experience was, it was yet another obstacle I had to overcome when the work wasn't quite feeling like a reward anymore. At least if I had to suffer, I didn't have to do it alone.

"Well, isn't this fun?" Antonio mumbled, arms crossed against his chest, legs stretched out wide. The moment the representative stepped out of the office to retrieve something she'd forgotten, my cousin leaped at the first chance to see himself heard. Like a fussy toddler, he could rarely sit still. "What a great way to spend my Friday morning. You know, this is exactly why I joined the family business. Nothing screams fun like learning insurance jargon and sipping cheap instant-made coffee in an office filled with," he gestured toward the strange knick-knacks on the shelf behind her desk, "whatever the hell that shit is."

"I take it back—I wish you had blown up in the explosion."

"You and me both," he snorted. "Especially if I have to suffer through this for another minute."

I glanced down at my watch. "Well, you have fifty-six seconds left. So, do us all a favor and end it now. I'm sure your mama will understand. The poor woman has had to deal with you for thirty-one years. Let her finally rest."

He leaned back in his chair and took a sip of the stale coffee. "Speaking of my mother, do you mind dropping by the bistro after this is over? It's only a few blocks away."

"Sure," I answered. "After we run a few errands along the way." Predictable as ever, Antonio tilted his head toward the light fixture above and groaned. Maybe this would teach him for refusing to drive because he didn't want to fill up his gas tank. Everything came at a price, and taking shortcuts meant he'd be stuck with me for the remainder of the afternoon until I'd checked everything off my list. "Walk home for all I care."

The fluorescent lighting had drowned out his olive skin tone, making him look like a ghost of his former self as he shifted under the harsh conditions. His dark brown eyes found mine, narrowing for a moment as he considered whether or not I was messing with him, and when he finally came to a conclusion, he spoke. "Fine. Okay. We'll have it your way. As long as we stop by to say hi at some point today, it will save me an ass-whooping. I love her to death, but damn, I swear that woman acts like not visiting her will send her into an early grave."

If Antonio was in trouble for not visiting his mother often enough, then I could only imagine the lecture I was about to receive. I had my reasons for not visiting as often as I should. Regardless of what animosities may divide us, I knew she was someone I could always go to, even if I rarely took her up on the offer.

Several signatures later, we were finally on our way, fighting the tail end of the morning rush hour. The city was alive and well with the congestion and chaos that made this place special in its own terrible way. We crept through traffic, making it a few blocks without seeing an end to the torment. By some stroke of luck, a parking spot opened up curbside just as we were approaching the shop, saving us the headache of finding parking elsewhere in this city.

"I really hope you aren't dragging me to a flower shop."

"Shut up and make yourself useful," I said, shifting the car into park. "Help me find some poppies."

Roses had once symbolized a part of myself that I refused to let go. A connection to a broken past that tethered itself in a mess of vines and thorns that didn't always look as beautiful as they appeared to be on the outside. My intention in gifting Krissy a singular rose after each performance was harmless at first, a way to bridge the distance between us before our time was ready. A token of my appreciation for a woman who'd stolen the show along with my heart. Now that I knew her favorite flower, I wasn't entirely sure I could ever buy her a rose again, knowing what I know now.

Antonio scoured the quaint little shop without a clue of what he was supposed to be looking for. It took five long minutes of searching before the young shopkeeper swept in to save the day, finding him a bundle of poppies before I could. With yet another thing checked off my list, we popped into the coffee shop a few shops down. The morning rush didn't deter others from joining in, finding odd places to stand in the cramped space while they waited for their order to be ready. It took another twenty minutes before the barista called my name.

"Is that it?"

"We're waiting on one more," I answered in a clipped tone.

Antonio frowned at the counter, looking strangely out of place, clutching the bundle of flowers close to his chest. I wasn't sure how much longer he could handle being dragged around town like this. It was only a matter of time before he snapped.

"Erick," the barista called my name again, placing the Americano within arm's reach. With both drinks secured, we exited the shop and made our way back to the car.

Antonio hummed, elbowing me in the side. "You shouldn't have. An iced latte and flowers, you treat me so well. I don't deserve you."

"You really want to walk home, don't you?"

He raised an eyebrow, acting as if he knew more than he was letting on. "So, I take it things are going well with Anna." In public, both of us knew better than to speak her name out loud, so the name Anna was born to hide her identity in case anyone was listening. "That poor girl was practically drooling over you; it was only a matter of time before you two finally accepted the inevitable. In all seriousness, it's nice to see you trying after your last failed attempt at love. Not all women are that cynical."

"That's none of your business. She and I–"

Someone slammed into my shoulder with enough force to send both drinks slipping from my hands. I caught one, and the other exploded as it collided with the concrete below. Scalding hot coffee came flying in my direction, burning my wrists in odd patterns and soaking the hems of my pants.

"Watch where you're going," Antonio screamed over his shoulder, searching for the asshole who'd hit me. As quick as he came, he was gone, swallowed whole by the throng of people moving about the city in clusters. "Shit, are you okay?"

"Yeah, fucking splendid," I murmured, clutching my already bruised ribs. Patrick managed to get a few good shots in, and I was paying for it now.

It was likely just an accident, but in a city where pickpocketing was on the rise, I handed off the latte and rummaged through my pockets to be sure. Keys, wallet, phone—-it was all there, which was a relief, but I didn't expect to find something that hadn't been there before. A single playing card—the Joker, to be exact. In the blank space above the fool's cap was a ten-digit number, handwritten in sloppy jagged lines. The last two numbers were smeared but still legible.

Chance was a silly word, used to explain the unusual and odd circumstances that came our way. It implied that had we been anywhere else but here, the entire trajectory of our lives would have been different. Had I left the coffee shop a minute sooner, none of this would have happened. I didn't have the luxury of believing in chance when I chose to take over the Destler family business after my father's passing. I would have found the card regardless because when it came down to it, this was a carefully orchestrated plan that would have always ended with the Joker staring back at me.

I didn't say a word as I led Antonio toward the nearest back alley. Giving us the illusion of privacy, but I knew damn well every waking moment of my life since the rehearsal dinner had been meticulously watched over, waiting for a slip-up that would never come. Only ever finding peace behind closed doors, where Krissy was truly safe. While the alley was a far cry from being inconspicuous, it would have to do for now.

For once in his life, Antonio was speechless. Utterly silent as I took out my burner phone, careful not to agitate the small burns on my wrist, and typed away. He made sure to stay close in hopes of catching bits and pieces of the conversation.

It took all but three rings before the line connected.

"That didn't take long," a voice said as a way of greeting. Although our paths had not crossed in person yet, I instantly knew who I was speaking with.

"Well, I work fast."

"If that's the case, then I suppose forty-eight hours will be plenty of time for you to decide whether or not you'll accept my offer," Charles said in a dry tone. "For reasons I don't understand, it seems as if you've caused quite the mess by kidnapping the one woman in the city everyone's so hellbent on rescuing."

My heart sputtered out of control.

"I've already been through this with Patrick. He couldn't give me what I wanted, and I doubt you can either," I interrupted, keeping my voice calm and unreadable. Originally, when Krissy and I had formed this plan, we never intended for this to be anything other than a fear campaign, a way to scare Patrick into doing our bidding, but now that Charles was involved, there was no telling where our mistakes would take us. Patrick knew I was the one responsible for her disappearance, and whether he had told his brother-in-law or not was up for debate until now. Charles knew, and there was no point in hiding it anymore.

"You'd be surprised what I'm capable of," he responded in a thick accent. "Patrick lacks self-control, all it took was one bitch to ruin him for–"

"Call her a bitch again, and I'll rip your fucking tongue out."

There was a pause. The longer it dragged on, the harder I gripped my phone.

"Ah, I see," Charles sighed. "This was never about the theater, was it? I didn't think so. Remember this: a caged bird may sing at first, but with time, you'll only kill its spirit. She'll grow to resent you if she hasn't done so already."

If that were true, it would imply Krissy was bound to her cage with no way of setting herself free. That I'd been the one to place her there against her will with no intention of ever letting her go. That couldn't be further from the truth, and with time, my little angel would be able to stretch her wings and fly. Until her safety was guaranteed, she would remain here.

"I'm hanging up. I don't have time for games."

"Without hearing what I have to offer first? What a shame that would be." He clicked his tongue, disappointed that he wasn't going to hear me beg for it. Charles took my silence as an invitation to speak. "Patrick tried his best to hide the injuries, but I'm no fool, and neither are you for keeping him alive. Release the girl, and you'll have the theater. Release her within the week, and I'll let you finish what you started."

I laughed, and Antonio leaned in more closely. "You've lost your mind."

"In the end, you'll be doing both of us a favor." Then the line disconnected.

I cursed, my voice bouncing off the tall brick building surrounding us.

Deals were meant to be broken by nature. They were presented as a glimmer of hope that promised the best of outcomes but always crumpled when they were within arm's reach. The deal seemed too good to be true unless his hatred toward his brother-in-law took priority over all else. What Charles offered not only guaranteed the theater would be mine but that Krissy would never have to look over her shoulder once she left the safety of my care. She would never have to worry about men like Patrick, who assumed they had any power over her again. I wasn't naïve enough to take the bait, but as I left the dingy alley, I couldn't help but wonder how long the caged bird could last before it stopped singing.

Chapter Thirty-Four

Krissy

Everything hurt. Each muscle ached down to the bone, and deep purple bruises ran across my skin in diagonal lines. Beautiful, little marks that reminded me that last night hadn't been a figment of my wild imagination. Everything had been real. Every kiss. Every whisper in the dark. Every promise he'd made when I'd been unbound and lying in his arms. Last night had been real, and so were the conflicting emotions that tethered me to the man who slept soundly above, completely unaware that I'd even slipped out of bed.

It was nearly noon at this point. Utterly exhausted from the night before, I slept as long as I could with Ghost curled up tight against my chest until she gently woke me up, demanding to be fed. Unlike most mornings, when I would typically wake up to an empty bed and a handwritten note explaining where he'd run off to, there he was, sprawled out on the sheets, sleeping like the dead. I loved this version of him, the one that spoke to his gentle nature and caring heart, but even in his state of vulnerability, the scars, new and old, gave him away.

Whatever happened yesterday had left its mark. Marring him with tiny cuts and deep bruises that made my mind wander with possibilities. It seemed to be all I could think about as I got ready for the day and prepared a late breakfast. Those troubling thoughts buzzed around my head like bees protecting their hive, relentless in nature. It wasn't until I noticed the vase sitting on the piano that the buzzing stopped.

The morning sun bled through the massive windows behind, hitting the vase just right so it twinkled the deepest shade of amber. Placed inside was a bouquet of poppies surrounded by different variations of wildflowers that brought life to the apartment. The sight of the vibrant red flowers made my chest tighten uncomfortably. The sensation didn't ease as I reached for the tiny note propped up against it.

I know this was never part of our plan. Somehow, we ended up here, nonetheless.

P.S. Check the fridge, there's an iced coffee waiting for you.

I stood there, staring at that silly little note for what felt like a lifetime, fixating on the first half of the sentence. All those weeks ago, everything felt so simple. Despite the odds being stacked against me, I sought out the help of a man I knew could very well be the death of me. Our plan had been nothing more than a cruel punishment for someone who undeniably deserved everything that was coming to him. No matter how terribly things had turned out, I couldn't bring myself to regret asking for help. What I regretted was not foreseeing Charles' connection to the Martin family and keeping my friends in the dark. Everything that came after was a tangled mess, so intertwined that I didn't know how to break myself free. With no end in sight, it was safe to say that if I could turn back time, I might have done things differently.

Somehow, we ended up here, nonetheless.

My heart sputtered within my chest as I reread that part. Although Erick had never hidden his intentions, seeing them written down made it all too real. What he was implying was that I had somehow made leaps and bounds in my own personal journey, meeting him halfway despite everything. I wasn't sure that was entirely true, but there was no denying the pull that dragged me toward him. At first, it was nothing more than sexual attraction and the idea of tasting forbidden fruit, but, with time and trust, something more had developed. I couldn't deny it, especially after last night. That didn't make it any less terrifying.

Accepting that felt like standing on the edge of a cliff and consciously taking that first step with nothing to catch my fall and no way of knowing if I'd survive the impact. For most people, I assumed half the thrill was taking that first leap, journeying into the unknown with the hope that the risk would be worth the reward. If they failed, they dust themselves off and make the trek back to the top to do it all over again. I wasn't sure I had the courage to willingly put myself in that situation and accept whatever outcome came next.

The note crumpled in my hand.

As much as I wished I could, I wasn't sure I could jump for Erick, but was jumping headfirst into the unknown the only way to go about this? It couldn't be. I refused to believe there wasn't another alternative. One that allowed me to move at my own pace and ease into whatever was forming between us. One that gave me a fighting chance.

Ghost darted from her place on the couch and raced up the stairs. From this corner of the apartment, I could barely hear it, but Erick was up and moving about the loft. My eyes frantically darted between the flower and the balcony, searching for an answer I wasn't sure I could find. If there was an alternative, shouldn't I have seen it by now?

Without a clear answer, I felt myself backing away from the cliff's edge, step by step.

"You look terrible," I said, leaning up against the door frame.

Erick met my gaze through the bathroom mirror, a smile turning the corner of his lips. He wore nothing more than a pair of navy-blue boxers, giving me a clear view of the bruises running across his ribs that I hadn't seen before in the poor lighting. The beautifully delicate wings sprawled out across his side were hardly visible amongst the dark patches of skin. While the Fallen Angel was depicted with an outstretched hand, in this context, it looked like he was pointing out the physical burden Erick was forced to bear.

The sight of the deep bruises made my stomach lurch.

"Well, I can't say the same about you," he responded. The way his eyes ate up the space between us made me painfully aware of how little I wore. While I didn't bother wearing a bra this morning, Erick didn't bother hiding the fact that he noticed. "You know, I have a hoodie you can borrow if you're cold."

I scoffed. "We can find you a matching pair of sweats while we're at it."

"Touché," was all he said before returning to shaving his face.

Daring to get closer, I entered the bathroom, not entirely sure what I was doing. I propped my hip up against the counter and sipped my coffee while I watched him work. There was so much left unspoken between us after last night, but instead of giving him the upper hand to stir the conversation, I took the reins first.

"I just wanted to say thank you," I cleared my throat, "for the flowers and coffee. You didn't have to get me anything. They're beautiful, though."

He set down the razor and smiled. "You're welcome, little angel. If it puts a smile on your face, then it was worth it."

Out of the corner of my eye, I caught a glimpse of my reflection. There was no hiding it, but I tried to, taking a long sip of my coffee to keep Erick from seeing the blush forming across my cheeks. Whether he noticed or not, he didn't make it as abundantly clear as he had in the past.

"Maybe you should have bought yourself a coffee while you were at it—you look exhausted."

"Well, for one, I think we both know why I didn't get much sleep last night," Erick smirked. With a clean-shaven face and messy hair, he looked strikingly beautiful. "And for the record, I did buy myself a coffee. I drank one sip before someone knocked it out of my hands. Not the best way to start the morning."

"I would argue waking up like that," I gestured toward his ribs, "isn't the best way to start your morning."

He waved me off. "Those are just cuts and bruises. They look worse than they feel."

That was a lie if I'd ever heard one. It was a surprise he could even keep himself upright.

"Here, have some of my coffee. It looks like you could use it more than me."

Erick didn't argue as he reached for the cup, and in that instant, I saw it. All across his wrist were tiny marks that looked as if his skin was melting away, exposing the layer below. The wounds were fresh, still moist, as the pink skin glistened off the bathroom lighting.

I lunged for him, grabbing the backside of his wrist, careful not to agitate the burns. "What the hell happened to you? And don't give me another bullshit excuse."

"Like I said, not a great way to start the morning."

"Jesus, Erick," I hissed, inspecting his skin. "You're going to get an infection if you leave it like this. Where did you put the first aid kit?"

Working in theater for so many years, I'd learned a thing or two about tending to injuries. While most dancers sprained their ankles at some point in their careers, there were instances where things could take a turn for the worse. Two summers ago, Amanda Benowitz tripped in her stilettos and landed headfirst on the edge of a table during rehearsal. In that instance, everyone froze, unsure how to help as blood gushed onto the stage. That's the thing about head injuries: once they start bleeding, they're hard to stop. After that fiasco, Lyra and I swore to take a first aid class so we'd never have to stand around like idiots again. The skill became especially useful while teaching youth dance—children are constantly injuring themselves.

I did my best to make it as painless as possible. Ever so gently, I washed the tiny burns sprawled out across his wrist and applied petroleum jelly in hopes of allowing it to properly heal. Neither of us spoke a word as I focused on dressing the wounds. While I kept my gaze fixed down low, I didn't need to look up to know he was watching me.

"You'll need to clean it a few times a day. If you notice any discoloration or pus, we might need to take you to the doctor, but I think you should be fine if you don't do anything stupid. The burn wasn't too serious to begin with."

"Thank you, Krissy."

"Consider us even."

Erick cupped my cheek, forcing our eyes to meet, making me confront everything I was avoiding up until that moment. The proximity. The tension. The way he consumed the space between us. I was starting to question why I'd even stepped into the bathroom when I knew my intentions weren't clear. There was no way I was willing to jump, yet I didn't move as his thumb brushed over the hint of freckles scattered across my cheek.

"What's wrong, little angel? I can't help but notice something seems off." I leaned into his touch. "Does it have to do with what happened last night?"

My eyes shot open. "No, of course not," I said without thinking. "Last night was...well, last night was something else. I'm fine, I promise. I think I'm just tired. I didn't get much sleep, as you already know."

"You would tell me if something was wrong, right?"

Would you?

"Of course," I lied so effortlessly, hating the way the words rolled off my tongue. It came so easily, which was scary considering how much we'd shared between these walls. Although I wasn't the only one withholding information, was I? The burns were accounted for, but what of the rest of his injuries?

He'll tell you when he's ready. Patience. Stop finding flaws that aren't there.

"Good," he sighed, then paused. "I can't get last night out of my head."

"Neither can I," I answered truthfully.

"I can't get you out of my head."

My breath hitched, and Erick took it as a chance to close the space between us. There was so much I couldn't say or do at that moment, but desire was a language I spoke. A path I could take without fear of becoming entangled in emotion, allowing my body to stop betraying me in ways that revealed my weaknesses. Sex was easy. Sex was safe. It always had been...until last night. That moment of weakness was a fluke, a moment of fragility that was purely carnal need.

I couldn't let that happen again.

His hand slipped to the back of my neck, bracing me for a kiss I expected to be rough and demanding. Instead, it felt like a plea. Soft and gentle, he took his time, savoring the taste and the sensation of our bodies connecting once more.

I stepped closer, pressing my hand between us, longing for urgency. Erick ignored my silent plea, maintaining his slow, deliberate pace even as my hand brushed over his boxers, demanding otherwise. He deepened the kiss, and my mind went fuzzy. I could hardly think as his tongue lapped over mine.

Erick pulled away, and for a moment, I finally could breathe. Or so I thought.

He burrowed his face into the side of my neck, biting and kissing the skin as he struggled to keep himself sane. I pulled him closer, and it was clear that whatever control he once had was slowly slipping away.

"Fuck," he groaned against the column of my neck.

"Does that feel good?" I asked breathlessly, struggling to maintain my own sense of control. Erick hit the sensitive spot just below my ear, and I bit back a moan.

"It's nothing compared to being inside of you, little angel."

Whatever control he'd been clinging to snapped. In one sweeping motion, Erick swung us around and attempted to lift me onto the counter, but failed miserably. Consumed by his own desire, he'd carelessly pushed his body toward a limit he wasn't capable of withholding. I tumbled down with barely enough time to catch myself by the edge of the counter before it could collide with my lower back.

"Shit," he hissed, clutching his ribs with one hand and reaching to protect me with the other. "I didn't–"

"You stupid idiot," I said. "Go lie down on the bed, I'll take care of you."

Erick wasn't the type to admit his weaknesses, but he allowed me to drag him from the bathroom into the bedroom. It nearly killed me to watch as he lowered himself onto the duvet cover with exasperated effort.

"If I remember correctly, I think you told me they look worse than they feel," I teased, lowering my voice an octave while holding up quotation marks. "Doesn't seem like that's the case, does it?"

"Ha. Ha." Erick huffed a laugh. "Fine. They hurt like hell, but as long as I don't agitate them, it's manageable."

Ah. The truth, there it was.

"God, you're stubborn. Now lie back, so I can make you feel better."

Erick flopped back into the mess of pillows near the headboard. One hand propped up behind his head so he could keep a careful eye on me, and the other resting on the chiseled definition of his lower stomach.

"And how exactly do you plan to make me feel better, little angel?" He smirked.

Tracing my finger along my collarbone, I studied his reaction as I let one strap slip down my shoulder. His eyes narrowed in anticipation, but I didn't give in so easily. Grabbing hold of the second strap, I hesitated, making a show out of teasing him. Suddenly, I was transported back to The Lotte, feeding off an adoring crowd, glued to my every move.

He laughed. The type that sounded like a low grumble deep within his throat.

"I think that will work."

The moment I saw his hand disappear below his waistband, I whipped around, letting my curls trail after. Knowing he was playing with himself to the sight of me was the audience I always desired. I fed into it, playing my part as best as I could. From the sway of my hips, the way my fingers traced over my curves, to the sensation of dragging the fabric of my clothing off my body and tossing it aside. By the time I glanced over my shoulder, I was wearing nothing but the lace panties I knew were already soaking wet.

Erick paused, completely bewitched.

"If you take them off, so will I."

It didn't take much to convince him. Erick shucked off the boxers and kicked them aside as I bent forward, hooking my panties with my thumb, and did the same. The sight of Erick lying there, stroking himself in slow, leisurely motions, was enough to bring me to my knees. Erick was a god, a formidable and unforgiving creature that had me crawling on all fours once I reached the foot of the bed so I might worship him.

I took my time, dragging my lips against his golden skin all while he pleasured himself to my touch. It would have been easy to give in, to lay the flat of my tongue just below the base of his shaft and make him bend to my will. Instead, I crawled over his torso and chest until I was positioned with my thighs bracketing either side of his head. Erick wrapped his arms around the underside of my legs for stability and yanked me down.

"Fuck," I slurred. "Shit. Erick."

There was no mercy. No sense of resistance as he devoured me whole.

Erick couldn't speak, but he groaned his approval against my skin.

I felt as if I was falling with no way to catch myself. Even as I clawed at his hair and screamed his name, I couldn't find purchase. Every moment trapped within his hold felt like a lifetime of building and building until he shifted his attention toward my clit, sucking and biting at the sensitive nerve. I rocked my hips and selfishly ground against his tongue, and I felt as if I was starting to crumble atop of him.

"Shit. I'm going to come."

I attempted to pull away. His grip tightened, and so did mine.

"Erick," I warned, giving him a chance to pull away. As stubborn as he was, he didn't.

Waves of pleasure washed over me, hitting their crescendo in an earth-shattering moment. A sob tore from my throat, and everything went a little dizzy. It took some time for the world around me to come back into focus, but when it did, I found his eyes peering up at me.

"Try to remove yourself again, and I'll tie you up next time so you can't," he growled, his lips moist with the remanence of my orgasm. He planted a gentle kiss on the inner part of my thigh, then urged me to move by patting my backside. "Give me a second to reposition myself."

"If you say so," I responded, biting back a smile while I watched him ever so gently position himself up against the headboard. Sitting more comfortably on the mattress, he dragged me into his lap, even though I did most of the work to save him the trouble of injuring himself any more than he already had.

I kissed him breathlessly, raking my fingers through his hair, needing more of him as I might never get enough. I could taste myself on his lips as he reached between us and lined himself up between my thighs.

"Oh, Krissy," he moaned into my mouth as I lowered myself flush against his skin.

Grabbing the headboard for stability, I rocked my hips, feeling the length of his cock slide in one inch at a time. Erick hooked his arm around my hip and forced my tempo slow and steady. There was no end to this desire. No reality in which this man could ever sate that need. I would always need more. I would always need him.

Erick bucked his hips upward, meeting me halfway. I threw my head back and moaned, exposing my throat enough for him to gravitate toward it. Each thrust simultaneously built me up and made me wither away. I couldn't survive this. Erick Destler would be the death of me.

"You make it so easy to fall for you," he whispered, hardly loud enough to make out.

"What?"

We both paused, unsure we'd heard each other correctly.

A long silence followed.

"I think you heard me," was all he said in return.

I felt myself pulling away in more ways than one. I slipped out of his lap with my heart lodged in my throat and frantically searched for my clothes so I could cover up. "Erick, don't," I warned, shaking my head.

Completely unashamed by his physical and emotional vulnerability, he lay on the bed unmoving and watched me pace about the room. I tossed him his boxers, unsure if he could have even gotten them for himself.

"I told you I was always going to be honest with you about my emotions," he reminded me, keeping his voice steady. "There's no point in hiding it. I knew it back at the club when you stole my breath away, and I know it now. Everything in between has only confirmed that I'm not crazy for believing it. Every smile. Every laugh. Every kiss—all of it. I can't help that I'm falling for you..."

The walls seemed to close in on me.

"This all feels like too much for me right now," I admitted, stumbling over my words. "I—I don't want to hear this."

Each gasp of air didn't feel like enough.

"Can I not speak freely about how I feel about you? It's not as if I'm forcing you to reciprocate anything," he snapped, matching my tone. Erick rose to his feet, managing to keep his strength as he towered over me.

"You're confusing lust with love. You aren't falling for me. I promise you that."

He stepped forward, and I stepped back.

The space between us felt suffocatingly small.

"Yes, I am," he insisted. "There aren't many certainties in this world, and I can say without a doubt in my mind that I'm falling for you, Krissy Davis. You can do whatever the hell you want with that information, but you don't get to dictate how I feel."

Whether I liked it or not, I was being pushed into a corner. The further I was forced back, the more distant the cliff's edge became until eventually I couldn't see it at all. Any hope of change was snuffed out in an instant before I even had a fighting chance to try.

"Erick, please do yourself a favor and shut up for once." I cringed. "You have no idea what it feels like to be in love. Don't you dare give me that bullshit."

"I was in love once before." He paused, studying me for a long moment. "Don't look surprised, I had a life before you ever stumbled into it. There were plenty of women who came and went, but above all, there was someone to whom I dedicated three miserable years of my life. And I was prepared to give her the rest until I found out she was sleeping around with someone else. None of that matters now, because when it comes down to it, Krissy, even when I was so certain I knew what love felt like in the past, it was nothing compared to this. *Nothing.*"

The truth felt like a blow to the gut. A devastating final blow that swept me up from where I stood and knocked me across the room. I wasn't sure what hurt more, the fact that he'd had plenty of opportunities to tell me about this mystery woman who had carved such a big hole in his heart but never mentioned her, or the fact that it wasn't me.

"Well, she clearly didn't love you back if she cheated on you," I blurted out, instantly regretting the words as soon as they passed my lips. And as much as Erick couldn't take back his confession, I couldn't take this back either.

I didn't wait for his reaction as I turned to leave. Erick caught me by the wrist, but in his weakened state, he didn't stand a chance. I broke free and fled for the stairs. Just as I was making my descent, I heard him call my name.

"Your self-destructive bullshit isn't going to work on me. I see right through the walls you're trying to build between us," he shouted, his voice shaky. "If you could work yourself around your commitment issues for one *fucking* moment, you might be able to see that someone loving you isn't as crazy as you think it is. Don't give up on us because you're scared." I paused about halfway down, gripping the railing so tight a blistering pain shot up my hand. "I know you're scared, Krissy, but so am I."

I didn't dare glance over my shoulder, because if I did, I knew I would go back on everything I said. "That's the difference between us, Erick." I shut my eyes. "You'll never understand, and I don't expect you to. I can build walls all I like because when it comes down to it, the feelings that you're harboring for me are as fake as the situation we created for ourselves. All of this was pretend. Everything."

There was no escaping him while being trapped in the confines of his apartment. So, I did the best I could by leaving him standing there on the top of the stairs without saying another word.

Chapter Thirty-Five

Erick

Taking it back would be a lie, and hiding it felt just as dishonest, and with one slip of the tongue, all that we had built crumbled at my feet. Every unspoken promise of understanding and compassion. Every bleeding heart left mended. Every insistence that we'd opened up to one another and revealed the rawest, most vulnerable parts of our souls. All of it crumbled around us, and no matter how much I scrambled for those falling pieces, I couldn't stick them back together again. Each attempt only drove a larger wedge between us.

Krissy gripped the railing with unwavering strength.

Darkness had been our greatest companion. Our sole confidant. My sweet little angel used the darkness to her advantage, whispering her most heart-wrenching secrets into that void to make susceptibility somewhat bearable. I ate up every word, clinging to the story of a young, broken girl tossed aside and disregarded by a world that gave little in return when it was kind. Krissy shared all that and more despite every instinct not to. I was willing to grant her patience, time, and understanding in exchange for the same. And while saying what I did was a mistake, given her past, loving her never was.

No, I couldn't take it back. I couldn't hide it, but the real question was: could I let her go? Could I have her walk away from this situation when every instinct was telling me to catch those falling pieces and find a way despite the odds?

"That's the difference between us, Erick." Her grip tightened. While she refused to give me anything other than her back, I could just barely make out the break in her voice. Nearly as broken as the soul she carried around—a spiderweb of cracks that she clung to so desperately, hoping no one would notice she was close to losing it all. The only reason I recognized it so clearly was because it was a mirror of my own past. "You'll never understand, and I don't expect you to. I can build walls all I like because when it comes down to it, the feelings that you're harboring for me are as fake as the situation we created for ourselves. All of this was pretend. Everything."

The spiderweb expanded, stretching out in jagged lines that served no purpose other than to threaten to shatter me altogether. She didn't mean that. She couldn't have...

Krissy didn't give me a chance to respond before making her final descent and disappearing into the kitchen, leaving me standing at the top of the stairs, utterly speechless and clutching my bleeding heart.

All of this was pretend. Everything.

Her voice roared in my ears, echoing until her footsteps dissipated into nothing.

I couldn't move—couldn't speak.

My head spun. So much was happening all at once, I couldn't make sense of a single thing. Gut-wrenching shame ate me from the inside out, frustration nearly drove me to my knees, and rage made the blood beneath my skin burn so furiously it promised to burn me alive. All three slammed into me all at once, leaving me a tangled mess of emotions. One wrong move away from letting them all spill out.

Shame was but a whisper, hardly audible amongst the chaos that had erupted within my mind. It demanded retribution for exposing her insecurities and being the reason distance grew between us. It reminded me of the humiliation of not only this rejection but all that had come before, and I swore I was the reason why. Frustration gnawed at my gut, digging its claws in so deeply it vowed to never let go, refusing to let me forget how little she cared to try to, and how frustrating it had been to care for someone who couldn't recognize how much you'd done for them. I'd given up everything for her. We were on the precipice of an all-out war, and no matter how many lives had already been lost, I did everything to make sure she wasn't one of them. I'd given her my heart, and she gave me little in return.

Loudest of all was rage. It was a selfish little bastard who only cared to be let free. While the others whispered their promises and swore to help if I only gave in, the fury that lay dormant for so long did none of those things. It swelled and expanded like a living beast, growing too large for its own cage. I didn't trust that voice—I never did. So instead of letting any of them win, I forced myself to move. Forced myself to collect my belongings and leave the safety of the loft. Forced myself to pass the bathroom that Krissy had barricaded herself behind without giving in. Forced myself to leave without saying a word, because as tangled as I was, giving in wasn't worth hurting Krissy any more than she already was.

As damned as I was, nothing was worth that.

I wasn't sure how long I walked. A couple of miles, perhaps. The soles of my feet ached, I was cold to the bone, and my surroundings became unrecognizable. Republic City was divided among different districts, each carving a slice of the city to claim as its own. I bobbed and weaved through the imaginary lines until I could make sense of my surroundings once more and found myself standing before a tall brick apartment. It sat atop businesses lining the bottom floor, each of them bustling with life. I bypassed them all, reaching for the door that was squished between a pizzeria and a liquor store.

Antonio buzzed me in a few minutes later.

I wasn't entirely sure what I was doing here, especially when I was so hellbent on putting distance between anyone and everyone mere hours ago. I didn't give it much thought as I mindlessly carried myself up floor after floor. While my head was still flooded with conflicting emotions, the walk had helped, giving me enough composure to face my cousin when I needed him most.

"Did you miss me?" he asked, pouting his lips in mockery. Clinging onto the doorframe with one hand, he swayed, his feet still in the apartment while his upper half hung out in the hallway. "It's only been a few hours since you dropped me off. Can't stay away, can you? I–" As I slowly approached, his eyes narrowed. "You look like shit. More than usual."

"You wouldn't be the first person to tell me that today." My voice felt like sandpaper sliding down my throat, leaving it raw and blistered with each word that broke free. "And don't flatter yourself, I only keep you around because you're a liability on your own."

I shoved past him despite the agonizing pain erupting at my side, knocking his shoulder in the process and sending him stumbling forward to steady his balance. As forcefully as I barged my way into the apartment, the scent wafting about smacked me right back. An explosion of herbs and spices danced around, making me suddenly fatigued after hours of walking the city.

The scent was unmistakable. It was the memory of a past unmarred and filled with potential when ignorance was still bliss.

"Dick," he hissed. "What? Trouble in paradise with our little prima donna?"

I shot him a look, and he raised his hands in surrender.

Beyond the living room was a small cut-out in the wall that gave a glimpse into the kitchen. A small figure danced about the room, checking on the various dishes she was preparing with the same level of care she always dedicated to her craft. The radio had drowned out our conversation, and she wasn't yet aware that Antonio had a guest.

My cousin clasped me on the shoulder when he noticed me lingering in the foyer. "You made it just in time for dinner," he said, ushering me inside as I fought the urge to turn around and leave.

As expected, the moment my aunt realized I was here, she put me to work. Nothing had changed despite the years since the last time I helped in the kitchen. Cooking had always been a production for her, a way to expel her loud and overbearing personality. Aunt Stella thrived in the chaos of a busy kitchen and continued to add to that chaos as the dish progressed. Unlike her bistro, Antonio's apartment lacked the commotion she was used to, so she settled on creating it herself by blasting the radio as we worked. I'd been assigned to cutting vegetables while Antonio sat on the counter and watched. My aunt didn't trust many to help and, unlike her son, I'd been given that honor.

"If you had dropped me off as you promised to, she wouldn't have shown up on my doorstep like this, you know?" Antonio said, then popped a black olive in his mouth.

"We were a little tied up to go visit."

Directly after the call, we'd tossed aside our plans to visit the bistro in lieu of returning to the club—or what's left of it. There were certain protocols and procedures that needed to be handled accordingly after Charles expressed his interest in an exchange. Granted, I wasn't planning to take it at the time, but we needed to be on guard in case his call was nothing more than a ploy. We eventually parted ways, and I found myself flopping into bed alongside Krissy, too exhausted to do anything else. It was a terrible morning, to say the least, and everything since then didn't seem to be much of an improvement.

"I blame you for this," he said. "I love my mother, but I can only handle so much. At least at the bistro, I could have left anytime I wanted. Now, if I want some peace and quiet, I have to kick my poor mother to the curb like an asshole."

We were just far enough away that Aunt Stella couldn't hear us over the music.

"Blame yourself for not visiting her often enough. Maybe then she wouldn't have to show up on your doorstep begging for quality time," I responded. "You should be grateful your mother can still visit you."

Aunt Stella glared over her shoulder. "What are you two boys bickering about over there?"

God, just looking at her made my chest ache. Although she and my mother were a few years apart, the similarities were uncanny. It was like looking into a strange mirror that gave me but a glimpse at what my mother might look like if she were still here. The rest was up to imagination. Would she have loose gray strands of hair brushed back into a braid like her? Would time have crept up as gracefully as it did for her younger sister? Would this room be filled with more laughter and warmth if she were here?

I forced myself to look away and continue working.

"Shit. You know I didn't mean it like that?" Antonio tried to reach for my shoulder, but I jerked away, not caring that our interaction was being watched.

Everyone fell back into rhythm, but the room was more noticeably tense as each of us pretended nothing had happened moments ago. It wasn't until Aunt Stella put the pot on simmer that she turned to Antonio and shook her empty cigarette pack at him. "Do you mind running down to the liquor store and getting me a new one, love? There's money in my purse, take an extra ten and buy yourself something while you're there."

Antonio rolled his eyes and pushed off the counter. As much as he loathed getting off his ass and doing anything productive, he knew he couldn't argue with her. I expected the tension to lessen once he was gone, but it strangely settled there in the kitchen, unmoving.

The flick of a lighter caught my attention. Aunt Stella leaned against the counter with a lit cigarette pressed between her lips. I raised an eyebrow.

She waved me off. "He was going to keep bugging both of us if I didn't get him to leave somehow. So, tell me, caro, what's the matter? Why do you have such a grim expression on that beautiful face of yours?"

There was no way I was having this discussion with her. Not now. Not ever.

"Nothing," I bit out, chopping the onion a little harder than necessary.

"Doesn't sound like nothing," she said, her voice thick with smoke. Up close, the differences between my aunt and my mother were more noticeable. Stella had slightly sharper edges and harder lines in her facial features, while her sister adored the softer side of their genetic pool. It was subtle, but I'd studied enough pictures to remember her face well enough to compare the two. "Does it have to do with the blonde girl Antonio was telling me about?"

I'm going to kill him.

"I don't know what you're talking about."

"He said some young dancer stole your heart. Is that true?"

"No," I said, struggling to keep my composure.

"Did something happen between you two? Did she break your heart? Antonio said she was full of spirit. I wouldn't be surprised if–"

"Jesus Christ," I slammed the knife down on the cutting board, "that's enough, Aunt Stella. You don't get to just stumble back into my life and act like nothing happened, all while you interrogate me on things that are none of your business. If you cared enough, you should have done it earlier when you had the chance."

The apartment stilled. Even the music dulled amongst the ringing in my ears. What little control I had over my own emotions was gone; years of pent-up frustration and sickening memories came spilling out all at once. And once it started, I wasn't sure I could stop because when it came down to it, regaining control wasn't worth taking back all that I had said. There was comfort in pain, there was comfort in darkness, and somehow addressing this heartache distracted from the other.

You were only a child, Erick. Someone should have been looking after you. Someone should have stopped him. Krissy's words rang in my ears, as painful as it was to hear her voice.

"Caro, I do care. How can you say that–"

"I needed you. I know you were too busy with your stupid restaurant and family to realize it, but I needed *you*. And despite being fully aware of everything my grandfather and father were doing to me, you did nothing and let me grow up in that hellhole after my mother died. I was just a child, and I had no one. No one. Do you realize that? I was absolutely terrified and alone.

You had every opportunity to step in and not only help your nephew but also your sister."

She studied me for a long moment, her face unreadable.

"Go sit down at the table. I'll finish up in here, and we can talk once you've cooled off. I refuse to talk to you when you are so determined to be an asshole just because you're hurting inside," she said in a calm tone, completely unfazed by my little outburst.

"I'm leaving. I said what I needed to say."

"Erick, sit down so I can make you some dinner," she said, wiping her hands on her apron and returning to her craft. "You've put off this conversation long enough. It's time you knew the truth." I paused under the archway. "The liquor store downstairs doesn't carry my brand. We'll have plenty of time before Antonio comes back."

My eyes darted between the front door and the dining room table. Two paths presented themselves, one meant slicing old wounds that never quite healed right. Jagged white scars that I hid well enough that even I was convinced they weren't there. And the other path meant creating new ones. I let out a deep sigh and picked the least threatening of the two.

A few minutes later, the music lulled to a standstill, and my aunt emerged from the archway with a handful of dishes. I helped her with the remaining plates of food until we were surrounded by more pasta and salad than the two of us were capable of eating.

"I'm not sure I want to have this conversation with you," I admitted, watching my fork poke a piece of lettuce.

"But you stayed, didn't you? That's a step in the right direction." She sighed. "Okay, look, this isn't going to be easy, but I need you to hear me out and understand where I'm coming from."

I nodded despite it going against my better judgment.

"It was no secret to our family that your mother was sick. We'd known for what felt like a lifetime before things started to take a turn for the worse. Hospital visits became more frequent, and breathing treatments weren't helping like they used to. It was a miracle she'd even had you in the first place, given all the complications," she started. "Despite all of that, she showered you with love and tried to be the best mother she could with what little time she had. She loved you, Erick. I mean it, she truly loved you with all her heart.

"That's why it became so difficult for her to accept that her own body was suffocating her slowly over time. Everyone knew it, even your mother, who refused to acknowledge it aloud. A few years before her respiratory system failed, I pulled her aside to have a discussion about what would happen next. She wasn't exactly happy about that." Aunt Stella choked out a dry laugh. "I warned her about what might happen to you after she was gone, and she screamed at me until her face turned blue. It wasn't a pretty conversation, but it was necessary when she had a child's future to worry about, but she didn't want to listen to me. I asked your mother to grant me full custody, and she said no."

I met her eyes, startled by the confession.

"You were going to adopt me?"

"Of course, I would have taken you in if it meant you'd be happy with my family. I knew there would be no life for you with your father once she passed on, but your mother was blinded by love. Gianna started to ignore my calls and avoid me at family gatherings—something must have finally snapped because she told your father about our conversation, and that's when things became hostile. My intentions were to always protect you from the future your father so desperately wanted you to have, but he had other plans.

"He threatened us, swore he had all the power, money, and resources to hunt me down if I even tried to take you away. I couldn't even call the police or CPS because of the connections he had with law enforcement. It was subtle at first, but he started to limit how often I could see you. He was keeping us apart, and I was terrified, Erick. You have to understand that, but I fought back in whatever ways I could. Keeping you behind for Sunday school, sending Antonio on playdates to defuse the tension at home, and even forcing your grandfather to have dinner with us once a week. It wasn't ideal, but I did all I could to keep an eye on you and bide my time until I could do something more significant."

A lump grew in my throat, swelling so furiously that it felt as if I was gasping for fresh air.

"So, instead, you just sat back and watched him do all of this to me?"

Aunt Stella chewed at her cuticles, tears brimming in her eyes. "I wish I had a better excuse, but I was in my early twenties with a kid and a deadbeat baby daddy who had just walked out on us. I was in over my head and had absolutely no chance against someone like your father. I failed you, Erick, and more importantly, I failed your mother. I know it might not mean anything now, but I'm sorry."

We sat in silence for a long time after that. What she was implying changed the entire course of my understanding, and while it didn't excuse her compliance, it was enough to make me question everything I knew about my aunt and the parts of my childhood I'd romanticized in my head. There was too much to unpack for one conversation, too many questions, too many accusations, and too many painful emotions that felt as if there would never be a reality in which I could stitch together the hole in my chest and pretend as if it wasn't bleeding with every step I took.

Antonio would be back any minute, and I would lose my

window of opportunity to speak to her alone. I broke the silence, desperate for more of her time.

"She had a chance to protect me, and she didn't take it. I want to hate her so much for it, but I just can't..."

With my elbows propped up on the dining room table, I sank my face into my hands.

"You and me both," she mumbled as she leaned back in her chair. The old wood creaked with the added weight. "Love blinds us. It keeps our senses dull to things that seem so obvious on the outside looking in. Your mother and father loved each other with such a passion that it made her blind to the type of man he was because, to her, he was everything she could have asked for. Gianna was distracted by the promises he made, the protection he gave her, and most of all, the family they created together. To her, it felt like a betrayal that I would even ask. How dare I demand she hand over her only son when the love of her life, the man she trusted with all her heart, would take care of you rather than of me? I desperately hoped I was being paranoid, that I was seeing things that weren't there, but after your mother died...well, let's just say he never seemed the same after he lost your mother."

I let out a long sigh and pulled my hand away from my face, finding that she was watching me. Those deep brown eyes of hers were silently searching for any sign of forgiveness or understanding. I couldn't give her what she wanted—not now, at least.

"How can you sit back and watch someone make the wrong choice when you know their actions will hurt them in the end?" I asked, knowing I wasn't asking about my mother anymore.

She took my hand, and I felt the rhythm of my heart beat out of place.

"For those that we love, there is only so much we can do before we have to take a step back and let them learn from their own mistakes. Forcing them to think a certain way will only make them resent you more. In time, they will learn for themselves, and if they don't...well, that was never your burden to carry in the first place, was it?"

The weight of those words hung heavy on my shoulder, weighing me down as I trekked through the snow to get home. If those parting words were to be believed, it gave few options other than sacrificing everything for a glimmer of hope. I knew what I had to do, but I wasn't sure I had the courage to let go.

Chapter Thirty-Six

Erick

I couldn't go home. The Lord knows I tried. I got as far as the lobby before I bypassed the elevators and made for the parking garage instead. Call me a coward, but I wasn't prepared to fully process all of the information my aunt tossed my way, let alone what that meant for Krissy and me. Rather than being where I wasn't wanted or forced to have a conversation that we weren't ready to discuss, I hopped in my car and mindlessly drove until I could make sense of the numbness that tingled through my limbs. Never in my life had I felt so shaken up. Never had I felt so unsure of myself and my understanding of the people around me. The lack of certainty felt like a foreign entity sliding under my skin, lurking just close enough to be seen, but I had no idea how to remove it. The closest thing I could compare it to was a bloodsucker—a leech that took and took and took, threatening to leave me half the man I was before our parasitic relationship began.

With nowhere else to go, I found myself in the district. Flickering neon lights and crowded bars paved the way down either side of the street. Despite the cold, young couples and groups of friends tossed on their warmest coats, braved the elements, and ventured off into the night in order to enjoy all the city had to offer. Normally on a Friday night, there would be a line wrapped around the building, swarmed with people trying their luck at getting in, but amongst the organized chaos and glittering lights, Don Juan looked like a blemish on the district. While there hadn't been any exterior damage, the lack of life made our portion of the block look dull in comparison.

It took a few more minutes, but eventually, I found a parking spot and let myself in.

Viewing the building from the outside was misleading. It stood like a mighty oak, unmoving and completely intact, with no signs of damage besides the notice on the door from the police. Inside, the club looked like an empty shell of its former self. While I was grateful the explosion was merely a fear tactic and most of the damage was cosmetic, something about that night had snuffed out the charm and soul of the building. Debris had been swept, blood had been mopped up, and broken furniture had been tossed away, yet it wasn't enough to restore it to its former glory. It would take months to open the doors once again. Money wasn't a problem, and I would do all I could to make that happen sooner rather than later, but the club was the least of my worries.

In the center of the dance floor was a chair lying on its side. I picked it up and set it right before taking a seat. Tilting my chin up, I let the back of the chair support my neck as I stared up into the darkness of the high ceilings and let out a shaky breath that I'd been holding in for quite some time. The silence that followed was nearly suffocating; it took everything not to feed into that nothingness and let all that I was suppressing win for but a second.

The building groaned in response, seeming to mock the silence. From time to time, the building would make strange noises when it didn't think anyone was listening. The closing staff was adamant it was a residual haunting that I wasn't entirely convinced was real. It did make me wonder if my great-grandfather was still here.

It was almost poetic thinking about his intention behind creating this place. Rosita Blanchet's relationship with her husband was a product of its time, where men took the privilege of sharing a life with another as an invitation to beat and cheat their way through their marriage. My great-grandfather created a safe haven for a woman that had captured his heart, and all he was given in return was a rivalry that outlived him—yet another instance of how love can blind those who least expect it.

It felt like that might be the true Destler curse, falling for a woman that we had no business pursuing. My great-grandfather chased after a married woman, praying for the day she'd leave her husband despite it being a time when divorce was out of the question, my father married a woman he knew he would have to bury one day, and I found myself pining for a woman that wanted nothing to do with me because of my inability to keep my damn mouth shut.

All of this was pretend. Everything.

I refused to believe that was true. Love may dull our senses, but it doesn't manipulate and alter our understanding of the people we choose to care for or create things that simply aren't there. Our weeks of isolation had proved that time and time again. It was real in the dead of the night while I held her tight, feeling as if the world was crumbling around us. It was real when we confided in one another, fearing that no one would ever listen. It was real each and every time she made me smile, despite swearing I would never find happiness. Krissy was the light that had always been absent from my life; she was the hope that would bring a better tomorrow, and she was the promise that there was a life worth living. To live without that light meant to lose a piece of myself in the process and give up on the only woman who had made any of this worth a damn.

Love may have blinded me. It kept me numb to the fact that Krissy might not be willing to care for me in the same way I did, but it never, and will never, make me a liar. All of it was real. Every damn thing. However, with that being said, what good was forcing someone to recognize their mistakes when they weren't ready to do so? Was it worth potentially losing her forever?

It was well past midnight when I pulled into the parking garage. Nearly fifteen hours had come and gone since Charles made his offer, leaving less than a day and a half to make a final decision. It was so simple at first. I had planned to decline his offer until I could find an alternative route that would ensure her safety— perhaps something involving Elijah's confession. But with each minute that ticked by, bringing us closer to that deadline, things no longer seemed as easy as they once had.

"Damn it," I muttered under my breath, entering the apartment.

I had every intention of sneaking into the apartment, hoping that Krissy was well asleep by now, except that couldn't be further from the truth. A somber melody drew me closer, compelling me to move against my will. I still had time to turn around and leave without her noticing, but after the way we left things, I needed to know if she was okay.

I let the hauntingly beautiful music guide me toward the living room. Krissy sat at the bench, wearing a pair of black leggings and a stolen gray hoodie from the closet, her posture stiff as a board. Her normally vibrant blonde hair clung to either side of her face in wet clumps, partially dried near the ends. The strands that framed her face blocked out the majority of her features, but from where I stood under the archway, I could just barely make out the tightness in her jaw and the downturn of her lips.

If she sensed my approach, she didn't show it.

Aunt Stella was a gracious host and refused to let me leave without some food to take home, never mind the fact that it had been sitting in my car for hours and was now disgustingly cold. I set it down on the island, hoping Krissy might heat it up for later. All it took was one look at the kitchen sink to know she hadn't set foot in here tonight. Normally, when she cooked, it was as if a bomb went off. Dishes were piled up in the sink, tiny crumbs of food were scattered about the granite countertop, and pans were left on the stove with leftovers for me to steal when I came home after a long day. The kitchen was spotless, and that didn't sit right with me knowing she hadn't eaten.

A small tapping drew me away from my thoughts. I glanced over my shoulder to find Krissy sliding across the bench. In a clear invitation to join, she patted the empty space to her left, all while keeping her gaze locked down on the ivory keys.

I guess she did notice after all.

I was at a loss for words as I sat down, struggling to break the heavy silence that clung to the air. I spat out the first thing that came to mind. "I brought back food if you're hungry."

Her fingers paused for a second before returning to their somber tune; only then did I realize how erratic my heart was beating.

"I hope you know buying me things isn't the way to my heart," she said, hardly loud enough to hear over the music. "I couldn't care less about things like that."

"I know," I responded. "It's not like I know what is."

I hardly intended for it to sound so cruel, but there was a bitterness laced in each word that slipped free. Krissy winced. It was subtle, but the wet strands of hair that broke free were a dead giveaway. Out of habit, I reached out and pushed them behind her ear, realizing my mistake too late. I might have pulled away had it not been for what I found without her hair hiding her face.

"Have you been crying?"

The whites of her eyes were bloodshot, and the skin around them was swollen.

"Don't worry, I wasn't crying over you," she said, leaning out of my touch just far enough that my fingers skimmed the round- ness of her cheeks, then fell right back into my lap. "I wouldn't waste my time doing that."

It felt like a punch to the gut, even if I wasn't entirely sure it was true.

"Then tell me what did, so I can help."

"Stop," she mumbled, shutting her eyes and savoring the tense silence that followed. "Please stop, you're doing it again. All I wanted to do was make sure your wrists were okay, but you're doing it again."

"Krissy–"

"This," she shouted. "You do this. You stumble into my life and pretend that you can fix all of my issues in the blink of an eye. You pretend everything will be fine as long as we stay between these walls and isolate ourselves for God knows how long. I came to you for help when I had no one else to turn to, but all it has done is create more issues. So much so that I can't even tell fiction from reality. I don't know what's real and a product of our circumstances."

She turned away slightly, blinking away her tears, hoping I wouldn't notice.

"I'm so tired, Erick. I'm tired of putting my entire life on pause for something I have no control over anymore. I miss my friends, my career, and the life I left behind. For almost three years, I'd dedicated *everything* to that theater and was given little in return. Then, as soon as I'm finally appreciated for all that I did, I'm running from the damn place with my tail between my legs. Everything was perfect until I fell for Patrick's tricks, and all I have done since is pay for that mistake."

"It's not your fault," I choked out.

She huffed out a dry laugh.

"It's not your fault," I repeated, gently placing my hand atop hers where it rested on the piano. Like a frightened deer, she stared at our point of connection, unsure of herself and whether or not she should pull away. "It's not your fault, Krissy. There are so many wonderful things that make you who you are, and your strength has always been something I've admired. You've always been a fighter, from the very beginning, and I think that's why it's so difficult to accept what Patrick has done to you. He took some of that power away.

"Abuse is never the victim's fault. I understand it might be hard to realize now, but in time, I hope you do. This was never your fault; Patrick made the conscious decision to lie and manipulate your relationship. It's his fault. It always has been."

Krissy refused to look away from our hands as she spoke.

"He never hit me. I wasn't abused."

"Little angel," I sighed, brushing my thumb over her knuckle. "Abuse comes in many forms. Someone doesn't have to lay a hand on you in order to leave a mark. Nor does it matter if it happened only once or a hundred times. Abuse is abuse. He was only starting to show his true colors. Take it from me, I would know..."

Scars and bruises aren't terribly difficult things to find. They are irrefutable evidence that could be seen and reported by others, but what of the scars that aren't visible? Concealed deep within, these wounds grow and expand like a living beast, threatening to consume us all. External wounds may heal over time, but internal ones don't mend quite as easily.

"I—I..." was all she could muster up.

"I know, little angel. I know."

Her hand slipped from mine, and a piece of me left with her.

"I think I want to be alone right now."

I felt her slipping away. Part of me wanted to take her in my arms and remind her that she didn't need to face any of this alone. Somewhere along the way, she'd convinced herself that this was the rule, not the exception. Krissy Davis lived an extravagant life filled with unruly parties that never seemed to end and lively friends that fed into the chaos; all of it was a distraction for the bits and pieces of her life that she tackled on her own or flat-out ignored out of sheer stubbornness. For once, I wanted her to understand that asking for help wasn't a weakness. I wanted her to know I was there for her.

The other part of me knew I was already overstepping my boundaries. I knew I had caused enough heartache between us for one day. So, I let her leave, hoping to give her the space she needed.

Chapter Thirty-Seven

Krissy

Erick didn't come to bed that night. I didn't expect him to, but it still hurt, nonetheless. Ghost was slightly conflicted and bounced around between the loft and the couch, unsure of where to be. Each time she jumped off the bed, I checked the time and made a mental note of how long I'd been mindlessly lying there with no hope of falling asleep. It didn't matter how mentally or physically exhausted I was; rest never came my way.

As dawn crept through the apartment and a new day approached, I felt too numb to pry myself out of bed and enjoy it. There didn't seem to be any point in doing so.

Compared to the woman who had made a deal with the devil all that time ago, I hardly recognized myself now. Years of suppressing a past filled with neglect and trauma were manageable when I could fill my life with exciting distractions. Without a class to teach, a party to attend, or a show to star in, it became increasingly difficult to push away emotions I kept locked away for a reason, especially when Erick was so adamant about facing them.

Imagine a tiny wooden box fitted with a large brass lock.

Before, that lock had enough strength to withstand all that rattled around within it, but over time it began to weaken. Now it shook with such fury, I wasn't sure how much longer the lock could withstand.

Of course, I knew the solution to handling the wooden box. I was stubborn, not stupid. Malik had mentioned plenty of times that our insurance covered professional help, but that meant handing over the key to someone I didn't know and trusting them to care for it when I couldn't even do that with people I was much closer to. Handing over the key meant addressing a myriad of issues: never properly dealing with the grief that riddled my soul, the years I wasted away in foster care waiting for something that would never come, replacing self-worth with stardom, the fear of giving myself over to someone just for them to leave me in the end, or worse, someone forcing me against my will to stay.

Jesus Christ, I was a mess.

It wasn't as if I wasn't aware of everything weighing heavily on my shoulders. It was an entirely different thing to willingly step out of my comfort zone and address it properly. Which was something I wasn't prepared to do just yet—maybe never.

In hopes of avoiding the unavoidable, I buried myself in a heap of covers and refused to leave until I was certain he was gone. Only then did I go in search of a different type of distraction that wouldn't take so much strength to keep the broken pieces from slipping free. Drinking was a double-edged sword; one end allowed for a level of dissociation that kept you numb, while the other threatened to knock the box over and care less if it shattered. It was a risk either way, but I took it, knowing anything was better than feeling so empty.

All was going according to plan as I curled up on the couch with a bottle of whiskey and last night's takeout—that was until I started flipping from channel to channel, trying to find something mindless to watch. I was hoping for trashy reality TV or maybe an old movie, but stumbled across the end of a news segment instead.

The bottle nearly slipped from my hand as Samantha Wilson stared back at me. I could hardly believe what I was seeing. Haloed around her curls was the outline of the theater in the background.

"You can only imagine my surprise when they invited me back, Barbara," she laughed. "It took some time for me to recover mentally and physically from the accident, and though I am still mourning his loss, I know my dear Aiden would want me back on that stage."

The reporter reached for a box of tissues and offered her one as a tear slipped free and rolled down her cheeks, her foundation ruined in the process.

"Well, Miss Wilson, we're all excited to see your long-awaited return. Mr. Hoffman will surely be watching over you tonight," the reporter said, patting her on the knee before the camera cut back to the studio.

"Thank you, Barbara. What a touching story," the news anchor cooed. "Now back to the scandal unfolding in Ohio's 9th district–"

I turned off the TV.

And the tiny wooden box rattled.

The room was spinning, and so was my mind. The alcohol was hardly helping, but that didn't stop me from trying. It wasn't until the bottle was nearly half gone that I found myself sitting on the floor perfectly still, every muscle in my body so tight that they were starting to cramp up. With my knees tucked to my chest, I stared at the far wall, unblinking for so long that I wasn't sure I could move even if I tried.

Ghost heard him before I did. She leaped from the couch to the floor so she could greet Erick as he tried to slip into the apartment in the dead of night, obviously trying to avoid me. I forced myself to blink several times, slowly returning to reality.

Erick stopped dead in his tracks, noticing the strange figure sitting in the dark. Dressed more casually than he normally did, Erick wore a pair of black jeans and a forest green hoodie that reeked of weed. I had no idea where he had been, but I knew what he was doing.

"Did you know?" I asked, refusing to look at him.

Out of the corner of my eye, I noticed him shift from one foot to the other.

"You're going to have to be more specific than that. Did I know what?"

"Did you know," I swallowed the lump in my throat, "that I've been replaced? Did you know that Samantha Wilson was headlining and didn't tell me? Apparently, it's all everyone can talk about. The *long-awaited return* of a grieving star to honor her dead lover. How poetic," I spat out.

He studied me from a distance, his eyes instantly finding the half-empty bottle of imported whiskey clutched tight to my chest. "Antonio sent me the article earlier today. So yes, but not much longer than you," he admitted.

I let out a humorless laugh and attempted to stand, not as gracefully as I had hoped for.

"The entire point of making this stupid deal in the first place was to help my career, not hurt it. I understand the theater had to fill the role, but of all the people to replace me with, they picked her," I slurred, slamming my palm to my chest. "I saved that theater, and this is how they repay me?"

Erick took a cautious step forward. "Krissy, you're drunk."

"You aren't listening. They replaced me, Erick."

He took another. "Whether or not they replaced you is irrelevant. You've been missing for a while now. They needed to hire someone in order to keep paying the bills, Krissy. They're doing it out of necessity, not to be cruel to you. And regardless of any decision they make, I'll have the power to kick Samantha off the stage, or anyone else for that matter, as soon as I take ownership of the theater," he explained, keeping his voice level and calm as if one wrong move might spook me. "The alcohol isn't helping you think clearly, little angel."

The conversation was quickly taking a turn for the worse on my part, but I didn't have it in me to care. The theater was merely the tipping point—the final blow to a seemingly endless string of unfortunate events. And Erick just so happened to be the poor bastard caught in the crossfire.

I took another swig from the bottle out of pure spite.

"I don't believe you. You can keep whispering all the sweet nothings to your heart's content, but everyone eventually leaves or tosses me aside. My foster parents did. The theater did. What's stopping you from doing the same once you have ownership?"

What's stopping you from leaving me if I take the final leap?

"That's not how this plays out, nor would I ev–"

"The funny thing is, I don't even know how long I've been *missing*. Has it been weeks? Months? I lost track of time, yet no matter how long I spent trapped between these walls, you continue to reassure me that everything will work out. How much more do I have to lose before I can leave? Huh?"

"I'm working on it," he answered, brows furrowed.

"Are you? Because it really doesn't seem like it."

He took two long strides before he was suddenly towering over me. The darkest corners of the living room welcomed him like an old friend, enveloping all of his figure besides the white glow of his ever-present scar. *Someone doesn't have to lay a hand on you in order to leave a mark.* Erick wore his with pride, letting it symbolize all that he'd overcome, while mine wasn't so easily seen. I wondered if there would ever be a time when I could do the same.

I wasn't sure who moved first, whether I anticipated what was coming for me and stepped back to keep the bottle out of reach, or the reverse. What I didn't expect was for him to grab either side of my face and draw me back in.

"Are you scared I'm going to leave, Krissy?" he challenged, my name sounding like a prayer on his lips. "Or do you want me out of your life? Which one is it, because it can't be both? I know you don't want to hear this, but I think it's easier for you to push me away first than wait around and find out whether or not I'll leave. It saves you the heartbreak you're anticipating but strips you of any happiness we could share.

"I told you this once, and I'll tell you again—it doesn't matter how long it takes, find me when you're ready. Find me when all of this is over, and you have the clarity you're searching for outside of these walls. Find me when you realize all that we share isn't a product of our circumstances but the reason that we were brought together. You have my heart, Krissy Elizabeth Davis, and it doesn't matter if it takes months, even years. It will always be yours."

The bottle slipped free, landing on the rug with a loud thud but completely intact.

I was falling, and all I could do was grab either wrist and hold on to him for dear life.

Walls were more easily built up than they were taken down. Erick, of all people, could see right through them. I hated him for being the one to call me out for it. And I especially hated him for threatening the very integrity of their strength. I imagined what it might be like to strip them down brick by brick—what it might be like if he were there to help me. As much as I dreamt of that type of freedom, I wasn't of sound mind, and as long as I was still trapped in this situation, I didn't trust myself to make the right choice.

"I can't promise you anything," I whispered, eyes shut, nails digging into his flesh. "I might very well leave this apartment and never look back. I hope you understand that."

Erick shifted his grip so he was cradling the back of my head and drawing me in closer. Selfishly, he kissed the top of my head before embracing me. Where words weren't enough, and promises could be broken, I gave in to the need to be closer without thinking twice.

"Then I'll die knowing what little time we shared was the happiest I'd ever been. I'll always cherish what we had, and pray that whatever happiness you find after this is enough." I couldn't see his face, but by the thickness of his voice, I knew he was choking up. It took all the strength I had left not to look because if I did, I wasn't sure I could hold myself accountable for what would happen next.

"I just want to go home, Erick. Please."

He kissed the top of my head.

"I know, little angel. I know. Tomorrow I'll have a solution to our problems."

Chapter Thirty-Eight

Patrick

The unintentional reminders of her were everywhere. While they were easier to avoid at home, they were inevitable at work. Little pieces of her seemed to be embedded in every corner of this place. There was no escaping her, especially when I drowned myself in work to keep distracted. It was difficult to stay positive when so much time had passed, but the theater gave as much as it took away. As much as I'd grown to love my role at this company, the people here were insufferable. The theater distracted me in the ways it needed to, but created more issues in the process.

I made my way backstage, hoping for a moment of peace and possibly a smoke break. It was a nasty habit I rarely partook in, but something about interacting with Samantha, Malik, and Lyra all at once meant it was necessary. Since Samantha's return, there had been a shift in balance that everyone felt but refused to acknowledge–

"Patrick," a deep voice called out amongst the masses.

The crowd parted like the Red Sea, and Charles ate the distance between us. Since assuming ownership by marriage, my brother-in-law had only been to the theater a handful of times. It was likely that an unannounced visit from him wasn't going to be a good thing, especially when my sister was nowhere to be found.

"Salut," I said, plastering a fake smile on my face.

"Salut, frère," he responded, slightly distracted by the theater manager passing on our left, doing his best to keep his head down and nose to his clipboard. "Malik, we're going to use your office if you don't mind."

"Go right ahead," was all he said before scurrying off. It was difficult to make out, but I could have sworn I heard him mumbling to himself about not having much of a choice in the matter.

"Rehearsal starts in twenty minutes. I hope to return before then."

"Hmm, yes," he hummed while leading the way. "Glad to see you're enjoying your new position. Seems like you've found your passion."

We made ourselves at home in Malik's office. I found a seat while Charles snooped through paperwork on the other side of the cold metal desk. The office was cramped, to begin with, and it might not have been as bad if Malik didn't keep his space the way he did. Calling it an organized mess would have been a compliment. There was stuff everywhere. All four walls were consumed by vintage posters and framed newspaper clippings. The pop of color made Charles' charcoal gray suit dull in comparison to the vibrant energy of the room.

"Does my sister know you're here? I haven't heard from her in a while. Is she well?"

He placed the knick-knack he'd been examining back down and turned his full attention to me. "You need to understand she isn't ignoring you because she wants to. She's at a crossroads with you—give her time, and she'll be fine," he assured. "And to answer your first question, no, she doesn't know I'm here, and I'd like to keep it that way."

Secrecy is the perfect way to uphold a marriage.

"I don't like lying to my sister," I admitted, hoping he would catch on.

"It's not lying if you don't bring it up." He paused. "Look, Patrick, I don't want her to worry any more than she already does. Destler contacted me, and he's ready to trade over the girl. I think we can both agree it's in our best interests to protect Josephine."

For the first time in weeks, I felt as if I could breathe. Rich oxygen filled my lungs, and it nearly drove me to my knees. In a world that was so determined to keep us apart, an end to our torment was nearly here. Krissy was coming home, and it took what little strength I had to mask my excitement for the sake of the conversation.

"Josephine was the mastermind behind purchasing the theater. Doesn't she have a right to know what we're doing? She's a big girl—you give her less credit than she deserves. My sister can handle this and anything else you throw her way."

"Destler wants you to make the exchange—not me." My smile faded, and ever so slowly, I could feel the blood drain from my face. Charles took note of the change and continued speaking despite my having trouble comprehending what I just heard. "He won't give her over unless you're there with the paperwork for him to sign. Those are his demands. We either take it or leave it."

I'm on my feet in an instant, pacing about the room in short, meaningful strides.

"Destler has threatened me multiple times, and he has made it perfectly clear he doesn't want me anywhere near Krissy," I admitted. "When and where does he want to meet?"

"Don Juan, the day after tomorrow."

I choked out a laugh, feeling delusional at this point. "It's a damn trap, Charles. I'm not risking my life for this. Are you mad?"

I'd do anything to ensure Krissy's safety, but walking into a situation where I would put not only myself but the woman I love in danger was out of the question. It was a suicide mission, and we both knew it.

"I know," he said, crossing his arms. "You're right, it's a trap and a terrible one at that. That's why we'll level the playing field."

"You'd better have something good in mind, because I refuse to put both Krissy and myself in a situation where either of us could get hurt, especially over a silly feud neither of us has anything to do with."

Charles laughed, scratching at his beard while considering the statement.

"She's been in danger this whole time." The polaroids were enough to confirm that. "You'll be lucky to find her the way you left her. There are whispers that Destler corrupted your little star. Whether they're rumors or not, it's entirely up to you to find out."

The term corruption could take on a million different meanings in all types of contexts. Based on the smug look on his face, I knew he only meant one. I wanted to strangle him for implying such a horrendous thing, but I needed to preserve what little trust and understanding we had for one another if I wanted Krissy back.

"Suggest anything of that nature again, and I swear to God I'll—"

Charles raised his hand. "Easy, Patrick. Surely, they're just rumors, and nothing more."

"What's the plan?" I bit out.

From his waistband to the table, the handgun landed with a thud.

"Do you know how to use one?"

Of course not.

That didn't stop me from assuring my brother-in-law that I was a quick learner and would have no trouble handling such a weapon with a little practice. After rehearsal, we would go to the range outside of the city so I could get familiar with shooting a gun. And although I wasn't comfortable with such a responsibility, it felt necessary. Walking into Don Juan without any form of protection would be a death wish.

"Per his request, you'll enter the club with four of my men serving as protection, plus the lawyer. Once everyone is disarmed and searched, you will present the paperwork and handle the rest. My portion will already be signed and notarized for the fraction Josephine and I own. All you'll have to do is sign over yours to Destler," he explained, fishing out a pack of cigarettes and a lighter from his suit pocket. "See, Destler was smart in demanding we make the exchange on his territory. However, for some reason, he fired a good deal of his father's men once he assumed his role. He is wildly understaffed but flaunting his legacy as if he weren't. Eliminating anyone he has posted outside the building won't be terribly difficult. The challenging part will be getting you to the subbasement."

He offered me a smoke, and I took it.

"Thanks to you and Josephine, we now know the location of the theater entrance. If we can corner them in the tunnel, I can close in on both ends. All you have to do is promise him whatever he wants to keep him distracted until we have our window of opportunity. The tunnel will provide you both safe passage, so I can do the rest."

In theory, it couldn't be simpler. Play along and pretend all is well. Make empty promises to gain his trust. And wait for

Charles to strike so Krissy and I can flee into the tunnel system, where he will be waiting for us. That didn't account for the millions of variables that could alter the course of the night; any number of things could go terribly wrong in a split second, but what other choice did I have? I lacked the resources and strength that Charles had built an empire on. With so many failed attempts to rescue my dear Krissy, I was now at the mercy of two men I didn't trust.

I lit the cigarette and savored the burn, knowing this hell was almost over.

Chapter Thirty-Nine

Erick

Lying is necessary from time to time—lies protect us until they don't. Telling Krissy I was falling for her was among the few. Like a fallen angel, I had plummeted from the sky and landed hard. From heaven to earth. The same had happened with Krissy—my time falling had passed, and I was undeniably in love with her. I thought there would be some kind of warning beforehand, but the moment I wrapped her in my arms and told her I'd wait a lifetime for her to be ready, I knew it for certain. Perhaps I'd been keeping the truth from myself to protect some part of my heart and reassure her hesitation, but lying wouldn't protect me anymore.

As much as it hurt to step back from this, I knew it was nothing shy of the truth when I promised her all that I did. I would wait for Krissy—and if she never came, then so be it. What little time we shared would never be enough, but if it meant she would be happy, then I would make that sacrifice for her.

Antonio followed me into the apartment, staying a few steps behind to give me space. Compared to the outside hallway, the loft felt suffocatingly hot and only grew warmer the further I climbed up. Krissy was lying in bed, her nose in a sign language book I'd purchased after meeting Damon, so I could teach myself the basics. Ghost was curled up in her lap and barely gave me a passing glance as I rounded the bed—I swear that cat forgot I existed the moment she stepped into our lives. She continued reading as I found a spot on the edge of the bed and prepared myself for what was to come next. I tugged at the collar of my shirt, feeling a bit constricted before finding the courage to speak.

"We are making the exchange in an hour," I announced with a heavy heart. "All you have to do is pack up your belongings and give them to Antonio so he can drop them off on your doorstep."

The book slipped from her fingers, and for the first time in what felt like forever, she smiled. The sight of it crushed me while simultaneously piecing me back together. On one hand, seeing her genuinely happy felt like an answer to a prayer, and on the other, it meant facing something I wasn't prepared for.

"Holy shit, you're dead serious. This is happening?"

"I made you a promise, didn't I?"

"Okay. Give me twenty minutes!"

She sprang out of bed with a type of excitement I realized had been terribly absent from her life here lately. It was one thing to accept the truth, and it was an entirely different beast seeing her light up the way she did, which only confirmed my worst fear. I did my best to bite my tongue and keep distracted while she sprinted around the apartment collecting her things. No matter how much it ached to see her smile, I knew I was making the right choice.

Twenty minutes quickly turned into twenty-five, then thirty minutes. Krissy had left her mark in this apartment; tiny reminders of her were everywhere. From the books she left lying on the island to the worn t-shirt on the floor, to the bathroom counter covered with skin care products. Each of them was collected and neatly packed away, making the apartment feel empty and dull without them. Antonio and I sat in silence patiently waiting for her to finish, hardly speaking a word to one another. When Krissy finally finished, she handed off the bag to my cousin.

"Jesus Christ, this thing is heavy," Antonio said, attempting to bicep curl the bag. "Don't worry, I'll only snoop through your stuff a little."

I spared a glance at the empty apartment. Nothing had changed, but it was as if Krissy had taken all the life from this cold place and stuffed it away with the rest of her belongings. Someone would have to look after Ghost because there was no way I was sleeping here tonight.

"Why don't you wash my clothes while you're at it, perv," she shot back.

"If anyone is a perv, then it's–"

"Antonio," I snapped before he could finish the thought. "Leave."

"Fine. Fine. I'll meet you two at the club after I stop by the laundromat." Antonio winked at Krissy, and I felt a pang of jealousy as he slipped out the door.

Her gaze lingered on the exit. "Shouldn't we be leaving too?"

Ghost seemed to sense the shift in the room and began relentlessly meowing as if she knew this might be her last time with Krissy. Like little tiny pleas for her to stay, she brushed up against her shins and meowed continuously. Krissy obliged by picking her up and placing a heartfelt kiss atop her head.

Rounding the island, I sat down and made myself comfortable.

"I told you an hour so you would have plenty of time to get ready," I explained. "We have an additional forty minutes until we have to be at the club for the exchange."

She cradled Ghost with such tenderness it made my heart

twist. After giving her another gentle kiss, she met my gaze. "Might as well tell me you don't trust me to be on time, Erick, instead of giving me the wrong time on purpose," she said, shaking her head and rolling her eyes. We were close enough to make out the hints of gray and green in the outer ring of her irises. So much emotion resided there without her knowing; all I had to do was peer into them in order to truly know how she was feeling.

"This has nothing to do with trust—I'd trust you with my life if I were being completely honest with you," I wholeheartedly admitted. "I wanted to give us time to discuss what happens next." Her pupils slightly widened, giving her away. "Before we enter Don Juan, there are a few things you need to know. Blanchet was the one to reach out and agree to my terms—not Patrick. For whatever reason, Blanchet is eager to put this whole mess behind us and give me more than I originally asked for in exchange for your safe return."

"Sounds too good to be true. What else did he offer you?"

"My thoughts exactly," I said, scratching the stubble along my jaw that I was too lazy to shave this morning. "Blanchet wants Patrick gone. I'm assuming it's easier for me to get rid of his brother-in-law than have to wash the blood off his own hands. At least then, he wouldn't have to hide the truth from his wife."

Those big, beautiful eyes of hers were as round as the moon.

"One of my stipulations was making sure you were safe when you returned," I continued. "Unfortunately, I can't do that if Patrick is still breathing. Blanchet made it sound like he was doing us both a favor by offering his head on a silver platter for me. I have my suspicions, but at least this way, you can finally have the freedom you deserve."

"You can't be serious."

Ghost jumped out of her arms and landed near my feet.

"Dead serious," I reassured her. "Patrick is being sent by

Blanchet, completely unaware he's part of the deal. The terms of the agreement state that each party can bring four members as protection, and each person will be searched by the other party before it even starts. I'll have to remove every weapon I have, which is why I'm giving this to you."

It didn't seem possible that her eyes could get any bigger, but Krissy proved me wrong as I pulled out my Sig P939 and handed it to her. I didn't know what to expect when I did, but it sure as hell wasn't this. She instantly checked if the gun was loaded and ensured the safety was on before admiring the weapon for herself.

"I was about to ask if you knew how to shoot a gun, but I think you answered that question."

She shrugged. "My dad grew up in a rural part of Indiana before moving to the city to appease my mom. As much as he hated it here, he compromised by taking me hunting from time to time," she explained, lost in a memory. "The funny thing is, I hated going hunting so much that I would purposely miss my shot so I wouldn't have to kill any animals, but now I'd give anything to camp in the woods with him one last time."

"You don't strike me as the camping type."

Krissy laughed. "You wouldn't catch me dead in the woods, but if my dad were still here, I would suck it up for the sake of spending time with him." She cleared her throat. "So, what do you want me to do with this? Shoot Patrick?"

Now it was my turn to laugh. "You would make my life a lot easier if you did, but no. In case of an emergency, I want you to have this for your own safety. Let me worry about Patrick."

The drive from my apartment to the club was painfully long – and I savored every minute of it. I indulged in the rich scent of her vanilla shampoo and stole quick glimpses of her fidgeting in the passenger seat. Although she refused to admit it, she was nervous. If she wasn't messing with the hem of her sweater, then she was obsessively checking the safety on the gun resting in her lap.

"Erick," she exhaled.

"Yes, little angel," I responded, gripping the steering wheel tighter.

"Do you regret what we did? Making the deal and all?"

I took my time forming a response despite already knowing the answer.

"Given all that Patrick had over you, I don't think there was a reality in which he would have let you go without consequences. I'm grateful you asked me for help, and I would do it again in a heartbeat—and I hope you know if you ever need anything in the future, I'll always be there for you. And I think Ghost is grateful too, I swear she likes you way more than she ever liked me."

Krissy laughed, but it was the sad type of laughter that didn't feel earnest. It quickly faded, and so did her smile. "I regret a few things," she paused for a long beat, "but overall, I'm grateful you were the one to help me. Thank you for everything you did. I have no idea where I'd be without you—scratch that, I do, I'd be absolutely miserable and forced to be in a relationship with Patrick to keep my career afloat. I owe you more than I can ever repay."

I intertwined my hand with hers, noticing there was a slight tremor in her fingers.

"You owe me absolutely nothing. As I said, I'd do it again in a heartbeat." She chewed on the inside of her cheek like she didn't love the idea of a free handout – even though I was getting the theater out of this deal like we originally agreed upon. I considered my options, then quickly corrected myself. "If you want, you can make me a promise instead, then we can call it even."

"I already told you I can't make any p–"

"This is different." I squeezed her hand. "Promise me you'll consider talking to someone about everything you've been holding onto for so long, preferably a professional who knows what they're doing. It's worth considering at the very least."

I didn't care that I might be overstepping her boundaries; it had to be said. It wasn't as if I was forcing her to go, but exploring her options wouldn't hurt when so much was weighing heavily on her heart.

She studied me for a long moment before she turned away.

"I'll try. I promise."

Chapter Forty

Krissy

Don Juan felt like a shell of its former self—still and desolate compared to the last time I'd been here. All the life had been gutted from the building and left to rot until there was nothing more. Had Erick not been as stubborn as he was, perhaps it might have, with time, but all it took was one quick glance at the club to know he'd rather die than let that happen. Reconstruction of the century-old building was in the beginning stages. Tools and heaps of building material were scattered across the main floor, preparing for what would later be a massive project to complete.

The sight of the damage was enough to make me pause. Erick, on the other hand, didn't even blink twice as he entered the building, leading the way. We were early, which I was grateful for. Each of us needed time to situate ourselves and mentally prepare for what was to come next; however, I didn't imagine there could ever be a scenario in which I would be fully prepared to face Patrick and all that entailed. Let alone one that didn't make saying goodbye to Erick any less painful.

Thoughts, emotions, and behaviors are all interconnected; none of them can exist without the influence of the other.

Spiraling thoughts shift into negative emotions, and negative emotions cause irrational behaviors. Irrational behaviors impacted contradicting notions and so on. It was a vicious cycle that continued on and on until you could finally disrupt it for better or worse. For myself, the moment I stepped foot into the club, my thoughts began to spiral, threatening to drag me down with them. I was beginning to feel a little nauseous when a hand brushed the place between my shoulder blades.

"Are you alright, Krissy?" Erick whispered, leaning in close.

"I'm okay. Don't worry about me." I forced a smile and allowed him to guide me inside.

While the club was mostly in disarray, the dining area below the balcony had been pieced together specifically for tonight. A large square table sat in the middle of the space with three chairs surrounding it. Lola and Damon watched from afar as someone I didn't recognize set out the supplies for the transaction. With the little Sign Language I'd learned over the weeks, I greeted Damon in passing before taking a seat.

Erick tugged at the material of his slacks so he could comfortably squat down, making us eye level with one another. From this angle, it would have been difficult for anyone to see him take my hand in a gesture that hurt more than it should have.

"I always worry about you." Erick paused, watching his thumb stroke the backside of my hand. "I hope you know it's okay to be nervous. I'm nervous too," he admitted, still refusing to meet my gaze. "Patrick will be arriving soon, and when he does, I'm going to have to play my part. Anything I say or do isn't a reflection of how I feel about you. I just need him to believe I'm the villain in this story, which means you have to believe that as well." His beautiful, deep brown eyes found mine. "Krissy," he sighed. "Just remember, no matter what, you're safe, and all of this will be over soon."

I swallowed the lump in my throat. "Do what you need to do to make it believable. He–"

Something snagged his attention over my shoulder.

It all happened so fast, one moment I was basking in what little time we had left, hoping either one of us had the courage to say all that was left unspoken, and the next, I was being yanked out of my chair, completely at his mercy.

"I hope you don't mind me bringing in the trash from off the streets," Antonio called out, a few people trailing in after him. Tall, brooding men filed in one after the other, each of them on high alert and assessing the building with each step they took. My heart quickened as the last man entered, his eyes instantly finding mine. The lining of my throat felt thick, like there wasn't enough room to breathe properly.

Someone doesn't have to lay a hand on you in order to leave a mark.

Safety wasn't always guaranteed. It was a feeble little promise that could be taken away just as easily as it was given. That felt especially true the moment I became face-to-face with the inevitable. Despite how far out of reach this exchange felt at times, I knew everything would eventually come down to this. I knew I would have to face Patrick once more, but that didn't make it any less terrifying.

Nor did it make it any easier to accept something that I'd suppressed for so long. Erick had breathed the words into existence, and I did my best to deny them each and every time, but denying something for so long will only get you so far. In the end, we all have to face our demons whether we want to or not. And for me, that meant facing the man who manipulated me one last time.

All it took was one look to know the truth. One measly glance to realize that I was so petrified by fear despite all attempts to convince myself otherwise. The sudden understanding was one thing; knowing what to do with that information was an entirely different beast altogether.

Patrick paused for but a second before he lunged forward, attempting to reach me as if the distance between us was merely the last obstacle keeping us apart. Antonio reacted nearly as quickly as he did, jutting out in front of him in an attempt to hold him back. There was shouting and arguing all around me, but I couldn't hear it over the ringing in my ears. Chaos had erupted near the bar, guns were drawn, and a deadly promise lingered in the air.

My back collided with Erick's front just as the cool bite of metal brushed over my temple, making Patrick and the rest of his men pause. "Come any closer, and this meeting will end before it even starts," Erick shouted across the room, pressing the gun more firmly.

Patrick raised his hands as guns were lowered. "There's no need for that. I just wanted to make sure she was okay." Then his eyes flickered down to mine. "Are you okay, sweetheart?"

Despite dressing his best for the occasion, the suit seemed to be wearing him instead of the other way around. Bags hung heavy under his eyes like he hadn't slept in ages, and there were loose strands of hair that had fallen out of place. Based on appearances alone, little had changed, but there was no denying my perspective of him had been forever altered. It was the same Patrick I'd known all that time ago, but I hardly recognized him now.

There must have been a long pause that followed, because Erick leaned in close, his breath hot against my cheek. "He's waiting, little angel. Tell him what he wants to hear," he whispered for my ears only.

"Yes," I choked out. "Please just hurry up."

"Good girl," he said in hushed tones.

"You heard the lady, let's hurry this up," Antonio said with a clap that echoed off the high ceilings. "If you don't like seeing your little girlfriend staring down the barrel of a gun, then I suggest we start the searches already."

The air felt thick, dense, and punishing as Antonio escorted the men toward the table designated for their weapons. To my surprise, Patrick pulled out a gun from his waistband and placed it down after a moment of hesitation, like he was wondering if he was a good enough shot to bypass me and hit Erick instead. Luckily for both of us, he didn't try his luck and allowed Damon to pat him down, then the others.

"You're shaking, little angel. Are you okay?" Erick tightened his grip around my waist, making the metal dig into my stomach a little harder.

I could feel Patrick's eyes boring into me, but I refused to look up.

"I don't want to be anywhere near that man."

"You have every right to be upset," he breathed. "Remember that you are safe, and if there's ever a moment you don't feel like you are, you have the means to protect yourself." A beat passed. "There were so many reasons to fall for you, Krissy Davis—your strength was but a fraction of those reasons. You are stronger than he ever treated you."

And just like that, he was gone.

Antonio was there a moment later to replace him, restraining me with only his hands to keep the illusion in place. It took everything not to call him back. It took everything not to watch him from afar as he willingly offered up every weapon in his possession. It took everything to force myself to lock eyes with Patrick and pretend seeing him was a blessing and not a curse. I had a role to play, and as much as it hurt to pretend, I knew my place in this game. It was only a matter of playing it well enough for this to work.

Once all was said and done, Charles' representatives sat

down with Erick and began the strenuous process of signing over the theater from one owner to the other. I wasn't exactly sure what to expect when I imagined the moment I'd regain my freedom, but it certainly wasn't this. The process was so mechanical and anticlimactic compared to the way the evening had started, with nothing but paperwork and awkward silence. The lawyer shuffled papers from one side of the table to the other, asking for signatures and clarifying sections of the documents that posed questions. I felt like an outsider, watching from the inside. Absent but painfully consumed by everything unfolding before me.

I kept my eyes glued to Patrick; on occasion, he would sense me staring and look up from his paperwork. In those brief moments of exasperation, I would force tears to swell in my eyes and grant him reassuring nods to keep him numb to the fact that all of this was a ploy. Men like Patrick victimized and targeted those whom they believed they could manipulate more easily than the rest, and as adamant as he was to hurt me, it's almost ironic how easily he'd believed it all.

I had no pity left for him. He dug his grave long before he was ready to fill it.

"Sign here, Mr. Martin," the lawyer said, pointing to the flagged area.

Patrick pursed his lips as he silently read.

"I'll admit, Mr. Destler, I was surprised when Charles told me you two had struck a deal of some sort," he finally said, breaking the painfully loud silence. "It seems as if all of this could have been dealt with properly weeks ago. It's a shame it took so long. Wouldn't you agree?"

"I can't say the same," Erick responded flatly.

He slid the paper across the table for Erick to sign next, then anxiously glanced over his shoulder. The strange gesture appeared to be nothing more than a nervous habit or a subtle way to communicate to the men accompanying him without using words, but the depth of that stare shot well over their shoulders. Erick seemed to notice at the same time I did.

"Do you have somewhere more important to be, Mr. Martin?"

He shook his head. "I'm sure Krissy would have appreciated it. It's just a shame she had to be dragged into the middle of this for reasons I still don't quite understand. Makes me wonder why you didn't accept my first offer?"

"Are you accusing me of something? Because I suggest you be a man about it and say it instead of beating around the bush."

The lawyer at his side stiffened at the sharpness in his tone and then quickly handed off the next round of signatures to Patrick. They were nearing the end of the stack, but the closer they got to the last page, the more tense the room grew. Each man might have been disarmed, but that didn't stop them from wielding their words.

"I don't know, you tell me. Why was Krissy ever a part of this deal in the first place?"

What the hell is he talking about?

"She was simply a means to an end—nothing more."

"Or were you hoping for mor–"

"What first offer?" I blurted out, and suddenly all eyes were on me. "What is he talking about, Erick?" I realized my mistake a second later when Patrick's jaw clenched, and Erick's eyes snapped in my direction. Jealousy was a nasty look on some, which was especially true for my former lover.

Antonio's grip tightened on my shoulders. "Easy, little one, you'll ruin the fun."

Patrick turned his attention toward Erick and spoke as if I wasn't even there. "Did you not tell her? Does she not know all of this could have been over weeks ago if you hadn't been so damn stubborn and refused to take the theater when we last met?"

I might have been shaking again. I wasn't sure. The hammering in my chest was drowning out all my other senses, making it difficult to focus on one singular thing happening around me.

"Is that true?" Patrick was about to speak, but I shushed him. "I want to hear it from him."

This deal had taken its toll. At times, it seemed as if it took more than it ever gave, stripping me down to the vulnerable layers I kept hidden for a reason. It reminded me how bruised and messy my past was and how poorly I handled it. It took and took and took until I felt as if I was crawling on my hands and knees, begging for something or someone to save me from this hell I'd created for myself.

To my surprise, someone had listened. Someone had stretched out their hand and offered me light in the darkest moments. Erick had been there with welcoming arms and reassurance that he was doing all he could for not only my well-being but the situation we were stuck in. Patrick's confession meant nothing to me—he'd lied to my face countless times before. But Erick? He had only ever been honest with me. I needed to hear it directly from him to know for certain.

I needed Erick to tell me the truth.

"Is that true?" I repeated with a sharpness in my tone.

This meeting was on the precipice of something much larger than our strained relationship. We spoke in heavy detail about how our actions could easily impact the outcome tonight, one way or another. One wrong move and all of this could have been for nothing. I'd selfishly asked for the truth at a time that didn't warrant that type of response, and Erick selflessly knew he couldn't resist leaving the question unanswered.

Erick snapped his eyes shut, took a deep breath in, and forced the words out. Before he could even answer, I already knew...

"It wasn't as simple as he's making it sound. You have to understand–"

The center of my chest tightened, and I silently gasped for air.

The lawyer cleared his throat. "This is the last document. If you'll sign here..."

Erick had a role to play, and he intended to play it well. Realizing his mistake, he stiffened his posture and cooled his expression, fixing himself with every intention of finishing what he'd started. His gaze found mine despite himself in an attempt to silently communicate all that was left unspoken. It was a plea for understanding. A plea for forgiveness, but I didn't have the patience to listen.

"Sign it already," I urged, forcing my gaze elsewhere.

"Krissy."

"Sign it, goddamn it!"

My voice echoed off the ceiling for a split second, then dissipated into utter silence. Eventually, the sound of paper sliding over polished wood broke that silence, then a swift stroke of a ballpoint pen.

Standing here, watching from afar, I felt helpless. I felt every emotion, every fear sparked to life and festered inside until it felt as if it was sliding under my skin, and the only way to get it out was to drag my fingernails over my flesh and claw it out myself. If I drew blood and broke the skin, it would hurt less than enduring another second of being near either one of these men, I thought to myself.

"Well," Patrick said, forcing a smile. "Congratulations, Mr. Destler, the theater is officially yours."

"Lucky me," he deadpanned.

As the lawyer spoke, Erick took one open palm and discreetly pointed it to the other in choppy, uneven motions. To an untrained eye, it was nothing more than a nervous fidget, but I recognized the sign almost instantly. My chest tightened.

A hand darted out, snatching the gun from my waistband before I could react. I jerked back in surprise, colliding with Antonio's arm. The motion sent a warning shot whipping past Patrick's head, the crack of the gunfire echoing in the room. A split second later, the bullet found its mark—the man directly behind him crumpled to the floor.

His skin paled, making the thick red blood splattered across the right side of his face pop with a gut-wrenching twist. Lifting a shaky hand, Patrick felt around his features, expecting to find a bullet wound that wasn't there. Blood was everywhere. I'd never seen so much of it before. Some of it had dripped into his mouth, and Patrick was struggling to suppress the urge to gag.

It was a swift death. It was likely over long before he even hit the ground with a resounding thud that shook the foundation of the old building. The ringing of the shot lingered for what felt like a lifetime after. In actuality, it was only a few long seconds that no one dared to move, too shocked by Antonio's mistake to do anything about it. Eventually, the world came spiraling back into place, and the severity of the situation hit suddenly as one of Charles' men side-eyed the weapon's table. I wasn't sure who moved first, but once someone stepped forward, the rest followed, creating a panic.

"The tunnel!" Erick screamed. "Go!"

But my legs wouldn't move.

Someone reached the table, and another earsplitting shot rang out. Unlike the first death, the body that toppled over wasn't lifeless. They flailed on the ground, screaming at the top of their lungs as blood pooled all around them, soaking them bone-deep. One shot to knock them to the ground, and another to silence them for good. By the third shot, I was sprinting toward the hallway, praying I wouldn't get caught in the crossfire.

Chapter Forty-One

Charles

Diminishing spirits prove diminishing endeavors. Keeping a spirit alive and well can be challenging when it is passed down from one generation to the next. It becomes the burden of another to keep it from dwindling. For all the Blanchets that have come before, their sacrifices did not go without notice, and when that burden was passed down to me, I welcomed it with open arms and praised it for what it was—a blessing, not a curse.

Unlike my father and his father before him, I had no intention to waste what was given to me. Although I wouldn't be the man I am today without them, I grew up knowing nothing other than their failures. What good was making a broken promise if it meant my future son or daughter would inherit something that was always meant for me?

I had no intention of being like my father.

The last few months have posed many questions that have kept me up late at night, turning them over one by one until it seemed to be all I could think of. Marrying Josephine meant starting a family of my own and recognizing what that meant for my legacy and the future of my bloodline. Most of all, what that meant for her safety.

While the months following our marriage should have been filled with bliss, so much weighed heavily over our relationship and the integrity of my name within the district. Blanchet was a name to be feared as much as it was respected, but lately, it didn't seem like that was the case. Patrick meddled in everything he could get his hands on, causing more issues than he was good for.

While marriage united us, that didn't mean he could get off so easily for his mistake. Destler, on the other hand, paraded around the streets pretending as if he didn't initiate an act of war the night of my rehearsal dinner, stealing something that wasn't his to take. While I couldn't care less about the girl, it was the principle of the matter.

Each had a price to pay for their actions.

A man is only as good as his word. I swore to myself all those years ago, I wouldn't waste the burden I was given. I bide my time, count my blessings, and wait for the right moment to strike. That patience granted me more than I could ever ask for. It brought me to this moment. It brought me here.

The theater was empty. The last of the staff had gone home hours ago, and I was all by myself, staring out into a sea of tables and chairs. From atop the stage, it all felt so feeble in the grand scheme of things. It was nothing more than smoke and mirrors, a silly ploy to trick the eye and create the illusion of class and wealth. A filthy trick that predated the construction of the building itself. A means to manipulate and cheat when arrogance got the best of those who were willing to cross the Blanchet name once upon a time. For myself, this building symbolized that continued disrespect and the promise to demand retribution. Wanting it was one thing, but taking it for myself was an entirely different beast.

With the absence of life, the theater felt smaller. It was as if all it was ever good for was stuffing as many bodies through the door and blinding them with god-awful music and suggestive dancing. Without a note to play or a dance to be spun, perpetual silence stretched to every corner of the building. I savored it for as long as I could until a familiar tone broke that silence. I glanced down at my phone and contemplated even picking it up.

In the end, I was too curious not to.

"Charles! Thank God," Patrick shouted, his voice hardly audible amongst the chaos in the background. "We need you. They hid a gun on Krissy, and now the club is a bloodbath. You need to send in your men, now!"

I held back a laugh. Hearing the tremor in his voice was music to my ears. If Patrick was so adamant about being a part of this, then I would make it my mission to give him exactly what he wanted. It was an opportunity to save the woman he claimed to love, and like all the times before when he went behind my back, he would simply have to figure it out on his own. Patrick dug his grave long ago. Now it was time to lie down and take it.

A shot rang out, and I heard a whimper on the other line.

"Charles, where are you?"

I sighed. "Sorry, frère."

Then I hung up.

It was well past nine o'clock. The outside of the building had been secured, and chaos had erupted within. Now it was time for my role in all of this. I made my way backstage, leaving a trail in my wake. The canister swayed with each step. When I finally reached the dressing room, nearly half of it was gone, leaving a pungent stench that burned the lining of my nostrils. The smell worsened within the cramped space, making it more difficult to breathe as the corner of my eyes stung. I blinked back the tears and continued to diligently work until every article of clothing, piece of furniture, and velvet curtain was soaked through. When all was said and done, the only thing left to do was move aside the sofa that concealed the entrance to the passages and douse it in a thick pool of gasoline that dripped down between the cracks in the floorboards, but that wasn't good enough for me. I dared to open the trap door and pour the last of the canister on the concrete floor.

A smile tugged at my lips as I admired my work—the way the subtle slant of the floor sent the pool trickling in thin lines toward the boxes and excess furniture cluttering the passageway, doubling as storage for the club. With any luck, their negligence would act in my favor.

My phone rang again, and it broke me from my trance—my sign to leave. I shut the door, turned my back, and reached for the pack of cigarettes in my coat pocket as I made for the exit. Once I was far enough away, I selfishly lit it, taking my first and last inhale. The crude burn filled my lungs, and I savored every moment before releasing a thick trail of smoke that danced around my face.

"Adieu," I said before flicking it away.

Diminishing spirits prove diminishing endeavors, but what if they never had to? What if there was a path that made that spirit burn as bright as the flames slowly engulfing the theater? What if it could all go to hell?

Every last one of them.

Chapter Forty-Two

Erick

"What the hell is wrong with you?"

Antonio struggled to catch his breath, heaving with each gasp of air he took. With only seconds to react, we lunged for the nearest booth and took shelter behind the massive piece of furniture once I was certain Krissy had made it down the hallway, and no one was following after her. It wasn't enough to protect us for long, but it gave us an opportunity to regroup and locate the guns I stashed within the rip in the cushion just in case.

"Krissy hit my arm. What the hell do you want me to say? It's not like I did it on purpose."

Hearing her name felt like a blow to the gut. I kept my eyes fixed down the hallway and waited for the sensation to lessen, but simply knowing she'd made it down there safely wasn't enough to ease my anxiety. I needed to see it for myself.

Mistakes were inevitable. It didn't matter how meticulously this meeting had been planned. There were bound to be a few, but what I didn't account for was foolishly seeing an opportunity present itself and being too stubborn not to take it. Safety was a promise I swore time and time again, but I broke that promise by putting Krissy in harm's way, attempting to take a shortcut and end our misery sooner. If anything happened to her, I would never forgive myself.

"Did you see where Lola and Damon went?"

Antonio checked his weapon before answering. "Lola ran for the table, and I have no idea where Damon went."

After the initial attack, the club fell silent. Anyone who was still breathing had run for cover or died trying. Those in my company were all well aware of what to do in such a circumstance. It was just a matter of who'd managed to reach their weapons in time. Careful not to make another grim mistake, I peeked my head around the booth and assessed the damage.

Three bodies: the man who was standing directly behind Patrick. Richard. And–

"Damnit," I cursed under my breath, flopping back into place. "Lola's dead, and I don't see Damon."

Antonio uttered a prayer and traced the sign of the cross.

There simply wasn't time to properly grieve. Staying alert and present in this situation took priority over all else, and as much as Lola deserved better, she would understand if the roles were reversed. I shoved aside the image of twisted limbs and the shock etched into her features and tried to focus on not spilling any more unnecessary blood. Our numbers were skewed; with Lola and Richard gone, we were now outnumbered.

I looked down the hallway again, and this time, Antonio noticed.

"You need to go after her and make sure she's okay," he whispered.

"I can't leave you."

He offered a weak smile. "She needs you. Damon and I can handle ourselves."

I stared down the hallway for a long moment, assessing the odds and weighing my options. In the end, it all came down to faith. Antonio and Damon deserved nothing less than to have my full trust invested in their abilities to handle this situation and anything else that presents itself. As careless as Antonio's mistake was, it was my call in the first place, and everything that happened after that was a series of unfortunate events stemming from it. I couldn't hold that over him. Trusting them was easy when I had no other option if I wanted to ensure Krissy had made it out to the other side safely.

I tucked my gun into my waistband.

"Okay. Cover me."

The path was short. Only a few meters separated the booth from the bend in the hallway. I took a deep breath in and held it, carrying the weight in my lungs until I found the courage to let it out. A second later, I was sprinting out into the open, chasing after Krissy with nothing more than pure luck to protect me. Two shots rang out, hitting the back wall and making the plaster explode in every direction. Bits of debris nicked my skin, but I hardly felt them as Antonio returned fire.

I took the first corner too sharply and nearly lost my balance. On the next corner, I did, causing quite a scene at the top of the stairs. Krissy yelped, then muffled the sound with her hand when she realized it was only me. It was never my intention to startle her, but here we were anyway, and the sight of it broke my heart. My little angel stood at the foot of the stairs, frantically trying to find a way out. The PIN pad had been flipped open, but she hadn't had any luck guessing the four-digit code. I could only imagine how frightened she must have been down here all by herself, shots slowly closing in, all the while she struggled to unlock the only thing separating her from freedom.

"It's okay, it's me," I said in a winded breath. "I'm here, Krissy."

She watched me descend the stairs with an expression I couldn't quite read. Eyes wide and lips slightly parted open. Time slowed, screams softened, and the weight of her stare bored into me, making me feel full of life while simultaneously shredding me from the inside out. I held her gaze as long as I could, trying to piece together all that wasn't being spoken.

"You came for me..."

"Of course," I mumbled, typing in the PIN with trembling fingers. "I promised I'd always be there for you, didn't I?"

She nodded, clearly suppressing as much as she could.

There was more to this than I was seeing. Something hung heavy between us, and I was about to ask when our moment was cut short.

Time rushed back into place, the sharp crack of gunshots slicing through the haze and jolting us back to the present. Screams bled through the fog, painting a picture of the horrors unfolding right above us. Reality had snuck up on us like a wave building in size, growing too large to hold its own weight, giving it no other choice than to crash down on the two people foolish enough to stand in its path of destruction.

A stray bullet hit the wall.

Then another, causing flecks of debris to rain down on us. The wounds sprawled out across my forearm, singed as fresh ones joined in, and I did my best to shield Krissy with my body, but as the screams grew closer, I knew the only way to protect the woman I love was to ensure she was as far away as possible from the chaos I'd created.

The short passage dragged on for what felt like a lifetime. Krissy kept one pace behind, our hands interlocked as the shadows of the tunnel swallowed us whole. The stairs leading out of the tunnel slowly came into view, materializing step by step. I slowed my pace as the last step bled through the darkness and urged Krissy to do the same. With so much uncertainty hanging in the air, I couldn't, in my right mind, leave things the way they were before parting ways. There had already been so many mistakes—so many regrets. If I returned to help Damon and Antonio, and something happened to me...Well, I just needed her to know the truth.

I grabbed her by the shoulders and forced her to look at me, taking in all I could one last time despite how overwhelmed my senses were. Gunpowder still lingered in my nose, drowning out the scent of her rich perfume. My skin felt flushed from running, adrenaline still pumping through my veins with no sign of stopping.

"As soon as you get out of the theater, you need to call the police," I rasped. "Hide in your apartment until I come and get you. Don't open the door for anyone else. Do you understand?"

"You aren't coming with me?" Her eyes frantically darted back and forth.

"There are people depending on me–"

"You could get hurt, Erick," she blurted out, voice cracking.

"There are people depending on me," I tried again, "and I left them to make sure that you were safe. Protecting you will always take priority, but I can't abandon Antonio and Damon while they fight alone. If something happened to either of them, I would never forgive myself for not being there. And if something happened to you...I couldn't live in a world without that light, even if it was never my light to hold in the first place. You need to leave, Krissy. I need to know you're safe."

Loving Krissy had never been easy. It was a constant push and pull that drew us closer together, making the inevitable happen. I never had a choice in loving her. It came as easily as breathing itself. It gave life and meaning to a world I'd given up on a long time ago. Loving her was never a choice. It was something written in the stars, meant to align for the two of us.

If this was what it took to protect her by sending her away, then so be it.

I leaned forward, resting my forehead against hers.

Heat licked down the side of my face.

"I need you to know, I never hid the truth from you intentionally. When I met with Patrick, I insisted on only making the deal if he swore to leave you alone after you were released. He refused, and I took the deal off the table. There was no point in making the exchange if I couldn't guarantee you wouldn't be trading one prison for another. I wanted to protect you, but I know it was wrong to leave you in the dark as I did. I should have told you. I should have given you that choice instead of making it for you. This deal between us was always meant to be a way to tether myself to a past worth forgetting, but somewhere along the way, I realized that the building means nothing to me unless you're safe within its walls."

Krissy was always full of surprises—unexpected moments that never ceased to amaze me, for better or worse. My little angel took either side of my face and pulled me in for a kiss before I could even register what was happening. By the time I came to, I savored all but a second of the sweet tenderness of her lips before she pulled away.

"You should have told me. You messed up, Frick. I hope you know that," she said. "But I can be upset with you after you come back and find me. I can be upset when I know you're safe."

"Deal." I couldn't help but steal one last kiss. One last moment where the world stood still and nothing else mattered other than being close to her. One last promise, I intended to keep but couldn't say aloud. Krissy seemed to understand, wrapping her arms around my neck and pulling me in closer.

"Don't you dare get hurt. Swear it, Destler." Krissy pointed at me with fire in her eyes.

With my index finger, I traced the lines over my heart, and that seemed to be enough to soften her gaze. It was a simple gesture, as unspoken as everything else that stood between us. Content with my promise, Krissy climbed the short distance up the staircase and threw back the hatch to find all hell had broken loose.

Chapter Forty-Three

Erick

A world filled with blistering embers and consuming flames erupted above us. A treacherous sea of orange that swelled with each kindling caught in its path. The flames would have been bound to the dressing room had the old ceiling not started to crumble under the weight of its own age. Debris rained down in sporadic fits.

A few pieces nearly hit Krissy as she jumped back. One of them tumbled down the steps, landing in a wet substance I hadn't noticed pooling around my feet before. Flames sparked to life within the tunnel, quickly eating up the space near us. Had I moved a second later, the death that would have awaited me would have been a fitting end to the life I'd lived. Making sure Krissy didn't face a similar fate, I grabbed her by the arm and sprinted in the opposite direction, making sure to stick to the edges of the passageway where the concrete was still dry. Whatever flammable substance soaked the ground hadn't reached the full length of the tunnel, but that didn't stop the flames from finding kindling, building in strength and speed as it turned into an impenetrable wall of destruction. There were enough boxes and furniture stored along the walls to ensure they'd never run out. While we were far enough away from it to breathe a little lighter, we realistically only had minutes to escape upstairs before the speakeasy and my office succumbed to the flames next. We followed the path until the tunnel spat us out on the other side.

I glanced over my shoulder to check on Krissy when I realized her attention was fixed elsewhere. She opened her mouth to speak, but before she could, a resounding crack splintered the air. Flesh tore, and ligaments snapped. Each one is shredding apart, creating a pathway for the pain to lodge itself more deeply within. The pain was like that of no other, erupting at the point of entry along my kneecap and spreading like wildfire in a blistering heat that threatened to burn me more fiercely than the flames licking at my back. I'd built too much momentum running through the tunnels to stop, so the next step I took, I crumbled under the weight of my own body, taking Krissy down with me.

"Fuck." The lining of my throat stung as a scream tore loose.

We all suffer in our own ways, and agony had taken hold, acting as an old friend greeting me once more. It had visited me in many capacities throughout my life, shaping itself into the jagged lines of a broken bottle, a final goodbye after years of suffering, and a lonely existence riddled with self-inflicted wounds. The most heart-wrenching of all was seeing Krissy crawl over me on her hands and knees, wading through a pool of my own blood. She was chanting my name over and over again like some kind of incantation that might reverse what couldn't be undone, her voice breaking between chanting my name and begging the shadow in the doorway to stay away.

The shadow didn't listen, and neither did I.

Plumes of thick gray smoke lined the ceiling, moving and shifting like a living beast as the flames slowly closed in. The dense cloud rolled overhead while thinning ones filled the space between us, partially concealing the man lurking in the shadows.

I didn't need to see him to know who was standing there, waiting for another opportunity to strike. My first instinct was to rise and fight, to find a way despite the overwhelming pain rippling through my limbs. Being closed in on two fronts left me little choice in the matter. It was either lie there and take it or die trying.

Krissy was there a second later, coughing up a fit as she struggled to hoist my upper body off the ground.

Another shot rang out, and a blistering white heat skimmed across my ribs. I toppled forward, any strength I once had diminishing in seconds. With my forearms braced on the cold, hard ground, I howled in pain, but with each cry, the side of my torso felt like it was splitting open. With the amount of blood loss, it seemed as if that was true. I clutched my side; thick blood seeped between my fingers and then raced down the length of my arm as more gushed out.

"Erick. Get up. Get up. Please," Krissy shuddered, attempting to lift me once more as if that would be enough to grant me the strength I simply didn't possess. The second shot had taken its toll, withering me down into nothing more than dead weight. We both went crashing down as a voice called from the smoke, making her arm stiffen around me.

"Krissy. Come here." Patrick called from behind the barrel of a gun. "Get away from him."

Agony takes many forms, manipulating itself against our own will. I thought seeing Krissy like this would be another one of those manipulations, but it wasn't until I realized what she was doing that I understood how much worse the situation was. Without hesitation, she threw herself between Patrick and me, using her own body as a shield.

She shook her head fiercely and extended her arms to block what her body couldn't.

The toxicity of the air was inundated. Our lungs filled with smoke upon each inhale we dared to take; it was becoming increasingly difficult to breathe. The poor air quality was but a reminder, a cruel sense of presage for those foolish enough to linger here long enough.

There was a pop in the distance. Pressure built and built within the furniture caught ablaze until it had no other choice but to release it. I was acutely aware of how the flames seemed to have a mind of their own, jumping from one thing to another, desperate to keep building in size. We had little time, and Krissy must have known that too because the next thing that came out of her mouth surprised me.

"Help me," she choked out, clearly holding back tears. "Help me carry him out of here."

A bewildering look glistened in his eyes as he took a cautious step forward. Shock, betrayal, and indignation hit him all at once, and I watched each emotion course through him as he took in the sight of Krissy kneeling before him. While the gun was still pointed in our direction, he slightly lowered the weapon with trembling hands.

"What are you doing? Get up, sweetheart," he snapped, a shaky edge to his voice.

"Help me," she shouted, tears spilling freely. "He's going to bleed out, and I can't carry him out of here on my own. Help me. Now."

He paused, eyes frantically bouncing back between Krissy and the flames behind her.

"You know I can't do that," he said, panic-stricken. The entire right side of his face was glowing orange as the flames danced nearby. He was close enough now to see the droplets of perspiration race down the profile of his face. "We need to leave right now. I'm not wasting my time or energy on a piece of shit like him, and neither should you. He could burn *alive* for all I care after what he did to us."

Krissy choked out a laugh and clutched her heart. "I'm not leaving him."

Their voices faded in and out, getting lost amongst the crackling of flames, but I caught bits and pieces of what was being said. Patrick's persistent questioning of why she wouldn't come, and Krissy's outright refusal to leave. The two danced around in circles, no closer to a singular decision that might very well save her life. She was too stubborn to leave, and he was too weak to make her go all on his own.

My eyes felt heavy as I leaned my head back and watched the smoke roll in thrashing waves high above. The room was becoming suffocatingly hot, but a shiver ran down my spine. Once it started, it didn't seem like it could stop. I was losing too much blood...

There aren't many certainties in this life. We're forced to navigate without clear direction or even certainty that our decisions will be the right ones. That grim truth can be frightening at times. We make predictions despite that fear and try our luck, but deep down, that truth always lingers. In one of those rare moments of clarity, I reached for Krissy's hand, knowing I was making the right choice for once.

The arguing abruptly stopped as her eyes met mine.

"Krissy," I rasped, squeezing her hand a little. "It's time to go."

"What?"

"You need to go, little angel. It's not safe down here."

"No." Hot angry tears slipped down her cheeks, and I couldn't help it when I brushed them away with my other hand. Every instinct told her to lean into that touch; she gave herself that pleasure for but a second before jerking away. "Don't you dare. Don't you fucking dare. I'm not leaving without you, Erick. End of discussion."

"I've made so many promises to you. Let me keep just this

one." There was a lifetime of confessions on the tip of my tongue with no time to tell them. I blinked away the tears as my vision blurred, knowing she deserved to hear every last one of them. Time had never been on our side from the very beginning, so I said what I could as time worked against us. "I'm sorry things had to come to this. You deserved so much better, and I can't give you that if I'm still holding you back." A single tear rolled down my cheek. "What little time we shared was never going to be enough, but I'll always be grateful that the happiest moments of my life were the ones you were a part of. If I could turn back time, I would do it all over, even knowing things would end like this for me. I would do it in a heartbeat if it meant I could fall in love with you all over again."

"I was wrong. I was so wrong. I can't do this without you. I need you, Erick," she panicked. "This isn't a goodbye. This isn't how it ends for us."

I blinked again, finding Patrick looming over her shoulder, unsure what to make of the interaction. Some may see him keeping me alive as a mercy, but he knew that by leaving me here, a fate much worse awaited me. I swallowed the lump in my throat and shoved that thought aside, forcing myself to nod in his direction. Something unspoken passed between us, and he returned the gesture.

"I love you, little angel. I always have."

She sucked in a breath. "You don't understand. I can't leave you knowing I–"

One moment she was there, and the next she was gone. Patrick saw this for what it was: an opportunity to catch her off guard and save her before it was too late. If I had to resort to tricks, then so be it, because I'd rather die a thousand fiery deaths before I let Krissy burn up with me.

Loving her was never easy, but what a life it was to have her be a part of it.

Chapter Forty-Four

Krissy

To fear death was to fear the inevitable. It's the only guarantee in life that each of us is promised. Death doesn't discriminate between race, gender, wealth, or even age—it comes for all of us in some capacity, whether we're ready or not. For so many years, that inevitable truth was tainted by distant memories of a childhood worth forgetting and the fear that death would come to claim the life he was promised when I hadn't perished with my parents that night. It became this entity that I felt like I was constantly running from while simultaneously feeling guilty for avoiding it for this long. Death had been a promise I swore to keep hidden in the shadows as long as possible, but as I threw myself between Patrick and Erick, I knew I didn't fear death as I once did.

Because the fear of losing him eclipsed everything else.

It was enough to drive me to my knees and make me beg a man who valued me more as a prize than a human being to save someone I knew I couldn't. What other choice did I have when the flames were slowly encroaching on the space, and too many factors were actively working against me to ensure I couldn't drag Erick out of here on my own? What other choice did I have than to exploit Patrick's weakness and manipulate him as he had once done to me? I would have promised anything in exchange for Erick's life, and that included myself. Staring down the barrel of his gun, I realized the power I possessed over him and how it could be wielded into a weapon far greater than anything we'd tried before. I could easily bide my time and strike when need be. Sacrificing my sanity and freedom was a price I was more than willing to pay in order to ensure the man I cared for didn't die in a pool of his own blood.

I would have given up everything if it meant taking a chance on us. Whatever the price, I would have gladly paid it, knowing there was a piece of my heart that wholly belonged to Erick and I was too stubborn to tell him before.

But that choice was ripped away from me.

Patrick had me by the waist, dragging me further away from his body. Plumes of thick gray smoke were swallowing up his lifeless form, drowning out the definitive features of his face until they were nothing more than a smoky haze. A sheer memory of all I'd fallen for and a promise to steal them away forever. While I'd spent so long running from death, Erick had welcomed it with open arms and accepted his fate without an ounce of fear. That choice came as easily as the one Patrick made, despite my objections to staying. Both men had made those choices on my behalf, but I'd be damned if I let either of them get their way in the end.

I thrashed within his hold, kicking and screaming with all my might. The more I struggled, the more he did too, forcing him to readjust his hold in order to maintain control. His arms felt like two boa constrictors squeezing my ribs nearly past the point of no return. Each breath was already ragged from the smoke, but with the added pressure, every cry that followed felt as distant as the last.

"Jesus Christ," he hissed as I kicked the heel of my boot against his shin. "I'm trying to save you, goddammit."

"Let me go!"

"You'll burn alive, Krissy. Is that what you want?"

"I can't leave him," I shrieked. "I'm not leaving him."

He turned his back toward the flames, and my kicking turned frantic without a clear view of Erick. The open doorway bled through the smoke, and the closer we grew, the more aware I became of the fact that if we crossed that threshold, any hope of saving him would be gone. Once Patrick got me past that door – the very one we'd foolishly left open—he could seal in the tunnel with no way of opening it again.

"I'll do anything you want. Please. Patrick. Please."

"Charles was right. He's corrupted you." He sighed as if he hadn't meant to say that out loud. "I'm doing this for your own good, sweetheart."

Underestimating Patrick was a mistake. Perhaps there was a reality in which I could bend him to my will if we had enough time, but time was scarce, and as the door came into view, I knew he was a lost cause. I needed to change tactics.

Twenty feet separated us from the threshold now. With my arms pinned to my side and my feet dangling off the ground, I did my best to fight my way out of his hold with what little leverage I had. In a desperate attempt to break free, I forced my leg up as high as it would go, then rammed the heel of my boot into his knee.

"Stop it," he howled. "Stop fighting me."

The first blow did nothing. The second made a popping sound that crawled under my skin. And the third had him crumbling to his knees at the foot of the stairs, taking me down with him. Patrick wasn't letting go, and I did the only thing I could think of to get free. I shifted as far forward as his hold would allow me, then I threw my head back, cracking the back of my skull against his nose. A splitting pain exploded at the back of my head and rippled out in violent waves, making my brain feel foggy as I tried to comprehend what had just happened. I was vaguely aware that I was crawling away, but my head was swimming, and it made my body feel as if it wasn't of my own.

"Krissy," he screamed at the top of his lungs.

A hand wrapped around my ankle, and I didn't hesitate to kick before scrambling to my feet. Each step was laborious in nature and entirely uncontrollable as I swayed back and forth, drawing closer to the flames. The sound of my name sounded like nails on a chalkboard. It chased after me, ringing louder in my ear as I struggled to find my center of balance.

I blinked rapidly, trying to gain back control of my vision and to make sense of my surroundings. The name was called out again, closer this time. Once I could piece together a clear image of Erick lying before me, I started sprinting for him, still a little too dizzy for my liking. Through the hazy smoke, something small and black caught my attention. I thought I might have been imagining things as I fought the lightheadedness weighing me down. But my suspicions were all but confirmed when I dropped to Erick's side and found his hand resting on the handle of his gun tucked in his waistband. It was as if he was reaching for it in a final attempt, but gave up halfway when his conscious-ness started to waver.

The name was called again, and I whirled around, weapon pointed in that direction.

"Krissy," Patrick yelped, raising his hands up in surrender. There was a slight tremor in his hands, hardly visible from my vantage point, but it was there, nonetheless. He chose his next words carefully, calculating the risk in every possibility as blood gushed out from his left nostril, leaving a thick trail that dripped down the contours of his neck and below his collar. "Don't you see what he is doing? You're so much smarter than this, Krissy. You're falling for his tricks."

"Patrick," I warned. "Carry him out of here right now."

With his hands still raised, he took a cautious step forward and then a half step back when he noticed my finger brush over the external safety.

"What you feel for him isn't real. You are a victim in all of this, Krissy, and it's okay to be confused, but you need to understand he's manipulating you into caring about him by making you dependent on him for emotional support and survival." A large beam fell from the ceiling and exploded into a sea of embers near the mouth of the tunnel, making us both flinch as the ground shook on impact. "Think about it, sweetheart. Destler has been isolating you from your friends, your career, and all the wonderful things that make you who you are. He's been doing it for months, and now he's using that against you so he doesn't have to die here alone."

As his gaze bore into me, it was as if he was picking apart my innermost insecurities and fears regarding loving Erick and was bringing them forth to confront. It was overwhelming and downright violating.

"I know it's hard to hear this, but he doesn't love you. How could he possibly care for you when all you've ever been to him is a bargaining chip? You're just a tool to him, and you're letting him use you over and over again," he explained, practically breathless. "I'm not going to help someone who takes advantage of people like that, and you aren't going to be able to carry him on your own. Is dying for him really worth it in the end?"

There was something to be said for my actions tonight, but no matter how hard I tried to reconcile my emotions, the fear had already taken its toll. So much so that I'd gone as far as to ask Erick for space to consider what falling for him meant for both of us outside of the walls of my isolation.

Patrick stepped forward, catching me off guard while deep in thought.

"We're running out of time. Is he really worth dying for?"

He was doing what he did best, and I'd be damned if I let him get inside of my head like that. Shoving those open wounds aside was more easily said than done, but I did what was necessary to maintain control.

"You're wrong," I shook my head. "And I don't have the time or patience to explain why. You have five seconds to decide whether you are going to help me or not."

My muscles strained, screaming in protest the longer I held up the gun.

"If I'm wrong, then why did you hesitate?"

"Five."

He dared to take another step. "There's actually a psychological term for this–"

"Four."

"–it's when a victim begins to–"

"Three."

"–sympathize with their captor."

"Two," I screamed, lining up my sight.

"We can find you professional help." Patrick offered me a smile. "All you need to do is–"

My finger slipped, and a resounding crack splintered the air.

Allowing Patrick into my life had taken so much in return. When I left, he'd taken a piece of me with him, leaving a hole I didn't know how to fill. Slowly but surely, I noticed the edges begin to mend—it wasn't enough to heal properly, but it gave hope of what could be. There was a long, treacherous journey ahead of me filled with promises to keep, but in that moment, as I watched Patrick's eyes widen in surprise and reach for his throat, it felt the most healing of all.

Old blood mixed with new, painting his skin and clothing a

deep red from where it gushed down his neck. Patrick grappled with his wounds, a silent plea on his lips, but his fate was sealed, and he all but accepted it as he sank down to his knees and sobbed. He attempted to speak, but it came out as a gargled bloody mess.

"You should have let me go." I took a step forward and reached down to sweep a stray hair out of his face. "The night I first met Josephine, I told you I was leaving, and you said *no*. I guess if things were different, I wouldn't have gone to Erick for help, and neither of us would have been in this mess in the first place."

Realization slowly washed over him, and I savored the way the light drained from the dullness in his eyes. He tried to speak again; this time, it came out like something vaguely resembling the word 'help.' I leaned in close and said, "I don't help people who take advantage of others. Rot in hell, Patrick."

Chapter Forty-Five

Krissy

K illing him was as much of a blessing as it was a curse. A double-edged sword that swore nothing good could come from either outcome. On one hand, the dividing force preventing me from coming to Erick's aid was gone, but on the other, the only chance I had to carry him to safety was lying in a pool of his own blood, eyes vacant, and neck still bleeding. We were damned, but with fate actively spinning its intricate webs, I didn't waste any time weighing the options— I simply acted on impulse and hoped for the best.

Erick was unconscious and still bleeding profusely. The amount of blood loss was utterly terrifying, and if it wasn't for the shallow rise of his chest, it would have been easy to assume death had already claimed him. My stomach whirled at the sight of him, and that feeling didn't lessen as I desperately searched for anything to stop the bleeding. The best I could do was a long strip of fabric and a ballpoint pen, both stolen from Patrick's lifeless body. I fashioned the fabric around his lower thigh and placed the pen on top of the knot. It took two tries to steady my shaky hands, but once the pen was tightened in place, I began the laborious process of twisting the pen over and over again until the fabric created so much tension it wouldn't twist anymore. The makeshift tourniquet was a far cry from what it should be, but it would have to do for now.

Erick groaned, and his eyebrows furrowed.

"I know," I mumbled. "I know. Stay with me."

The flames were close enough to reach out and touch. It was a miracle we hadn't been swallowed up yet. While they were just far enough away to taunt us for testing fate, it was the smoke that was all-consuming and unforgiving. I felt it everywhere. The dryness in my eyes, the way it clung to my skin and hair, and the thick layer of it coating the bottom of my lungs. I tried to cough it out as I leaned down over Erick and hooked my arms under his armpits.

"This is going to hurt," I said, knowing he couldn't hear me.

In any normal circumstance, I don't think I could have done what I did next, but when faced with unthinkable feats, the human body can do extraordinary things in return. With adrenaline coursing through my veins and a heart beating so furiously, I feared it might burst, I did the unthinkable and began to drag Erick backward toward the doorway. The position was awkward and incredibly taxing on my weakened body, but each inch I recovered felt like a small victory. My muscles ached, my back strained, and my lungs shricked in protest with each mouthful of smoke I inhaled.

I slowed at times, but I never stopped.

A long, thick trail of blood followed after us. Each time I picked up my gaze to check on Erick, I saw that trail and was reminded that death chased after us. It was close—all I could do was drag his lifeless body toward salvation with a prayer on my lips and hope that there would be a tomorrow for us to celebrate. Hope kept me pushing through it all despite every element working against me. The blood loss, the flames, the smoke, the concussion I was struggling to keep at bay—I could handle it all, but what I didn't account for was how I was going to lift him up the stairs.

I paused on the first step, taking a deep breath in before throwing my weight back. It was a miracle to have made it this far, but I couldn't help feeling like our luck had finally run out when little happened. Erick was a dead weight in my arms and unbelievably heavy. Dragging him on the ground was one thing, but climbing a steep set of stairs like this was an entirely different beast I wasn't equipped to handle. Adrenaline had only gotten me so far, and while my body had surprised me with what it had accomplished while faced with incredible odds so far, there was a limit to everything.

But I didn't get where I am today by abiding by limitations.

"Come on, you bastard." I pulled again. Each individual muscle felt like it was being plucked apart, fiber by fiber. I screamed through the pain, and when I gained one step, that scream turned into something that couldn't quite decide if it was a sob or a laugh. One step had taken so much out of me that I had no idea how I was going to make it up fourteen more.

Patrick had once asked me if the risk of dying was worth saving Erick's life. I knew the answer then, and I was certain of it now. Because that's what I was fighting for, wasn't it? The reason I was willing to risk life and limb was to act on everything I couldn't speak aloud. Every confession. Every dream. Every shred of happiness that had come before and all that wasn't promised tomorrow. There was a life waiting for us at the top of those stairs, and it wasn't worth reaching without Erick at my side.

That's what kept me going.

That's what pushed me past each step.

"Stay with me, Erick." Five stairs left.

The flames were at the threshold now. Long black scorch marks were creeping up the stairwell, making the corners of the wallpaper curl up before crumbling into ash. Every so often, an ember would trickle down and land on a step. Each time that happened, I would hold my breath and wait, praying it would fizzle out and nothing more. Had the circumstances been different, I might have been able to close off the passages to slow the inevitable from happening in order to buy us time. The thought had crossed my mind no less than a dozen times since starting our ascension, but I was already fighting gravity as it was; letting go of Erick to seal the door shut would have only ended one way, and I wasn't going to risk all the progress we'd made to test that theory.

Three steps.

"We're almost there. I got–" The word turned into a shriek as I lost my footing and smacked the small of my back against the hard edge of the stairs. Everything happened so fast, one moment I was gleaming with pride and utterly exhausted, and the next, I was sliding down the steps on my ass, struggling to find traction. Each second wasted brought us closer to the flames. Step by step, I saw a future I only dreamt of being ripped from my hands. In a desperate attempt to slow us both, I reached up for the railing, relinquishing part of my hold on Erick. The moment I wrapped my hand around the wood, all the momentum we'd built sent us swinging sideways.

I howled in pain as my hip bone rammed into the wall.

All the progress I'd made had been lost in the blink of an eye. We were mere feet from salvation, and one mistake had cost us so much in return. Five steps. Five *fucking* steps. I was choking back my tears as I dangled helplessly from the railing, one arm still hooked around Erick with no chance of regaining a proper hold or footing. Everything about the way we were positioned was designed to weigh us down, promising that one more misstep would be our last. Carrying Erick with two arms was difficult but manageable with enough force; carrying him with one was a death sentence. Both of our weights were being supported solely by the strength of my grip, and the longer we held on, the more that strength wavered. Letting go meant losing everything, but hanging on meant death would still find a way.

A sob tore at my throat as I lost any sense of control. I was utterly helpless, and there was nothing I could do about it. There wasn't a shred of hope to clutch to when death hung over us like this. I couldn't lose him. I couldn't let go.

"Help," I cried as my body shook. "Please help us. We're down here."

A long moment passed by, and nothing happened. I wasn't even sure there was anyone left to hear me scream or if my desperate pleas were even audible over the crackling roar of the flames. I screamed until my throat turned raw and every pathetic shriek sounded more like a choked-out cry. Most terrifying of all was when my throat stung so ferociously it felt like claws were being dragged down my windpipes, and I needed to pause for a second to rest. Those brief moments of weakness felt the longest for I feared some part of me would give up, whether it was my voice or my grasp on Erick. The human body has limits, and I was terrified I was nearing mine.

I screamed again, and just like all the times before, no one answered.

Because no one was coming for us, and when that grim realization settled in, I couldn't tear my gaze away from the beautiful features of his face. It was as if I was trying to commit it to memory one last time.

"I'm sorry." I inhaled a shaky breath. "I'm so sorry. I should have told you I loved you when I had the chance. I thought we had time. I thought I could give us time. I'm so sorry, Erick."

In the end, death is inevitable. It comes for us all. I had accepted that fate, as cruel as it may be, and welcomed it for what it was. I didn't fear death as I once had because I knew I didn't have to face it alone anymore. "Please forgive me."

It was hard to hear over the roaring flames, but I could have sworn I heard someone whisper my name. The sound was distant. It was as if I were standing in a dark room consumed by my own isolation, and no matter what path I took into that darkness, I couldn't pinpoint the source. I strained my ear searching, nonetheless.

I thought to call out to the voice, but when I tried, nothing came out but a strangled sob.

"Help," I wheezed. "Down here."

The voice called over and over again, growing louder than the beating heart in my chest.

What happened next happened in a blur. I was faintly aware of a weight being lifted off my shoulder and a hazy dark figure near my side. They were difficult to make out amongst the shifting smoke, ever-changing forms that didn't seem to hold any mass until a strand of smoke wrapped around me. I was weightless for a long moment as the smoke took hold. It cradled me and whispered sweet nothings in my ear. That warm embrace felt eternal and everlasting until a breeze sliced across my cheek, snapping me out of the haze.

Reality shifted back into place to the distant sound of wailing sirens and flashing lights.

The hospital wanted to keep me for some additional tests. With the amount of smoke I'd inhaled, the concussion I had, and all the minor cuts and bruises riddling my body, it seemed like a reasonable decision to make. However, the longer they kept me back, the more I was itching to be let free. The instant the paperwork was signed, I found myself down the hall, locked in another room much larger than the one I had slept in the night before, though it looked identical. It was well past noon at this point, and the sun was gleaming through the window; despite the natural lighting and pristine white furniture, it felt stagnant and cold. Like the room itself was holding its breath, waiting for him to wake too.

Seeing him hooked up to all these machines was my worst nightmare while simultaneously being the thing that breathed life into my weak lungs. It bred hope while withering it down with each passing night he spent lying in this godforsaken hospital. Each time a nurse or doctor would enter the room, I would get the same response as the last time I'd asked. He was in stable condition, recovering well from surgery, but they feared complications on the rehabilitation side that came after. How he recovered long-term would be solely based on his will and ambition. Knowing Erick, that wouldn't be a problem.

Eventually, no news had become good news, but the fact that he was still sleeping was concerning. Until I saw him conscious once again, I didn't think I could rest easy.

Someone entered without knocking, and I assumed, like all the times before, it was a staff member making their rounds until a hand lightly gripped my shoulder a moment later.

"I'd say I'm surprised you're still here, but I'm not," Antonio said from behind. "You should rest or at least take a moment to call your friends. I'm sure they're worried sick about you, especially after I dropped off your belongings on their doorstep without a word after."

"They can wait," I answered dryly. Given all that had happened, I knew they would understand once I gained the courage to finally reach out and talk. That was a problem for another day.

"I figured you'd say that." Antonio handed over a measly sandwich from the hospital cafeteria. It was nothing to write home about. A poorly made, poorly constructed ham sandwich that surely sounded better on the menu than it did when it came out. I took it despite how bad I knew it would taste because my options were limited and I was too hungry to complain.

"Thank you."

Antonio took the seat beside me and stared absentmindedly at the mess of blankets I'd placed over his cousin. It was a bit of an overkill, but the place was freezing, and every so often I would notice a shiver run down his spine. I assumed he was thinking the same thing until I saw his throat work out of the corner of my eye. I turned and gave him my full attention.

"When I close my eyes, I still see the image of you dangling onto the railing for dear life with my cousin nearly slipping out of your arms," he started, taking a much more serious tone than I was used to from him. "All I could think about at that moment was the fact that Erick was gone and how eternally grateful I was that you'd saved his body—that I would have a part of him to bury and mourn after all of this was over." He let out something that was a cross between a sigh and a laugh. "I was wrong, of course, and thank God for that."

"I wasn't going to let him die, but for a moment back there it didn't really feel like I had much of a choice in the matter." I brushed my thumb over the back of Erick's hand "How long did it take you to realize he was still alive?"

"Damon had Erick in his arms, and when we both exited the building, I could tell by the look in his eyes that he wanted to communicate something with me, but couldn't over the wailing sirens. I wasn't one hundred percent sure until the EMT showed up and there was enough light coming from the ambulance to see his chest rising. It was faint, but there he was. Stubborn as ever."

"My first instinct is to thank you for saving us, but that doesn't feel like enough," I responded, averting my eyes to keep my voice steady. "There is virtually nothing I can say or do that could repay you for what you did for us."

Antonio rose, brushing off his pants as he stood tall. "I guess I can say the same, but I'll still thank you for saving my cousin's life. What Damon and I did back there meant nothing if you hadn't held on as long as you did." He made for the door. "I'd say we're even, but I want you to make a promise for me."

With so many to keep, what was one more?

I nodded, and he smiled.

"Tell him the truth. Someone doesn't risk as much as you did for someone they don't care about. Tell him the truth. He deserves that much after going through hell that night and all the nights before."

"I'm well aware."

"Good," was all he said before leaving.

With so many to keep, this one didn't feel quite as daunting.

That felt especially true when Erick's hand tightened around mine.

Chapter Forty-Six

Erick

"This seems dangerous."

"It's not like we can do any more damage," Krissy said, striking a match. While the conversation was lighthearted and fun, the theater seemed more visibly tense as it sparked to life. A single flame was nothing more than a promise, a mere whisper that swore nothing good. That promise grew louder as the match landed in the pile of wood below and erupted into a sea of hypnotic shades. I stepped back out of instinct and forced my thoughts elsewhere. She must have noticed because she intertwined her fingers with mine, and the flames noticeably drew back.

"Are you ready?"

Beneath my fingertips, I could feel the blood-soaked fabric, now dried after months since the last time they were worn. I gave the clothes little regard before nodding.

"Okay. On three," she started. "One. Two. Three."

The flames engulfed the clothes a second later, catching fire almost instantaneously. They pounced on the fabric like a beast starved after a long, harsh winter, and once it had its prey, it took its time savoring the kindling. The entire process was slow and methodical, and all we could do was watch as the remnants of the night turned to ash and dust. Mere articles of clothing that meant nothing to us outside of those blood-stained memories, ones that could only be rid of by burning them. I'd be lying if I didn't admit I thought there were holes in her logic the last time I'd witnessed the strange ritual, but standing here now, I understood the weight a few articles of clothing could have over someone.

We were silent for a long while, patiently watching the flames consume the last of them.

"Good riddance," she spat.

Her gaze lifted from the fire ever so slowly, as if she was taking in her surroundings for the first time. While parts of Don Juan had been spared after the first responders swept in to extinguish the flames, The Lotte wasn't as lucky. The theater felt like a shell of its former glory, scorched into obscurity. Decades of rich history gone in the blink of an eye, and had it not been for the brick exterior, there might not have been a building left to stand within. "I'm really going to miss this place," she sighed.

"I still technically own the building. Unless I decide to bulldoze it, the theater will always be here," I reminded her. There was some truth to that statement, but I refused to elaborate any more than I already had. There would be no fun in ruining the surprise.

What had started as a selfish endeavor—fueled by spite, foolish rivalry, and a desperate pursuit of broken memories—had evolved into something far greater. Gaining ownership of the theater had come at a steep price, forcing me into deals I'd rather forget, but none of them were the reason why I'd begun secretly reaching out to contractors. That choice was entirely because of the woman standing beside me.

The months following the fire hadn't been easy on either of

us. Countless doctor visits, physical therapy appointments that took more than they gave on a good day, and times where all I could do was lie in bed because the pain was too excruciating to bear. While most of my hardships were physical, Krissy had her own demons to face. Her recovery process was quick and relatively painless; however, it was the stories she retold in vivid detail that truly painted the horrors of that night. Unsung terrors that I wasn't conscious of remembering.

Then she was forced to relive those terrible memories over and over again while being interrogated by the police numerous times. At first, it seemed like she was being called to the station daily, but over time, the calls became less frequent. From the few times I'd reached out to Sanderson, I'd gathered enough information to know that without a body to autopsy or any viable evidence leading to the causes of the fire, Krissy wasn't being considered a suspect any longer. Sanderson had also mentioned there weren't any whispers of Charles retaliating, so I took it as a sign to rest until I was healthy enough to finish what he'd started. The investigation was still ongoing, but it didn't seem like RCPD was doing much to solve it either.

The road to recovery was not without its difficulties, but we had each other every step of the way. She kept me going in my darkest moments, insisted on being present at every appointment, and bounced back and forth between her apartment and mine, so I wouldn't have to sleep alone. In exchange, I did all I could to soothe her tattered soul and begin to mend the remnants of our relationship. Some days were easier than others, but overall, we were caught somewhere in the middle—not together but not without each other either. It was strangely intimate and confusing at times. It was all the comfort and support with none of the lust or fear that nearly drove us mad—neither of us was willing to address all that had happened before the accident as we cared for one another, and for a long while, I was content with just that. As the weeks dragged on and the pain started to lessen, I began brainstorming how to repay Krissy for everything she'd done. Nothing would ever be enough, but restoring the theater was a start.

My little angel had given me life, and I vowed to spend every waking moment of it ensuring her happiness took priority over all else. I vowed to give her my heart, yet she'd stolen it long before she'd even realized it.

"Maybe you should just take it out of its misery already."

I smiled, feeling the warmth of the dying flames. "My great-grandfather was the one to build it. I don't think I have the heart to be the one to tear it down. I guess it will just have to be the eyesore of the entertainment district."

"Yeah, an eyesore I'll have to walk past every week on my way to therapy."

"Therapy? That's news to me."

"I made a promise to someone that I would try. Remember?" Krissy shrugged, biting back an obvious smile. "My insurance finally kicked in at the dance studio, now that I'm full-time. It took some effort to find the right therapist, but I start on Monday."

"Sounds like a smart someone."

"More of a stubborn bastard with a hero complex and a death wish, but he gives good advice from time to time."

"Ah. So, he's smart *and* noble. I should really meet this mystery man," I teased, then lightly squeezed her hand to get her full attention. "In all seriousness, Krissy, I'm extremely proud of you for taking this big first step. I know this decision wasn't made lightly, and just know I'll be here for you too, if you ever need me."

Describing what I was feeling as pride felt like a gross understatement. Her journey had only begun, one that very few were willing to take and accept all the raw vulnerability that came with it. There would be challenges and roadblocks along the way, but maybe with a little time and healing, she'd see herself for who she truly was. She'd finally recognized the strength I'd always admired.

"I know. The same goes for you," she mumbled. A beat passed. "Do you think it will ever get better?"

I had her in my arms a second later, wrapping her in an embrace despite the blistering pain near my ribs. Krissy gently leaned in, careful not to agitate the healing wound. The scent of vanilla and spice quickly replaced the remnants of smoke and ash—I could have stayed like this forever if it meant being this close to her. Hearing her heart quicken. Feeling the warmth of her skin. This was exactly where I was meant to be.

"Yes," I answered truthfully, then kissed the top of her head. "Some days will be tougher than others. I can't promise there won't be times when all you want to do is give up, but it isn't the negative thoughts that define who we are. It's what we do with them that promises a future worth living. Like I've always told you, Krissy, you are stronger than you think, and I've never known you to give up when things started to get tough. Things will get better, maybe not today or tomorrow, but one day they will."

She released a shaky breath. "When I was dragging you up those stairs, I told myself there wasn't a life worth living if you weren't at my side when I reached the top. I think it's what kept me going despite all the pain. Imagining a life with you kept me from giving up."

I forced myself to take a step back so I could get a better look at her, and those vibrant blue eyes struck me dumb. It was the type of beauty that was bound by no limits, and no matter how many times I caught myself staring at her, it would never be enough to comprehend how stunning she truly was.

"And what kind of life do you imagine for us, little angel?"

There was a pregnant pause that lingered for what felt like a lifetime.

"I love you, Erick," she said without a hint of fear in her wide eyes. "I told you that once before, but I was a coward for only saying it when death crept around the corner, and I've been a coward ever since as I sat by your side for months knowing that I was madly in love with you but too scared to say it. Do you have any idea how frustrating it is to want something so badly just to have your past take that away from you?"

I wasn't entirely sure I was breathing.

"I'm absolutely terrified, but I can't give us both the future we deserve if I don't tell you the truth—if I can't tell you how much you truly mean to me. I love you, and my future is nothing if it isn't with y–"

There was nothing tender or sweet about the way I kissed her. It was pure desperation for the happiness we deserved. It was salvation after a life of hell. It was a promise for all I swore to keep. And it was gratitude for a second chance.

By the time I pulled away, I was finally breathing—gasping for air as I rested my forehead against hers and whispered, "I should have died that night. Do you understand that? There is no reality in which I could be standing here today without the sacrifice you made in order to save me. You are many things to me, but a coward is not one of them." Her cheeks turned a deep shade of pink, and I couldn't help leaning in to kiss her again. "I love you, Krissy. You gave me something I can't even begin to imagine how I might repay you for, but for as long as I live, I swear to spend my every breath loving you."

"Every breath?"

"Every breath, little angel."

We lost ourselves in one another's arms. Neither of us was willing to pull away.

But as the flames finally died and the warmth left the

theater, there came a time when we both knew. I took her hand and led her from the shadows of our past, leaving behind everything that didn't fit in the future that awaited us. As we passed through the theater doors, I was reminded that just because something is broken, it doesn't mean it's not worth fighting for.

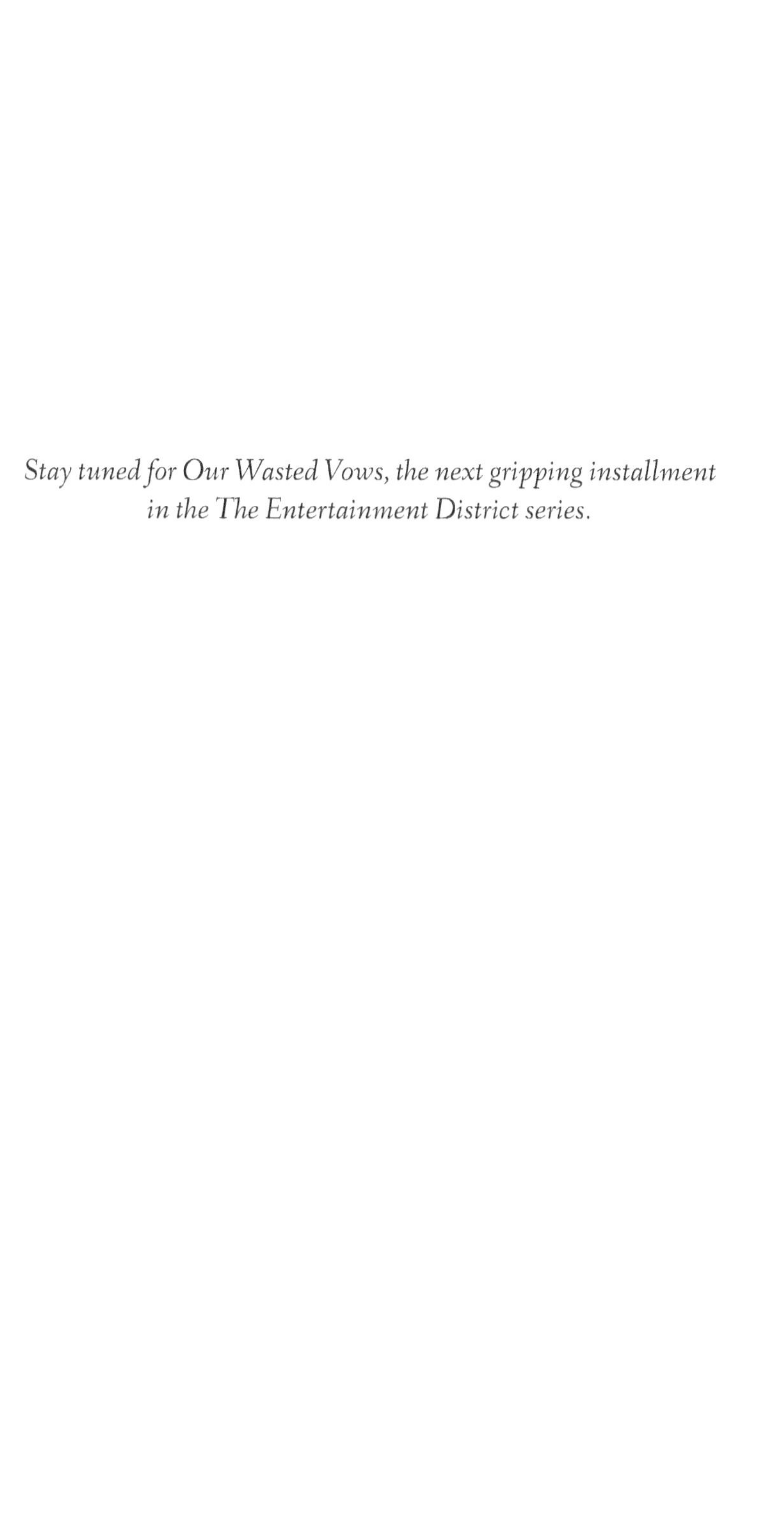

Stay tuned for Our Wasted Vows, the next gripping installment in the The Entertainment District series.

Acknowledgments

At a time when I felt hopeless, I turned to writing as my escape. From my internal frustrations and obsession with the Phantom of the Opera came a passion project I always intended to keep hidden like my dirty little secrets. As the months turned to years and that passion blossomed into a raging need to publish, it was my husband who stood by my side and kept me going despite every doubt and hateful word I cursed at my computer screen.

In the two years it took to develop this story from a pinprick of an idea to a full-fledged novel, our relationship has shifted and grown along with it. I've had the pleasure of calling you my boyfriend, then fiancé, and now husband during the course of the writing process. And every step of the way, you were there for me when fear had wedged itself so deeply within my mind that I nearly gave up. Thank you for your continued support of my dreams. I quite literally couldn't have done it without you.

Jennifer Herrington, thank you for guiding me through the editorial process. You were my first introduction to the publishing world, and I will forever hold onto the things you taught me as I navigate the beginning stages of my career. It was a dream to work with you, and I couldn't have asked for a better editor.

And lastly, thank you to the people in my life who were unaware of my writing journey but whose love and support they showered me with, inadvertently led me down this path, and gave me the strength to make this dream a reality. I will forever be grateful for the opportunities they have blessed me with.

About the Author

Riley Andrews was born and raised in California, then moved to Arizona for college and never left. She is a young author who has a soft spot for morally gray characters and fantasy novels with too much romance. If she isn't stressing out about her next project, you can find her snuggling up with her two dogs, who think they are both lap dogs.

 instagram.com/rileyandrews_author

 tiktok.com/@Rileyandrews.author

* 9 7 9 8 2 1 8 4 4 3 5 5 9 *